RECLAIM THE STARS

RECLAIM THE STARS

17 TALES
ACROSS REALMS & SPACE

Edited by

Zoraida Córdova

W
WEDNESDAY BOOKS
NEW YORK

First published in the United States by Wednesday Books, an imprint of St. Martin's Publishing Group

For everyone who's ever dreamt about magic and space.

CONTENTS

OTHER TIMES, OTHER REALMS

INTRODUCTION

Dear Reader,

Do you remember the first time you believed in the impossible?

I do. When I lived in Ecuador as a little girl, I believed there was a duende that stole my dolls. That might steal me away. When I didn't want to eat my vegetables, and I begrudgingly did, I remembered that the cuco and el tintín would come and bite off my toes or scare me in the middle of the night. If I cried, I'd be reminded that my wailing would attract the legendary crybaby herself, La Llorona. Duendes, cucos, tintíns, La Llorona. These are the creatures of nightmares that appear throughout Latin America in different stories and iterations. I believed in them then, and I believe in them now.

I often tell people that being Latina means that magic is inherently part of my existence. Not necessarily the wand-waving and rhyming couplets associated with witches in media, but magic that is woven into every part of my being. I never set my purse on the floor because it's bad luck. I know that dropping silverware comes with omens. I don't leave dishes in the sink because it attracts poverty. I *did* sweep over my own feet with a broom to upset my mother because I was sixteen and proclaimed I never wanted to get married. I light candles when my friends need some luck and love and happiness. I believe in ghosts and evil spirits. I believe in superstitions. I am Latina, but I know that this is not the only way to be Latina. I believe—I know—that I am not the only one who dreams in magic and stars.

When the seeds of this anthology first came to me, I wanted to bring together a collective of science fiction and fantasy authors who spanned the Latin American diaspora. Each of them has a unique perspective and that is the magic they use to bring these stories to life. It is my hope that it sparks something in others to write their magic, too.

For many people in Latin America, and those living in the diaspora, science fiction and fantasy is the now. Communities ravaged by climate change. Myths that live in our islands and rivers and seas. Violence that leaves the imprint of ghosts through generations and into the future. And yet, when it comes to our literature, there are a million stories that have yet to be told. Let's start with these seventeen.

I hope that *Reclaim the Stars* is only the beginning.

Con amor,

Zoraida Córdova

author and editor

Write what should not be forgotten.

—Isabel Allende

TO THE STARS

REIGN OF DIAMONDS

by

Anna-Marie McLemore

Even a princess going to her death must appear worthy of her title.

And so, as the ship streamed against the cold velvet of space, my mother laced me into a new gown. It was the blue of a frozen sea, and something about how soft its many layers felt against my fingertips made me want to beg Mamá not to make me do this.

"Remember the fate you carry today," she said, tightening the bodice. "The livelihood of nuestro planeta and everyone on it depends on your victory."

"So does my life," I said, failing to keep the bitterness from my voice.

She cut a glance at me. She always hated when I was sarcastic.

"This is how disputes have been settled for centuries. Accept it with grace." She adjusted the blue stones of my necklace. "This is greater than you, or me, or your father." She looked into my eyes, the same chilled brown as mine. "Whoever controls La Ruta controls everything. We cannot cede it to the Masielas."

I could have recited her impending speech by memory. The

route between our planets provided a vital shortcut away from one of the most dangerous asteroid fields in the galaxy, one that had broken into pieces more ships than it had let through. Many an astronave would—and did—pay dearly for an easement to use La Ruta, sparing them the danger of that asteroid field or the costly amount of fuel needed to go around it.

I glanced out the window of the astronave, looking to the ice crystals on the glass for some comfort. We were so close to landing, and the red-tinted surface of the moon below looked so forbidding and cold. Not cold like our home, not with endless life in the oceans beneath the ice crust. But like a place so dust-dry that nothing survives.

This was precisely the reason that the ambassadors, the ones from our planet and the ones from the Masiela family, had agreed on it. Only a place given neither to ice nor fire would be a fair battleground.

My mother gave the laces one last pull, so vehemently that the blue layers of my skirt, some as deep as the sky, some as pale as the crust of saltwater ice on our home, ruffled.

I thought of my rival, my enemy, how soon Ignacia de Masiela would sweep out of her own family's ship to face me. The brown of her eyes would be as hot as the brown of mine was cold. Imagining her left my ribs and lungs tighter than the worst Mamá could do with the corset.

The ship rumbled to a landing. Just before los embajadores came for me, Mamá neatened the dark curls around my shoulders.

"Shouldn't I wear it up?" I asked. "The better to fight?"

My mother gave me the kind of fond smile I only got when I showed perfect posture or the most delicate curtsey.

"When you win"—she drew a few curls to the front of my shoulder—"I want you looking every inch a future queen."

Papá warned me what the moon would be like. I was, of course, ready for the cold. It's so cold at home that frost collects on my parents' thrones. But if he hadn't told me, I wouldn't have been prepared for the air—so thin I had to draw each breath hard. Riosar was a moon so dry that the only plants that survived could condense water out of the air, their sword-sharp leaves a little like the agave I'd only seen rendered in books. My throat felt tight, and my skin parched almost instantly.

The ambassadors escorted Ignacia and me to the agreed-upon place, a rocky plain between the two landing sites. She emerged from the dull landscape, a sweep of dark hair and a fire-bright skirt. Her hands looked both delicate and strong, like the sea stars that survive in our freezing oceans. She wore a simple fire opal, raw and hanging just beneath her collarbone.

The ring of jewels around my neck felt suddenly gaudy and showy like I had something to prove, and she knew it.

I tried to keep my face impassive, the demeanor of a princess. But the embajadores must have seen my fear. One gave me a look of barely-veiled pity—the other, an encouraging nod.

"Buena suerte, princesa," the ambassadors said as they left me.

Ignacia de Masiela and I watched our respective families' astronaves starting up again, rumbling the ground beneath our feet. They propelled away from the surface, and we watched.

The ship carrying away my mother, painted in blues that matched my dress, trailed a stream of ice like a comet's tail.

Ignacia's eyes followed her own family's ship, gleaming red

and orange against the dark sky, powered along by a column of fire.

There was something a little heartbreaking at that moment, the two of us staring like that. Like we were not princesses but children who watched our parents leave us—like Ignacia was now my playmate on this barren planet.

It made me newly sad that I would have to kill her.

Neither of us moved. The ruffled edges of Ignacia's underskirt were as light as fire so that even the thin air stirred them.

We regarded each other. She lifted her chin, not as though looking down at me, but as though appraising me. She had an odd look, as though sizing up an opponent when the truth was she knew me already. We had been around each other enough since we were children—from our families attending the same balls in all corners of the galaxy to the many failed attempts at treaties—that the sight of me was nothing unfamiliar. She knew my weak places already. She knew my strongest sinews and softest points. She knew where I was sharp and where my body yielded.

But she did not know what brutal will I brought to this fight. That was the one surprise I could still have for Ignacia de Masiela.

As the debris from the launches cleared, we saw it for the first time, the prize one of us would claim. La astronave that would go to the victor. The ship stood against the rocky landscape, gleaming pale gold, its fins adorned with what looked like pressure-made diamantes.

Only the victor would board it. The other would be left dead in the red-tinted dust, her body preserved in the cold, dry air for millennia.

The ambassadors had decided that our battle would not begin until we saw the signal overhead. They would be watching to ensure we obeyed, along with every spectator who'd come from all corners of our star system.

As we waited, I did a deep curtsey, the gesture I was told would befit either a gracious winner or a brave loser. Ignacia must have been told the same. She gathered her dress and gave her curtsey.

I shivered at the sight of her hands clutching the fabric. Those palms had been on my waist, tight against the bodice of my dress. Those fingers had brushed pieces of hair away from my face. I had rubbed those hands between mine to warm them; even in heavy layers, she was always shivering when her family visited our planet, and always too stoic to admit she was cold.

I shrugged away each memory as fast as it came to me. The feeling of pulling her body against mine to warm her. My family visiting her luminous planet, and her taking me to her room, helping me out of my dress when I overheated.

No one watching knew any of that. They didn't know about her drawing me around corners to kiss me, me tying strings of delicate blue stones around her ankles because that was the only jewelry of mine she could wear without anyone seeing.

Those watching were busy considering their wagers. It was little wonder that most spectators hovering in the sky had put their faith—and, for the betting men, their money—on Ignacia. Ignacia, after all, came from a planet of fire, and I from one covered in a shell of frozen seawater. And she, far better than I, fit their image of a queen. She stood tall, branch-thin, where I was short and curved. I was a deeper brown while she was pale, with a nose as long and elegant as an icicle. Her hair flowed down straight as falling water, while mine moved in currents like oceans beneath the ice.

I may have been half a head shorter than Ignacia de Masiela. My chest may have been pounding from the thin air, but I kept my princesa's posture—straight as the espada plants. I stood upright even in the face of the dress they'd put Ignacia in, reds and ambers and golds that reminded me she could vaporize me.

If I didn't align my will with the ice in my blood, she could burn me up by pulling fire down from the sky.

What no one watching expected, what I didn't expect, when the burst of flare light in the sky signaled the start of our battle, was for Ignacia to run.

The moment the signal painted the air, Ignacia de Masiela fled from me. Light layers of her dress trailed behind her, so much like a flame, I wondered if she had a train of fire.

Then she vanished into the crags of the landscape.

To pursue her as ruthlessly as I knew I would have to: there was one last memory I had to shrug away, the one that would weaken me if I did not cast it onto the fine dust of this moon.

The last time I'd seen Ignacia, she told me she would never touch me again.

I let this last memory fall from my fingers and felt my heart become a fist of ice as hard and cold and perfect as my home.

I followed Ignacia de Masiela deeper into the rock hills. And I did it while giving everyone their show.

I tracked the steps of Ignacia's finely sewn boots in the soft dust, and I drew down frozen rain from the uppermost layers of the atmosphere. I followed the places her wide skirt had disturbed the dewed blades of the espada plants, and I spun a storm of whirling ice through the sky.

Without my hands to warm her, a princess accustomed to fire wouldn't last long.

As I rounded every crag and boulder, I tensed, expecting to be ambushed by a column of flame.

But I did not cower.

"Ignacia." I called out to her through the thin air so loudly it pinched my lungs. "Ignacia de Masiela, show yourself!"

I hoped to find her shivering behind a field of rocks, shielding herself against my storms.

I was half-disappointed and half-insulted when I found her perched on the edge of a low crag, the red flames of her skirt fluffed around her. She was drawing constellations in the now-damp earth.

"Que espectáculo," she said, dry as the air. It was the first indication that she sensed me at the edge of the rock ring. "You're giving them quite the performance. They'll all be pleased."

Rage rose in me. Did I inspire no fear in her at all? Was she really so calm that she could just sit here and draw?

The only thing that stayed my anger was the shiver that went through her shoulders, her skin paler from the cold.

As though sensing the anger vibrating my heart, Ignacia de Masiela looked up. The hard, perfect black of her eyes pinned me where I stood.

The sheets of frozen rain settled behind me. The ice-sharp wind fell at my back.

"I'm not going to fight you," she said.

That fixed my heart in place.

No.

Not my heart.

My will.

"That's too bad," I told her. "Because I'm going to fight you."

With those last words, what should have been impossible in these atmosphere-depleted skies began to appear, the condensing water I was shaping into silver clouds.

They glinted with a warning as though studded with the bluest ice.

Ignacia looked up, more with pain than fear.

"Don't do this," she said.

"Why not?" I asked, that beautiful blue ice shimmering in my blood.

"Because this is what they want," she said. "You're playing by their rules."

"*You* decided we would follow their rules." I didn't mean to yell it, but I did, as loud as I had called her name.

Ignacia's shoulders rounded, a flinch that was more in her body than her face.

"You decided they would never accept us together," I said. "You decided we'd be enemies."

"No." She was yelling now. "I decided that they couldn't know I loved you."

I loved you. The words bit into me. She had never said them to me in the present tense. And now they were already in the past.

"What kind of show do you think they'd have made of us

then?" She glanced toward the sky. "You think we have an audience now." She gave a bitter laugh.

"Get up," I said, "and fight me."

Ignacia lifted her eyes to mine. "No."

My rage swirled the cold clouds above us, turning them brighter blue.

"No me engañes," I said.

"I'm not," she said. La piel de gallina dotted her arms, from cold or fear or both.

The cold glint above us grew coarser. Fierce blue winked through the clouds.

I would bring down on Ignacia de Masiela a storm neither she nor the watching galaxy ever saw coming.

"You can't fight like this," Ignacia said. "And neither can I."

"What do you mean?"

"You have no control."

The clouds deepened along with my anger, not because she was wrong but because she was saying what no one else knew.

When it came to Ignacia de Masiela, I had never had any control.

"And you do?" I asked, my voice snapping back through the thin air.

"Of course not," she said. "Why do you think I'm hiding? I can't do this. I can't end this because I can't end you."

"*You* ended us," I yelled. La galaxia could listen in for all I cared. What did it matter now?

Ignacia rose to her feet.

Finally.

She saw me as something other than a lovesick girl. She respected me as the rival I was.

She came closer, said my name.

"Stay back," I yelled. "We fight from a distance, como princesas."

She moved closer still, fast enough that my body reacted before I could think.

I knew what was in my blood by growing up among the ice planets of our region—the deep blue of our atmospheres. I knew the stories of how, sometimes, when the pressure and gravity and composition of our worlds were just right, the atmospheres compressed molecules of carbon into the same glittering rocks adorning the victor's astronave.

Sometimes, on our blue planets, the sky rains diamonds.

And because I had learned, and studied, and practiced, I now did that which neither this enemy princess nor the watching galaxy thought me capable. With the flinch of my instinct, I tore open the clouds above us and brought down a storm of blue diamonds on Ignacia de Masiela and me.

A rain of jewels, blue as our oceans under ice, fell from the highest layers of the atmosphere. Hard as hail but with the sharp facets of cut gems, walls of them poured from above. For a moment, it looked as though the entire sky was crowded with the glitter of blue stars. More sparkling blue than I ever thought was in me or all the ice planets of our line.

But I did not cower. I stood tall to meet my rain of diamonds. They might crush us both, bury us under a mountain of blue and sparkling rubble, but I would not shrink from my bright wrath.

I only saw the fear, the reaction, in Ignacia's face for a fraction of a moment before her instinct met mine.

A line of flame streamed up from the ground into the sky. It rose, obliterating the storm of blue gems. It was a veil lifted off a star, a sheet of fire from a sun. It burned brilliant and hot as a wall of lightning.

It registered as only a flash before its heat blew me back onto the rocks, fast and hard as if I'd been thrown. Before I landed, one of the flames licked out. A searing feeling crawled along my arm.

When I struck the ground, the slick of something hot and wet underneath me told me it was the fall, not the flame, that would be the cause of my death. The side of my body had struck a jagged rock, and I was bleeding through my dress. But it was the throbbing from the burn along my arm and bare shoulder that forced my eyes shut. Every thought I had was on that burn. I barely felt the wound that was draining the life from my body.

In these moments before my death, I thought of my mother and father. I thought of Mamá teaching me that I may be as short as the smallest of nuestros ascendientes, but that I carried their blood, which was reason to stand tall. I thought of Papá, teaching me our night sky and commanding me to turn my back on anyone who claimed a woman could not map it as well or better than a man.

But most of all, as I lay on the dark earth, I thought of Ignacia de Masiela. I thought of how I had loved her, how the exchange of glances began the first time we were brought to a convening of our two families. How I once kissed her behind the gleaming silver wall of our palace gate and then tried to run, and she grabbed my arm and stopped me and kissed me harder than I had kissed her in the first place.

I pretended I stopped loving her a year ago when she said

we could not pull each other into corners anymore—when she feared the star building between us would be used against us. And I hated her for it. But at this moment, I knew she was right. If everyone had known about us, one daughter of blazing planets and one of frozen ones, we would have fought each other far earlier.

I had loved Ignacia since our families forced us together during ambassadors' visits, los embajadores demanding that we smile politely at each other while hoping we would stoke their rivalry in our hearts.

Ignacia ran to my wounded, bleeding body, which probably already looked like a corpse. Even with telescopios, no one could have seen through the swirling atmosphere that I was still breathing. They could not have seen the shape of Ignacia's lips, how many times she said my name.

She breathed hard, tearing pieces from her skirt. "Is this what you wanted?" She held them against the wound the jagged rock had left. "For one of us to die for a stretch of airspace?"

I couldn't tell if she was yelling at me or the sky.

I cried out at the pressure of her hands. "You've won." I squeezed my eyes shut. "Take your victory."

My body was too weak to resist her wrapping cloth around me, tight against the wound. I wanted to fight her. What would she do with me? Keep me alive longer? Make sure I was awake and alert enough to watch her take off in her victor's ship?

"I thought this was the worst they could do to us." She tied the ends, and I clamped down my teeth not to scream. "Put us on a moon where we would think we were the only two souls in all these stars." She put her hand to the side of my face. "Did you ever think maybe that's what we needed, for it just to be us, a world that's ours?"

My eyes worked to bring her into focus. "What?"

She was still breathing hard, her lungs fighting to get enough of the thin, chilled air. "We've wanted this for so long, for it to be just us, just once. All those moments sneaking around corners while our parents and their men screamed at each other. What would we have given for a world of our own?"

I looked at her, at the tears that dried so quickly in the parched air they didn't fall. "Don't leave me here," I whispered, pain choking my voice. "Not like this."

Ignacia pressed her lips together. "Nunca," she said.

I breathed out. So there was at least this much love left between us. She wouldn't leave me here still alive, bleeding into the dust as I watched her go.

My body tensed, bracing for however she would end me.

But then I felt my body move. I felt her lift me from the scorched ground and take me in her arms. Pain shot through me, making me scream loud enough to reach the asteroids. My limbs were so slack only that pain reminded me I had not died yet.

When the searing ache of being moved let up enough to open my eyes, I saw the astronave. Ignacia carried me, as gently as a flickering candle, into the jeweled ship. She ripped open the supplies meant for the winner to patch herself up, tearing gauze with her teeth, spreading the hearts of sábila on my burns, closing my wound with a flame-cleaned needle.

The next time I woke, I found her sleeping alongside me. The stars floated outside as the astronave followed the course Ignacia had set.

Blue glinted from under the hem of her dress.

"You kept them," I said.

"Of course I did," she said.

I kissed the bone of her ankle, not to thank her for her mercy but because I found a string of blue stones right where I had tied it so long ago.

By now, everyone on my home planet is wondering what has become of me or my lifeless body. The Masiela house wonders what has become of their victorious princess who flew off in a jeweled ship with the body of her enemy. They want their fierce princesa, the one who defeated her rival with a wall of flame so bright it was seen from stars away.

I thought it was the cruelest trick of our two families to make us the only two hearts on a lonely moon. But Ignacia was right. Us being the only two people in our world was what we had needed this whole time.

My mother and father raised me to be a proper princesa, stoic and beautiful, never making a scene. So I can imagine their horror that I have not only made this recording, that I have not only sent it out through our entire sector but that I have beamed it throughout our swirling branch of the galaxy. I want everyone who watched that day to know. I want all who hovered above that barren moon, waiting for the show of two girls destroying each other, to hear this. After all, they came for a show. How ungracious would it be of me to deny them the truth of how it all turned out?

Perhaps we are on some distant moon. Tal vez, on a shadowed planet. Or maybe we're on the other side of the asteroid field that so many navigators fear. For now, we will not tell you where we are hiding. Not yet.

Send word in the stars if you all—ambos: her family, and mine—can accept that we will reign together.

When you can, your princesas, your precious heirs, will come home.

FLECHA

by

Daniel José Older

How do you mourn someone who's not dead yet?

This is the kind of question too much time in space gets you. Too much waiting, too much boredom. Weird music filters through the starboard side speakers over the forever-growl of that relic of an engine. Too much floating through too many stars will have you thinking too many damn thoughts, and finally, eventually, you'll get to the terrible ones. Like this.

I click off the music, which is the only thing that'll get Grengraf's attention, and ask her the thing that's been circling my mind for the past, oh, ten hours, as we hurtle back toward a more civilized corner of the galaxy to find a black market outpost and offload some of this plunder.

Grengraf grunts. It's almost all she ever does when I ask her ridiculous existential questions. It's almost all she ever does at all, actually. To be fair, she's eight feet tall and looks as if someone mated a walrus with a yak that then ran off with a giant gorilla and made Grengraf.

"Music," Grengraf growls, a sound that is raspy and low and bereft of coffee, and look—I get it. Tunes are important, especially to break up the monotony of all that emptiness. But this shit, which we have to listen to at least once a day, apparently, sounds like sirens howling over a hundred very sad fiddle players who have been up all night drinking. It's not bad—like, at least they're in tune with each other, and that heavy booming drum in the back gives it some kind of shape—it's just, enough is enough.

But Grengraf has both horns, eight medium curled ones across her head and down her back, *and* tusks. So I click the music back on but lower it a few notches. *Whaheeeeeeeeeeeee* wails a siren as the fiddlers go deeper into their cups.

"You didn't answer my question," I say.

"Is which outpost, we head for?" Grengraf asks.

"Delbar Font is the closest. Why?"

She stands, all six hundred pounds of gray fur, muscle, and sharp points, brushes past me, and swipes my legs off the control panel where they had been very comfortably resting, thank you very much. "Hey!"

Grengraf ignores me because she can and taps something into the autopilot navigator system. Then she turns the music up a few notches, lumbers back to the massive seat we had installed for her near the cannon computer, and flops back down. "Answer to your question."

"What did you—?" I swivel my captain's chair around to glimpse the screen.

This beast set our damn course for the one place I swore I'd never return.

Earth.

• • •

My mom was the ice cream lady in our barrio.

Let me try that again: my mom *is* the ice cream lady in her barrio. I mean, probably still is. Seemed like a lifetime gig. She loves doing it. Brings smiles to the faces of all the local kids, yadda yadda, okay, cool.

She was a devotee of Ochosi. Our apartment was small, but a good chunk of the main room was filled with various implements of the hunter god: deer antlers sprouting from cowry shell–adorned cement in a large plate, a bow and arrow, beaded gourds, and blades. Over and over, she said: Ochosi watches over us, he protects us, the patient warrior, he bides his time, waiting on the wind, waiting on the moment. And then he strikes.

But where was he when our world fell apart? All those magical weapons and fancy tools, and still the microeconomies collapsed one by one around us as one neighbor after another fell sick with the Silent Cough. We made it through that impossible summer somehow, but nothing was ever the same. I thought it would be. Things started to get better, it seemed like. Then mom took me out to the landing pad at the edge of town. A crisp fall twilight, that hazy flutter of rain in the orange fluorescents of the control tower. A ship was waiting there—a small freighter—and some tío I'd never met stood on the gangplank, trying to muster up a smile.

I was twelve.

"You'll never be safe here," Mama said, and, just a few seconds too late, it dawned on me what was happening.

"But I . . . I don't want to go," I choked out through sobs. She kissed me on the forehead, her face stone. I want to believe there was sorrow there, hiding, that she refused to show it because if she let a tiny crack in, the whole façade would crumble and her resolve with it. But her resolve to what? Abandon me to the stars?

I wanted to run back to the house and knock over her altar, feel those fancy beaded implements she cherished so much crack and become dust in my hands. *Where is your hunter god now?* I wanted to yell, but instead, I just whimpered. "No . . ."

"I'll come find you," she promised, but it felt like a lie.

And then she turned, and the ship swallowed me whole, and the sky swallowed the ship, space swallowed the sky, and the rest of my life began.

I remember the Orion Arm checkpoint from when Tío Eugenio and I zipped through on our way out of the system five years ago. It was a goofy little outpost—I think he just waved nonchalantly as we whizzed past, no big deal. The thing looming toward Grengraf and me is a whole other beast entirely—a giant steel blockade with a single guard station in the middle. The promise of many, many guns. Some kind of hypermilitarized death zone, basically.

"Um . . . why did you bring us here, Grengraf?" I say, slowing us to a more innocent-looking crawl.

"Tired of same question over and over."

"I . . ." Okay, she might have a point. But space is monotonous, especially with just two people, er . . . one person, and one Grengraf. And perhaps my internal monologue slips out more often than I realize. Fine. "But—"

"Only way to stop mourn something not dead is to face." A pause, and then: "To say what one has to say."

What *do* I have to say? I wonder as a dozen satellite cannons spin on their axes and direct bright red laser beams into our cockpit. *I hate you, Mama,* is the first thing that comes to mind. *I love you, Mama,* the second. Both are true, I guess. She never came looking; the lie was worse because I never believed it, not really. Maybe somewhere deep down, I'd held out hope, though, and maybe being the one to come looking for her is the one thing that means it's over. It truly was a lie. Maybe I put off coming back so she could always have that chance, just in case . . .

And that's why I hate her. Because now I am coming back, and that means she missed her chance.

"This is a restricted zone," an irritated and entitled little voice fizzles forth from our codex. "Chemical Baron jurisdiction."

Chemical Baron? Grengraf and I trade a look. Nobody likes the Chemical Barons. They're a galactic joke, basically—an Earth-based conglomerate that cares about nothing except profits—but also incredibly powerful and known to have a small private army that has set off more than a few minor resource wars. The Star Guard used to have jurisdiction here, though. That's who was running that lax little checkpoint Eugenio, and I blasted through. I can just make out the aggressive sneer of the Chemical Baron guy glaring out from his switchboard.

"Okay," I say. "And?"

"We are participating in the ongoing maintenance efforts on Earth, and no one is allowed nearby right now."

"What maintenance efforts?" I demand. "What are you maintaining?"

"A slight communication error is all. The comms units are down. Now, I'll be the one—"

"Which comms units?"

"Well, all of them," he admits. "Now! I'll be the one asking the que—"

"There's a planetwide comms fail?" I gape.

"Identify yourself," the guard demands, finally fed up with my pushiness and probably more than a little alarmed by the starship we're in. "And explain how you came to be in possession of such an elaborate war machine."

Let me tell you a thing or two about the *Ramshackle Bonanza*, or *RamBo*, as I like to call her. You know how people used to think they were slick and say, *Wow why don't they just make the whole plane out of the little black box-majiggy that can survive any kind of explosion?* Yeah well, obviously that would be too heavy, an aerodynamic catastrophe (remind me to name my next ship that). However! Some genius in the Star Guard space military tech department figured out a way, and for a brief period about ten years ago, they manufactured a hundred or so of these unstoppable flying death fortresses. I think it ended a few wars a little too suddenly because the Triumvirate put a sanction on the things pretty quick, and anyway, the things were just too damn expensive to make in bulk. The firepower alone is unheard of—enough to take out a medium-sized squadron without too much trouble, so you can imagine how the whole known galaxy had a shitfit.

They melted down the lot of them. Well, almost the lot of them. You know how these things go. And how does a seventeen-year-old castaway get her hands on one of the most destructive war machines ever invented, you ask? Easy! Justifiable homicide. But that's a story for another time.

The point is, *RamBo* is mine, all mine, and no dingy Chem-Bar-check-point douche has any right to question why. Even a super militarized dingy Chem-Bar-check-point douche. By way of an answer, I signal Grengraf, and with a satisfying click and then whirr and about sixty more clicks, our front cannon system spins fully to life. *RamBo* is built like a medusa head—there's a globular cockpit in the front, about a thousand mechanized death machines all around it. Sleeping quarters and a rec room are down the stairs behind Grengraf's huge gunner seat, nestled safely away under layer after layer of unbreakable steel. It takes less than a second for the additional shields to reinforce the pilot area, but I don't think that'll be necessary in this case.

"Why have you armed your—" the checkpoint douche begins, but it turns into a shriek as simultaneous cannon blasts hurl outward from our cannons, demolishing all twelve satellites. The point of running around in a space tank is that you don't actually have to kill that many people. It's the Blackbeard method: scare the ever-loving shit out of them for their own good and yours. Take what you want—less trouble, less murder, less messy. Sometimes you have to put on a good show, is all. And it's for the best, really. Chemical Barons are the most highly protected people in the galaxy. They've rigged interstellar legislations to wrangle ridiculously high penalties for anyone who kills one of them, and the bounties levied instantly on us if we kill this guy would mean a lifetime of ducking and dodging. Or, even more ducking and dodging than we already do. Way more.

"Scamper back to your little Chemical bros," I say, revving back up into a full-throttle charge and blitzing past. "You're in our way."

Fortunately, he does.

• • •

I swivel around in my seat as we blast by Venus toward the place I once called home. "The way you said, *To say what one has to say*, earlier. . . ." The swirl of stars must make a brilliant halo around me; somewhere up ahead, the Sun peers out, its radiance glinting off various rocks and planets, stretching through the celestial nothing to find us, even all the way out here.

"Yes," Grengraf says, not looking up from some dime-store novel she's always reading.

"*Yes*, what?"

"Yes, Grengraf also left a world behind. People who are not dead but must be grieve."

"You left your homeworld? By choice?"

She's never talked about her life before. I've never asked. "Choice . . . is complicated thing. But yes, Grengraf left. In Faydomar, all world must be scared of one terrible monster. Is . . ." She looks around, waiting for the word to appear. "Custom. Old custom."

I wait. Clearly, there's more. Grengraf will either tell me or not, but there's no pushing her.

For a few moments, it's just stars and the hum of the engine, the impossible foreverness of the galaxy. "Monster was Grengraf."

"Ah shit," I say. "I was afraid that might be what it was. What do the other Faydomar people look like?"

"Like Grengraf," she says, shaking her head. "But they shave all hair."

That's actually terrifying, but I keep that to myself. Sometimes I'm diplomatic.

"As cub, Faydomar elders select Grengraf for honor of to be monster. To send away. To terrorize town. Unshorn. Is meaning of name, Grengraf: unshorn."

"And?"

"Elders leave official star cruiser unattended after ceremony."

"No!"

"With ignition card on dashboard."

"You didn't!"

Truth is, we've been partners for like six months now, and it's probably the best six months of my life since I left home. Earth. Whatever. And most of that is because both of us mind our damn business and just do what has to be done. A shady customer has some cargo to move; cut the deal, head to the site, pick up the shit, head to the drop site, drop the shit. The shady customer gets a little too shady: spin the play some other way. We just knew, almost immediately, how to move as one without speaking. It's a necessity when there's contraband and assorted crime lords in the mix. If there's an easily snatched trawler, snatch it. Take their shit. Leave 'em with enough fuel to make it to a checkpoint but not follow across the system. What's to talk about?

Things are different now. Proximity to the place I once called home, proximity to the person who shoved out into the galaxy and carved a galaxy-sized hole into my heart. And yeah, the Chem Barons are some bullshit, mostly, but the danger feels different here. It prickles. "What was this like two or three hundred years ago?"

Grengraf hunches over and makes an alarming click-click-click noise that takes me a few moments to realize is her laugh. "Last year."

I gasp. "Shut up! How old are you?"

"In Earth years?" She elaborately motions with her claws, counting, I realize. "Sixteen."

I damn near slide off my chair and onto the floor. "Stop!! I'm older than you? I thought you were ancient!"

She keeps clicking, her shoulders bouncing up and down, eyes closed.

"It's the gray hair! On Earth, people's hair gets gray when they get old."

She holds up an arm, suddenly serious, and directs sad eyes at the long strands of shaggy fur draped off it. "Ah-hm. Is actually what you call silver. Grengraf need shower more often."

And then she's click-giggling again, and I'm cracking up, because oh my god! And then both of us stop laughing very suddenly because we're coming around the Moon and Earth has just slid into view and . . . something is *very* wrong.

Every year, on the day before my birthday, all of San Norberto would gather for a huge celebration to honor our benevolent god of the hunt. People would bring flechas—sacred, decorated arrows for Ochosi to reap his divine justice with—and roasted pigeon offerings. It used to bug me when I was little. How dare they pay attention to anything *but* me so close to *my* special day, right? Typical Gemini shit, I know. But Mama said to think about it as if they're celebrating me, too, like I get a whole festival to enjoy, and that Ochosi must think I'm very special if he decided to share his big party with me and only me. That did it. She knew who she was dealing with. From then on, I walked around the fairgrounds like the Queen of the World, the hunter god's one and only chosen child. Made her dress me up in my one little gown and everything. Everyone played along too—Carolo, the meat man, would bow elaborately and cut a special slice of something just for me; the marching band crews would parade along in my wake, blasting jazzed up birthday songs for all the world to hear.

At night, there'd be a huge bonfire in the main yard of our apartment complex; a lone elder would sit by it and toss herbs in; you could smell that fresh, woodsy scent for miles and miles. Mama and the other priests would set up their Ochosi altars in a ring around it, and everyone would bring gifts and salute, whispering prayers for justice that I imagined rising up to heaven on the wisps of the scented smoke.

I prayed back then too—for toys I wanted; for my mama to stop having to work so hard and not worry so much; for love, when I got older—but now . . . there's no prayers for something like this, no words. My mouth just hangs open as we zoom closer to the planet I once called home. "It can't be," I gasp. "Where's the . . . where's the land?"

Grengraf just shakes her shaggy head. She'd stepped up beside me and leaned over the control panels, squinting out as if somehow that would make it make sense. "Is no."

The whole planet is just a hundred different shades of blue and gray, the swell of the ocean, everywhere, everywhere.

There's nothing. No mountains, no cities. Not even an island. Earth has become one big water planet. Everything, every*one* I've known, is beneath those waves.

"No," I say, more as a sigh—a moan. "Mama." The chair catches my fall, and Grengraf's huge claw is on my shoulder, warm and strangely comforting, and then I just double over and sob and sob and sob.

I don't know how much time has passed when I finally look up with puffy, tearstained eyes. Grengraf had pulled her huge chair up to the pilot's station and taken over flying duties. She'd also apparently placed me in her lap while I was too distraught to notice, and there's something to be said for the comforting power of being surrounded by a big cozy fur monster. The rich smell of fresh soil is everywhere, her natural scent, I guess.

Outside the reinforced cockpit glass, the sun sparkles off crashing blue-green waves beneath us. They go on and on and on. I glance my question up at Grengraf, and she shakes her head ever so slightly. Nothing. No life. No land.

Sniffling, I slide into my own chair beside her and just try to take it all in. Mama's gone. Along with the whole population of Earth. Or maybe it's the other way around? The whole population of Earth is gone. And so is Mama. Grief makes the tiny details into giant, insurmountable cliffs and turns the things that really matter into meaningless afterthoughts. I can't keep track of where I am or what's important. The waves zoom past, the shadow of *RamBo* flickers along across them, our superpowered killing machine that suddenly seems very tame compared to the wanton destruction below. All those lives. All those hopes and fears and dreams and plans. All that history, all those gods, all that art, all that love.

Just gone.

The next thing that rises in me is a killing rage.

When I left Earth five years ago, the environmental doomsday that everyone had been so worried about a generation earlier was basically under control. Sure, there was instability, huge storms and mass floods, and fires here and there. But they'd regulated the shit out of most industries and figured out ways to make it profitable and *not* be an absolute ecopocalyptic monster. Folks pretty much got in line. *No one* talked about polar ice caps melting or whole continents sinking like they had been when Mama was growing up. And that means . . . that means something happened that someone did. Someone did *this*—the genocide of an entire planet. And whoever that is . . .

"Had you . . . had you heard anything?" My voice hoarse, a thousand tears still wait within it.

"Not this." Grengraf waves a long arm across the waters. "Just what small Chemical Baron say. Something about comms fail. Is all."

"*Liar!*" I spit, clenching the dashboard so hard my fingers ache. The whole Baron operation is one big liar. All of it. The word feels like a curse, and I mean it that way. It's a curse that fills my whole heart and expands outward. Because if it was the Chemical Barons that did this . . .

"Ship," Grengraf says, glancing down at a radar report blipping across our monitor.

I look up, squint toward the far-off horizon. The sun has started its slow descent, casting sparkles across the waves through orange clouds. People should be shielding their eyes and gazing over the water, walking out on piers, taking holo-pics to send to loved ones, writing bad poetry. Instead, they're all corpses at the bottom of this rotten sea.

"Intergalactic academic frigate," Grengraf reports. "The *Gallant*."

"Academic?" I growl. There: a blotch hovering just over the waterline. "Anyone who's here to study this probably had something to do with it happening." I reach over and adjust our course.

"Ah," Grengraf says quietly. "Is careful."

Be careful, she means, but I have no need or desire for caution right now, only blood. "Prep the cannons."

When she looks slowly down at me, I add: "Please."

Grengraf lumbers off, taking her chair with her, and the clicks and beeps of our full artillery arming sound from behind me.

The *Gallant*, huh. Not for long. We're already closing with it; tiny lights blink serenely from the dorsal wingtips. The ship's just cruising along at a slow glide over the waters as if nothing's wrong.

Everything's wrong. And if it isn't for them, then it's about to be.

"Mayday! Mayday!" blurts a high-pitched voice over our codex. "Come in, please! Unidentified hunter-class destroyer, come in!"

It sounds like a damn kid, but that doesn't mean anything.

"We are a civilian vessel!" The voice is stern, urgent. "But we are armed and don't want to hurt you."

"You don't want to hurt *us*?" I say, but just to myself. "Cocky." Then I glance back at Grengraf. "Arm lateral disablers and lock on to target."

"Ah," she says, and then, "Hrmmm." It's a low, gravelly growl, and I take it to mean she's not so sure about this.

"Repeat," the voice says. "We are the *Gallant*, a civilian ship full of school children. We're just kids! Most of us. We are the last survivors of Earth, as far as we know."

I've played that game too. It's easy when you're short and scrawny and still a teenager. Play them—their deepest fears, their fleeting morality. Play their need to protect, and when they get close enough, do what you have to do to stay alive. We're right on top of them now, and I'm not the one. I won't be played.

"If you are a bounty hunter in the employ of the Chemical Barons, please know they are not people of their word." Our board lights up with alerts about the *Gallant*'s weapons system coming to life.

"Grengraf!" I yell. It's not that they could actually do much damage. It's just . . . I don't want them to even get a single shot off before turning them to flaming wreckage.

"We're just trying to find a home!" the voice yells as all the upper cannons on the *Gallant* whir around and lock on us.

It's the word *home* that gets me. Everything seems to stop, and I realize tears are sliding down my cheeks. I put my head down on the dashboard and just let the sobs rock through me again.

"Hello?" the voice says. "Destroyer?"

I don't have to tell Grengraf to disarm everything. The clicks and power-down hums sound all around me as we glide toward the frigate's topside landing pad.

So, turns out they weren't lying. A crew of about a dozen kids stands waiting for us when we land. Most of them look to be about twelve or thirteen. They're all various shades of brown. And armed to the teeth with a thrown-together patchwork of weaponry. They remind me of me.

"We have eyes on you," the girl I take to be their leader says, stepping forward. She has a metal bat with some kind of bison skull fixed to its business end and a massive fro. "And by *eyes*, I mean snipers."

I put both hands up, walk slowly down the gangplank. "Whoa

whoa whoa." A slight smile creeps out, but I can't help it! They're all so cute and dangerous, and anyway, nothing makes sense.

"Where are the adults?" I ask.

The girl glances back at the others. One wears a space suit, the face shield opaque. That could be a very short adult, I guess. Another, I just now realize, is, in fact, a very old man. He's in one of those hovery-chairs they used to make, head bowed.

She turns back to me. "There's a few left. The others ... there was a fight." She shakes her head. "We had to kill them."

"Shit." The planet-sized graveyard we're sitting on top of seems to rise within me, and everything feels like it's shattering again. "What ... what happened?" My voice a raspy whisper. I nod out at the endless water.

The girl sees it all over me—that I'm just coming to grips with the same reality that they've been trying to survive for ... however long things have been this way. She softens. "I'm Sarita." She shakes her head sadly. "There's not much to tell. It was a few months ago, I guess? I lost track. We were about to take off on an interplanetary field trip when the floods hit. We left, hoping to find salvation on some outpost, maybe settle, but ..."

"They were waiting for us," another kid says, stepping forward, fists clenched around an archaic machine gun. "The Barons."

"They'd blockaded the planet," Sarita says. "We watched them shoot down a slew of fleeing civilian ships. They came after us. We got away. Been running ever since. Looking for land or ... anything. We can stay afloat for a while longer, but ... every couple days, we end up have a close call with another Baron raider squad. We don't want to make a second run at the blockade, but we can't keep doing this forever."

I hadn't seen it coming in, but that doesn't mean anything. Those blockades will be deceptively absent and then suddenly swarm whatever poor fool slips into their grasp. They probably wouldn't want it with *RamBo* and me anyway, but a civilian frigate like this wouldn't stand a chance. And it's too big a target for Grengraf and me to run interference for.

But anyway: the Barons. I let out a snarl. "It was them."

Sarita nods. "Some chemical they were developing, sythilium or something? Tipped everything over the edge, apparently. They were mass producing it in secret for a bunch of years, had some secret government contracts. I dunno. Dr. Bayaro taught us some about it." She nods at the old guy. "He's been teaching us medical stuff too. And survival skills." She looks hopeful for a moment, then lost—as tired as I feel, as if all that water and death is on top of us both, our burden to carry. "What about you?"

"I . . ." I shake my head. Where to begin? I don't know if my mom ever would've come looking for me like she promised, and now I never will. It's all empty—the past, the future, all these meaningless hypotheticals. Everything, swallowed up by the sea and the Barons' endless greed. "I've been gone five years. My mom sent me away, and I came back to . . ."—probably to curse her out, if I'm being honest, but that doesn't seem like the right thing to say.

Before I can find the words, the other kids start yelling and hold up their weapons. I look up to see Grengraf standing on the gangplank, a fully armed shoulder cannon aimed at the sky.

"What the hell is that?" Sarita gasps. I'd forgotten how cut off Earth was from the rest of the galaxy.

"She's my friend," I say, following the trajectory of where

Grengraf is pointing to a small, single-pilot stealth-craft hovering not far from where we stand. "What the hell is that?"

The cockpit slides open, and a gregarious-looking man with an audacious mustache steps out holding a laser-sighted sniper rifle.

"Oh, that's Corrales," Sarita says. "He was the janitor back when we were a school. Now he's been running scout missions for us, trying to find land."

"What's, ah, what's happening here, kiddos?" Corrales says with an accent that reminds me of home. He's still smiling, rifle aimed at Grengraf. "Making new friends?"

"Everybody stay cool," I say. "This is Grengraf. She's my partner. My . . . my friend. And I'm Taya. I'm here to . . . to help, I guess."

"Good," Corrales says. "Because I found something like land."

All the fear and uncertainty of the moment flutters with the explosion of joy and questions from all the kids around us.

"I know, I know," Corrales says, waving his hands. "But don't get too excited. A Baron patrol found it too. It's a slew of 'em. Too many for me to handle in this little spy ship. Probably too many for the meager little gun system on this ol' girl too." He glances over at me, then eyes *RamBo*. "Our new friends, though . . . that's another story."

"Just send us the coordinates," I yell, already halfway up the gangplank. "Grengraf, you drive. I'll take the guns."

There's a story my mom would always tell about Ochosi: he had hunted down a special bird to present as an offering to Olofi— God. He left it on the table and went out to do an errand, but when he came home to get it, the bird was gone, taken! So he shot his arrow into the sky with a prayer that the arrow would pierce the heart of whoever had taken that bird. As it happened, his mother had come home, found the animal, and cooked it up into a delicious meal, not realizing it had been marked as a sacrifice. The arrow did as it was told, and of course, Ochosi's heart broke too, shattered by guilt and his own stubborn sense of right and wrong.

The setting sun cuts through the tops of buildings up ahead. They rise from the water at odd angles, like jagged teeth. A city made up of smashed-together ruins, the possibility of life amidst all that death. Perhaps, a home for these wayward wanderers.

A fluttering of hope unravels inside me, but I push it away because right now, it's not time for that.

Right now, it's time for war.

Five Chemical Barons warships hover in the air around this final broken city of floods. They're small, one or two pilot fighters. Built for battle. They know, I'm sure, that the *Gallant* is out seeking a safe haven. They're waiting for their prey and probably staking out territory to begin reclaiming the planet they destroyed. They're banking on the rest of the galaxy not knowing anything about what happened until it's too late and then skewing the narrative to make themselves victims.

And who knows? It just might work, especially if they wipe out whatever survivors are left, which is exactly what they think they're about to do.

They think they're the hunters, that waiting a few hours or days makes them patient. They think they've won.

But I am the hunter. And though I've lost so much, this is a battle I've already won.

Ochosi, still grief-stricken, went into exile, roamed the world. I imagine his broken heart trailed behind him like a song, that sorrow seeping out everywhere he went. Water spirits took him in, healed him, repaired him. Eventually, he rose, a god, a broken-hearted warrior, master of the hunt, holy saint of divine justice.

The fighters see me coming, but it doesn't matter. It's already too late. They hover into a loose triangle formation—two in front, three spread wide behind; they ignite their shields and cannons. My first barrage leaves our starboard cannons with a rumble and flash. It gobbles up the pair at the vanguard, turns their sleek warships into mutilated smoking catastrophes in mere seconds. They cascade from the sky—the Barons' charred remains indistinguishable from the rest of the debris.

The Ochosi story used to just seem sad to me—can't someone come fully into themselves without all that tragedy? Stop shooting arrows at the sky, heroes of yore! Well . . . it hits different now, surrounded by all this suffering. Now, I'm glad there's a story that can whisper to me about greatness after a fall, that there's an answer to the gnawing, impossible question: *what now?*

The other three scatter. One loop-de-loops niftily upward, spraying the whole world with a desperate scattershot of laser fire. I trail it on my screen, hear the escalating beep and then hum as the target computer locks on. I let off two torpedoes. One clips the fighter's wing as it levels out. The other smashes directly into the hull. The force of that explosion catches another fighter, which plummets right into a splatter of laser cannon fire I laid out; then it crashes somewhere amidst those buildings.

The last fighter climbs, climbs, climbs into the darkening sky, but it can't outrun the immense sonic combustion blast I send booming out in an unstoppable wave. It would've leveled this crumbling city of the sea if we'd been pointed the other way. Instead, it crushes every gear and pipe, each wheel and shard of machinery in that ship, along with every bone of every body that's on board. The fighter falls silently, slips beneath the waves, and is gone.

What now? A million voices demand inside of me.

How do you mourn someone who you thought you were going to curse out but now would give anything in the world for a chance to forgive?

I'll escort these lost children and their wayward guides to the strange city on the sea. They'll ask us to stay, I'm sure, and it will be tempting. I could see calling this place home one day. But no. There is more for me to do now.

How do you mourn one person among ten billion dead?

How do you mourn at all when it seems like the very waves that closed over the heads of so many others are calling out to you too?

What now?

You mourn by living, of course. You honor the dead by not joining them. Not yet.

I'll become that arrow of Ochosi, launched for divine justice—sacred, razor-sharp, unforgiving.

I'll hunt down every last one of the people who let this happen to my home.

And I will live my best damn life each step along the way.

THE FIRST DAY OF US

by
David Bowles

It wasn't love at first sight. No.

There was no first day we met. Not really.

But there *was* the first day of *us*.

It wasn't the first day of our junior year, though that second-period class opened the door.

Almost exactly twelve months ago, I walked into the one course I hadn't chosen on my own—Corporate History and Field Integration—and started sizing up the other students. Only one of them was from my career path, Joaquín Valderrama, that weird kid who's obsessed with waste disposal.

The rest of y'all were strangers. So, like I do when facing any new problem, I started with the superficial.

Looks.

A couple of gorgeous guys with administration patches. Ugh. Power trips.

Nondescript everybodies studying transportation and civil defense.

Then there was you, Mar.

Tall, thin, your curls streaked with purple, big eyes framed by long lashes, thin mustache emphasizing pouty lips. Way too much glitter on your sandy skin. A uniform that had been specially tailored, almost too sexy for corporate regulations.

Whoa, I thought. *They really must like to push the limits.*

Turns out, your pouty lips had something to say to our instructor.

"Mr. Sánchez, for the life of me, I can't understand why Enjovian would force me into a room with people I will never see again after this year."

That haughty tone made everyone turn to look at you with disbelief.

"Señorite Mostrenco," the instructor warned. "The corporation expects its salaried families on this orbital platform not only to be familiar with its history and divisions, but to work well with all Enjovian employees. Many students in this room will have contact after graduation, via memoranda and interdepartmental collaboration. Even those as famous as yourself."

Just then, a girl a few seats away gasped. I hadn't noticed her before, but she was incredibly cute. A black stream of hair, delicate and dark features, compact and curvy form, rooted in an Indigenous heritage like my own.

It was you, Atzimba. Small. Quiet. So adorable and sweet that anyone would want to wrap you in their arms and protect you.

"Are you Mar Mostrenco?" you asked. "I've always wanted to meet you!"

And Mar smirked at you. "I can't imagine why. What could a girl from Pedagogy and Therapy discuss with someone like me?"

Your face scrunched up like they had slapped you, Atzimba. I couldn't keep my mouth shut, even though I knew exactly who they were. Who their family was.

"From that passive-aggressive superiority complex of yours, I'd say you'll be needing her counseling services in a few years, science brat."

Oh, that pushed your buttons, Mar. Your blazing gaze fell on me, and your lips curled into a twisted smile.

"No one asked you for your opinion, techie," you said.

"You'll want it if there's ever a Systems Control issue in your family's lab," I shot back. "Bio-engineering can't reroute power or reboot crashed consoles. So maybe don't be such an asshole."

"Enough!" Mr. Sánchez demanded. "However you may personally feel about it, this course is required of every junior on Plataforma La Mancha. It's written into your families' contracts. Save your weak barbs and transparent flirting for lunch or after school. Right now, eyes to the front. Let's watch this holo introduction from Enjovian's CEO."

For the rest of the first month, our roles were defined by that initial interaction. Cautious Atzimba tried to have conversations with you, Mar, but you were busy acting stuck-up or flinging witty putdowns. I would parry and return the attack, hoping Atzimba would find me heroic or handsome or *something*.

Day after day.

Mr. Sánchez tried to take control of the situation. No luck.

Finally, when the class had to research and present on one of the founding board members of Enjovian, he pulled an ace from his sleeve.

"Mar Mostrenco, you will be working on Sandra Lovato."

An audible groan escaped your pouty lips.

"And Diego Quispe will be your partner."

You were *not* happy. When I joined you at the workstation, tablet in hand, you rolled your eyes flamboyantly.

"First, he assigns me the one founder who knew *nothing* about science. Then, he makes me work with a repulsive techie who probably doesn't know the difference between a stop codon and a nullomer."

"You're a real jerk, you know?" I told you. "But you're right. I'm just a techie. No famous fathers. Not the wealthy heir to reams of valuable genetic IP. All I know is that both stop codons and nullomers are nonsense sequences in DNA. But only one of them ends the process of translating information into proteins."

That got your attention.

"Wait, how—?"

"Mar," I told you, leaning close. I could see you swallow heavily. Pheromones. Always my secret weapon. "Engineering excites me. Electrical or biological. I know you're brilliant enough to see the overlap, lovely."

Your eyes were wide, a little red, and glued to my face for way too many seconds.

Then you gave a dismissive laugh.

"Compliments will get you nowhere, techie. I have standards. Now pull up the public-facing dossier on Lovato and read it to me."

Despite your bluster, you kept stealing glances at me as I recited her biography.

I could see through your facade.

You were falling for me.

We finished that research project with just a few emotional scratches. After we presented and got the highest marks in the class, we became begrudging friends.

One day I was sitting alone in the cafeteria, feeling frustrated at my dads, who had interrogated me relentlessly before heading to school.

Unexpectedly, you set your tray down in front of me, Mar. With that careful elegance of yours, you folded your slender limbs into the chair.

"You look positively miserable," you remarked.

"Just annoyed at my dads. All four of them quizzed me this morning about my love life. Do I have a crush on anyone? Am I secretly dating? When am I going to finally have sex?"

You leaned your head back, half-closing your eyes in exaggerated empathy. "Ugh. I know the feeling. My mother constantly bombards me with those sorts of intimate questions. My fathers never would have. They would have stopped her from making me miserable. But . . ."

Your voice trailed off. Mentally, I finished the sentence for you: . . . *they're dead*. I could see tears trembling in your eyes. My chest ached at the idea of you crying.

"I guess we'd better start looking," I said, sitting up, trying to distract you. "There's got to be a couple of contenders in this goddamn cafeteria."

Sniffling a little, you laughed and turned in your seat.

"What about that one? The redhead by the view port?" you asked.

"Mmm, they're not bad. A little too obsessed with Jupiter's atmosphere, though. Maybe the girl in the anti-grav chair?"

Your tongue flicked out as if by impulse, the sexiest thing I'd ever seen.

"Yes, she's luminous. Techie, I think we have the same taste."

I reached out, my hand trembling a little, and touched your arm.

"It's Diego, Mar. Please."

You looked down at my hand, then raised your gaze to meet mine. Your bronze cheeks were flushed.

Someone walked by at that moment, drawing my attention away.

It was you, Atzimba.

For a second, you turned and looked at the two of us, hopeful and happy.

But then you saw my hand on their arm, beautiful contrast of mahogany and cedar.

Smile fading, you turned and headed off in a different direction.

"Mother of God," I whispered. "Now, *she's* on a completely different level."

You watched her walk away, Mar, nodding appreciatively. "You're not wrong."

Then, with no warning, you grabbed my hand and stood, pulling me to my feet.

"Come with me. Now."

No idea how, but you knew the ins and outs of that level as well as any technician. In a matter of seconds, we had ducked inside a dusty diagnostic niche in an empty service corridor.

"Don't say a word," you breathed as you reached up and twined your fingers in my hair. "Just kiss me, Diego. Kiss me."

My heart aching with the frenzied beating of my heart, I pressed my mouth to your pouty lips, felt them open with intoxicating hunger as your warm tongue twisted against mine. My arms went around you, pressing your body close, the fluttering of your pulse a dizzying counterpoint to my own.

When our tablets signaled the end of lunch to us, we ignored them till their AIs threatened to alert school counselors. Then, reluctantly, we pulled away from each other and hurried to our next class.

You in your career path, me in mine.

It became a pretty regular thing, consuming more and more of our lunch period until finally, we skipped the meal altogether.

Atzimba, this was about when you had a breakthrough with Mar.

"Mar?" you asked one morning, having screwed up the courage to strike up a conversation again.

"Yes, sweetie?" they answered, not with arrogance but with genuine friendliness.

"Um, is it true that you engineered the pazbosa when you were just ten years old? Our psychopharmacology instructor mentioned you the other day."

Mar smiled at you, pleased. They love to be reminded of how badass they are.

"Well, Aztimba, is it? May I call you Zim? You see, Zim, I was really just assisting my fathers in the lab, but yes, I came up with the sequence that made the slugs secrete mood-altering proteins."

You brightened like the petals of a *rozochi* when UV light hits them. "You are a *pinche* genius!"

Mar waved the adulation away, though they couldn't help grinning. "Tell me more about how y'all use pazbosas in therapy. I hadn't even thought about such applications."

And just like that, the two of you became friends, spending more and more time together in class every day. I'll admit I was a mess. I was doubly jealous.

On the one hand, I wanted to get to know you, too, Zim. At the same time, I was afraid you might come between Mar and me.

You always make fun of me for this, Mar, but I'm a big believer in fate.

I think mine was sealed on that evening near the end of the first trimester. I was helping Papa Manny in our kitchen when a call came through from Papa Santos.

"Diego," he said, "can you meet on level 12, section E? There's been a glitch that's sealed the doors to all the households. I could use an assistant."

I headed down five levels and hurried to the right spoke. There were people, mostly children, and teens, milling about in the corridor. Some were banging on the doors to their households.

Papa Santos was at a diagnostic station, looking frustrated.

"Son, it looks like I'm going to have to crawl into the access tube. It's a physical short, and I don't want to leave all the kids in the hall waiting for automated repairs."

I nodded. "Okay. Want me to monitor from the diagnostic console?"

"Yes, that would be great. Field questions from folks as they come up, too."

After he disappeared into the access tube through a nearby panel, a familiar voice called out.

"Diego Quispe?"

I turned. It was you, Zim.

"Atzimba Sainz!" I said, a little too excited. I tried to recover my cool immediately. "Um, what are you doing here? It's a little dangerous."

You smiled, and my heart skipped a beat. "My family lives here, in 1212-E. I was just about to cycle open our door when they all sealed up."

"Oh, shit. Are your parents freaked out?"

"Yeah. They're super paranoid about possible raids."

I raised an eyebrow. "By?"

You shrugged. "Pirates? One of the syndicates? Papá has been convinced for years that La Ermandá wants to push its way into Jovian space."

"Station security is pretty good, Atzimba. And the UJH Constabulary has patrols near all Enjovian platforms."

You smiled. "I know. But Papá's been preparing me, just in case."

I couldn't help but laugh. "How?"

Looking me up and down, you took a step back. Then, before I could even blink, you spun toward me, aiming a kick right at my head.

Your little booted foot hovered there, centimeters from my face.

"He's a captain in Station Security, Diego. Taught me capoeira."

As you lowered your leg, I struggled to find a response. Anything. It didn't even have to be snappy. But I was too surprised. Fortunately, Papa Santos spoke over the diagnostic station com right then.

"Okay, Diego. Found it. Check the power levels. I'm going to bypass the short."

There was a crackle of energy, then all the doors up and down the corridor hissed open.

"Good job," you said, Atzimba. "I'm going to head inside. But first—do you, um, have your tablet with you?"

"Huh?" I muttered stupidly. "Yeah, in my back pocket."

You pulled out your tablet, and with a flick of your wrist toward my butt, you sent your percom ID to mine.

"In case you want to give me a call," you said, ducking your head, "or message me."

Then you rushed to your household, not waiting for an answer.

Needless to say, I couldn't get Atzimba out of my head, Mar. Not even when you and I were kissing the next day during lunch. You noticed I was distracted.

"What's wrong, Diego?"

"I . . . well . . . is this it, Mar? Is this what we are, two virtual strangers who make out every weekday?"

You looked at me with the gentlest expression I'd ever seen on your face.

"I *do* want something more."

"Like, what, dating? Should we start?"

You pursed your lips, thinking. "I'm not sure. I like the idea, but something's, you know, missing."

It took me only a few moments to understand what you meant.

We were both raised by polyamorous parents. The most loving relationships in our lives have been bigger than two people. It wasn't that something was missing.

Some*one* was missing.

"We won't be satisfied with just each other, will we?" I asked you. "Won't feel complete."

Relief bringing tears to your eyes, you shook your head. "No. We won't."

We stood there for several minutes, staring into each other's eyes.

Then, at the same time, our lips moved by fate, we whispered her name.

"Atzimba."

The last week of the trimester, right before First Break, our Corporate History and Field Integration group went on a tour of the central hubs of the station. Mr. Sánchez organized us into triads.

Again, fate. Laugh if you want.

He put the three of us together.

You two.

Me.

Yes, I showed off a little when we were in the Systems Control Hub. I'd been there so many times that I wanted to let you in on all the hidden secrets and cool backstories.

Atzimba, come on, you did the same thing when we were in the Station Security Hub. And we almost got busted checking out that weapons locker.

Your father's boss came around the corner, and you screamed, "Run!"

Laughing like weirdoes, we hurried back to the main group, hand-in-hand.

Did you two feel it then? The spark? I sure as hell did.

It lit my damn blood on fire.

The Administration Hub was so freaking boring. Ditto Pedagogy and Therapy. Sorry.

Then we came to the Science Hub.

And everything changed for everyone, but especially for the three of us.

"Come with me. Now," you said, Mar, taking us both by the hands again. We were at the back of the crowd of students, so it wasn't hard to slip away. You dragged us through a twisty labyrinth of narrow hallways and then dropped my hand to punch a code into a lock.

On the other side of the door was an empty office with a massive viewport overlooking Jupiter's kaleidoscope clouds.

"My fathers used to work in here," you explained as you herded us in.

"Uh," Atzimba asked, "why are we here?"

You gestured at the viewport. "If we stick with the group, you won't get to see my family's most amazing creation close-up."

Zim looked at the chronometer on the wall. "No way, Mar. They're about to breach, aren't they?"

I was clueless as per usual. "What are you two going on about?"

"The *sipacas*," Atzimba explained. "Mar's grandfather Bartolomeo engineered them fifty years ago."

"Ah, the gas whales," I blurted.

Mar, you rolled your eyes at me. "Sipacas, Diego. Our organic solution to mining—rather than human-piloted ships or AI scoopers."

You didn't add that the creatures had made Enjovian very profitable—and your family very rich, as primary stakeholders in the technology. We already knew that. Everybody does.

"Look," you told us, tapping a nail against the viewport. We crowded close, Atzimba in the middle. She glanced first at you, then at me. It felt like sparks were arcing between us. "A school of sipacas, gliding just at the edge of the atmosphere, buoyed by the massive gas bladders in their guts."

Gas whales, I was tempted to repeat. But the sight shut my big mouth. Even a future engineer like me had to admit that the wetware folks had outdone themselves.

The creatures were magnificent. Bursting through the exosphere, their colossal blue bodies trailed ions and heated plasma like ribbons of rainbow fire.

Atzimba gasped and grabbed both our hands. "It's beautiful!"

You looked at her as she turned her pretty face up at yours.

"I so want to kiss you right now," you muttered.

Atzimba looked over at me, eyes wide.

"Me, too," I added. "Can we?"

Trembling as she squeezed our hands, Atzimba nodded.

"Yes," she whispered. "To both of you."

And she stood on tiptoes and kissed you, Mar.

I don't think either of us was expecting that reaction.

Zim, your black eyes closed, and you gave yourself over completely to the moment, eating Mar up with your pomegranate lips.

I could hardly breathe, watching you—the two people I most desired in the world, in each other's arms. The fire in my veins threatened to set the whole world ablaze.

Mar pulled away, glancing at me. Then you reached up, pulling me down. When our lips met, it felt so right.

As we kissed, Mar wrapped their long arms around us, and there was no doubt in my mind. Fate.

Perhaps ten seconds later, the Science Hub was rocked by a series of explosions.

The lights in the office shut off, leaving us in total darkness.

I could feel the two of you. Mar, you started to shiver with fear. Atzimba, you tensed up as if ready to spring into action.

Then the emergency lights came on, casting a purple hue over everything.

"W-what the hell?" you muttered, Mar.

Atzimba pulled away from us, walking over to the door and peering outside.

"I think we're under attack," she said. "I can hear hissing like they're pressurizing a new airlock."

My ears suddenly popped. "Ugh, yeah. Someone's connecting a ship's narthex to this level."

"Papá was right," Atzimba said, cycling open the door.

"Wait!" you shouted, sounding frantic. "W-what are you d-doing?"

"Mar," Atzimba said calmly, "pirates or syndicate criminals are about to pour into this level, and the other eighteen students are wandering around with Mr. Sánchez and a couple of scientists. We have to warn them. Just stick close to me."

I took your hand, and we followed you. I knew then, I'd follow you anywhere.

Zim, you had no problem remembering all the twists and turns that Mar had led us through. Soon we were peering around a corner into the main corridor.

Figures in black jumpsuits and masks were herding our classmates at gunpoint into a lounge. Most of the students were crying or begging not to be hurt.

"I don't get it," I muttered. "UJH Constabulary is probably just minutes away. Station Security will get here soon as well. Why would pirates risk an attack?"

Mar was still trembling, but they cleared their throat and said, "It's probably corporate espionage. All they need to do is enter the lab, grab a couple of specimens and a computer or two. Then they take it all with them, sequence our proprietary DNA, and steal our genetic IP."

"Shit," I muttered. Enjovian was widely known for its bio-engineered solutions to all sorts of gas-mining problems. The sipacas were too big to fit in a lab. But there were plenty of other creatures in there, weren't there?

"The only good thing," Mar whispered as a pair of intruders

fiddled with the access panel to the main bio-lab, "is that the access codes rotate daily. They can't get in."

I grunted. "They'll just blow the lock."

With a gasp, Mar pulled us down a side corridor.

"There's another entrance. We've got to reach the lab before they do. Stop them, somehow."

"But," you protested, "didn't you just say the access codes are changed every day? How do we get in?"

"We've got Diego. Show us some of that technical prowess."

Finally, you were giving me my due, and I couldn't quite appreciate it. I took a deep breath. "Okay, I'm not supposed to, but I may happen to know the master code that chief system analysts use to bypass security protocols. I saw Papa Santos punch it into a diagnostic station the other day."

We reached the anterior entrance. I closed my eyes, hand above the access panel, trying to remember the numbers Papa Santos had entered when we were down in Atzimba's level a few days earlier.

You kept talking to yourself, Mar, reciting the different bio-engineered species housed in that lab.

"The tragones. They eat industrial waste. Lure the assholes to them? No, I don't think I can stand to see anyone die. Plenty of pazbosas, but even calm corporate spies can steal. Oh! I know! The afferadores."

"What do they do?" Atzimba asked.

"Rescue. When technicians spacewalk, if something happens and one floats free, an afferador can seize the person with long tentacles, pull them into a pressurized bladder and return to the station by expelling air from another bladder."

"Shh," I hissed. "Trying to remember."

You both fell silent, and the image of my father's hand moving over the keys came into focus in my memory.

Quickly, I entered the code, holding my breath.

The door slid open.

The next things happened in a blur.

Mar, you flung a pair of gloves at me and pointed me to a huge vat.

"That's full of pazbosas. Grab a couple of handfuls and get ready. That misty zero-gee chamber behind us has a half dozen aferradores inside. When those assholes come through the door, distract them long enough for me to open the chamber with your father's code, then get the hell out of the way. Zim, honey, I'm not sure what you . . ."

Atzimba tilted her head back and forth, popping her neck. Then she raised her fists and assumed a capoeira stance.

"Don't worry about me, Mar. I'm going to kick some pirate ass."

I think you were about to give some witty reply, but then the corporate spies blew the lock, and they came spilling in.

I slammed my hand against the release button, opening the lid of the vat. Reaching in, I grabbed a handful of the slimy drug slugs and started flinging them at the invaders.

A few landed on bare necks, foreheads, and forearms. Those spies became immediately bewildered, their steps slowing.

Zim, meanwhile, was kicking weapons from the hands of the others, punching a few in the throats and groin, generally wreaking havoc on the unsuspecting invaders.

"Out of the way!" you screamed, and Aztimba and I dove for either end of the lab as you opened the chamber.

Out of the foggy interior shot long, gelatinous tentacles. They encircled the corporate spies and dragged them, kicking and screaming, into the zero-gee containment area.

Then you slapped the button for emergency seal and trapped those assholes inside.

I took a couple of seconds to catch my breath and clamber to my feet. Atzimba, you had kept your wits about you and were already contacting your father on the lab's com system.

"Yes, Papá. I'm serious. We just trapped them in the afferadores chamber. I'm fine. We're all okay."

Mr. Sainz's voice sounded thin but relieved through the speaker. "Okay. Stay put. They put up a barrier, but we're almost through. Constabulary ships are inbound."

"Okay. Over and out, Papá."

I pulled the gloves off my hands and carefully stepped around the pazbosas that covered the floor, heading toward you.

Mar fanned themself and sighed as they walked toward us.

"That," they said, "was entirely too freaking close."

"Yup. But we make a great team, don't we?" I asked.

Mar gave a weak laugh.

"You'd better believe we do."

Then, Atzimba, you whispered nervously, as if afraid we might say no.

"Are . . . we . . . *together* now?"

Both Mar and I took one of your hands in ours.

"Yes, our beautiful Zim," Mar answered.

"Mark the date on your calendars, lovelies," I added.

Then the three of us—novia, novio, and novie—kissed one another gently to make it official.

That was the first day of us.

THE TIN MAN

by

Lilliam Rivera

First thing you do is drop to your knees and give thanks. Every morning. Hit them knees on that cold ass floor. Ignore the goose bumps playing a raunchy bachata on your arms and legs, and recite a few words. The words? Honestly, I don't think it's important. I recite the lyrics to the classic song "Bodak Yellow." Some people might say the tune is not very spiritual, but who can argue with "I'm a boss, you a worker bitch" as a daily affirmation? Not I.

Then the day begins. There is a whole list of things needing tending to. I peek out the window, and a radiant beam of light pours through. I let it rest on my hand for a few seconds. Then I splash cold water from the container on my face to wake me up. I make a note to refill the barrel before the end of the day. I get dressed and drape my utility jacket over my shoulders. The last thing I do is strap them to my back. They usually don't like that part.

"Good morning. We're late," I say. "Let's go."

Silence.

"I'm serious. Don't give me that look," I say. "You know today is a busy day for me."

I pat down my pockets and make sure everything is secure. Open the door and head out. The first stop is always the roof. It's where we keep the food. Before La Gran Fuga, residents grew their own on the roof, community-style. Everyone had shifts to take care of the garden, and we all shared the haul. Now there's only us. We don't have to share.

Our apartment is on the last floor but getting to the roof is no easy feat. The stairs are but crumbling facades of their past life, the result of an explosion done in anger by past residents. The make-shift bomb was strong enough to destroy the adjoining hallways that, at one time, connected the other projects to this one. The drop down to the lobby is ten stories. If I don't hoist the rope to the right spot, it would mean bye-bye Alida. No one wants that, especially not the silent ones riding on my back. I tie the rope tightly around my waist and fling us across. I've done this hundreds of times.

"Here you go," I say.

I unstrap them and gently place them on their favorite spot on the roof. From there, they get the best view of our abandoned solitary borough. Blocks upon blocks of empty buildings and stranded cars. No signs of life. Not a pigeon, a squirrel, or even a rat. It's been like this for a year ever since La Gran Fuga. Those who couldn't bounce out of the city, like most in the BX, stayed behind, suffering for their choice. Once the coughs came, your timeline mostly ended in RIP.

Well, most timelines anyway.

I brush the dirt off a couple of carrots. I still have leftovers from the beans I heated up yesterday and eat those. I sit by them and close my eyes to let the sun caress my thin cheeks. With a wet finger, I wipe a smudge off their face.

I always press their right paw before I leave. If I don't, my day feels off. I press it, and the sound of their laughter fills the air.

"*Everyone, come in! Get in closer! Ay dios mío. You guys! Pay attention.*"

First, Mami's voice comes in loud and clear. She always had a commanding tone. In the background is Papi and Little Jonah.

"*Happy birthday to my beautiful nena. You are my sunshine and my future. This might not be what you had hoped for in a quinceañera, but we promise to throw a big party after everyone gets over this flu.*"

"*Happy quince!*" Jonah and Papi scream. Little Jonah coughs.

"*You used to love bunnies, so here's the biggest bunny ever. We love you, Alida. We will always be here for you.*"

Then the recording stops.

The giant stuffed bunny is called Jumbo Pawlette. There are three recordings on it, and depending on which paw I press, I get to hear them. One of them is of Jonah reciting a rap birthday song he made up. There's a lot of rhymes with the word cat: THAT, MAT, SAT. The third recording is of Papi singing a slow jam, "Love Love Love" by Donny Hathaway. Papi loved Hathaway. I try not to listen to that one too much because I get choked up every time I do.

Only three recordings to remind me of my family and my broken heart. Only three.

"I'll see you guys later. I'll be back in time for dinner." I head out to the stairs.

One apartment I converted into an exercise room. I located

every piece of equipment I could find and set it up in this one-bedroom. In another, I lined up a bunch of mirrors for the dance room. The classroom is located at the far end of the hallway, where I set up with chairs. I use large slabs of white paper in the front of the kitchen. Depending on the day, I might study English, history, philosophy. Today is English, and I'm discussing who the true villain is in the novel *Les Misérables*. (Capitalism, of course!)

And then there's the Crying Room. Everyone needs a Crying Room. Actually, it's more of a spiritual center, a place to meditate and think about things. My sign is Cancer, so waterworks are non-stop, but I only allow emotions in the Crying Room for five minutes. There's work to be done, and tears will not help bring them back.

I climb down the stairs to the empty streets. Water is the biggest issue. I'm lucky. The city upgraded the housing projects into a green living situation. The building has its own water system. It was one of the last city initiatives, that and the rooftop garden and the solar-powered heating system. The big drag is hauling the containers up to my apartment, but it has to be done. Keeping a schedule is key. I've got to keep us clean. Healthy. Focused.

It wasn't always like this. The Bronx just happened to get hit the hardest. We're always known for going hard, but the sickness slowly took us out. First, my cousin got diagnosed. Then the neighbors. The family two floors down went out one by one. Papo who was a boxer. His brother Christian who was into singing R&B songs. The bodega owners. And so on.

Hospitals couldn't handle the influx of sick people, so they just sent them home to deal with it. We tried everything from isolating the person to taking the drugs people on the streets were using. All the while, I never once got ill, not a cough or a fever. My family got worse, and I tried my best to save them. It wasn't enough. Everyone got hit until there was no one left but me.

Funny how there was a time when I wished more than anything in the world to have my own bedroom and not share with Jonah. If only we lived in a regular apartment and not the projects. Funny how things change.

You get used to it. The silence is deafening at times, but your body can get used to anything, even this.

I walk to Associated supermarket to pick up a couple of cans. I stick to mostly vegetarian meals high in protein. The good thing was I was already on that veggie kick, although Mami was highly offended. "You're Puerto Rican. If you don't eat meat, you're going to get sick."

I grab enough food to last me for the week, and then it's back home. A quick detour to drop off my loot. When the sun sets, I heat up a dish and head up.

"I'm back! There was a long line at Associated. You know, cashier training," I joke.

They are not on their stool. Instead, I find them on the floor.

"Did a wind knock you off?" I ask, picking them up and dusting off the dirt. Weird. That's never happened before.

"You okay?" Their silence has a bit of an angry tinge to it. "It wasn't my fault you fell."

The chilly April is enough for a light sweater and jacket, but there's no forceful wind, not enough to move them.

"Let's go inside. It's been a long day, and we don't want to say something we might regret."

I strap them on my back and go home. Inside, I place them on the bed I used to share with Jonah. I document the day in my journal and try to get some sleep. I feel off, but I'm not sure why.

The next day is dance class and history lessons—no shopping for food or water. It should be a more relaxing day, but I still feel this unease as if I should be doing something more.

This time when I return to them on the roof for dinner, I find them back on the floor.

"What the hell? What's going on?" I rush to the bunny. I don't get it. I left them right where I always do. There's no wind. The weather is perfect. Am I losing my mind? Maybe I should rest. Take a break from the work. I must be doing too much and not paying attention.

"Excuse me."

A voice. Not mine. I stare at the giant bunny.

"Did you say something?" I ask.

"Yes. I said, excuse me."

I turn around so quickly I trip over my own boots. Oh my god. What the hell is that? What the hell am I looking at? I can't believe what I'm seeing. A type of machine stands erect before me on this very roof. The machine is about my height, five feet, with robotic arms and legs. A humanoid robot straight from every Netflix movie I binge-watch where they end up overrunning the place and killing humans. This can't be real.

I pull out the gun. It's not my family's piece but one I found during the many excavation trips I've taken.

"Yooooo! Don't freaking move, or I'll shoot." I scream so loud the heavens can surely hear me. "Move the fuck away from us."

"I'm sorry to have startled you." The robot's voice sounds like the autotune used in all those horrible songs. It stands there, and I keep thinking, there must be more of them. Maybe hundreds ready to invade. A whole army of killer robots.

"Where did you come from?" I ask, then I can't stop myself from asking all the questions. "Who programmed you? Are they looking at me right now?"

"From the planet humans titled Gliese 3470c. My owner. Yes."

There is no way any of this is true. This isn't a robot from planet G or whatever. This is a toy that someone somewhere encoded to come here. An upgraded drone meant to end me.

"How did you get here? Tell me right now!"

The machine turns around, does a flip, and falls off the side of the building. Oh my god. I run to the edge of the roof to look, and there it is. Just as it lands on the ground. The robot turns back and starts grappling up the side of the projects, climbing it like a metallic spider. There isn't any time. I need to go. I grab Pawlette and head to the exit. But before I can make it, the robot lands in front of the door, blocking my way.

Nah. I'm not about to let this happen. I managed to keep us alive this long. I won't let this Goya tin can replace me. No sir.

"I'm going to need you to step the hell away from us. Right now." I cock the gun.

The machine nods its head and takes two steps away from the door.

"I have a message."

The robot pauses, and there is a clicking sound. It projects a video onto the side of the wall. I keep the gun pointed at the robot while trying to watch the recording. Materialized on the wall is a woman about my mother's age. She wears a colorful long flowing dress that would definitely drag on the floor. Her hair is long and wavy, reaching way past her shoulders. It looks as if she's broadcasting this from in front of a regular ol' apartment building.

"My name is Sule, and it is really good to see you," she says. "I apologize for not meeting you in person, but we don't have much time, and we're still hoping to find others. We're a very small bunch of survivors. Earth is no longer a viable place for us. We're offering you safe harbor."

The woman in the video turns as if someone is calling to her. "I'm sorry for the briefness, but we hope you will join us." The transmission ends, and I'm back to staring at the robot. Safe harbor. No. This is my home, and I don't care where this thing came from or what this stranger is offering. I'm not leaving to go to some unknown. All I can think of is someone will convert me into a robot or a zombie or a slave or whatever.

"You said you're from something, something Guise. Where is that, and why doesn't your owner meet me in person? Why send a messenger?"

"They don't want to scare you."

"So, they decided to send me a killer Threepio instead? Unbelievable," I say. "Is she from Jersey or something?"

"No. From the planet humans called Gliese 3—"

"Yeah, I heard you the first time." I interrupt the speech. "If I don't return with you, what happens?"

"Your survival rate will diminish. In five days, the earth will shift."

The earth shifts. What is this thing talking about?

"What do you mean, the earth will shift?"

"A massive earthquake will destroy this building and you."

This is a setup. This walking drone and its owner Sule are liars. There's no way they would know any of this. An earthquake? Get out of here with that nonsense.

"Tell your owner no thanks. I'm good. You can leave now."

The robot turns around and does a whole parkour flip off the side of the roof. I run and catch it as it lands perfectly on the courtyard below. The machine starts running until I can't see it anymore. If the thing says it's from some planet, why is it roaming the BX and not flying off? I don't believe any of this. This is a horrible dream where my own private dystopia has transformed into a science fiction slash horror documentary.

I stay on the roof for hours, listening and waiting for the almost certain ambush. It's only a matter of time before this silver army invades. An earthquake. Never mind that sorry tale. We haven't felt an earthquake in years. This is New York, not California. And if there are all these survivors, why haven't I seen them? Whoever programmed Robo should have come up with a better story.

For the first time in months, I lock everything up on the roof. I secure myself tightly and double-check the building's entrances.

The Crying Room feels crowded today. I plop down on one of the cushions and light one of the botanica candles—blue for calm. I've been waiting so many months for any sign of life to deliver me from this nightmare. I should be happy, right? Instead, I'm stuck wondering if there is a diabolical mastermind lying to get me out of this building—a weird Elon Musk type who will probably convert the pjs into the luxury high rises with personal robot servants. Him and his army of tin cans.

I press the left paw, and Papi's singing lets the tears flow even more. What I would do to have him by my side right now. He would know how to handle this. Protect me from this uncertainty. Every day has been a struggle. I stopped asking why I survived this and not my family a long time ago. I went down that depressing path already. The conclusion I came up with was it didn't matter. And now I am being forced to make a decision. The tin can spoke of other survivors but offered absolutely no proof. It talked about a planet and the threat of a trembling earth. I'm scared because if there's anything I've learned from Papi, it's that strangers are out for themselves. When death is near, people get really desperate. I don't want to think back on those days when I barricaded myself in this apartment while those out there thought I held the key to their salvation. If they could have spilled my blood, then maybe they could have saved themselves. I did things I never imagined I was capable of doing to prevail, and now this?

"Tell me, Papi. What am I supposed to do?"

My neck is stiff from sleeping on the floor of the Crying Room. There's no way I can follow a schedule when nothing is certain. I scrap my usual plans and decide on taking a different route. If there are survivors, then they must be set up nearby. I need to see for myself.

"No roof for us," I say. "We're going on a mission."

I never take them with me, but things are changing, and I don't believe we are safe on the roof anymore. I leave equipped with weapons. I don't even know how to use any of these things.

Guns? Knives? My family wasn't about that, and neither were my friends. But I have to be.

We slowly patrol our block and then add another street over. I don't enter the abandoned buildings. I'm not exactly sure what I'm doing.

"Hello, Tin Man! Are you there? I got questions!"

Nothing. Quiet. My legs hurt after hours of walking. No sign of any life. Eventually, I collapse in front of a bodega.

Maybe I dreamt it all up. A really bad trip of some kind where a robot spoke to me about safe harbors. I don't know. How is it that I could accept being the only girl in the world, or at the very least the only girl in the Bronx, and I can't accept a robot appearing to me on a rooftop?

"What do you think we should do?" I ask. Their floppy ears practically reach the sidewalk. I gently push the ears away from getting dirty. Then I move them closer to me and drape my arm around their shoulders. "Why can't you give me a sign? Do I go with them or do we fend for ourselves, like we've always done? Talk to me."

The giant bunny just stares at me with that cute face. I lift the stuffed toy and hold it tight. There was a time when the rabbit smelled like home. Now it smells like me, and I hate that.

It's been five days. No sign of the robot or of earthquakes. Not much sleep either. I've done my patrols and been ever vigilant but found nothing out of the ordinary. All the while, I kept thinking, we made it this far without the help of anyone.

Today is the day, and I woke up angry.

"No one is going to chase us away from our home," I say while strapping them to my back. "We're having breakfast on the roof."

The rooftop garden is exactly the way I left it five days ago. I take care of the neglected soil. Water the plants that need watering. Cut off dry leaves. It feels good to pull out a couple of carrots that are perfectly ready for me to enjoy. I peel the carrots and cut pieces to add to my bean salad. A few clouds obscure the sun, but the weather is pretty normal. I sit and wait because what else is there for me to do? Something is going down, and I'm not ready for it, but I can pretend that I am. What kind of sign would an earthquake give?

I press the right paw and listen to Mami's voice just like I've done every day. I only have their voice in this stuffed animal— this memory. I mouth along to the words I've listened to countless times. I let their love surround me and try to quell this growing fear.

The metallic sound is unlike anything I've heard before. One robotic claw appears on the ledge of the roof and then another. I stand, clutching the rabbit's paw with Mami's voice still wishing me a happy birthday. In my other hand is the gun. I shoot and completely miss. The robot continues forward.

"There is no more time. The building will not survive the forthcoming tremor. You must leave."

"Get away from us!"

The robot inches closer, and I keep moving farther back to the other end of the roof.

A loud crashing sound drowns everything around me. And then, it happens. The shaking is sudden, and I am unable to hold my balance. The robot comes closer, and I'm on the ledge of a moving roof.

"Come with me," it says.

I shake my head.

The earthquake intensifies. I can't stand up for much longer. The building sways, and I drop to my knees. I'm sliding. My whole body is sliding. We're slipping off this building. Oh my god.

I grab hold of the ledge. I'm going to die here, fall down with this building to my death. I can't hold on to both of us. It's not possible.

"No!"

The giant stuffed bunny. I can't hold on to it for much longer. My hand is getting sweaty. I'm slipping from this ledge. I can't hold on to both things, the ledge and my family.

"You have to let go, or you will fall." The Tin Man stands above me on the moving roof, its claw extending out.

"I can't. Please save my family."

I'm losing my grip on their paw. I've protected them for this long. I can't fail now just because of an earthquake. I will not. I don't care if it's me that falls ten stories. I will not lose them.

"Please help me."

The robot grabs hold of my wrist, and I scream out in pain because it's not human hands but a claw trying to keep us all from sliding off this roof. But the robot can't do both, and we tumble. I scream as my hand lets go of my family.

Ten stories are nothing. The sidewalk quickly approaches. But the Tin Man runs down the side of the building, pushes off of it, then cradles my body. Within mere seconds of hitting the ground, I am, instead, being held by the robot. A few steps away, I see the giant bunny given to me by my family. Parts of the project come crashing down on it, but I run toward it anyway.

"We must leave now," the robot says. "Another shift from the earth will happen, and it will be the final one."

"But my family!" Rocks continue to rain down from above. I ignore the pounding from the stones on my body and dig, trying my hardest to reach them. The earthquake is relentless. It's impossible to keep steady, but I can't leave them behind. I won't.

The robot urges me to go. "You will be reunited with the other survivors. You will live only if you leave now."

Not much of a living if I can't hear my family's voice. What is there to look forward to? The building I grew up in, where I shared so much joy with my family, crumbles. A large piece of the roof teeters on the brink of collapsing, aiming right down on me. Another thundering crash alerts me to what will surely be my end if I stay here. I scream out in anguish.

"Where?" I finally say in between sobs.

"This way." The robot goes forward, and I try my best to keep up with it, but it's hard. The earth still shakes like a bouncy house. I don't scream. I just follow the Tin Man and pray I make it out in one piece.

Later, I'll mourn again. Later.

Right in the middle of the Grand Concourse is a large rustic ship, levitating like some sort of futuristic *Titanic*. It envelops the whole avenue, and the vastness of it takes my breath away. The woman from the video stares down at me from the bridge of the floating ship. Various people peer out from small oval windows. A young boy my age. Two slightly older girls. An abuela. A man. Everyone's different. Survivors like me.

"Welcome!" Sule shouts from this strange ship. "Welcome!"

The Tin Man offers its claw to help me board. I turn to face my former home as it sways back and forth. I hold on to the robot and take a step forward.

THIS IS OUR MANIFESTO

by
Mark Oshiro

In Containment 7, spinning around Saturn, Ramona Quiñones misses pupusas.

She has not eaten solid food in over a year, and yet, she can taste them again, the masa rolling over her tongue, the sharpness of the pickled carrots bringing her to salivation. It lasts half a minute before she feels the electro-baton on her spine.

"Are you daydreaming, 981?"

A number. Not a name. A number. She sits up straight. "Just reading, Wilpers," she says, then points to the message on the holoscreen. "You know how Warden Treymond can be. A little wordy."

Wilpers nods, and Ramona turns and notices that he's had a haircut recently. Must have been another guard who gave it. Her thick black hair has grown halfway down her back. She would enjoy it more if she had chosen to let it grown long.

"Well, you've got an hour left, 981," says Wilpers, removing the baton, and relief floods Ramona. "I need these communications and invoices organized and sent for execution for tomorrow's shift."

She wants to say

"I know, puta, because we do the same thing every day."

or perhaps

"Why don't you do it yourself, baboso?"

But she doesn't because she has seen what happens then. She would rather be alive.

(Though she doesn't know what it means to be alive anymore.)

He steps out, his boots sharply echoing off the metal floor, and that's when it arrives.

The message.

She knows it is different. It doesn't look right; the font is too large and bolded. The timestamp confuses her. It says it was sent sixty days ago, yet it appears at the top of the inbox.

There is a subject line: THIS IS OUR MANIFESTO

No one talks like that in these messages.

She should report it. That might grant her some reprieve from Wilpers, as he's done in the past. He might look the other way while she and Teresa push their bodies together, relish in the thrill of human touch, and then make another invasive comment about how much he wants to watch. She's heard stories of him doing so.

And she definitely believes them.

Her cortical implant can't look away from the message. It is like it is speaking to her, begging her to open it. And what harm will there be? At the end of the shift, Wilpers will wipe her memory of what she's done. She's a prisoner. She doesn't get to know things.

She touches it.

It springs to life.

There is a voice-over coming from the electronic delivery system.

There is a voice in her head.

And before she can stop it, before she can disconnect the system and begin to formulate a story so that Wilpers and the others do not shower her with batons and fists, the message plays.

This is our manifesto.

If you are reading this—

If you are listening to this—

If this has been downloaded to a cortical device and the words are flowing through your body—

you need to know who we are.

It doesn't matter who I am. What my crime was. What my journey consisted of. How I have suffered.

What matters is

Us.

We are the children you tried to throw away.

It never mattered whether justice was served.

Whether we were innocent or guilty.

Whether our lives had any value outside of this system.

(And we do not mean monetary value, for we are not a product to be sold, a means to an end, a price on a digitag.)

You have convinced yourself of this illusion of justice and fairness as you vote for the politicians who tell you that the Galaxy Incarceration Program is making the world a better place. That your neighborhoods are safer. That with each ship sent away—Earth approaches perfection: a life without crime. And that you trust the program that finds us, that identifies how each of us has violated the Planetary Code, that refuses to see complexity or exception or humanity within its analysis.

It's sad, really. You were all able to imagine a beautiful world, one that is technologically advanced. Implants that regulate and heal. Mods and tweaks for a prosthesis. Instant communication within a heartbeat to any human on the planet. You reversed the climate disaster that nearly destroyed us all in 2045. We could go on and on and on.

And yet.

And *yet*.

You could not imagine a world without prisons.

Technically, we are not quite correct. You *did* imagine a world without them: by shoving them all out into the solar system, spread among the moons and satellites of Saturn and Jupiter. The Galaxy Incarceration Program meant to catch those children who were prone to breaking the law, who were prone to acting out, who were prone to being . . .

Well.

Human.

Did you know why we were on *those* moons? Did you know why Herman McConnell chose such distant locations? You probably don't, but it is one of the first things we learn in this place.

We are shown a video after we are processed. Herman is laughing. All of those men . . . they're laughing. Herman sips something out of a small glass and then gestures toward one of the service bots, which whisks over to refill it. "Thank you for the kind words, gentlemen," he says, and the camera pans out to show that he is on a stage, that he is surrounded by innovators and chairmen and the greatest scientists in their respective fields, all of whom have undoubtedly changed the world for the better. "But you can't replace poetry," he continues, then takes another sip. "When they look outside of their containment units, they will see, if they are lucky, the swirling gases of Saturn or the dust ring of Jupiter."

The men nod.

They look upon him with veneration.

"But most of the time, they will see the endless expanse of space, a reminder that their behavior is small, infinitesimal, and meaningless."

He laughs.

They laugh.

"They will never see Earth again."

Who are "they"?

Who are *We*?

Well.

We are the prisoners of Gee-Eye-Pee Containment 1, located on Dione, a moon of Saturn. There is nothing else on this moon;

it is just us. Seventeen prisoners, forty guards. More than two guards for each prisoner.

We are considered the worst.

We are the activists who tried to free the West Oakland 12.

We are the hackers who erased four decades of e-credit debt in fifteen seconds.

We are the students who fought back as your racist AI was installed in our high school.

We are the accused, all of us from what used to be the San Francisco Bay, but is now an occupied zone. You took our home from us, labeled us the Oakland Terrorist Collective, and then you kidnapped us, one by one, charging us with every possible crime you could make stick.

We are everything you think is unnecessary, that was "solved" by world peace and technological advancement. "Latinx is useless," you told us. "Why must you call yourselves Black? Color doesn't matter anymore."

All those words:

Queer.

Disabled.

Not you.

You say there is no need for labels.

We are evidence to the contrary.

We are the children you tried to destroy.

Did you know we are sent to these containment units upon ships that are not fit for long-term space travel? Most of us die on the way to these moons.

Recuérdalos.

Timoteo Sánchez, who tried to stop a guard from suffocating one of us.

Rosalie Miller, who developed space rot and was ignored by the ship medic.

Kasper Nilsen, who died of a broken heart after they were separated from their boyfriend.

Recuérdalos.

Because we began our journey with forty strong, and only seventeen arrived. Their names are in this message, and soon, you will be unable to forget them.

Because this is your fault.

We are the children you tried to diminish.

It did not matter what we had done or that the AI bots had mistakenly grabbed other kids as part of our "collective" when we had never met them before in our lives. Jesús Alvarez, fifteen years old, ripped from his family, all because his skateboard had a sticker on it:

Free the West Oakland 12.

He was wrongly arrested for protesting a group of activists who were . . .

. . . wrongly arrested.

There is no room for error in your computations. There is no possibility of a mistake.

We are evidence to the contrary.

But then there is me. No necesita saber mi nombre. It's not important. But I was not wrongly arrested.

I entered the line of code that disrupted your databases.

I deleted hundreds upon thousands upon millions of lines of records.

I liberated people from a lifetime of servitude to debt.

I would do it again.

And yet, it doesn't matter what we did. We arrive at these moons, and we are assigned a public defender.

This defender is not a person.

It is barely a machine.

It is one AI in conversation with another. We stand in a room of four metal walls behind a plexiplastic screen as we are scanned and analyzed. Our case details are fed into the system, and they are precise and exact and uncaring. Our defender appears on the screen, and it is not lost on us that they are designed to be comforting—

a tall white man with blond hair and a big smile

—to *you*.

Even though you will never come here.

Our defenders make our case to the projected AI judge.

Both of them are made by you.

There are no people

no witnesses

no hope

because we can't speak, unless we want to feel an ungodly pain through our bodies and clutch ourselves, crying on the floor as two artificial intelligent bots debate the merits of theft or sedition

or "potential criminal proclivities."

They argue about us.

Never *for* us.

We are the children you tried to exploit.

No one is ever acquitted. They don't tell you that. Not one case out of our seventeen ends up with anything other than a conviction. Our records are in your mind now, too. Every charge. Every verdict. What we've done while in the Galaxy Incarceration for the last year. Read them. Feel them. Commit them to memory.

We spend eight hours of each Earth day—even out here, we cannot escape Earth and its standards and rules—in solitary confinement. Our containment pods are state of the art: everything is monitored. Our nutrient levels. Our oxygen intake. How long we are in REM sleep in our cots. The right drugs, the right vitamin inductions, all of them are doled out in exact measurements thanks to the all-seeing eye of the system that watches over us.

We have not eaten a single piece of solid food since we left Earth.

We spend eight hours a day working. It does not matter what skill set we came equipped with. I excel at computers, but I am forbidden from ever touching one. Each morning, after a dose of nutrients, we are brought to a large room full of artificial sunlight meant to boost our emotional state.

But you didn't account for what it would feel like to sit in one spot for ten hours; no amount of sunshine can liberate a heart like that.

We sit in silence as the day's task is downloaded to our cortical devices, along with the requisite knowledge to complete it. We have no questions to ask because we know everything about what we are to build.

And we build.

Everything.

The clothes you wear that turn sunlight into nutrients.

The security nodules you install in your homes.

The air filters you place over your nose and mouth to allow you to breathe in the areas that are still recovering from climate damage.

The wearable infoswatch that provides you with a constant feed of news and entertainment.

And we do it all while basking in a light that warms but doesn't penetrate, in a silence interrupted only by tools clanking, parts clicking, fabric tearing.

Because we are not allowed to talk.

Some of us learn it the hard way. Through well-timed swings of a baton, through flashes of e-tasers and brainstuns, and, more often than not, from the force of a human fist.

At the end of our shift, we are fed more nutrients through induction, and then we return to our pods. We are allowed six hours to do as we please, or at least this is what the guards tell us. But we cannot do as we please because there is nothing to do. We have no possessions, no entertainment, no access to one another.

What are we?

The irony is that we are surrounded by technology that can do things indistinguishable from magic.

But you use *us*.

We are the solution to your problems.

And in a few weeks, when the ships return to Earth, they will be loaded with cargo that will enrich your lives, will make you feel fulfilled, will keep you safe.

And you will never know the cost we paid to give it to you.

We never got to say goodbye.

We are the children you forgot.

This is enough to ruin a spirit, to grind hope to dust. An endless repetition, acted out so that you can feel safe at home, assured that the bad seeds and the nasty spirits have been properly excised from your communities. You are told that we are taken to be reeducated.

To be turned into better members of society.

And that someday, we would be allowed to come home, and you would all see the benefits of this experience.

This is the story you are sold, with images of us working peacefully and happily alongside our fellow captives, attending school, learning where we went wrong and how we will do better. It is precisely why you all voted for the Extant Incarceration Initiative, the law that opened the door for this program's creation. Because prison would no longer be inhumane, would no longer be punitive, would no longer be the cruel institution of decades past.

We know you are sold this story because we make it.

Ah, maybe you were counting. Maybe you figured out that my total was short a couple of hours.

You are right.

Because for two hours a day, we are ordered to shower.

Apply makeup to hide our bruises and cuts and the swelling, whatever the guards decide to give us that day.

And we create the films you watch, ensuring you that what you voted for is what you got.

We sell you the lie because it's so very easy when you

when *we*

are so very far away.

But.

But.

We are the children of the reckoning.

You tried to send us away. You tried to destroy us. You tried to diminish us. You tried to forget us.

This means you never believed what we were capable of doing.

Such as when Jesús realized that one of the components we were assembling was the control for our containment pods.

Or when Raquel pocketed an infoswatch, which she used to sync the locks across the station.

Or when Miles placed a piece of nutrient cloth under his tongue every day for seven months. This fabric, this beautiful technology, binds to living cells, growing with whatever organism it is in contact with. Miles was so smart; he would wait until the final minutes of his shift, cut off the largest section he could without detection, and within months, he had enough to pass them to others so they could bind it to their skin.

When the time was right.

There were our hours and hours of silence each day, which were a chance for Wayne and Cecilia to teach us a modified form of sign language, something your surveillance AIs were not programmed to read.

And then we spent the last forty-five days slowly taking over Gee-Eye-Pee Containment 1, first by sabotaging the AI systems.

I did that. The code was rough but elegant, as vicious as a hammer, but fine as a needle, written underneath my cot with the tiniest shard of metal that I pocketed during a work shift. You will never know the joy I felt plugged into a computer after over a year without one. You will never know the elation as the memorized code left my cortical implant and rushed into the system, as it changed line after line, as it evolved the system to recognize *us* as the arbiters of power—of change.

The guards' weapons ceased to work after we pushed an update to their internal software.

The guards' screams weren't heard as the door to the airlock opened, and their bodies floated away.

Why are we telling you this?

Why have we revealed to you all of your flaws, all the ways you have failed to consider that we, the children you wrote off as criminals, have power in numbers? Surely it is a foolish thing to do, to spell out our sabotage in excruciating detail, to allow you to course-correct and snuff us out.

If you are reading this—

    If you are listening to this—

    This has been downloaded to your cortical device, and the words are flowing through your body.

Know that this message was sent from Tethys, the ice moon.

    Know that this message was composed by all of us, even though I coded it into the proper format.

    Know that we transmitted it sixty days after the liberation of Containment 1.

    Know that we transmitted it forty-seven days after the liberation of Containment 6.

    Know that there are now fourteen empty Gee-Eye-Pee Containment facilities spread across the moons of Saturn and Jupiter.

    Know that we have repaired your ships.

    Know that we have repurposed your propaganda machines.

    Know that

You have no idea how many Containment facilities are left under your control.

    How many lies have you been fed?

    You won't know.

    How long will it take you to respond properly, with an equal or greater amount of force?

    You won't know.

How will you know which Containment facility is next?

You won't know.

There is one thing we—the abandoned, the diminished, the harmed, the forgotten—want you to know.

We will dismantle them all.

And when we do

we

are

coming

home

This is our manifesto.

And you'd better be fucking afraid.

The door bursts open.

Ramona's heart is racing, but not out of fear.

She can hear Wilpers screaming at her, asking how she allowed that message in, but it doesn't matter. There is a smile on her face, one she can see reflected on the screen in front of her.

She reaches down the front of her nutrient cloth jumpsuit and pulls out the weapon.

The sharpened holodisk she stole weeks and weeks ago.

When she rises and faces Wilpers, his pale face is now red, and his eyes go wide when he sees what she is wielding. His hands shoot for his baton.

He doesn't make it.

Because he never saw Prisoner 522 behind him.

Teresa kicks his body aside.

They kiss. It is a kiss of revolution.

And then the prisoners of GIP Containment 7 decide that it is the last day they will ever be prisoners again.

THE MAGICAL
NOW

CREATURES OF KINGS

by

Circe Moskowitz

Vada Rivera is fifteen when she dies for the first time.

It doesn't feel any different from sleeping—blackness, velvet and complete, on the cusp of something other.

Then he comes.

The column of a spine. The marrow of a skull. Black eyes that glitter like gems in a fleshless face. He opens his mouth. Calls, *Vada*.

She has never felt more alive. Though she does not understand Death, she knows him. Energy thrums, feathers her skin, feels like the cradle of a homecoming. She wants to stay in this blackness, this *elsewhere*, never return.

But return, she does.

Everything halts. The light arrives, the blood pounds. The world falls back into place, has the brutality of a bludgeoning. Far worse than the gallows could ever be.

Death held her.

Now, he's gone.

Mama just stands on the curb, stares, does not speak.

Vada looks at her ruined shirt, watches the blood crawl back into each wound. It is something out of a superhero film, but a deep sense of wrongness has filled her chest. Though she is back where things are supposed to make sense, it does not feel like she belongs.

Possibly, she has never belonged.

She expects Mama to fall apart. Instead, she comes closer, says, "Well, mija? Do you see? We are creatures of kings. Death fears us, and he will not keep us."

Vada knows of normal girls. Their lives, their dreams—how flowers grow from their bodies when they die until they are forgotten. Now, she stands on this curb and sees the shadows in the daylight, understands that she is one of them—an unknown variable.

This is how a story begins.

Vada does not go to school after that.

She is taught from home and hidden away from the world. Not that Mama does much of the schooling part, but she gets away with it in Texas, where she can dictate a curriculum.

Vada does not long for mathematics or science, does not desire English papers or gym shorts, does not care for making friends. No, what she wants is simple: the art of Mama's tacos, how she knows the amount of sofrito to use without a tablespoon, or the way around their mother tongue—to learn more about the pictures of Mama barefoot and barelimbed in Puerto Rico.

But those words are never given. Vada's Spanish is broken, her understanding of her family limited, her culture curled around her shoulders like a ghost. Mama likes her less when she asks such questions, so one by one, she leaves them behind.

As she does, Mama grows closer to the liquor, worshiping the bottles like books in a library. Every day she wonders what story Mama will tell, in what new way she will make her liver fail, only to sit up, eyes dark with the return.

It does not take Vada long to realize just how much Mama wants Death. She speaks of him more than she speaks of Vada's father. Calls to him intimately, knows him, as Vada does. The same way she understands a night sky: the blackness may go on forever, but she still sees the stars.

A year goes, and they become better at this dance. Another, and she learns how best to love a mother who is a carcass decorated in warm flesh. She, too, hungers—for that face in the dark, that voice in the *elsewhere*.

Because deep down, she knows—she will never go to Puerto Rico, never fit in with the neighborhood kids who take one look and say, *You are not normal.*

She will always be the girl with a funereal heart.

The girl who cannot die.

Desperately she wants to scream, *Who are we? What are we?*

But she does not say those things.

She holds onto another year.

Then she turns eighteen.

She learns that it is not much different from seventeen.

She is sprawled out on the couch with takeout, watching *Gilmore Girls*. Not for the first time, she wonders what it would be like to know her mother, to know herself.

She goes and stands on their porch, looks out at the street, feels the dark gather and press around her. It is New Year's Eve. Teens run across the street, on bikes and skateboards and heavy feet.

Vada just stares.

Some stare back.

Most are familiar, will say, as they often do, *Ay*, *that's just the Riveras*.

Quieter comes the rest.

Locas.

Brujas.

They understand that Vada and Mama are different, but they do not see the truth.

When Vada was sixteen, she hung out with the boy next door, Oscar. She was curious, and so, she kissed him. Once. The feel of his lips was a brief, sunken moment. Like the sun and moon colliding. Warm where she was cold. Alive as she would never be. She couldn't bring herself to pretend she enjoyed it, or him, so he told the other boys after *That girl doesn't have a heart*.

He was wrong, of course. Vada does have a heart.

It just doesn't throb.

It whispers.

The night of the kiss, she came home and fell into Mama's arms. Together, they listened to their cavernous chests. Now she stands here, raises her hands skyward, wonders when Death will finally accept her.

He does not.

And does not.

Still does not.

She goes back inside.

. . .

Two hours pass, and Mama comes home.

The door bursts open just as Vada finishes the lo mein.

She carefully considers the woman who stands in the doorway. Her face is narrow, chin pointed. Eyes lighter than Vada's, but they have the same brown skin, full lips, and wild curly hair.

Mama mutters something she cannot hear, before rushing into the dining room, arms draped in shopping bags.

She leaves the door gaping. Vada stumbles off the couch to close it, keep out the biting wind. Then she trails after her, wary. Mama is bustling around the kitchen with a lighter in her hand and . . . *number candles?*

Mama whips off the lid to a birthday cake, tugs on one of many unruly curls on Vada's head. Their gazes lock. In Mama's, there is complete lucidity.

Vada knows what this means.

When Mama gets like this, it means stories. More about where they come from. Or her father. Or Death.

She's getting that on her *birthday*.

This never happens. Nor does birthday cake. It is this that makes the tears well up, spill down her cheeks. It even has her name on it. *Happy Birthday Vada* spelled out in crisp blue icing. Then Mama sticks in the number one, the number eight—lights them with a shaky hand.

She pulls Vada into her arms. They feel like bone trappings, but she does not mind. This is Mama. No matter that, most days, they don't feel human at all. At least they are not human together.

"My baby," Mama coos.

"Thank you, Mama." Her throat feels swollen. "It's beautiful."

"Eat your cake," she says. "Then we'll go watch fireworks."

Vada eats two slices. Then Mama is tugging her out the door, and she can't stop the childish hope that wells. That maybe this time will be different. Mama will tell her the whole truth, not odds and ends of it.

They can stop living in this void.

In the car, she says, "How did you meet him?"

"¿Qué?"

"Death. How did you meet him?"

The silence stretches for so long that she is sure Mama won't answer. But then: "I was dying. Cancer."

"You had . . . ?"

"Long time ago. Before you were born."

"Why did he leave?"

Perhaps it is her tone, so eager, that disrupts the spell. But she can't help it—she wants to *know*. So badly.

Mama's expression shutters. "He left. What else do you want?" She turns up the radio.

Vada could push further, but it's pointless. She knows what Mama will say. *The time for truth is not now.*

But she is so tired of lies.

They do not speak again.

The park is colored in moonshine and people waiting for the show. Some sit at park tables while others are spread out on the grass.

There is one wooden park table that sits empty near a willow coppice, which Vada promptly claims. Mostly, they are separated from everyone else—except for a young couple that sits two yards away, playing with their toddler.

Vada watches it with the destitution of someone who is stranded on an island. It is full of life and color. Enough to keep her going.

Yet, it is nothing she wants.

Always, she longs for *elsewhere*.

Because *elsewhere* felt like her own heartbeat. Her flesh and blood coming to life. Missing pieces falling into place. She doesn't know what's behind that veil of blackness, in *elsewhere*. Nor does she know why Death is so determined to keep her away.

But no matter how she tries, this place and these people, so alive, will never feel like home. There will always be this *wrongness* crawling inside her bloodstream, telling her the truth.

Vada says, "We don't belong here."

Mama's gaze is a lightning strike. "No, we don't."

Fireworks break across the inky sky like flowers, their petals weeping. There is marigold, then rose—an iris, perhaps an orchid.

It is midnight.

It is a brand-new year.

Mama smiles big and wide. Their hands reach for one other as if electrified, moving on pure instinct, and Vada falls into a daydream. Imagines them fighting like mothers and daughters do, making up in a fit of tears—the kind of relationship she sees on a show like *Gilmore Girls*. But she knows that path would be as empty as the one she's on now. A half-life. Because something is missing. Always *missing*.

She cannot figure out if it was stolen or simply lost.

It is at this particular moment that a *bird* falls into her lap.

Vada can only stare as its little blue body twitches violently, going utterly still.

Another comes down.

Another.

Then, it's so many that Vada loses count. One pelts her leg while another hits her arm. All around her—*birds*. Dead and terrible from the sky.

Vada recovers from her shock as the screaming starts. The toddler is wailing, his parents rushing away from the scene. Everyone else scatters and runs, shielding their heads.

She stumbles away from the table, but Mama is still staring at the sky, expressionless.

"Mama!" she exclaims, tugging on her hand. "We have to move!"

Mama rises at a languid pace. Vada pulls her through the park, passes a man who is frantically gathering his camera equipment.

As she brushes by him, he clutches his chest, wheezing violently. Face-first, he falls to the grass, stiff.

Dead.

Mama stops walking, yanking her hand from Vada's. Her eyes are wide. She spares no glance for the people around them who are running and screaming, nor does she seem particularly bothered by the birds, still falling. She is just staring at the dead man.

She is not afraid.

She looks . . . *happy*.

"He's calling us, Vada."

"What?"

Mama turns to her abruptly, hands landing roughly on her shoulders. "*He's calling us.* Do you see? All this pain ends now."

She grabs Vada's hand and leads her back to the parking lot. When they arrive at the car, the birds have stopped falling, but their bodies litter the ground. An ambulance has arrived.

Mama pushes Vada toward the passenger seat. "Siéntate."

"No," Vada snaps. "What do you mean, he's *calling* us? Tell me what's going on."

"Tell you?" Her voice hardens, taking on a mocking lilt. "You're not one of those gringas on TV. You don't speak to me like that. I am your mother. I don't *tell* you *anything*."

"What if more people die?"

Mama's face softens. "Trust me. Please."

Vada's shoulders sag as they settle in the car. She turns and watches the park disappear as they hit the road. She trembles, unable to get the birds and the man out of her mind. If Mama is right and Death is calling them, why now, after all this time?

Something doesn't feel right, but she can't figure out *what*. Instincts are but inklings of the truth, not born in words.

As they drive over the bridge, Mama slams down on the gas pedal.

Vada's body jerks forward. They begin to accelerate. The yellow lines on the asphalt come faster and faster, turning into a luminous blur.

"Mama?" Her knuckles grip the steering wheel as she stares at the road. Vada begins to shake. "*Mama?*"

"I'm doing this for you, understand?" Mama's voice is ragged, but there is no fear, only *longing*. Vada feels her stomach drop, her limbs becoming phantasmal.

"I'm doing this for us. He *left* us here. But he's calling us back. *I swear, we're going back . . .*"

She jerks the wheel sharply to the right.

They go off the bridge.

Vada has died before, is familiar with how everything happens in quick succession, how before one can even process it, the gallows arrive. But as the car is submerged in water, something feels different.

Something is off.

The glass begins to crack, expands like crystal veins.

It shatters.

There is only *elsewhere.*

Vada is greeted with dim light when she regains consciousness. The world is gold and green, and the shapes of trees come into focus, cocooning her.

She is in a clearing. In the woods. Beside a rotting well.

She is not alone.

Mama stands a foot away, staring ahead. "We're finally here."

"How are we . . . are we . . ." Vada struggles to form the words. "Are we *dead?*"

"Sí." Mama's eyes are full of pure joy as she jerks Vada up by the arm, pulls her into a tight embrace. "Are you happy?"

"No," Vada snaps, pulling away. "You *killed* us. You drove us off a *bridge.*"

"*To bring us home.* Don't you feel it? Right now?"

Vada wants to deny it, but she can't. Home is a grave she's been clawing at for years. She knows the feel of its absence, has gotten so used to the gaping hole left behind.

This is different.

That hole has been filled.

Her heart knocks around her chest with the force of an earthquake. Each beat vibrates to the tips of her fingers, hot and *loud*.

She chokes on the first tears. So many emotions rage through her that she feels overly full. Glutted on sensation. She sinks to her knees.

"Home," Vada whispers. "We're home?"

"Yes." Mama smiles, tears falling down her cheeks. "We're *home*. It is time for you to claim your place. Your father is waiting."

Vada's father.

The word does something to her. All these years, the questions that were never answered. This pain that never made any sense. Now it wells up, this great wave. She shouldn't hope, but she hopes anyway, like every time she begged after a story—even one that was near rotten the moment it was told.

She wants to know, is scared to know.

Regardless of how she feels, this is not a choice.

"My father knows Death?"

"Mija," Mama says. "Your father *is* Death."

Mama guides her through the trees, hand gentle. The energy is different between them, all the tension now reduced to vapor.

They move forward to a path in the trees. Vada feels like she is floating on a cloud, but Mama is determined and quick on her feet, her entire body spirited. It is unnerving.

When they reach the end of the wood, they come to stand above a city.

It is unlike any Vada has ever seen. Of course, she only knows

Dallas, but this one is special. The streets below are glazed in color, neon signs beaming and disintegrating into the air like smoke—wisps of light dance in the misty air. At the center is a dark skyscraper towering high against a black sky.

What is peculiar about this sky are the large cracks slabbed in the middle. It looks like obsidian glass, this world encased in a box.

Mama pushes ahead, down the path. It is weaved with tree roots, transitioning into pavement once they reach the bottom.

Vada keeps close.

Through the streets, the people are fleshless, their faces skeletal, their hands bone. It is quiet as a grave because no one speaks. There is a system here as they weave around one another. Vendors in the streets wait stock-still, watch people browse but do not give a sales pitch.

This is mourning.

Vada knows because it is what she has felt her entire life.

She feels close to these people—though they are fleshless, and she is not. Like them, she is wrapped in Death. The putrid impressions are contagious, consuming Vada's heart. She is *awake*.

Mama is the same. She bounces through all of it, coming alive. She looks as young as she is, eyes light, like all the weight has gone. This place is a tomb, but somehow, it is where they belong.

Twenty minutes pass, and Vada understands—they are going to the skyscraper.

When they reach the glassy doors, her mouth loosens. Two bouncers stand at the entrance.

They are not like the people in the streets. They are larger and lupine, with monstrous faces made of ivory. Their glittering black eyes bring her to a stop, but Mama marches right up to them, hands on her hips. Something changes in their expressions when they see her, understand her. They exchange a glance.

Then, they wave her inside.

Mama smiles.

They know her. She knows them. She turns and waits.

Vada wants to follow, yet she is still so afraid. She thinks about her body, lying in that lake right now, cold and lifeless.

She won't return this time.

But that isn't what scares her.

What scares her is that she feels more alive than she's ever been, and it's only because she's dead.

"Come, Vada," Mama says. "It's time for the truth."

She expects something gaudier than an office space, but that is where they end up. It is small and sleek. A steel table in the center of the room seats three. Two skeletal wolves and one skeletal boy playing a game of cards.

These cards are made not of paper but glass. Enameled with gold, painted in strange symbols.

The boy is not much older than Vada, if older at all. His black eyes flicker away from the game, settle on her. He sets his cards facedown with a quiet *clink*.

"Out. Both of you."

The command is authoritative. The wolves obey and exit the room. The boy smiles. He rises from the table. Though he speaks to Mama, he stares at Vada. "She's beautiful."

Mama is frozen. "Where's Avel?"

"I never understood his fascination with you . . ." He trails off. "A mortal. He never wanted my mother, but he wanted a *mortal.*"

He says *mortal* with disgust as if they are something dirty on the bottom of his shoe. Whoever he is, he is not who Mama hoped to see. It is clear in her posture, all that hope long gone, in its place reservation. She is hiding what she really feels.

She is afraid.

"What is that tale of star-crossed lovers in your world?" The boy snaps his bone fingers, trying to think of it. "*Romeo and Juliet.* Here in Undar, we have one that is much the same. What happens when a god of death and a girl of flesh fall in love?" He spreads his arms wide as if he is conducting a performance. "*It breaks the world.*"

"It was you," Mama says. "Calling us."

"Yes."

"MATIAS!" a voice thunders.

A tall skeletal man stands in the doorway. He is broader, but he is hunched over, clutching his chest. He looks ill. But he comes closer anyway, his face full of anger. "What the hell are you doing?"

"*Avel,*" Mama gasps. She rushes to him, buries her head in his chest. He is frozen. But eventually, he moves, and his hands find their place at Mama's sides. But his face. *His face.* It is that face she saw in the dark.

Death.

Her father.

What happens when a god of death and a girl of flesh fall in love? This is him.

It hits her all at once that he is not human, which means that *she* is not human. At least, not entirely.

His eyes soften as he takes her in, but they harden when they land on Matias. "How did you bring them here?"

"Our world is crumbling," Matias says, rolling up his sleeves. "None of it can be fixed until the abomination is gone."

"You will not touch them," Avel states as if it's a simple matter. "Get out."

Matias smiles.

Too late, Vada realizes when the two wolves return. They pin Avel down, and Mama stumbles to them, screaming, "Don't touch him! Don't—"

A flash of silver, a gush of red.

Matias stands above her with that same wicked smile, his fingers no longer fingers but sharpened glassy blades.

She crumples to the floor in a dark expanding pool.

Avel weeps. Vada screams.

And when she does, the room tumbles, rumbles, quakes.

She screams and screams and screams until she is hollowed out and cold. It is not enough. If she could scream a deathless scream, she would.

But it cuts off, and the quaking immediately stops.

Avel and Matias are staring at her. So are the wolves. As though she has grown three heads.

But she only has eyes for Mama. Tears fall down her cheeks as she sinks to her knees, cradles her limp body. They've died, sure, but what is it to die *here*? What's after?

Is there an *after* when they're already in the *after*?

It feels impossible that Mama could ever be gone. No matter

how dark and twisted they were, she is the only home Vada has known.

And without it, what is she?

It all happens quickly.

Avel rises, shoves the wolves back, crushing their skulls. They crumble like sand before he turns to face Matias.

"How many years have you fretted over this mortal?" Matias demands. "It would have come to this eventually. No matter how many times you kept her away."

"And you thought to kill me for it?"

"You know very well we cannot be killed. We must *rebuild*. This world needs a new king."

They clash. Vada flinches, watching the violent struggle, still holding Mama in her arms—the blood has gone cold. Avel shoves Matias so hard he flies, hitting the opposite wall.

Avel bounds to Matias in a few quick strides. Like the wolves, he will crush him.

"Stop," Vada chokes out.

Avel goes still. Both of their skulled faces turn in her direction. "*Stop*," she repeats.

They are both parts of the truth, and the truth is what she needs.

Avel risked everything to hide it. Matias killed to bring it forth. Mama died to ensure it was received. It would be safer for Vada to go on denying everything she is—but she can't.

Not anymore.

"What happens," she whispers, "when a god of death and a girl of flesh fall in love?"

Avel hesitates. With his hands around his dead son's neck,

staring at his half-dead daughter, he no longer looks strong, only lost.

But the hesitation passes.

Then comes the story.

INTERLUDE:
THE GOD OF DEATH

It began as it always did.

But when I came, she did not beg for her life. Instead, she said, *let me tell you a tale*, and I learned to love what fades.

It was a bruise, something I did not understand. I wanted to pull away, but there was something hooking about this pain. I thought, is this what it is to be human? Though I cannot see it, have never known it, though it is like trying to see through murky water, I want it.

What an ache it was. A glinting apple. Hurt that I wanted to consume my entire body. I wanted every bone to break, then break again. As long as I could feel it wholly, no longer a whisper.

I needed more. I needed *her*.

So, she came.

So, we were happy.

A god of death, a girl of flesh.

It brings a thing of love, a thing of horror.

When our child was born, she wailed until the sky broke. As the light vanished and the warmth was ripped away from her bare skin, it was at once forgotten the name of this domain. It became something different. Limbo. And perhaps that is because the child herself was Limbo.

The hands that held her were no longer hands, but cages and the voice that crooned a cradlesong was no longer a voice but a shadow.

Such is the wound of things that are stolen.

That's the story, really, this matter of stolen things. Because the child grew up and all was taken. Her power, though bestowed by a god, was sooner abandoned than seen.

What was left was a boneyard, a catacomb, a memory. This was the way of it.

But it is not what they will tell you.

"Instead, they will say she broke the world," Avel finishes. "And that is also true."

It all falls into place.

She was born of love so ruinous *it broke the world*.

A god of death, a girl of flesh.

A child of horror.

Abomination, Matias called her.

But she never belonged anywhere else, has never been at home with the living, has spent every day trying to get closer to the unseen.

The shadows called, and she did not know what to call them in turn, had no name other than Death. But she always knew it was here.

She cannot go back.

What would she go back to when Death is the only thing she understands?

Now that Mama, the only one who felt real, won't be there?

"I was selfish to take her away." Avel looks at Mama in her arms. "She was never the same."

"You kept us away."

"Yes," he said. "To protect you."

"To protect me?" Vada wonders. "Or Undar?"

He looks at her, then really looks at her. "Both."

"She used to say we were creatures of kings. That we'd shape the world. I used to think it was a metaphor."

"Kings are broken. They do not live, and live we all should. You will eclipse me."

Mama stirs.

It shocks Vada to the core as she lifts her head.

Though the shape of her elegant cheeks remains, the flesh is gone. In its place, bone. The shine of her skull makes it all too real. There is no undoing. Mama is dead.

Yet, she is not gone.

Here, the dead remain.

"Racquel," he says. "I am so sorry."

Vada gazes up at him, tries to make sense of his face, to find herself in his features. She wants to ask him so many questions, to *know* him.

But she broke the world.

"Avel," Mama says. "You cannot send us back."

"Then she must claim the blood."

At these words, Matias struggles against Avel's grip but loses and slumps, demoralized. "She is a *scar*. You do not know what it will do. It could destroy us for good."

"She has the gift," Avel disagrees. "Stronger, unpredictable, because she is flesh. But she can deal in matters of death. I thought it was right to keep her away, but perhaps that is what held us in the dark. She is firstborn. It is rightfully hers."

"Blood?" she echoes. "What blood?"

"The power of a king cannot be taken. It must be given—and accepted. It is an agreement between you and me."

"You do not have to claim it," Matias insists. "You can renounce it."

"Is that why you brought me here?" she demands, getting to her feet. "Because you want it for yourself?"

"To be king is not to rule. It is to *mend*. If the blood is mine, I will send you and your mother home—and this world can be restored."

Vada could leave this all behind, go back to being normal. But she's here now. She can't turn away.

Avel suddenly weakens, his palms leaving Matias and hitting the ground. He coughs violently, clutching his chest.

"Avel." Mama rushes to him, and once again, it is disconcerting to watch the way of her skeletal face. "You're not well. What's wrong?"

"It's her," Matias accuses, nodding at Vada. But he doesn't look as angry now, just exhausted. For the first time, Vada notices that his bone arms are scarred.

Avel stops coughing, but he looks weary as he struggles to his feet. "Is it true? Is it me?"

"It is complicated, mija."

Mija. The word stuns. It is the first time he has called her that. Matias bristles. "Nothing changes, does it?"

"What do you mean?" demands Vada.

"Just what I said."

"Was I really such a threat? Was it really so hard for you?"

"You think it's been easy. Being here. With him." His voice is dangerously cool. "You're just a girl. You don't know *anything*."

"Because I've been kept in the dark!" she exclaims. "So why don't you tell me, Matias?"

He blinks—startled—opens his mouth with a hesitation that makes her realize he is not often asked to speak. Has he lived like a ghost, the way she has? Suddenly, he looks no more than the boy he is.

She would have thought him just that if he hadn't killed Mama moments ago.

Yet even monsters have stories, and perhaps it isn't really the monster that's terrifying.

But how much of herself she can see in a monster.

INTERLUDE:
THE HEIR AND THE SPARE

A world is dead. It is also dying.

It has a god who should be bound to duty. Instead, he is bound to love. It does not matter that his firstborn, the heir, is Destroyer. He retreats further into his skyscraper and allows her to live as she should not.

But there is another child.

A spare.

The spare used to laugh. He remembers, barely, when he knew happiness. Back when he was not so tired and broken, and love had not stolen God's sense. Now, sense is long gone, and the cracks in the world grow ever larger. The spare tries to pick up every broken piece, but there are too many, and they slip from his fingers.

He tries to hold up the sky.

It is so damn heavy.

The spare wishes he could grab the heir by her shoulders and scream. *Look at the mess you've left me.*

Because while she sits under God's protection, the dead begin to fall through the cracks. He sees how the damage weighs, an execution blade waiting to descend. He must act, for what is he, if he sits by and does nothing?

Yet, what *can* he do? Three months is the age difference between them. So small, yet enough to dictate him *secondborn*. Unless she renounces her claim, the power can never be his.

This gives him an idea.

A terrible idea.

But an idea need not be good as long as it is forceful. This one settles in his mind with the leisure of a beast, and he can think of nothing else.

One night, while he sits across from God in the dining room, he finishes his meal promptly. And like most nights, God does not waste words on him.

For the first time, he does not mind.

He dons his jacket and sneaks into the house.

The house sits at the center point of Undar and Earth atop a hill, sharp and imposing. But it is not quite Undar, and it is not quite Earth. It is an in-between, untouched by death—and it is sacred. Where the memories of everyone who has ever lived are preserved forever.

It is how the dead continue to exist in Undar, everlasting, never dying.

Yet it is also dangerous to enter the house because one could gaze upon a life that isn't theirs and lose themselves—wander the halls for so long their bones will wear to dust.

But the spare is special in a way that no one sees. To be so discarded and forgotten means that when he enters the house, he weaves through it with ease. The house is far bigger than it appears on the outside and goes on for miles.

The walls and vaulted ceilings are coated in crystals of different colors and shapes.

The spare cannot bring the heir to Undar without the power of a king. But there is something else he can do. Something abominable, but it could save the world.

He studies every crystal.

He learns that a violet crystal belongs to a person who is still living, and when that person dies, it will vibrate—turn a blinding white—then settle into the crimson shade of the dead.

When he looks closer, he is able to discern the difference in the grooves, see the exact person who exists in it. Their life laid out like a deck of cards.

He must find the crystal that belongs to the heir.

It takes him weeks to find it, and when he does, he sees Vada Rivera to her core. That's her name—*Vada*.

Today she turns eighteen.

The spare feels hate roll through him with the force of a boulder.

Because the heir is so fleshy, so completely ordinary, so much *less* than everything he is. What has she done, other than sitting on this couch, watching television? While he has been *here*, trying to fix the world she broke.

He cannot reap the dead, but if he destroys her crystal, she will be erased.

Entirely.

But when he tries, nothing happens.

Every time he attacks, Undar quakes so hard even the house trembles. Awful wounds crawl up his arms, and a pained gasp escapes him.

God has placed excessive protection on the heir, which means even here, the spare can do nothing. For a moment, he feels helpless.

Until he notices the other crystal beside hers—so close it nearly merges.

It is her mother.

Strangely, her mother vibrates white *three times* in quick succession. She tries to die, often. She loves God, with her entire being. She wants to go to him.

The spare picks up both crystals and is submerged in a vision: fireworks. The heir stares at her mother, and her mother watches the sky. Through the crystal, he can feel the other organisms that are present. Each has their own distinct feeling that he tracks across the room.

It leads him toward a group of crystals in the corner. He must create such a spectacle that it cannot be ignored by even God.

The spare claws at one crystal, then another—they go dark and vanish.

These crystals, these lives, these memories, belonged to birds.

He destroys them until he sees it dawn on the mother's face— all this death falling on their heads.

He destroys them, even as Undar continues to quake, even as screams erupt outside of the house. Is the world finally ending? Nobody but him knows what is happening. Each crystal annihilated is a sin—and they all leave their mark on him. In the end, he will save more lives than he took.

At least, this is what he tells himself.

The heir's crystal vibrates in his hand.

It is no longer violet.

It is bright red.

Matias's bone lips have flattened into a thin line. "The world is still crumbling. Because you won't face the truth. *You do not belong there.*"

"You're right," Vada says, her voice shaking. "I don't belong there."

"It doesn't matter whether she belongs there or not," Avel says, angry. "You have ruined yourself, Matias. The house is sacred, and you went in there to destroy. There will be consequences for this. *Severe consequences.*"

"I'm not saying his actions were right. But you would let this world fall just to shelter me—and that's not right, either."

Matias looks surprised, Avel goes silent.

"I have never lived," she went on. "I have *endured*. The moment I was born, it sealed our fate. It cannot be undone."

Mama and Death, star-crossed and doomed from the beginning. Their love was so fierce it culminated into ruin, held off by Matias all these years. Denial was a prison of their own making, had them all suspended in purgatory, averting destruction.

But let it come.

Let it come.

To wait is not to live.

"No more hiding," she says. "I will claim the blood."

"Kings, mija," Mama chants.

It is no longer a choice. It is what happens when fates are forged.

Matias's grandeur fades in an instant. She expects him to rage. Instead, he *laughs*. He no longer looks at Vada like she is a shadow.

Now, he knows she is as formidable as the moon.

Death, flesh, horror—she is all.

The god of death holds out his wrist to the child of horror, says, "Drink."

The child drinks.

This is how a story ends, and another begins.

This is the child who broke the sky. She was born of love and death. But she can be more, will claim every stolen star and face the world from which she was taken.

This is how she comes home.

This is how she becomes king.

ETERNO

by

J. C. Cervantes

The Dark sounds like this.
Quiet. Still.
It starts out as poetry that shifts like falling snow. And then . . .

NOW

I stand on the bridge above the empty highway. Bits of snow begin to fall from the dark sky, slow and graceful, clinging to my thickening beard.

Soon the forest will be choked with white, a sharp contrast to the last year I've spent in the endless dark of the Hollow. The prison where my older brother locked me away all because I broke the cardinal rule—*never get involved with a human.*

I grip the icy railing and take in a lungful of air.

Was the world always this dark? This empty? And then the words float up from an unknown space, *empty without her*, and it hurts worse than the hunger burning a hole through my stomach.

With a deep breath, I hang my head and wonder how it all got so bad.

An inner voice provides the answer I've always known.

I ~~was~~ never meant to fall in love.

THEN

It was a wrong turn. Or at least that's what I tell myself—a turn that led me to the boy.

He's a mere ten years old, wearing blue pajamas with rocket ships and a T stitched on the collar. His face is ashen. The machines he's hooked up to don't register what's about to happen. I look at my pocket watch. The boy has three minutes before he leaves this world.

I'm not here to consume the Dark. Children aren't capable of it. I should go, make my way to the right floor, but I decide to sit with him, so he won't be alone. I watch his chest move up and down.

The boy cradles a tiny stuffed fox with bald patches where he's clung to it tightly.

The seconds tick by. So slow in the human world. I rub my stubbled chin, staring at the colored drawings taped to the wall—balloons, trees, a family of three holding hands.

In the same moment, a girl steps into the room. She's six. Her hands are stuffed into white socks with painted smiley faces, and she tacks another drawing on the wall: the outline of a child's hand.

If she could see me, maybe she would think I was a guardian angel. But she can't. And I'm not. I'm a devourer of the Dark. I'm a memory thief. I am Eterno.

Slowly, she climbs onto the foot of his bed. She stares at the boy. Her dark eyes are filled with an intensity beyond her years.

She crawls closer to her brother, lays her head on his chest, and whispers, "You said you wouldn't leave."

She knows what the machines don't.

A strange silence closes in. It's everywhere. Between the dark and the light. The rise and the fall. It fills the room.

The girl's eyes are closed as she clings to her brother—as she wills him to live. If I could, I'd grant her wish. I want to promise her things, promise her he won't feel pain. Tell her I'm sorry that she'll feel an emptiness for the rest of her life because when he dies, a part of her will die too. She won't be able to name the emptiness. She'll just know it's there.

In that moment, I make the choice that will be my undoing.

I reach into the boy's chest gently, past blood and bone. As always, the music only I can hear comes first, the air hums, and time stands still. Every human is different. Some souls release their last memory by playing a distant hymn, some a rhapsody, or a whispering melody. Others play the dull beat of a somber drum or a chaotic blast of horns. Some are pleasant. Many are not.

The boy's is light and airy, like a flute.

I hold tight to the memory, removing it slowly. The small orb of light pulsates in my hand as the boy's music fades away on his last breath. I turn back to the girl: Layla. I wish I didn't know her name. She looks through me as if she can see me.

But it's impossible—as impossible as the new melody that now fills the room.

I shouldn't be able to hear it and yet . . .

It grows into a song that is both soft and sudden. The notes spaced perfectly like nothing I've ever heard, filled with a yearning that pins me to this moment.

The girl unfolds herself from the bed. And his lifeless body.

The machines, inevitably, are blaring now. Nurses blow into the room. They push her back. All hands are on the boy. A man with graying hair rushes in. He's screaming at the others to do something to save his son.

The music washes out the human noise and chaos. It's only the girl and her haunting song. She stands in the corner, taking in the scene with a sort of anger too old for someone so young. Her dark hair falls across her face in a heap of waves. She clings to her brother's toy, but she doesn't cry.

The music gets inside of me, drawing me to her like a moth to a flame, and I don't want to leave because I know the moment I do, her music will be gone too.

I take a step back, and as I do, her eyes meet mine.

She can't see me, I tell myself. There's no way. Not unless I allow it.

And then a strange feeling rises inside of me. A want. I need to give her the boy's memory before it dies.

The girl begins to walk toward me. Her eyes lock with mine. But how . . .

She holds out the fox as a peace offering. I kneel, holding the memory out to her. An unfair exchange because what use do I have for a toy?

"What's your name?" she asks.

I shouldn't tell her. "Sebastián."

Her small mouth moves, working out the syllables. "Are you an angel?" she whispers, her voice nearly swallowed by the panicked noise of death.

I shake my head. How can I explain to a child that I was born fully grown from the *dreams* of an invisible moon only a few years ago? How can I tell her that my sole purpose, like my brother and sister, is to consume the Dark that humans grow inside them like weeds? We keep it from leaking into this world because when it does, it attaches itself to some unwitting fool who has no idea why their lives have changed so dramatically—why their existence has twisted into an unknowable thing, why they yearn for something they can't name.

She shrinks back as I kneel, reaching out to place the memory inside of her. "Will it hurt?" she asks.

"No."

With a nod, she comes closer and takes a deep breath as I gently set the memory inside of her heart. There is a tiny shudder, and then, "If you're not an angel, what are you?"

I stand, towering over her. "I'm no one."

NOW

I reach into my coat pocket and tug free my silver pocket watch.

In exactly thirty-two seconds, two cars will sail toward one another on the highway below. They will collide. There will be one survivor. But I'm not interested in her. I'm here for the one scheduled to die. I'm here to consume *his* Dark. Even though I know it will never be enough to stop the light growing inside of me. Not anymore. Exile didn't get rid of it. My will couldn't kill it either. I begged my mother, the unseen moon, night after night, day after day, to extinguish the flame. But she ignored my petitions.

Tick. Tick. Tick.

The snow whips around me in swirls that take the shape of

memories I don't want to look at. I see her face. Layla. Olive skin. Wide midnight eyes. A straight, proud jaw.

I had always meant to leave her behind, to never think about her again. But that song, her music I somehow heard, I couldn't let it go. And so, thirteen long years ago, I returned to her. It was the week after her brother's death. I rationalized that it was best for her because memories are too easy to lose, and I needed to make sure her brother's memory was unbroken. But one visit turned into many. Moments turned into years of friendship—talking, laughing, dancing. And then, two years ago, she turned seventeen—that was the year of promises, stolen kisses, and a love I wasn't built for. But mostly, it was the year she got sick.

Promise me you'll be the one, Bas.

How could I promise something I wasn't strong enough to carry out? To consume her Darkness would be my ruin. But she's dead now, and I'm ruined anyway.

The cars are five seconds away from impact.

Five

Four

I will myself to the middle of the highway—the engines roar across the dark. My driver will never see the other car until it's too late.

Three

Two

One

Tires screech across the slick asphalt. Steel crashes upon steel. The car with my driver catches air, rolls three times, and slams onto its side. The engine erupts in fire.

His heart is still beating. I wait.

There.

It slows and then . . .

I'm in the car next to him now. He's young. Twenty-seven. The smell of gasoline and singed flesh cling to the air. A photo of a girl hangs from his mirror. I'm not supposed to pay attention to the human details, but I can't help it. I try not to imagine her face when they tell her he's gone.

The man is bleeding. He fights against the pain, against the inevitable outcome. It's always the same. Humans cling to life. I've seen it a thousand times. I've stood in the debris of flames and ash where humans cry out in agony, wishing for death, and yet when it comes, they abandon their wish like poison.

The man's heartbeat slows with more time between each, and I wish he would just let go. It would make this easier. Then I realize—it's her. She's what he can't let go of. "I understand," I whisper. I would give my last breath to have been there when Layla left this world. But my brother stole that from me.

The snow's coming faster now, clinging to the forest trees.

Layla's voice echoes through it all. *Take me to the sea, Bas. I want to see it before . . .*

The man's eyes flutter to a mere squint.

He senses my presence, so I allow him to see me, a seventeen-year-old boy. Arduously, he nudges his chin to the photo of the girl. I want to tell him I'm not what he thinks I am. I'm not an angel.

"Tell . . ." His voice is weak, strained. I know what he wants.

I don't have time to deliver a memory. But I'm already nodding.

The rush of music floods my senses. It drowns out the Dark— a guitar gently strumming under the shade of lime trees. I hesitate. Then as always, I reach in, past the flesh and bone, past the shadows and the light. His last memory clings to me.

In the same instant, he takes his last breath, a tremor. The Dark emerges from deep within him, rising to the surface. I stop it from coming into this world, absorbing it as I'm supposed to. Its claws cling to me, ripping through me like shards of ice, splintering my bones. But it's trapped. My body aches with its added pressure, and a moment later, I'm on top of the bridge again, heaving—steeling myself against the thrashing monster inside of me. It's all anger and fear. At least there isn't hate. That's one of the worst. With forced deep breaths, I wait for the moment to be over. For the Dark to realize I've won. For my soul to digest its power and accept its strength.

I pocket the memory just as the air ripples. My sister Amaya appears next to me. She takes me in with expectant and distant eyes—not the demeanor of someone who hasn't seen me in over a year. For a moment, I think she might say something kind, but in the end, she chooses neutral. "You're looking better than expected, Sebastián."

"You missed me," I say.

She fluffs the brown fur shawl she's wearing, sighs, and nods to the car still on the highway. "As entertaining as you are, little brother, I'm here—"

"—to confirm my present state of mind."

"To prepare you, to make sure you're ready to face Gael."

Our brother.

"Ready?" I don't bother to mask the hate. "He ripped her away. He locked me up." *I never got to say goodbye.* "No, Amaya—I'm not ready." *I'm going to split him apart.*

· · ·

Amaya's brown skin glistens in the moonlight. Snowflakes cling to her lashes as she glances at her timepiece. It's different from mine—gold with filigree and burned edges as if it survived the fires of hell. Gifts from our brother. Well, *tools* is more accurate. We are only to use them to slow or stop time if we have to chase down escaped Darkness.

"I thought that might be the case," she says, "so it's a good thing I'm here. To stop you from doing something foolish." Amaya reaches up and moves a piece of hair from my eyes. "Self-pity isn't a good look, Sebastián."

I move her hand away slowly, catching her gaze with narrowed eyes. She's wrong. It's not pity I feel. It's barely contained rage.

"Besides," Amaya adds, sliding a pair of cashmere gloves over her delicate hands one at a time. "I've been doing this for hundreds of years longer than you, and, believe me, humans aren't worth the attention you give them." Then she gives me a half-smile to take the edge off her words.

One human was worth it.

My sister had been the one to teach me how to consume the Dark after I was created. She's flawless, detached, and gifted at predicting behavior—a thoroughly useful skill unlike mine: the power to transfer human memory. For me, memories are malleable as clay. I can read them when I'm invited to; I can carry and deliver them, and I can manipulate them, but only with the aid of a power that I no longer have. It would be easy to blame the Hollow, but the truth is my power to manipulate memory died when I allowed the love in.

My hands begin to tremble. I stick them in my pockets, away

from Amaya's careful gaze. Then the familiar burn begins at the center of my chest, and I focus on anything but the pain. The icy rush of a nearby stream, the distant hoot of an owl.

Amaya flashes her heavily black-lined eyes my way, studying me. "Bas, how in the hell did you ever survive the Hollow?"

She means exile. A place of utter emptiness where there is no sleep or memories or light. But for me, there was one memory I clung to: Layla. She's the only reason I survived.

THEN

She's sitting on the roof, legs curled into her body, head tilted back at the sky. She's nineteen, but for a sliver of a moment she looks as she did when she was ten, wide-eyed, staring at the sky like there are answers to all her questions wedged between the stars.

I sneak up behind her and wrap my arms around her waist. "Happy birthday," I whisper.

Laughing, she pushes me away. "Not for another ten minutes. Did you bring them?"

I set the paper sack in front of her. "Hot Tamales, Sour Patch Kids, and gummy worms," I tick off proudly.

She rips open the box of Hot Tamales and throws her head back to catch each piece. "This is perfect," she says through a mouthful of candy. "*You* are perfect."

I laugh. A deep foreign sound that fills me up.

Her dark eyes catch my gaze. Pools of the universe untouched by light.

Then with an amused expression, she says, "I have a joke for you."

"Layla, please. Your jokes are really awful."

"Why was the skeleton afraid of the storm?"

I pull her to her feet and twirl her once. "No idea."

"He didn't have any guts." She begins to laugh, a contagious sound that has me cracking up in less than two seconds. We stand like that under the stars, laughing until our energy is spent. She leans her head on my shoulder with a deep breath.

"When the time comes," she begins.

"Don't say it."

"Bas—I want you to be the one."

"Layla." My voice quivers.

"I'm sick." She wraps her arms around me. "And you can't save me."

But my brother can, I think, too afraid to let the words out. The risk is enormous, but what if it saved Layla? I'd pay the price. I'd pay any price just to know she was still breathing.

Before I can say another word, she kisses me. Deeply. Longingly. And I'm lost, drowning in a sea of emotion I've denied for so long.

She pulls free first. Eyes locked with mine. Then she smiles that disarming *everything-is-possible* smile. "Sorry. I know you hate the taste of Hot Tamales."

I touch the side of her face, gently sweeping her hair back. There is a painful stab in the center of my chest, an aching that runs through me. And I know—this is the moment I finally ~~realize~~ accept that I love her.

NOW

Amaya pulls me back to the moment with a sock to the arm. "Did you hear anything I said? You can't go on like this."

I level her with a steely gaze.

Amaya returns the iron will, but behind those eyes, behind the facade, I see my mentor and teacher. Her eyes rake over me with a knowing that's unnerving because she knows about my weakness.

She knows my secret.

While I once thrived on the Dark, now it merely keeps me half alive. I have become a deep well of both darkness and light, and the two cannot live together. I clench my fists inside my coat pockets, trying to ignore the slow burn snaking through me like a stream of lava.

The rage speaks to me in shadowy whispers. "I will never forgive him." *For robbing me of whatever time Layla had left on this earth.*

"Sebastián." Amaya's eyes have a faraway, nearly terrified look, and I have never known my sister to be afraid. "I didn't come here to just check on you," she says. "I have another purpose."

I grow unnaturally cold. Waiting.

"There is a truth you should know," she says. "And I wanted to be the one to tell you."

I prickle with anticipation, knowing it can't be anything good. "What truth?"

"She's alive."

Everything stills. There is no sound, no breath, no cold or hunger. I think she's being cruel, gaming me for some sick sport, but then I see the gravity in her expression, and I know.

I grip my sister by the shoulders. "What do you mean? She was sick—she was . . ." *Dying.*

Amaya breaks free of me with one hard twist. "Well, Gael fixed all that."

Why would my brother save the one person he blamed for my greatest weakness? Falling in love. I had gone to him, had pleaded with him. He had refused.

I don't have to say the words for my sister to fill in the blanks. "Don't you see? Layla is Gael's new pawn."

I feel sick. Battling between despair and hope, but I'm too afraid to believe what Amaya is telling me.

"Why would he do that?" My voice breaks.

As a lesson to you, so you will know your role and who you answer to in this life and the next.

The words aren't my sister's. They belong to Gael. The memory of a once-forgotten whisper, while I was in the Hollow, rises just out of reach but close enough to taunt me.

"You've forgotten what we are," Amaya says with no trace of regret. "We are Eternos. And Gael wants you to remember that. To make sure you comply."

I realize the gravity of my situation. One misstep on my part and Gael will drain Layla's life away slowly, worse than the illness that once possessed her body.

Amaya rubs the dead animal draped around her neck. And the way she looks at me, the way her eyes see beyond me is unsettling. The strength of the unseen moon runs deep in Amaya. She is a favorite. I am not. I've strayed too far from who we are.

"Don't be a fool, Sebastián."

Amaya is right about one thing. I'm a fool if I think I could ever be with Layla again. She's human. I'm a monster. It's ironic, really—there is no place or possibility for love in my world and yet . . . it found its way inside of me, poisoning my purpose.

"I know you want to go to her," Amaya says flatly. "But if you do, Gael will make her suffer."

I know this. I would expect nothing less from my brother. And yet. Layla is alive. Her illness is gone. *She's ALIVE.* A wave of emotions rises inside me—joy, shock, anger, all vying for my attention, but the one I feel the deepest is also the one that cuts me to my core—hope. I have so many questions, but the only one that makes it to the surface is, "Is she happy?"

Amaya sighs. "I don't keep tabs on her, and I wouldn't know what real happiness looks like. Humans wear ridiculous masks their entire lives, hiding their internal worlds from the world outside."

If Amaya had said yes, if she had given me any morsel of hope that Layla is whole, then maybe I could have let it go. But instead, she serves me another plate of cruelty.

"You don't have to worry about her anymore, little brother. She never thinks about you."

"I thought you didn't keep tabs on her." I tighten my jaw, waiting for the blow I know is coming.

"Her memories of you are gone," Amaya says coldly. "Gael took them all."

I fight the primal urge to tear after Gael, but what good would it do? When he has the most powerful piece on the board. Layla would only pay for my sins. I convince myself it's better this way. That memories of me would only bring her pain and suffering.

And yet, I can't figure out how he did it. Gael is powerful, but his isn't the gift of memory. That is mine and mine alone.

I don't realize I'm still gripping the orb until the warmth of the dead man's memory pulses in my hand, reminding me it has somewhere to be.

"How did he do it?" I have to know.

Amaya swipes the memory away, gripping the tiny orb of light that belongs to someone else. "Humans are so pathetic, and you cling to them as if *they're* your family." She turns the light slowly in her hand. It casts a small shadow, and if it doesn't get delivered soon, it'll die. "Such an ordinary thing," she says distastefully.

"How did he do it?" I ask. More forcefully this time.

"I don't know," she finally says, answering my question. She's lying. But why?

Amaya steps back. She gives me a cold stare, and I see it—the disdain for humans that always makes an appearance. "We aren't the monsters, hermanito. They are. Killing each other over insignificant gains like shoes or a new car. Or how about those humans that murder for the fun of it, or because of someone's name or skin color or . . . ?" Her eyes harden. "Their sins run deeper than murder. Their atrocities are only limited by their sick imaginations. They—*they* are the ones who gave rise to the Dark. So, you tell me who the monsters are."

Taking advantage of Amaya's distraction, I lunge for the orb, but she's fast. Too fast. She disappears the moment we connect. By the time I catch on, she's next to the car on the highway below, calling me, taunting me to come closer. So I do.

"You want it back?" Amaya says, closing her fist over the light.

"I'm not in the mood for games."

With a heavy sigh, Amaya says, "Your soul has always been made of water. It's time it's made of fire."

Her gaze meets mine, and she holds it there for a while as if she is deciding what she will tell me. She nods to the woman pinned in the car. "Take her."

"Her Dark isn't going to be enough," I argue. Not to heal me, not to put me back together again. Amaya knows this, so why is she provoking me?

"Who said anything about the Dark?"

A pause.

"But she's alive and . . ."

And then I see with absolute clarity what she's asking me to do.

"No way," I say, shaking my head. "I can't take her life force."

"You can't or you won't?"

I see the gravity of her expression, the near pleasure radiating at my dilemma. My mind reels, and I can't find a solution fast enough.

In a rare unguarded moment, her face softens. "I don't want to lose you again, Sebastián."

A thought blooms inside me: *you can either be imprisoned or free, but either way, you'll always be a monster.*

In a surprising move, Amaya opens her palm, and when I reach for the memory still in her grasp, she tosses it into the car window, where it lands on the passenger seat. I will myself into the car and pocket the orb. The woman, fifty-four, is slumped against the door, unconscious. The smell of fresh blood fills the air, inviting me closer to the rising Dark.

She chokes out small breaths.

I won't do this.

Layla's memory reaches for me. It's a living thing, stretching inside of me, urging me to choose another way.

Do you love me, Bas?

Amaya appears in the backseat. "Never hesitate."

Before I know it, she thrusts my hand into the human's chest, and a wave of unimaginable power grips me. It's Amaya's power that guides my reach, holds it there. The Dark knows I'm here. It rises until we're touching, and only then does Amaya let go. But instead of the Dark peeling away as always, I have to rip it away. It's like nothing I've ever felt, not at all like what I've consumed before. That was like carrying a tiny flame. This is like carrying countless blazing torches. There's no music. No memory to catch. Only terrible static. And then comes the scream of a thousand agonizing deaths—shattering me into a million pieces.

I want to let go, anything to get the screaming in my mind to stop. But it's too late.

Darkness, pain, agony, and beautiful fear race through me at the speed of light.

And then it happens. The last of the woman's energy drains into me, feeding an ache in me that's always been there. Instantly the frenzy begins. Slow at first, then so fast I welcome it.

The pleasure, the want rips me to shreds. Burns me alive. Makes me whole.

And then, only then, does the world fall silent, and I let go.

Amaya is gone. Breathless, I look at the woman now, slumped like an empty sack. Small whimpers fill the car. I stare helplessly at the effect of my unspeakable crime. She's still alive. The terror of the moment crashes into me with mind-numbing force.

She's. Still. Alive.

If I let her live, she'll be catatonic, an empty shell. The human mind can never come back from what we do to it, which is why we only take Dark from the dying. But I've done more than that. I've just stolen most of her life force.

I stare at my hands, teeming with power, knowing the choice before me is no choice at all.

Never hesitate.

I snap her neck.

Amaya is standing outside the car. I pin her against the passenger door. My newly fed strength is no match for her. "You set me up!" Even my voice sounds like a monster's, vibrating with hate and anger and the kind of heat that could burn up the world.

Her eyes are empty, unknowable. "And look at you. I can see the immense power vibrating inside of you. Do you feel it?"

Yes, I feel it. It's both intoxicating and nauseating. And I hate myself for it.

"You ripped Dark from a . . ." I can't even bring myself to say the words. "That woman was alive!"

"Oh, Sebastián. You're too sentimental. She was going to die. Someday. You just helped her along. And it really was gallant of you to end things so quickly."

"You gave me no choice!"

"You could've released her any time you wanted. I may have led you to her life force, but no one made you consume it. And now you know, you can see and feel who you *really* are. You're not like them!"

Her lies are so good I can feel myself nearly nodding until I realize I never had the strength to release that woman. The second I tasted the power, I lost myself, gave in to the hunger and the want.

"Look, little brother. We're at the top of the food chain, and that means—"

"No! We were never meant to steal a life!"

Amaya's lips part slightly, and I can see the smile hiding there.

"Your innocence has always been your greatest charm and your worst trait. It has also made you so easy to predict."

The snow tumbles faster, clinging to the road, to the car where the woman's hollowed-out body is all that remains of her. Anger and guilt compete with the power pulsing through me. Dead is better than catatonic. This is what I tell myself.

Do you love me, Bas?

I never told Layla the truth. I never said yes. Why the fuck didn't I say yes?

I grip the memory in my pocket, feeling it pulse in my hand, wishing I could take back the last few minutes. "You knew I wouldn't be able to let go," I say.

A rare instant of regret passes over my sister's face, and I can only wonder what she is up to.

I shouldn't be here. I tell myself it's to prove I'm not a monster. That what I have just done can be erased. Or maybe old habits die hard.

The house I've come to is their house. The dead man and the girl in the photo.

The messenger will arrive soon to tell the girl he's gone. They will never marry in the spring as they'd planned. They will never have children or grow old together.

I step inside the bedroom. The walls are yellow, and there's a small corkboard filled with photos of smiling faces, the Eiffel Tower, a shaded kiss, the ocean, two different feet with a word written across each: *one* and *heart*.

The messenger is already on her way. These are the girl's last minutes of peace, of not knowing he's no longer in this world.

The girl is sitting at her desk. Her eyes are locked on an astronomy book. Dirty blond hair, cut at odd angles, falls around her full face.

The knock at the door comes right on schedule.

The girl looks up.

Soon she'll share this little room with only grief.

Pulling the pink robe tighter around her waist, she answers the door.

A cop with thinning gray hair stands there. Her mouth moves, but I don't listen to the words because they're all the same. They're always the same no matter what the language—no matter who the messenger.

I expect wailing.

But the girl, this girl, shakes her head slowly. The anguish washes over her, through her. She grabs hold of her stomach, folds herself in half, and opens her mouth in a silent scream.

The cop tries to hold her up before she falls to her knees.

The girl is lost in despair and doesn't feel the feeble attempts to comfort her. This is what love reduces humans to.

I turn away and wait. When the words have been said, when the tears are still flowing, when the girl is alone again, I pull my stopwatch from my pocket.

I have ten minutes before Gael knows I've stopped time.

The girl's lying on the floor, knees curled into her chest—frozen in time and grief. I stand over her, place my hand on her arm and tell her the memory the man shed as he died. Most humans leave at least one memory. Some aren't worth sharing, but this one. This one is a gift. One she'll see and feel and smell for years to come, never knowing how its vitality came to her.

I take the dying memory from my coat pocket and hold it in my hand, the same hand I place over her heart. Slowly, the light seeps in, and I close my eyes, infusing the memory to her very bones.

You were in a shady park. His hands were shaking, and you were eating ice cream, chocolate. You didn't know that the ring was in his pocket. You were talking about some poem you'd read. He was terrified . . . not to ask you to marry him, but that you'd say yes. Because if you said yes, it meant you loved him as much as he loved you. And that meant he finally had something to lose.

Right before he took the ring from his pocket, he watched the way the sunlight spilled through the trees, touching the tips of your hair, and everything stood still for him in that single moment because he knew it was perfect and nothing would ever be so perfect again.

I stare down at her bare feet. The word *One* is written across her left foot, and that's when I realize it's a tattoo.

One Heart.

Something gnaws at my core. Their feelings, this love they let in, only made them vulnerable, only paved the inevitable path toward pain.

And then I wonder if she would have chosen differently, knowing how things would end. My own choice stands before me, raw and repulsive. I begin with the rationalizations: *I'll stop time. Gael won't know if I keep it under ten minutes. Just to see Layla one last time. I have to know she's okay.*

In an instant, I'm standing in the shadows of Layla's small home. But she isn't here. I know because I can't hear her music. Unimaginable strings wrapped in a distant chant that rises slowly into an aching crescendo.

In the shadows, I seethe. Lost in a sea of questions with the same one rising to the top.

Amaya appears next to me.

"Where is she?!" I demand, taking a forceful step closer. She recoils as if I am a threat. Maybe I am. For once, her strength is no match for mine, but she did that. It's her fault I am momentarily more powerful than she is.

"I knew you would come here," she says. "Just like I know that you will be devoured by your"—she swallows as if she can't bring herself to finish—"your love for her. These feelings will consume you, and you'll never be one of us again."

Before she spills the last word, I'm already shaking my head. "I would never risk her. I just need to know she's okay."

A sad smile tugs at my sister's lips. "That's what you will tell yourself, but in the end . . ." Amaya's knowing eyes search my face in slow concerned circles. "Look inside."

It takes a moment for me to grasp what she is asking me to do. Amaya has never invited me into her memory. "Why?" I ask, suspicious that this is some kind of trick.

She grips my hand tighter. "Because your strength will only last for so long and because I want you to have a choice."

I think her mind will be an iron wall, but getting into Amaya's memory is easier than expected, as if gliding through clear water.

Layla sits at her piano. There is a slant of sunlight, cool and distant. Feathery shadows crowd the edge of the room and its details. All I can see is the back of Layla. I want to move closer, but an invisible force holds me in place.

This means my sister doesn't want me to get too close, so I stand in the corner.

Waiting. Watching. Wishing I could see Layla's face.

She touches the keys delicately as if they are made of sand. I have lis-
tened to her play a thousand times, and every time feels like the first time.
This is her gift. The thing inside of her that was meant for the world.

Why are her fingers trembling?

They press on the keys. But it's wrong. The notes are sharp distant
incoherent cries.

She tries again and again, but there is no music—only noise. Soon she
is on her feet, fists pounding the piano. A wine glass I hadn't seen crashes
to the ground, spilling red onto white tile.

Layla is on her knees, hands over her face, sobbing onto the glass.

The room's details come into full view. The memory rushes me as
if the chains holding me in the corner have been broken. Instantly I am
at her side. Her face is pale, her eyes sunken. She reeks of alcohol—of
hopelessness and despair.

And the walls. They are filled with music sheets taped at awkward
angles.

Layla is crawling over the broken glass, searching for the wine bottle
under the small window.

Desperation claws at my heart. I want to reach for her, to hold her,
to tell her I love her. But this is a memory, and there is no place for me
here.

And then I smell it—the Dark. It consumes her, thrashes around
inside of her like the unwelcomed intruder it is.

Amaya releases me.

Angry tears burn my eyes. My sister watches my suffering,
watches as the realization dawns slowly, painfully.

Ask me about Layla, Gael asked every time he visited me in the
Hollow. He knew I would cling to her memory and he used it to

mock me. *Ask me how she died.* I refused, day after day, month after month. Until this last visit, when he leaned close and whispered, *She was swallowed by the Dark.*

I didn't see it then. I was too lost in the chaos and suffering. Now, though, the awareness blooms through me with the power of a thousand suns.

My brother didn't have the power to take her memories of me. He sent the Dark to do it.

The monster inside of me heaves in the shadows. Waiting to be unleashed. "Why?" I ask even though I know the answer. My brother is cruel. Unfeeling. A beast.

"Control," Amaya says coolly.

"You told me you didn't know."

Amaya deadpans, "I went to see her . . . once. Because I knew we would end up here. Because I was hoping I was wrong, that you wouldn't take this path. That maybe you really could let her go."

"Why did you show me?"

"I told you. I want you to have a choice . . ." She hesitates. "A choice I never had."

I don't need to ask. I see it in her eyes—an unfinished life she left behind. That the monster has swallowed.

"It was never love," she assures, standing taller. "But . . . it was something."

"Amaya," I say, trying to keep pace with my racing, desperate thoughts. "If I consume her Dark, it will leave her worse off than she is. You know that."

"But this isn't Layla's Dark," Amaya says in a near-urging tone. "It's Gael's unnatural creation, and that means you can take it all. But it will hurt. Worse than anything you've ever experienced."

And then I see with painful clarity. Amaya used her gift of perception to tell her exactly what I would do. And then she fed me the power she knew I would need to do it.

I stand in the shadows one hundred yards from a small adobe bathed in moonlight. I stare up at the midnight sky. The unseen moon is watching me. Knowing what I am about to do. Tonight, my mother is red and lustful.

Layla is so close I begin to hear the music that has always radiated from her. Except for tonight, it's merely broken, hollow notes smothered by the Dark.

I feel nothing and everything.

With each step I take toward Layla's new house, I allow the memories to wash through me as if they can cleanse what I've done, who I am. The laughter and joy and dreams that two hearts share as naturally as the rain nourishes the sea.

The mist thickens all around me in a blur.

I'm inside now, following the sound of her. I stand outside a door, terrified to open it. Knowing that on the other side is a pain too great to bear.

My stomach roils, and the shadows begin to crawl. I unpocket my watch and protect the moment by stopping time.

I have ten minutes, too small, too big.

Layla is asleep. Her dark hair spills across the white sheets. Her face looks older, hardened. So many emotions flood through me: Regret. Anger. Love.

I kneel next to her, the words stuck in my throat before I force out, "Layla."

For an instant, I worry her name is a magic charm that will

unlock time, but everything stays frozen—everything but me. With an unsteady hand, I reach out and move a stray hair from her face before taking her hand in mine.

Gently, I reach into her heart, searching to confirm what I already know. The Dark is there, sleeping inside of her. Its belly full on our memories.

And it knows I'm here.

Leaning close, I whisper, "I wish I could change what happened. I wish I could love you the way you deserve to be loved."

The Dark is rising, gathering its strength.

I close my eyes, and my head drops with some kind of defeat that I'm terrified will define me.

Then, without thinking, my hand reaches deeper, past her heart and blood and bones, into the place I know Gael would have planted the Dark. Her very soul. Instant hunger burns through me as I touch her life force. The monster inside of me climbs to the surface, screaming *YES*.

All coherent thoughts vanish. There are only instincts now. The frenzy begins, drowning me, pulling me under. I rage against the desire.

Then, with every ounce of strength I have, I force myself into perfect stillness. Brace myself against the agony.

THEN

She's lying with her belly pressed against the floor, tapping her pencil against the hardwood.

"Are you writing a song for me?" I ask.

"Nope." She keeps her eyes fixed on the paper in front of her, but she can't hide the smile curling up the corners of her mouth.

"You should," I say, planting myself beside her. "It'd be a good song."

She rolls over, pensive but playful. "Tell me again what my music sounds like."

"Perfect. Beautiful. Painful."

"Bas."

"We've been over this."

She gives me a pleading look. So, I try to hum the melody, but it comes out all wrong.

"I have an idea!" Layla jumps to her feet and goes to the piano in the corner where she sits, fingers hovering. "I'll play each key, and you tell me when it's right."

"I know you're a musical genius, but I'm pretty sure you can't replicate it."

With a smug, determined expression, she says, "Or I could tell you jokes for the next few hours."

My frown is a playful one. "Are those my only two choices?"

She presses a key and then another. I shake my head over and over as she plays a new note. And then . . . "Wait! That one. What is that?"

"C-sharp." She pats the bench next to her. I oblige. Knowing what Layla wants is an impossible feat.

"Why do you want to play it so bad?" I ask.

A pause.

"I want to hear what you hear." She lays her head on my shoulder. "To feel what you feel."

NOW

I let the memories quiet the monster. But the pain remains.

You're going to need a greater power than you've ever known.

"You will be happy," I manage. "You will laugh and . . . you will love."

The Dark inside of Layla thrashes as I reach for it, rip it from its home, and consume it whole.

My agony deepens. But I don't let go. I can't. Not until it's done.

The Dark heaves inside of me, watching, waiting to see what I am about to do. My God, how did she survive? My brother's cocktail is made of contempt, rage, and endless fear.

I momentarily start time again to be sure that she is free.

There. Something gives way inside of her. I feel it. Like bits of stone falling away from a mountain. Wonder and stillness and light. Her breath comes in a steady, peaceful rhythm.

She stirs—sighs quietly.

My breath catches in my throat. I want those eyes to hold me again, to reflect the person only she could see. How easy it would be, but at what cost?

"Bas," she mutters softly, still asleep.

I go stone cold. It's not possible. My brother . . . he buried every memory of me with the Dark.

"Please," she whispers.

I feel so weak at that moment that I'm terrified I will give in. I'll do whatever it is that she is asking. But the Dark is pulsing, reminding me of her endless suffering. And I know I will never put her at risk again.

That's when I see it. The single memory of me she has hidden. It's in the deepest recesses of her soul. Damn stubborn girl.

I nearly give an appreciative laugh at her ingenuity. A human who deceived Gael. Priceless.

Do you love me, Bas?

I trace the memory's edges—the beauty and hope of it. It clings to her, and I know even I can't free her of its power. But I can change it. I can change everything so that she will finally be safe. And Gael will get what he wants. Me.

I lift my face to the window, to my mother. I don't know what I'm asking for—strength? Courage? The ability to just . . . let . . . go. I bring time to a standstill again, knowing I am doing more than letting Layla go. I am letting myself go. I lean down and kiss her softly, slowly. Feeling the warmth of her lips.

To create a memory takes the power of a thousand others. It's a trade—all of mine for a single one for her. By doing this, I will save her, but I will also forget. Layla's laugh. Her touch. The way she smells like green apples in the fall. The way her hair favors the left side of her face. The way she clings to the tiny toy fox, still. Its glass eyes stare at me from the side of her pillow now.

I draw up every memory I have of her to create a new one. My memories come slow and silent, tiptoeing through me. Gathering strength to feed the only one that matters.

We're standing at the edge of the sea.

Layla tilts her head up to the sky, where the full moon shines brightly. "Show me the location of the hidden moon again."

I take her hand and point her finger to the sky. "There, to the right, near the north star."

We're quiet for a moment before she utters, "You were born from her dreams."

The way she says it sounds romantic, but it's not, so I correct her. "That doesn't mean I'm not a—"

She whirls, pressing her finger to my lips, but she doesn't look at me. Instead, she takes several deep breaths then raises her gaze. Those eyes. "Don't say it."

"Okay."

She traces her thumb over my lower lip. "Tell me something else. Tell me how you feel."

"Layla."

"Do you love me, Bas?"

I stare at her stone-faced. To tell her will rip me open, will force me to admit a truth that could be my demise.

In the actual memory, I didn't answer. But in this one . . .

Do you love me, Bas?

I smile. And wrap her in my arms. In her ear, I whisper, I will always love you.

And then I let her go.

I stare at the memory I just created with the power of all the others. The one I know will nourish her. She won't remember me as the monster who loved her. She will only remember someone who made her whole. Who filled her heart with joy, not fear. She will remember me as a pleasant dream that gives her permission to live, to make music. And to love.

Gently, I cup the circle of light and place it into her heart, clinging to the memory—to her.

My time is up.

Slowly, I release one finger.

And then another.

Tears sting my eyes. "You're going to be safe now," I whisper.

God, I want to hold this moment forever. Hold Layla forever. But I can feel the memories of her fading like the sun dipping into the horizon. Trembling, I release another finger. And another. I stare at the last one through blurred vision.

Let her go. And so I do . . .

I stand.

Shaken by what, I don't know. A silver beam of the unseen moon's light illuminates the sleeping stranger. The girl looks so young and beautiful and in possession of peace I will never know.

Unhurriedly, I walk into the night. Where it's just begun to snow.

There is a foreign weight inside my pocket—a small thread-bare fox. I grip it tightly, and the most beautiful music wraps around me as I make my way home.

WHITE WATER, BLUE OCEAN

By

Linda Raquel Nieves Pérez

When Abuela told me she loved me, we all ignored the putrid smell that filled the room. Her eyes seemed happy, but there was a tremble in her hands as she examined our faces. It was obvious she was trying to see if we could smell it.

The lie.

Panic urged me away, the usual reaction to the cursed foam that was slowly pouring from her eyes and ears, surrounding both of us in a bubble of rotten clouds. I clenched my back muscles and managed to accept her hand as she caressed my cheek. I curled my lips into a forced smile and kissed Abuela, holding my breath so the worst of the smell didn't hit me, but the white fumes settled heavily in my lungs, weighing down my chest.

That was as much as I could take. My eyes watered with the vapors, and it took me a second to collect myself and say, "Bendición, Abuela," before leaving, making my escape.

Outside, the strong sun brought me back to another reality. The salty ocean breeze provided a sharp contrast to the poison inside the house, but it carried too many other implications to be comfortable. I could breathe clean air, but my chest wasn't any lighter.

The short steps of my mother followed me outside, and she looked around the street to make sure no one could see us before grabbing my arm.

"Gabriel, you're *not* making a scene in front of everyone," she hissed as she tried to control her hair from getting in her face. Her eyes looked angry, but her voice was pleading. I didn't know which emotion was stronger nor which one was directed at me, and which one was directed at the situation. She didn't want me to go back any more than I wanted to but knew she needed to try. "Go back inside and smile. How hard can it be to stand beside your primas and give your abuela the respect she deserves for five minutes?" I could hear the words she wasn't saying: *don't let them think they are right about us.*

Her voice had lowered to a whisper for the last words, her eyes focusing on Don Julio, Abuela's neighbor, across the street. She loosened her grip on my arm, and I shook it away. I took three steps before she whispered my name again.

"Ma, I'll be back for dinner. Let me get away for a few minutes. You know," I spied Don Julio crossing the street toward us as I spoke, "I *can't* be there right now. I just need to breathe for a moment." If only air could help me escape everything hidden in that house.

Don Julio had reached us and gave us a warm greeting before asking about our life "allá afuera" to my mother, who watched me for a few beats as I stepped away before turning her attention to him.

That was the famous question. For some reason, everyone

wanted to know about the differences in gas prices (¿tan caro?) and milk (¿tan barato?). Life "allá afuera" seemed to consist of those two things, with the occasional question about sports teams thrown in. Ma, always obliging, answered all the questions with a smile, laughing at the right moments even when she'd heard the same jokes and replies a dozen times. Usually, I dreaded the question, but today I would take any opportunity to run away.

The beach seemed to call my name with the low, rough whisper of a wave, and I followed.

No one in my family remembers how the curse started. My mother and tías have refused to address it beyond the nature of the curse. "Eso es buscar lo que no se te ha perdí'o," they used to whisper to us when we asked questions. The only answer we ever received was this: *the García family, with girls as beautiful as the moon and bodies blessed by the Earth, can't lie.* Which is, ironically, the first lie we're told: we can lie.

It just kills us slowly.

When that didn't calm us, the tías started telling us the second lie: *the García family, with boys that shine like the sun and hands that build dreams of light, can't fall in love.* This seemed to terrify my primas, but I was never satisfied.

But what about me? I started to ask. *What about the Garcías that don't fit those categories?* At that, my tías would shush me and walk away, whispering among themselves about the problematic sheep of the family.

As time passed, the only one that kept asking questions was me. They couldn't lie and make up something that would satisfy my curiosity because whenever they tried, the traitorous white snitch would cloud their eyes and start leaking from their ears. So they took me to Abuela, sure that she could scare me into silence.

"Tu madre . . . she's scared of what she doesn't know, so she holds to what she does. To her, the reasons this curse exists are not important; she focuses on the fact that it exists. She doesn't need to ask more questions, just live with what she got. You must try to understand that. She's forgotten the Ocean to create her happiness," she told me as we swung on the hamaca behind her house. "Now your tías . . . Your tías are scared of what knowing could mean, which is a curse in itself. In this world, we are constantly hurt by what we know; it's terrifying when you can't put a name to the source of your pain."

And so Abuela told me the story of a young woman whose love for a goddess was so strong that it damned her family for eternity. Pushed between family honor and the love of her life, the lies her family forced her to speak turned into daggers in the goddess's heart. Those same lies would doom them: every García who lied was engulfed in a cloud of putrid hate that poured from their eyes and ears. *White lies*. The vapors of this cloud were poisonous; no lie could pass unnoticed. Their lives were changed forever, and every generation after that carried the weight of a broken heart.

She took me to the beach and taught me to hear its voice, following the soothing melodies of the Ocean. She taught me the language of the water and its hidden messages. She taught me never to fear the water and its love. And she taught me how to fear expectations, for they only brought heartbreak.

It felt like a fairy tale, where love could cure and curse. I used to love the story as a child. But one day, Abuela lost her connection to the Ocean, and not being able to hear its voice broke her. Whenever I tried to talk about it, my tías would get her away, saying the stories of deities and siren songs were the reason we remained cursed, that we needed to forget about those old sayings. Ironically, that was the most I'd heard them say about our curse in years.

The words of the story became too personal and raw. Abuela grew weak, and the waves stopped calling her name. Not soon after, she lost her ability to see the white lies. But only to see them: the poison stayed with all of us, a constant reminder of what we carried, of what was inside of us.

My tías rejoiced in their rightness seeing her like that. With condescending voices and smiling lips, they reminded her of their cautionary tale and blamed love for it. More specifically, her love for *us*, for *me*.

They also blamed *my* love. I wasn't in love with someone else. I was in love with *myself*—with who I knew I was. And that, for some reason, made my tías angrier.

It turned out that the García family hadn't changed much since they angered the goddess: they wanted to continue to force people to lie for their convenience.

History repeated itself.

I could feel Ma getting frustrated by the situation, so what happened next didn't take me as a surprise.

We moved away to a place where the Ocean whispered no secrets, and the water sang no music.

· · ·

The rough sand welcomed me as I tried to listen closely to the Ocean, attempting to decipher the words it whispered one step at a time. Deep, salty air filled my lungs, and, unlike earlier, when the ocean breeze reminded me of cages, I felt at home. Free. I sat down, trying to get used to the voice of the Ocean again. It had been so long since I'd listened to it that the words felt far away, tangled. The sun burned my cheeks as I longed for the cold caress of the water. Frustration was building inside me when I saw a dark figure make its way from Abuela's house.

My father walked over and sat by my side, giving me a silent nod that said more than any words. *I am here.* He couldn't hear the Ocean's voice, but I knew he tried for me.

When the sun didn't warm my face as much, he stood up and extended his hand toward me. "Let's go, Gabo. Your mom has probably been expecting us for a while." I took his hand and shook as much sand as I could from my shorts, but not much could be done. Before entering the house, I found my voice.

"How do you do it, Pa?"

"How do I do what?" he shot back, confused.

"Stay with us with all this . . ." I moved my hand around the air in front of me, unable to explain so much in a few words. "*This.*"

He seemed to weigh my question before looking me in the eye. "I do it because I love you, and I feel your love for me."

The answer seemed so obvious, yet so strange. I recalled what my tías had said and heard myself ask, "But I thought Garcías weren't supposed to fall in love."

At this, he gave me a sad smile.

"Look around us, Gabo. The curse isn't being unable to love. The curse is not letting yourself love, hiding behind a white curtain, and blaming it for everything wrong in your life. The Garcías prefer perfect illusions to real feelings, and anyone who doesn't follow that pattern is deemed wrong." He glanced around, looking like he'd said too much. "I'm sorry, this house makes me ramble."

His words fell heavily on my chest as if answers to questions I didn't have the words to form.

My father seldom spoke about the curse, letting Ma take the lead. After all, he didn't live with the poison inside us; there was just so much he could say about it. But after leaving the family, Ma refused to speak about the curse or the voice of the Ocean. Like my tías, she wanted to ignore the curse. Unlike my tías, who constantly said they didn't want to talk about it but brought it up at least twice in every conversation, she did. *Building yourself around a curse only makes the poison stronger*, she constantly said when I asked too much. *There's more to life than lies, Gabriel.*

Scratching his head, he took a step forward and opened the door, making me focus on reality again. We could hear my primas across the hall, so he stepped to the right, heading for the dining room. "Entra. I'll go around and look for your mom." Before taking too many steps, he added, "And Gabo? I don't think you and your mother are as different as you think. Your love just shows differently."

My primas Nahima and Soé were in the living room as I entered. Soé had recently turned seventeen, like me, and Nahima and her were talking about senior year excitedly. Most of the García family had been homeschooled through childhood and then attended college or university online, but tía Rocío had agreed to let her go to their local high school to see how well she could manage the environment. Her goal is to study biophysics to find a cure for our "disease," but considering our situation, it's hard to be in a classroom full of people that could crack our shell if they tried too much.

I tried my best to listen, but my mind was still trying to make sense of my father's last comment, and I found it nearly impossible. Excusing myself, I walked to the kitchen, sure that a glass of water could help clear my mind. As I grew closer, the voices of my tías reached me. It was my mother's name muttered with strong aversion that stopped me.

"Marisol did it again. She's there with Mami setting the table like she isn't the reason our mother is so ill. That Patricia has grown to be the most disrespectful girl of this family y Mami le pasa la mano."

"Lorena," tía Rocío's voice interrupted, "cálmate. They mean no harm. Let us have a nice family dinner and be done with it. They'll jump back on a plane, and you won't see them for another year."

"That is my only consolation. I'm tired of Mami pretending Mari is her perfect little princess all the time. She left the house with *that* man. Dañando la raza, ignoring their roots, and—"

Loud steps from the dining room interrupted tía Lorena's tantrum, and I hurried away for fear of being found out.

Tía Lorena treated me with such politeness as we gathered for dinner that my heart wanted to justify her earlier words. *Surely I misheard her. Surely she couldn't pretend so well. The curse would betray her.*

I had started to think that we could be civil for the rest of the day, but then my tía's voice interrupted the peace.

"Patricia, pass me the water, please," she said, eyeing the gigantic bottle of water beside me. I wanted to make my hand move, but I was frozen in place. Hearing that name this many times in a day was catching up to me. "The water," she repeated, apparently growing impatient.

"Their name is Gabriel, Lorena," said my mother as she passed her the cursed bottle.

"*Her* name," Lorena spat as she stood up, the loud scratch of the chair against the floor adding an out-of-tune cord to the wild beat of my heart, "is Patricia, no matter what she's led your husband and you to believe."

Mom stood up and grabbed her food, ready to move outside. I had seen this scene many times growing up: tía Lorena would say something hurtful, and Mami would go outside to eat, trying to keep the peace between sisters.

"There she goes, con el rabo entre las patas. She can never have an actual conversation," tía Lorena whispered, putting another bite of my mother's potato salad in her mouth. Mom turned around.

"I'm only leaving because you can't seem to respect anyone but yourself in this house, *hermanita*. But if you want me to stay, you can start by calling my child by their name."

The next things passed like a blur. I was still trying to escape the physical pain my deadname brought me, but tía Lorena screaming, "Vete con los negros esos," and insulting my mother for ruining the family rang clearly in my ears.

"Esta maldición es eterna, but the worst thing I have to endure is the talk of the neighbors," Lorena said, standing up to meet my mother face to face. "My life might be miserable with the poison inside me, but at least I'm not flaunting my curse. ¿Dios no nos ha castigado ya lo suficiente? Is it necessary to turn us into a circus?"

I had been silly thinking what she'd said earlier in private was the worst she could throw at me.

This time I had no doubts about it. As I followed my father out of the room, I kept waiting for the smell to change and tell me at least a little of what she had said was a lie. I would take anything. But the door closed after my mother followed us outside with no change in the air.

The stench so hated only a few minutes ago turned into the only thing that could keep me from breaking down.

And it never came.

Waves crashed in the backyard of my mother's old house as we opened the door. Mom was still fuming from titi's words, but she hugged me and whispered a short "sorry" before going to her room. Dad stayed with me a little longer, but after my assurances of being fine brought no foul smells, he followed Mom and tried to calm her as well.

Although it's impossible for me to lie, I've learned to hide small lies in bigger truths. That was one of the last things Abuela told me before getting sick: the curse makes us unable to lie directly, but the best lies are the ones told through truths. I'm not okay. But I can say I'm fine, because, in a way, I was expecting everything that happened.

Before long, I could hear Ma's angry whispers through the door and the low soothing words my father said to calm her. And soon, her sobs fill the room, drowning even the coquíes that sing under the windows.

Although I knew those were tears of anger and not sadness, I needed an escape.

I opened the back door and went looking for my mother's hamaca.

It's strange how being with the people who are supposed to understand me the most feels so *other*ing. We are cursed by the same fate, but somehow they are able to justify their existence while invalidating mine. To them, it's only natural to think in pairs, in dual sides, in black and white. Truth or lie. But doing that closes the door to all the beautiful hues of gray and completely deletes the color from our lives. Painting over my skin won't make me white. Painting over who I am won't remove my colors.

I sat up in the sand and tried to make designs with my feet. I felt defeated in a war I didn't understand. My back arched with the weight of everything Lorena said. There, surrounded by the salty breeze and the crash of waves, it was easy to see how simple things would be if I listened to her—if I did what she wanted me to do: let go of the love I felt for myself. Blaming love seemed like the clear choice in the middle of this chaos.

But then a familiar voice interrupted my thoughts.

The Ocean called to me like raindrops dancing with the wind, and I listened. With a crash, it asked me to walk toward it when it saw that it had gotten my attention.

It's been years since I'd heard such a clear message from the water. It felt like coming home. I wouldn't say it's a song, but describing it as words doesn't feel right, either. It felt like my essence was being called by its essence, and I could only follow the soft whispers of the waves licking the shore. My feet were hit by the water, and I shuddered. The water was treacherously cold, but it seemed to ease a little of what I felt inside. So I listened to the Ocean and continued walking, listening to the voice that used to soothe me as a child until I'm gone.

Someone was standing in front of me, but I couldn't make out their details. That's the first thing I realize once I've been completely engulfed by the waters. I would look at their face and find it different the next second. Sometimes they looked like a young woman, and then I would find wrinkles lining their face the next second, only to morph into a man's face right after. Sometimes the face would seem like a collage of mixed parts, feeling eerily familiar and alien at once. Then their face would look like something so unnatural, so divine it made my eyes burn. I had to tear my gaze away. I focused on our surroundings, finding it easier to look at the changing walls than their changing features.

The water moved around us, creating shapes and paintings on the roof of what seemed to be a bubble, sharing stories of the past and promises of the future. Lights shined through it, and I could almost swear that other things moved behind the curtain of water, creating our safe space. I couldn't help but take two steps forward and touch the wall, sure that it would break and fill the space with water. Instead, a sharp coldness electrified me, and I brought my hand close to my chest. Then they spoke, making me turn around and look into their eyes.

"Gabriel," they acknowledged me, putting a hand over my head. Their voice was running water, changing from waves to river flow to rain between syllables. Like everything about them, it seemed to be always changing, always evolving. "My dear child of Ocean. I'm glad you've come back home."

They stood there, looking like they expected me to answer, but I didn't know what I was supposed to say. My silence seemed to remind them of something, and their hand fell to their side.

"I suppose you don't know my name yet. Not in this state. So be it. It will be revealed to you soon enough. I'm afraid when you do, you will hate me," they said. I felt the air in our bubble change, and their appearance started to change faster, as did the images around the walls. They stayed that way, lost in themselves until their voice interrupted the chaos once more. "This must be very confusing to you. Let me explain as easily as I can: I'm one of the reasons why the bitter *jagua* has been cursing your family for decades."

"*Jagua?*" I asked, the first word leaving my mouth since getting there. They smiled, pleased at hearing my voice, and inclined their head.

"The white water. The cursed water. I forget the name they use now, as they change it every few decades."

"The white lies?"

A laugh escaped them, or what I felt was a laugh. It sounded like a thousand raindrops hitting the ground at the same time. "You have really simplified the names. Yes, the *white lies*," they answered. "The *jagua* was given to you out of love."

For the first time in my life, I'd found someone who answered my questions instead of deflecting them. Seeing this as the only way I would know the truth, I dared to raise my head and ask them: "But why? Why curse us if you loved us?"

Their voice, like the crash of many waters, reminded me that I was not talking to another person but a supernatural being who I didn't know well. A goddess, if Abuela had been right all those years ago. Their face changed in flashes, barely letting me process what I saw. I could see their mouths moving, but the only thing I heard was the flow of a river after a rainy day in the mountains. Realizing I couldn't understand what they were saying, their voice changed to the liquid clarity of a calm ocean.

"I have known love, but love hasn't known me," they whispered, and the water around us completely changed. I saw them through a distorted glass, running through the beach, laughing with the sound of waves. Their happiness was such that it could seldom be contained, even as they started walking calmly over the sand, leaving behind them drops of water that turned into pearls as they touched the floor.

The houses were scarce and looked different. The shape of the trees had changed too, but everything looked strangely familiar, even the girl standing in the distance.

"Abuela?" I asked, looking at the girl in the vision. She had long dark hair and wore a dress unlike anything my abuela would use now, but the similarities in the face left almost no room for mistake.

"*Ana*," was their only answer.

As the image of them got closer to the girl, the details came into focus. The girl's beaming smile seemed to fill them with stronger happiness, but soon it was muddied by tears. Nothing could be heard from their conversation. They seemed to have a small discussion before the god-like creature disappeared on the beach, their scream thundering like a hundred storms.

"I loved your family and kept them from all evil they could encounter, but they paid me by marrying my one love and taking her away from our Ocean. Our home. Yet . . . I still loved them."

Their voice took a sense of urgency. "*Jagua* is not meant to hurt you. It was never meant to be a curse. It's meant to keep you from having to lie for others. Ana was forced to lie and hide our love out of fear of being killed by the family. It was my weakness that made her make that decision. I didn't want her descendants to suffer the same fate."

Unable to completely grasp the pain in their voice, I kept my eyes glued to the vision.

"Was that my abuela?"

"No," was their quick answer. "Ana lived a long time ago. I've forgotten the years and the times, but Ana always comes around. And you, my dear Ocean child, come back as well. It's always a pleasure to meet you. But no one can break the blessing I've given you. I am as tied to these waters as your family. Sorrow, grief, and anger make us hostages of this curse."

The scenes before us started to change. I could see the beach and the houses around it changing through time. More families, more buildings. The thing that remained unchanged was the deity that appeared walking on the beach every once in a while and the scene where they were left alone by a crying person. This person changed with each scene; their clothes, hair, and expressions were different; the outcome wasn't.

"Every time we meet, your family tears her away from me again and again. Instead of using my blessing to accept themselves, they use it to shame those of you who don't fit their idea of normality." Hearing their voice rise, I tried to look at them, but my head felt like it was being compressed from all sides. I held a groan down. "Someday, you'll be free from this, but not before understanding that not being able to lie only affects those that

wish to deceive." They were interrupted by a crash before focusing on me again.

I tried my best to keep my eyes glued somewhere that wasn't
moving, but the pressure I felt and the movements of shadows
in the water were making me dizzier with each passing second.
It took me a moment to understand that the crush had been me
falling to the ground.

"I have to let you leave now. More time on this side of existence could fragment your soul." Caressing my cheek just like
Abuela, they took a step back. "Take care, Gabriel. I'm proud of
who you are."

"Guabancex," I said, but I felt, more than heard, my lips form
the name, but I was lying alone on the beach. I blinked quickly,
gathering my surroundings, getting used to the unchanging sky
and the soft purple hues of a summer sunset. The sand was hot
under my legs, and it scratched my arms as I stood up. I could
feel my curls were full of sand and tried my best to shake it off,
but it fell to my eyes, and for a few moments, the burn reminded
me of the goddess.

I'd really met them. I'd finally understood the voice of the waters.
A burst of laughter escaped my throat. I felt giddy, the memories of
my tías erased by the magical scenes I'd seen with them.

I heard some ruffling to my right and turned around to find
my abuela searching for something on the shore, walking slowly
with her arms to the side, balancing her body in the sand. Her
eyes scanned the sand until they found me. Her gasped reached
me as she fell to her knees, and my body finally woke from the
daze and let me run to her.

"¡Abuela!" I screamed as I approached her. Once I was beside her, I kneeled down, trying to see if she was hurt anywhere. "What's wrong? Let me call Ma. She has to be around the house, I can—"

Her hand interrupted me, caressing my cheek in the same affectionate way she had that morning. She seemed . . . lost.

"Hush, my child. Your mind is always running too fast. I am fine," she said, changing her position and sitting down on the sand, almost mirroring my pose before meeting with Guabancex. "I thought I had seen someone I used to know, and I was too impressed to keep myself up. Now sit with me for a while. I haven't been to the beach in a long time."

We sat down, looking at the stars, ocean, and clouds, feeling close to nature but away from each other.

"Te mentí, ¿sabes?"

Those three words squeezed the remnants of the dream-like joy that had been in my heart, and I gasped. I could only think of my tías looking at me as the *jagua* made Abuela's feelings clear; I could almost hear them saying, *Of course, she doesn't love them. It's impossible to love someone like that.* I wanted to run, to scream, to step away from her. But the waters whispered that I needed to listen.

My gasp must have been louder than I thought because something that can only be described as a mix between a sob and laughter shook her shoulders.

"The Ocean didn't stop calling me. I decided it was easier to ignore it, just like your tías. Just like your ma," she said, her voice gaining strength with each word, her eyes turning glassy. Registering my surprise, a melancholic laugh escaped her throat. "Sí, they could hear it before, but the Ocean doesn't always say things we like. And sometimes we prefer to give up some things to gain others. I . . . I gave up a lot without knowing if I would get anything. At some point after that, the water gave up on me. But not before I gave it up to appease my girls. Pero tú, mi tesoro, you refused to ignore its voice." At that point, she turned away from the ocean and the stars and focused on me. "I resented you for that."

Somehow I found my voice to ask a simple "Why?"

Abuela weighed the question before answering. "To me, from the outside, it looked like you had it so easy, so . . . effortless. I let my jealousy cloud my eyes and ignore what happened, that *I* had taken my happiness from myself, not you. I placed my burdens on your shoulders without telling you, and then I got angry at you for not doing anything about them. Then your parents took you away and . . . It was easier to build this image of someone ungrateful and conceited when I only had my daughter's words to go by."

She looked away for a moment like she was gathering her courage to continue speaking.

"But today after you left, I heard the Ocean call me for the first time in years, begging me to come here. I knew I had to follow its voice. And it brought me to you."

This time it was me who looked away, focusing on the waves crashing against the rocks on one side of the beach. Guabancex had talked to her again? Was that the reason they had called me, too?

"I owe you an apology," she said, breaking the silence.

"Abuela . . ." I tried to stop her, caught off guard by the words, but her hand silenced me.

"Let me finish. I'm not above accepting my mistakes. My old

age doesn't excuse me from saying sorry. Especially when I've hurt my family. I've been ignorant and naïve. I've let fear take the best of me. I swear I will change that." She took a deep breath like she was finally letting invisible chains fall from her shoulders. "Gabriel, I love you. And I would be blessed if you gave me the chance to prove it to you."

I held my breath and waited. The stench would be overwhelming being this close. Closing my eyes, I counted to ten, hoping it wouldn't last long. But, like before, the rotten smell never came.

For a moment, it crossed my mind how much an action can change depending on the circumstances. The lack of *jagua* had destroyed me earlier, but now it reminded me of the words of Guabancex: knowing the truth behind my abuela's love wasn't a curse but a blessing.

With Abuela's arms around me, ocean breeze tangling our hairs, and sand getting in our faces, I felt the caress of the Ocean through her.

Even if it wasn't perfect, it was a gift.

LEYENDA

A WOLVES OF NO WORLD STORY
by
Romina Garber

Y saldrán mis raíces a buscar otra tierra.
—Pablo Neruda

And my roots will set off to seek another land.
—Pablo Neruda, as translated by Donald D. Walsh

PHASE I

Zaybet knows her classmates' applause is born of respect, not affection, but for a moment, she allows herself to imagine they're friends.

"Nada está decidido todavía," she insists, her metallic gaze bright as she enters the dining hall. Still, their clapping persists, none of them wanting to hear her protests that nothing is official yet. Not when she's the obvious choice.

The academy designates seven graduates each year as Marina's Leyendas. Six of them are lobizones, but the seventh spot goes to a bruja, and there's no better candidate than Zaybet. She's the most powerful Congeladora—*water witch*—to have graced the school's halls since her mother, who was the seventh Leyenda of her class, as was her mother's mother and her mother before her. It's an honor Zaybet was born to earn.

She has no backup plan.

This is *the* plan.

As though reading her mind, Fabián says, "Sos demasiado inteligente como para dudarlo." *You're too smart to even doubt it.*

Zaybet's mouth spreads into her roguish smile, an almost feral grin that lurks beneath her surface and makes it impossible for her classmates to figure her out. Is she a role model or a rebel? Does she mean the things she says, or is she just being provocative? Sometimes she can't tell herself.

"What about you?" she asks Fabián in Spanish. "You get applauded when you walked into the dining hall, too?"

He frowns like he doesn't understand the question. Leyenda status is expected of the most powerful werewolves, so it's not considered a victory.

"Don't you think it's strange that we only celebrate the girl?" Zaybet presses.

"You're going to fault us for being too chivalrous?"

"I prefer the term *patriarchal.*"

The students around them begin to disband, chasing the scents of entrañas and chorizos and milanesas and empanadas. This is their last week of school, and tonight's Class Dinner is specially catered to include all their favorite foods.

Yet a small group of spectators remains gathered around Zaybet and Fabián—mostly werewolves and Aurelia.

"Why can't you just be a normal bruja?" asks Fabián, his tone sharper now that their audience has shrunk. "Keep this up, and no one will ever want you."

Zaybet's fingers curl until her nails dig into her skin, but she has no retort.

Fabián's boys hiss like they can't believe he went there, and they cover their mouths to conceal their smirks. Aurelia doesn't bother hiding hers. She's been coming in second to Zaybet for years, and by now, she can barely bridle her resentment.

"Or maybe you're like this because you really believe in the Coven," says Fabián, and the wolves snicker harder.

The Coven is a made-up, bruja-led resistance group that will supposedly launch a revolution one day. It's a long-running joke among wolves—and a secret hope among some brujas.

Unclenching her fists, Zaybet extends a hand to Fabián. He looks at her in confusion.

"You're top of the lobizones, and I'm top of the brujas," she says, sparing Aurelia a glance for the satisfaction of seeing her grin wilt. "But by definition"—her attention returns to Fabián—"there can only be *one* number one. So, let's settle it: Who's more powerful?"

His frown deepens as the guys around them fall silent. "You can't compare wolves and witches. We're different—we don't have the same abilities."

"Let's keep it simple then." Zaybet takes a step closer, her outstretched hand now inches from Fabián. "First one to overpower the other wins."

None of his friends are smiling anymore. Even Aurelia seems concerned—she's not raking a hand through her coppery curls the way she usually does when Fabián is nearby.

"I'm not fighting a *girl*."

"What century are you in? Fight me, or admit defeat."

Their enhanced hearing means that within seconds, all the werewolves in the dining hall have abandoned their food and formed a ring around them. Fabián flashes the crowd a grin like this is part of some grand performance.

"When Señora Serafina comes around," he says to Zaybet in a lower register, "make sure you tell her you asked for this."

Zaybet doesn't blink as she says, "With this handshake, we *both* consent to whatever happens next."

Fabián's fingers close around hers, and his nails curl into claws.

He's smiling as his midnight eyes swirl with light. Fangs descend from his lips as facial hair sprouts, and his body lengthens and curves and grows hairier—

His transformation stalls. Fabián's grin droops into a grimace, the expression freezing on his face.

Literally.

There are gasps as Fabián's brown skin turns blue, his dark eyes lightening as they frost over.

Zaybet's metallic irises glimmer like moonlit oceans. She's numbing Fabián's power and keeping him from shifting.

Her magic is wrestling his brawn, and at this moment, *she's winning.*

"That's enough."

The students break away at once, like a school of fish scattering before a shark, except for Zaybet and Fabián, who are still holding hands. It looks like he's trying to speak, but even his vocal cords have iced over.

Señora Serafina touches Fabián's arm, and instantly, the light of Zaybet's eyes flickers off. She loses her balance and steadies herself against a table while the directora's moss-green gaze brightens, and what looks like vines grow from her hand to Fabián's skin, healing him. She's a Jardinera—*earth witch.*

"What happened here?" the head of the school demands.

"She went hysterical!" Fabián sputters, pointing his finger at Zaybet. "Just because we did something *nice*! We congratulated her, and she attacked me for it!"

The directora narrows her gaze at Zaybet. She doesn't look surprised or amused. "You know better than to use magic on another student."

"I'm sorry." Zaybet directs her apology to Fabián. "I promise to never emasculate you again."

He glowers and spins toward the directora. "You keep asking us to try being her friend! *Now, do you see why she's alone?*"

Zaybet's eyes flash to Señora Serafina, the air catching in her throat at her teacher's betrayal.

"Let's go," says the directora, and Zaybet considers not following. But she's in enough trouble as is, and she's not about to risk making it worse.

They pile their plates with the specially catered food and carry their trays through the Castillo de Cristal to the headmistress's office. Then they sit on the couch, around the crystal coffee table, and eat in silence. Zaybet knows from experience that Señora Serafina doesn't like to debate and digest at the same time.

Zaybet's eyes rove across the familiar space as she chews, and she wonders if it's her last visit to this office. The past five years, she's spent more time in here than any other room at the castle, save her own.

Señora Serafina's space is overrun with plants. She likes to swap them out according to the seasons of Argentina, and as it's currently fall, the foliage has a golden tinge.

A window occupies one full wall, but it's not the view outside that Zaybet is going to miss. She focuses instead on the directora's wall of words. Brown-green veins of ivy climb up to the ceiling, and flowery letters are netted among the vines.

At the very top, near the ceiling, is the name of their species— *Septimus*. A pair of categories branches out from the heading: *Bruja* and *Lobizón*.

Señora Serafina is a big fan of labels. She likes their clarity.

Jardinera is the largest word on the wall. There's also *Encendedora*— fire witch—and *Invocadora*—wind witch. *Congeladora* hangs closest to Zaybet's head, like a coronet.

"I'm going to have to report this to your mother."

Zaybet pushes away what's left of her chorizo. "And who do I report you to for going behind my back to my classmates?" She crosses her arms. "I don't need your charity. Did you ever think maybe *I'm* the one who doesn't want to be friends with *them*?"

"Zaybet, as a Leyenda, many doors will open to you. I hope that when you walk through one, you won't do what you did here." Señora Serafina's thin hair falls over her face as she leans in, her tone more intimate. "Don't shut everyone out. We're a pack species, so that change won't work alone. We need our communities, and our communities need us."

Zaybet knows the directora is right, of course. Leyendas get their choice of the best apprenticeships, and Zaybet plans to move away from Marina to La Rosada, the capital of the Septimus world, to become a legislator.

Her future plans are to change, well, *everything*.

And she's never doubted things would work out exactly as they have.

"I've proven myself harder than all the brujas here, and it's still not enough," she hears herself say. "No one cares, not even *them*. They're fine with their lot in life. Like being second to the lobizones is the best we can expect. Doesn't anyone want more?"

Señora Serafina exhales, for the first time seeming tired to Zaybet. Her green eyes soften into the borderline-parental affection that's become a blurred line between mentor and mother. "You're smart, and I've no doubt you'll shake up our world. I'm excited to see all you will do. But if you keep talking this way, you're going to attract the wrong kind of attention."

The directora is the only Septimus Zaybet has encountered who believes the Coven is real. She fears Zaybet being led down a dark path.

Yet at the notion of the Coven existing and wanting to recruit her, Zaybet feels what she didn't feel when her classmates celebrated her: nostalgia for something she's never experienced. It's the kind of pull on her heart she only ever senses at the full moon.

"We don't know our own power," warns Señora Serafina. "We must be careful." From the tone of her voice, Zaybet senses her dismissal.

"You can leave your plate here," she says as Zaybet rises to go. "Graduation is in seven days. I need you to keep it together until then."

Before shutting the door behind her, and without waiting for an answer, Zaybet asks, "I'm curious, Señora. If we're so powerful, why is it we don't have any power?"

PHASE II

The next day at breakfast, no one sits near Zaybet. It's not as if her classmates were clamoring to be near her before, but at least they weren't avoiding her then. The message is clear: Conform or leave.

It seems nobody wants to be infected with an original thought.

Zaybet wouldn't dare give them the satisfaction of reacting. She drinks her mate and eats her facturas, dipping the baked goods directly into the jar of dulce de leche since she doesn't have to share it with anyone. She can't believe the directora tried to make friends for her. At least in a week, she will be far from this place and these Septimus.

As if summoned by Zaybet's thoughts, Señora Serafina approaches her. "You have a visitor."

Zaybet's face is stoic as she gets up to meet her mother, but inside, her stomach squirms with nerves. If Esmeralda made the trip here, she must be especially displeased.

Zaybet sucks in a long breath as she enters the parental lounge, with its crystal tables and leather sofas.

Her mother is the room's sole inhabitant. It's not regular visiting hours. But then, there's nothing regular about the bruja standing by the windowed wall, back ramrod straight and hair pulled into an impeccable black bun.

"Hola, Mami."

Esmeralda turns toward her daughter and presses her cheek to hers in a perfunctory greeting. "I heard about your outburst," she murmurs as she tucks back a strand of Zaybet's unruly black hair.

Small talk is a crime in their family.

"It wasn't an outburst. Fabián and I were just messing around. It was a friendly competition."

"*Don't* lie to me," warns her mother, her jaw as taut as her hairdo.

"I'm not—"

"We both know you don't have friends."

Zaybet opens and closes her mouth, but no sound ekes out. Like a pen that's run out of ink.

She and her mother look like a pair of paintings of the same person at different stages of life. They have the same olive-brown skin and black hair, and even their eyes are matching steely seas, which is rare. It's typically only sons who inherit their mother's eye color.

"I don't have time to come here to satisfy this cry for attention," Esmeralda says, leaning in for a whisper of a goodbye. This was a record visit—sixty seconds, tops.

Instead of kissing Zaybet's cheek, Esmeralda presses her lips to her daughter's ear.

"*Do. Not. Test. Me.*"

The warning clangs through Zaybet's bones, and her pulse races with the intensity of her longing to be far from here. Once she's named Leyenda and has the power to choose her own future, she'll sail as far from home as the sea will take her.

"Sí, Mamá."

Her mom is already headed for the door. "I spoke to Serafina, and your tantrum will not impact your standing for Leyenda. But you are not to set a *single foot* out of line until graduation." Her silhouette is framed in the doorway. "Am I clear?"

She stares at her daughter as she awaits her answer. Zaybet thinks she sees a flicker of movement in the hall beyond.

"Sí, Mamá," she says again. It's only once her mother has walked away that she steps out to see if anyone is there.

Aurelia stands at the end of the hall, pale blue eyes piercing through her curtain of coppery curls. She must've tailed Zaybet here. It appears she plans to keep their rivalry alive to the very last day.

Part of the reason Aurelia takes it so personally that Zaybet is the better bruja is they're both Congeladoras. Zaybet just has a stronger connection to their element.

Yet it's not envy that now softens the lines of Aurelia's face, but pity. And while Zaybet may dislike the former, she won't put up with the latter. "Disappointed to hear I didn't ruin my chances for Leyenda?" she snipes.

Aurelia looks like she's been savoring a remark of her own. Instead, she slinks off without a word, leaving Zaybet more upset that Aurelia gets to be the bigger bruja.

They're not doing much in class these days, and Zaybet is in no rush to get back. Alone in the crystal hall, she stares at the ice-like wall, and her blurry reflection stares back.

The closer she gets to graduation, the more Zaybet has been thinking about a young girl she met years ago. A stranger she feels she knows intimately.

They met on La Isla Malvada, the most dangerous place in the world. It's a wintry island so hazardous that witches who visit must have a wolf escort. Yet Zaybet and her friends, back when she still had those, decided to ditch their dates to make the wolves chase them. It's a time-honored teen courting ritual.

That's when she came across a girl named Saysa. Brujas inherit their power with their first period on the first full moon of their thirteenth year. So, at age eleven, Saysa didn't have her magic yet. Still, she'd ditched her brother to take on the island alone.

And she wasn't doing it to flirt or fit in or show off. The only being Saysa was interested in impressing was herself.

Zaybet invited the girl to join their group, but Saysa preferred to race ahead, defiant and free—until she ran too far, and the ground beneath her melted.

She would have plummeted thirty feet, but Zaybet managed to solidify a thin sheet of ice from the moisture in the air. It held long enough for Saysa to leap back to safety.

Zaybet and her friends escorted the girl back to the entrance hall, where their frantic and furious dates were waiting for them, along with two ticked-off Cazadores—*law enforcement*. While the guys rounded on the brujas, and the Cazadores rattled off the dangers of what they'd done, Zaybet watched Saysa slip away and break into a sprint.

Unnoticed due to her tininess and undaunted by the near-death experience.

Free.

Zaybet is so lost in her reminiscences that it takes her a moment to spot the condensation on the crystal wall in front of her. Droplets are coming together, like they're magnetized, to form words.

Hola Zaybet.

She scans the empty school hall, but no one's there. The droplets move again.

We have been watching you.

"Show yourself," says Zaybet out loud. When nothing happens, she crosses her arms. "Who are you?"

You already know.

Her heart skips a beat. Was Señora Serafina right?

If you want to join us, we need more.

Zaybet knows she should keep walking, that in fact, she should be *running*—but far from feeling afraid, she is invigorated. The chance that the Coven might be real is exhilarating in a way nothing else can rival.

"What do you mean?" she asks the empty hall.

Prove to us that you're serious about making a difference.

Then the water droplets splash to the ground, and the hall falls into deeper silence.

All day in class, Zaybet can't stop thinking of the Coven. Can she really throw away all her hard work and sacrifice, her family legacy, her promising future? Risk it all just for the chance that this ghost of a group might be real and could tap her to join?

Again, Saysa comes to mind.

Something about her encounter with the girl changed Zaybet. In the two years that followed, she began speaking her mind more. She questioned the injustices they were expected to accept, like how brujas earn less than werewolves in the workforce and occupy fewer than five percent of all positions of power. How all brujas are expected to become mothers, even though they suffer from severe postpartum depression that shuts off their magic for a few years.

Over time, Zaybet lost all her friends.

Yet as lonely as she was, she kept telling herself she would meet her true pack once she left the academy. But will she actually find like-minded Septimus at the capital, working with law enforcement? Or is she more likely to find her place among the rebels of the resistance?

Zaybet thinks of now-thirteen-year-old Saysa and envisions the five years that lie ahead for her at school. The idea of that fearless young bruja's bravery getting stamped out with age and social pressures and the Septimus system is unbearable.

"We don't know our own power."

Señora Serafina's words of warning sound in Zaybet's mind, and a scheme begins to take root in her thoughts. Maybe there is a way for brujas to gauge their power and for Zaybet to show the Coven how serious she is about disrupting the status quo.

But it will mean enlisting the help of all the brujas—even Aurelia.

Especially Aurelia.

That night, all eighty-four brujas of the graduating class gather in their common room to elect their speaker. The wolves and witches must each collectively choose a representative to speak for them at the ceremony.

As president of the brujas' student council, Aurelia is the obvious front-runner. "It would be my honor to be our class speaker," she says after calling the meeting to order.

She stands at the front of the room—curls corralled into a messy bun that can barely contain them—while the others squeeze onto heated couches or sprawl across thermal blankets. "Would anyone else like to declare their candidacy?"

Zaybet is the only other bruja standing. She's at the back of the space, leaning against the wall.

Aurelia pans her blue gaze across her classmates. "Anyone?"

When it seems there are no challengers, Zaybet steps forward.

"I declare my candidacy."

Everyone turns to stare at her, except Aurelia, who's already scowling at Zaybet across the sea of bewildered brujas. "You're *unbelievable*. You know that?"

"I do."

"We all know this ceremony is a joke to you—just like everything else. But we won't let you ruin it for the rest of us."

"I'm serious." Zaybet strides toward Aurelia, the room's eyes following her movements. "I really want to speak—"

"Then you're more arrogant than a lobizón! You barely know us, and you think you should be the one to speak for us?"

"That's not—"

"You think because you were born into a powerful bloodline, you're better than the rest of us?"

"*No!*"

Zaybet's voice rises in pitch, making the word sound like a plea. It lingers in the air as Aurelia crosses her arms, lips sealed like she has nothing left to say.

Zaybet now holds everyone's attention.

This is her chance.

"I-I know I've messed up," she says, her voice thin as she faces her classmates. "I've been speaking for you without knowing how you feel. I've shouted at you to listen, only I'm the one who's not hearing you. I'm sorry."

Her mouth is dry, and her heart is thudding. She can't tell if she's going to pass out or float off the ground, so she just keeps talking.

"I know we like to relive our inside jokes in the class speech, but we can do that at any of the after-parties. Graduation is the one time we have everyone's focus. Why waste this opportunity by making it about us when we can make it about the real *us*?"

All eighty-three witches remain silent—even Aurelia. Emboldened, Zaybet begins to pace the front of the room.

"The moment a girl becomes a bruja, her only value is as a wife and mother. As soon as we leave this school, we'll be measured by the suitors we attract and the offspring we produce. Our passions and potential are irrelevant. In the patriarchy, our wombs are worth more than our magic. So I say we refuse their offer."

These are the sorts of things she says that usually make the brujas turn away, only this time they're staring at her the way they do inside the classroom. After all, Zaybet is no ordinary bruja.

She's pulled off feats even the instructors still whisper about, like when she manifested a thick fog that stubbornly clung to the castle for days or the morning she accidentally set off a tsunami.

"Speak plain Spanish, please," says Aurelia, rolling her light eyes. Yet Zaybet has piqued her interest, or Aurelia would be demanding silence instead of clarity.

"We'll never have the same opportunities as the Fabiáns of the world so let's reject the narrative that we're equals. Let's show the wolves we're not going to play the parts they've written for us." Zaybet's voice deepens with urgency. "We're going to shred those roles and design ones that fit us. We'll take back our magic even if only for a moment."

"How?" asks Aurelia, no longer sounding disinterested.

"We'll prove to the wolves who really powers their world by declaring a *bruja strike*."

The room itself trembles, like it's experiencing a minor earthquake, and the temperature rises and falls. The witches' heightened emotions rattle their magic, but their mouths remain sealed. They just stare at one another, waiting for someone else to act.

Aurelia's voice cracks the silence.

"I can't say any of that."

Zaybet's chest deflates with disappointment, her hope snuffed out.

"But I think somebody should."

At Aurelia's course reversal, Zaybet's jaw drops. The two Congeladoras lock eyes, and when gleaming metal meets icy sea, Aurelia announces:

"I retract my candidacy and nominate Zaybet for class speaker."

PHASE III

Zaybet's last week of school is also her happiest. Aurelia invites her to sit with her friends for every meal, and the brujas actually listen to what she has to say. It makes Zaybet wish she'd dropped her guard sooner—a mistake she won't be repeating at the Coven.

Señora Serafina is right: *change won't work alone.*

"Sounds like you're ready," says Aurelia, who's helping Zaybet memorize her speech. Everyone else went to bed hours ago.

"I can't wait to ruin the lobizones' fun." Zaybet's grin is feral.

Yet Aurelia's gaze is grave. "We'll all go on strike together, but you're the one who has to deliver the words. Are you sure about this?"

Aurelia's concern still jolts Zaybet. Just one week ago, both girls would have reveled in their rival's downfall.

They spent their whole time at school competing when they could have been working together.

"I'm more than sure. *I'm ready.*"

"What difference will it make, though?" whispers Aurelia, for the first time sounding vulnerable to Zaybet. "No one's going to listen to a bunch of brujas. The only ones with the power to change things are the wolves."

Lightning sparks in the steely seas of Zaybet's eyes, a sign of the storm to come.

"But aren't you tired of waiting?"

The morning of graduation, Zaybet wakes up feeling the way she did when she turned thirteen. Like a new world just dawned with her.

All this time, she thought she wanted to be a Leyenda, so that she could move to the capital and apprentice under a legislator. But the truth is she has no interest in working within a wolf-dominated world, struggling to earn enough respect to be worth listening to, forced to compromise her values to forge the alliances she'll need to effect some modicum of change.

Now that the Coven exists, there can be no other path for her.

She practices her speech enough times that she's worried she's forgotten how to say anything else. She's so frazzled she mixes up where the brujas are meeting before the ceremony, and she winds up arriving just in time to hear the directora finish announcing their class. She files out with the others.

Graduation takes place atop el Castillo de Cristal. On all sides, they're surrounded by the light blues of the sky and the deep blues of the sea. The graduates are slightly elevated, on what looks like an enormous open-face clam. Wolves are on one shell, brujas on the other. They sit on pink velvet benches that are plushy and heated. Behind the students is an audience of loved ones who are spread out on puffy thermal blankets all across the icy ground. Most families greet each other, capture the moment on a device, and fill calabaza gourds with hot water for mate.

The brujas' speaker goes first, so Zaybet steps up to the elevated dais, where her voice will be amplified. She stares past her classmates until she meets her mother's eyes. She's sitting on a long blanket with Zaybet's father and brother and grandparents and aunts and uncles and cousins.

Esmeralda might never forgive her daughter for this, but at least Zaybet isn't alone. She finds Aurelia in the front row, and at her friend's encouraging nod, Zaybet begins.

"It's fitting that the brujas and lobizones are sitting on different shells because even though we're students at the same school, today, our paths diverge. The world waiting to welcome the wolves is not the same one that awaits us witches. Guys are expected to transform into leaders of their pack, while girls are expected to grow the pack."

The brujas sit still, but the wolves begin to shift around in their benches. Zaybet doesn't look beyond the members of her class because she can't risk crossing gazes with her mom or Señora Serafina. Not if she's going to get through this speech.

"Brujas brew your potions. We heal you. We transport you. We fuel your technology. We give up *our* power to birth *your* children. *Your* world runs on *our* magic."

A stabilizing sense of purpose seems to settle on Zaybet as

she speaks. Rather than setting off a monstrous rage inside her, the words cool the flame of injustice that burns at the base of her throat.

She's so used to being silenced every time she tries to share her thoughts that she had no idea how good it could feel to have listeners.

"Why is only one Leyenda a bruja?"

She pauses like she's expecting an answer.

"Why can't there be years when three or four or all seven Leyendas are brujas?" She begins to move around, growing more comfortable as she gains command of her stage.

"Leyendas are tomorrow's leaders. Yet brujas don't lead. In fact, the only brujas allowed into positions of power are the ones who uphold the status quo. They're more conservative than their wolf counterparts. It's all performative inclusivity."

Zaybet's gaze meets Aurelia's. "It's not enough for one of us to land a seat at the table. As long as we're always forced to compete for the same spot, the lobizones' power is unchallenged. We won't be equals until we *all* have access to *all* the seats."

She turns to the wolves now, meeting Fabián's round eyes. He's stunned, her speech freezing him as effectively as her magic. "You guys define chivalry as pulling out a girl's chair, but what we actually want from you is a bigger table. We'll pull up our own damn chair."

Even Aurelia's gaze has grown wide with awe, and Zaybet wonders if some part of her didn't think she would have the guts to say these words to the world. Or maybe Aurelia is just anticipating what comes next—the moment when Zaybet and her sisters make history.

"I refuse to uphold an unjust system." Zaybet takes a deep inhale. "As of this moment, I am a bruja on strike."

The castle grounds have gone completely quiet.

Now it's the others' turn.

When each bruja declares herself on strike, they'll be sending the message that this new generation of witches has come to demand better. Zaybet nods at Aurelia to begin.

But she's still just staring at her in stupefaction.

Zaybet's gaze pans across the other girls.

None of them will meet her eyes. They're staring at their laps, their hands, each other. Why won't they look up at Zaybet? Why won't they stand?

The seconds elongate into months. Zaybet has no idea how long she's been standing there, holding everyone's awestruck attention.

The brujas are betraying her. *Aurelia* is betraying her. Biting her inner cheek, Zaybet forces her expression not to break, so her emotions won't betray her too.

At least the Coven has to know she's serious now. She may not have displayed any ability to lead or inspire others, but she's clearly willing to risk it all for the cause.

Zaybet looks to Aurelia again. The latter's shock is thawing into something more knowing, until the blue flames of her eyes glow with magic.

Something moves on the podium by Zaybet. Droplets of condensation dance around to form letters.

Read any good messages in the water?

Zaybet's head snaps back up. Aurelia gives her a small smile.

The Coven wasn't real. Nothing about this past week was.

Aurelia just made her final move and won the game.

Zaybet grips her stomach, this deception stabbing too deep. Then she meets her mother's murderous metallic glare in the audience.

In her face, Zaybet sees that she's acted unforgivably. Something has been forever lost to them.

She feels the yawning of a chasm in her chest, and she needs to find safe harbor in a friendly face, someone who will make her feel like she's not dying in front of the entire school. Her sight lands on Señora Serafina.

The directora's expression is Esmerald*aesque*. The same disappointment that broke something between Zaybet and her mom has crushed something here too. In one gamble, Zaybet lost *everything*.

Devastated and desperate, emotions roil inside her like tempestuous waves. The icy water below and the moisture dappling the air fuel her magic like oxygen until power tingles from her fingertips.

Her hands shake as the clamshell where the brujas sit begins to frost over with the release of her magic. The witches' eyes flicker with light, but the cold front is too sudden and strong, and it crystallizes their skin, like the blast from a freeze-gun.

Aurelia is an ice sculpture whose mouth is shaped in an O.

Zaybet's winter storm crashes across the wolves next, freezing Fabián right as he's transformed, mid-pounce toward her.

Zaybet is pure power. She's lost all self-control, and now her magic heaves on her insides. Like it's consuming her.

The pull of her element is too strong in the watery world of Marina. The ends of her black hair turn snow white.

Zaybet's life force is being drained. The dual pull of her emotions and her magic is destroying her. She opens her mouth to scream—

And everything goes dark.

PHASE IV

When Zaybet opens her eyes, she's in a glass globe suspended in an indoor lake, like an inside-out fishbowl. She's lying on a bed, and through the transparent walls, she can smell the salty sea and hear it lap against the glass.

She's in a healing center. They've placed her in a room for Congeladoras. It takes her another moment to realize she's not alone.

Esmeralda sits in an armchair across from her daughter, the coldness of her metal gaze hard to take. As memories of graduation flood Zaybet's thoughts, her body grows heavy, and she sinks into the mattress.

Then she catches sight of the ends of her hair and sits up, running her fingers through the black locks that look like they've been dipped in a shock of white.

"Your hair has experienced true death," says her mother. "It will never grow again."

Zaybet frowns, trying to process some kind of pain or surprise, but she feels nothing.

"We'll get the white lopped off. You'll have short hair forever, but at least you won't be marked."

Zaybet's about to ask for a mirror so she can look at herself, but her mother says, "You didn't get Leyenda."

Even now, she has no time for small-talk.

"We gave a big enough contribution to the school to keep them quiet about this whole thing. It's the only reason they're letting you graduate. And none of the parents will talk to the press. We're not interested in other packs picking up this news and coming to Marina to make a spectacle of you. *Community comes first.* Something you forgot last night. Do you understand you could have faced criminal charges?"

"For speaking my mind—?"

"*For attacking children!*" Esmeralda's voice shakes, and lines crease her face, like fabric testing its seams. She takes a breath before continuing.

"Do you think you're special for possessing a radical opinion? We're *all* idealists when we're young. But you used your magic against your classmates. And the only reason you're not being arrested is our family's impeccable, multi-generational reputation, which you selfishly nearly shredded."

Even though her mother pauses, Zaybet knows better than to speak. That's what Esmeralda wants: entrapment. Her scolding isn't over, but she's giving Zaybet a chance to worsen the situation. Anything she says will be heard as a declaration of war, so the smart thing to do is stay quiet.

"You're going to remain in this healing center until the full moon," Esmeralda goes on. "We'll say the stress of being the best got to you, and given the strength of the magic that runs in your bloodline, you were overcome by your power."

Another pause.

Even if Zaybet wanted to argue, what could she say? Where could she go? She has no friends, no future, no hope. And she would much rather be here than at her parents' house.

"Next moon, we'll organize meet-and-greets with potential suitors, and with any luck, you'll be engaged by the end of the year. Any chances of a great career may be shot, but you can still bring esteem to the family by making a powerful match."

A third pause.

Zaybet feels herself sinking into the mattress again. She's devastated and distraught, humiliated and directionless. Yet, the numbness from this emotional cocktail is, strangely, empowering.

If she's lost everything she ever wanted, why should she hold on to what she doesn't?

"I'm not doing that."

When Zaybet speaks, Esmeralda's eyes flare open in a way that would have made her daughter cower before today. Yet this dead-hair Zaybet finds her mother's expression almost comical.

"I'll go along with your plan of staying here for now, but next moon, I'm leaving Marina."

"To go where?" Her mother's voice is deadly even. "Who will take you?"

"I've got a couple of weeks to figure it out," says Zaybet, adopting the same emotionless tone. "I think visitor hours are over."

Esmeralda stares at her daughter as if she'd just transformed into a lobizona.

"I'm appalled at you, Zaybet. You have no respect for me or your grandmother or any of your ancestors. We struggled to make things better for you to have more opportunities than we did, and this is how you honor us? By throwing away your potential?"

"But there's still only *one* bruja Leyenda!" Zaybet blows out a hard breath. "If we keep doing the same things, we'll keep spinning in the same cycles." She raises her voice when she sees that her mother is about to argue. "There are other ways to win, even if it means giving up our privilege. You may not see it yet, but this is me carrying the torch."

It's only after her mother's left that Zaybet stands up and approaches the table beside the armchair, the sole furniture in the room. And she reaches for the handheld mirror.

When she brings it to her face, she gasps at the sight of the girl reflected.

She's never felt more seen.

Seven days later, Zaybet leaves the healing center for the first time. It's part of her recovery. She is to spend a few hours by the real sea, not the imitation inside the center.

She's sitting on the icy banks, unbothered by the cold, and contemplating where she's going to go next moon when bubbles break the water's surface.

Zaybet gawks as a giant, half-fossilized seashell spirals into view. It looks like it belongs to an ancient world. Clearly, the healing has backfired if she's now having hallucinations.

A face pops out from an opening in the shell. The bruja has ebony skin, crunchy curls, and eyes that look like a firestorm in outer space.

"You Zaybet?"

Her voice has a honeyed sound, like a toasty afternoon on the banks of a warm lake.

"Who wants to know?"

The girl smiles, and Zaybet feels actual warmth on her skin, like sunlight. "I'm Laura. I've come to offer you a ride."

"Where?" But even as Zaybet asks the question, she hears the answer in her heartbeat.

She's already creating an ice pathway along the water's surface to board the ship when Laura says the most magical words she's ever heard:

"Your true home. *The Coven*."

COLOR-CODED

by
Maya Motayne

"It usually happens to girls when they're older. Fourteen's a little early, but that's okay," Flor's papá had assured her when she woke up for school with a head of silver hair.

Flor buried her face in her pillow, holding back the urge to scream into the fluff. She wanted her hair to be black like everyone else's. Her papá had to lean close to hear the muffled, "I'm not going!"

"You are going to school today, Flor."

"I don't want to."

"Why not?"

"No one else in class will look like me! Everyone will think it's weird!"

At fourteen, Flor was the youngest freshman in her class, thanks to her post-Christmas birthday. At the earliest, she'd heard of a girl going through the Change at fifteen. It was almost always sixteen, never fourteen. What would everyone say when they saw her? The boys were going to think she was fast or something. Her face went hot.

Flor felt her papá's hand on her back, moving in slow circles. "No one will think it's weird, and don't you think Mateo will be sad if you don't go to class today?"

Flor thought of Mateo with his normal black curly hair, his gap-toothed smile, and his peanut butter and banana sandwiches. She raised her face out of the pillow. "Yes."

He pressed a kiss to her forehead. The bed creaked as he stood. "Okay then, muñeca, time for you to get dressed for school."

Papá had always told her that she was the quietest baby on the planet. Barely cried or anything. He would take her to double-features at the movies, and she would sit through them without a peep. She was so quiet that he'd wake up in the middle of the night just to check if she was breathing. She'd seemed more like a little doll than a baby, so his nickname for her had always been muñeca, but him calling her that gave her no comfort this morning. While she dressed, she heard her papá speaking on the phone downstairs in the kitchen. Their house was squat with low ceilings, so they were always in earshot of each other. He yelled on the phone as if he thought his voice had to power through the curled cord to get to the other side.

"Hi Mrs. Vidal, this is Flor's papá . . . Yes, buenas! I just wanted to let you know that Flor's hair changed this morning . . . Yes, she is quite early. Her mamá was an early bloomer too, actually! . . . Yes, yes, of course. In any case, I wanted to ask if you could maybe talk to her this week. I think she needs a woman's touch . . ."

Flor rolled her eyes. Papi was talking to her old babysitter.

Whenever something happened that required a so-called "woman's touch," he would call her. Flor loved Mrs. Vidal. Some of her favorite childhood memories were colored with Mrs. Vidal's laugh and slices of her famous flan, but she didn't need a speech about how she was a "very special girl" who had just become a "very special woman."

Flor dressed slowly, careful to choose clothing that bore little to no color. She stared at herself in the full-length mirror. Her silver curls were a stark contrast against her brown skin, and she felt that everything, from her white T-shirt to her blue jeans, clashed against the silver. She teared up again and stepped out of the mirror's eye.

"Baby!" her papá called from downstairs. "Breakfast is ready! Come on down!"

The change in hair color was just the beginning. Flor was nervous about what would happen next. Sometimes other things besides hair changed for girls Flor's age. When Mateo's older sister, Gaury, was sixteen, her hair turned from black to magenta, and she could make flowers bloom or wilt just by walking past them. When Mateo beat her too many times at Monopoly, she'd thrown a fit in their backyard that killed every flower in the neighborhood. Maria, a girl two years older than Flor, got a shock of firetruck red hair, and she could make you sneeze just by looking at you. When Miguel Sosa told her he didn't like her new shoelaces, she made him sneeze until his nose bled, but it was allergy season, so the principal couldn't be sure. Nuriya, who once had a black cloud of soft, corkscrew curls, returned from spring break last year with a blue halo of hair that reminded Flor of how water was colored in anime. Whenever she got in a pool, Nuriya could sink to the bottom and run around without difficulty moving or breathing. Sometimes, she snuck out of class to sit at the bottom of the school pool and blow bubbles, startling the swim team during practice.

Some girls were excited for their hair to change and the new strengths that came with it, but not Flor.

Flor was afraid.

Flor's mother had had long grass-green hair, and she'd been a flyer. She would float around the kitchen while she cooked, her toes barely even skimming the floor. Sometimes she would forget she was floating, and when she flipped pancakes, they would smack against the ceiling. When she took on a gardening project, she would shoot high above their lawn to see how the flowers looked to the birds. When Flor had nightmares, her mother would gather her in her arms and sit in the air, curved like a crescent moon. She would rock back and forth like she was Flor's personal hammock.

But soon, her mother became more interested in the sky than the ground. She would disappear for days on end and return with leaves and bird feathers in her hair and starlight in her eyes. At least, Flor thought of that glint as starlight. Her papá had called it mania. He'd explained to Flor that it ran in Mami's family. When Abuela was alive, she'd had the same condition that made her talk very fast without stopping, see things that weren't there, and get mood swings that led to family visits being cut short.

Papi had tried to get Mami to take medicine for it, but the medication made it harder for her to fly.

"Mi amor, it's worth it. The pills keep you here with us, present in the moment. They keep you grounded—"

"Grounded," Mami had said, gritting her teeth, the sign of a coming argument.

Every day she refused the pills, and the longer her mother spent in the sky, the more she and Flor's papá fought on the ground. Slowly the starlight in her mother's eyes became brighter, hungrier. She would babble about the sky, the stars, and the wind as if they were her friends. She would float around the house like a lost ghost and forget to pack Flor's lunch before school.

When Flor was eight, her mother carried her onto the roof and dropped her. "If Mami can fly, so can you. You're just like Mami, aren't you?" her mother had said, the starlight burning bright in her pupils. When Flor woke up in the hospital with a sore head and two broken legs, her papá told her that her mother was gone and she was never coming back. She'd flown away. All evidence of Gina Fuentes had been erased from the house as if she'd never floated through the kitchen searching for her keys every morning.

She'd chosen flying over them. If her mother had never gone through the Change, she never would've learned to fly. She would've taken her medicine. She would never have left.

"Flor?" her papá poked his head into her room. When she buried her face in her hands, shoulders twitching with suppressed sobs, he kneeled in front of her and pressed her face into the soft juncture between his shoulder and neck. "It's alright, muñeca. It'll be alright."

"It looks like—you look like," Mateo stammered, fingering one of her silver curls at lunchtime. "It's like you caught moonlight in your hair."

"You can't catch moonlight in your hair." Flor rolled her eyes.

Mateo always talked like a book, and with his obsession with aliens and black holes and planets, of course, he would say her hair looked like moonlight. "It's not like how you can get leaves stuck in your hair."

"You know what I mean." He dropped the curl and bit into his peanut butter and banana sandwich. The first half of the school day had gone by fairly well. In homeroom, everyone had stared at her, whispering behind their hands. Ms. Esposito, who herself had a pixie cut of radioactive green hair, had been kind and complimented Flor's hair before turning the students' attention elsewhere. As Flor made her way out of class, she'd even given her a cookie and said, "Keep your chin up, Fuentes."

Flor dutifully split it with Mateo during their math lesson.

Several girls had flocked to Flor, telling her that her hair looked cool and asking her if she felt different. Flor could only shake her head, bewildered by their excitement. Tired from the frenzy of questions, Flor avoided the more crowded area of the cafeteria, walking toward the back where Mateo waited for her.

"Maybe she got it early because of her trauma . . ." Rocio, a girl with baby-chicken-yellow hair, said from a table as Flor passed. "Because of her mamá, you know?"

Flor stiffened, anger bubbling inside of her. Rocio was a year older than her, and her mom was a psychiatrist. She was always throwing around words like "trauma" and "catharsis," and every time she did it, Flor wanted to throw her out a window.

"What do you mean?" another girl asked Rocio.

"My mom says trauma can have unexpected effects on people and can even manifest physically. Maybe her mamá throwing her off that roof is why she changed early. She might even have the same thing her mom had," Rocio said with the authority of a doctor. "It's probably hereditary."

With her knuckles tight around her tray, Flor sped toward Mateo, leaving the girls to discuss her like a patient on some sort of doctor show.

"You okay?" Mateo asked when she approached him, his eyes scanning her face. He always knew when she was upset. Flor hated that.

"Fine," she bit out.

"Okay," Mateo said quietly, knowing better than to press her. Mateo led her to the back corner, where they sat at a table with one leg shorter than the rest.

"No one likes to sit here since it wobbles," Mateo promised her as she stared at the rinky-dink table skeptically. "No one will bother you here."

"Alright." Flor sighed and dropped her tray on the table. It squeaked and slouched to the right. Mateo sat beside her and unfurled his brown lunch bag before methodically spreading its contents across the table in his usual order: drink, fruit, sandwich, then cookie.

"I wish I could go through the Change too." Mateo sighed. "Any day now, you could get your ability—could be anything! Must be exciting."

"It's not," Flor huffed, flicking a chicken nugget on her Styrofoam lunch tray. "I hate it."

"You always hate everything at first. You'll probably like it later," Mateo offered with an easy grin.

"I won't," she said, her voice snapping like a whip. Mateo quieted and looked down at his sandwich. Silence stretched between them.

"Do you want some?" he said, holding the unbitten half of his sandwich. He knew she loved peanut butter, but nuts made her papá's throat all itchy, so they never kept any in the house. Sometimes Mateo would come to lunch with a sandwich for her, slathered with extra peanut butter. "I'll trade you for some chicken nuggets."

"Deal," Flor said, pushing her tray toward him. As she took her first bite of the sandwich, Pilar Perez walked by, her hair still black as ever. Flor thought of the picture Pilar had drawn in art class today, big red roses that the teacher had complimented her on. Red like the blood she spat into the sink when she brushed her teeth too hard. Flor had worked on a flower drawing too, but the teacher didn't seem as impressed, and hot jealousy had trickled down Flor's spine like water down a drainpipe.

"Flor . . ." Mateo said quietly, his voice hushed with awe.

"What?" she asked, but her question was answered when she looked down at the sandwich in her hand, and it was bright red, from bread to banana to peanut butter. With a gasp, she dropped it into her lap and, slowly, it faded to its original colors.

"Did you—" Mateo began, his hand reaching for the sandwich before he thought better of it and pulled back. "Was that on purpose?"

"No!" Flor shouted. One of the teachers that supervised the cafeteria during lunch period, Mrs. Malta, glared at her and raised a finger to her thin lips. Flor lowered her voice. "It wasn't on purpose!"

"Do it again!"

"No!"

"Come on, Flor! That was so cool! Here!" Mateo stretched his hand out to her. "Do me!"

Flor could see Rocio and her friends pointing and staring. The whole cafeteria was looking. The more Mateo begged, the more people looked, and the tighter her stomach felt.

Flor shoved her lunch tray at him, sending her chicken nuggets all over him. "I won't! I don't want to! I don't want it!"

"Flor Fuentes!" the supervising teacher rounded on their lunch table. "Did you just throw your lunch at Mateo Suarez?"

The whole cafeteria fell silent. Flor felt embarrassment burn through her.

"I didn't mean to—I'm sorry I—"

"It was nothing. We were just playing around—" Mateo began.

"Hush, Mateo! Flor, you will be receiving a lunchtime warning—your second this semester! Oh my . . ." Mrs. Malta said, her voice petering out as she blinked down at Flor. The other students in the cafeteria started whispering, leaning forward to catch a closer look. Flor looked down at herself. Her entire body had turned a bright pink, the shade of an embarrassed flush.

Flor was given permission to go home early that day.

Mateo sat with Flor on the school curb. He'd asked Mrs. Malta if he could be a little late to his next class to keep Flor company. Feeling guilty over triggering Flor's color shift, Mrs. Malta had said yes. While they waited, Mateo said nothing, which is exactly what she needed to hear. Her papá pulled into the empty bus loop to pick up his blush-pink daughter. When she got in the passenger seat, Mateo leaned his spindly frame against the window. His fingerprints dotting the glass, he said, "Feel better."

"I'm not sick, dork."

"You know what I mean."

Flor's papá gave Mateo a nod before driving away. Flor reclined her seat all the way and turned her back on him, not wanting to see him stare at her skin.

"It'll be alright, sweetheart. We'll get you right home and have pancakes for dinner! How's that sound?" he said, sounding overly perky. Flor said nothing. He placed one hand on her back and kept the other on the steering wheel.

Flor couldn't help but remember another time that her father had been forcing himself to be chipper for her sake. It was after Mami had disappeared, and Flor's legs were still in casts. After she'd been brought home from the hospital, Papi had worn a smile so tight that Flor thought it might snap. Only when she pretended to fall asleep on the sofa did he let the mask slip.

"She'll come back," he'd said, his voice thick as he sobbed on the phone to his sister, Tía Marina. "She'll remember that her family needs her, that that's more important than anything. She'll realize she needs help. She'll knock on that door and come back."

But there was never any knock on the door, no hugs, and kisses, no promises to be better. Mami never came back, and if the Change was enough to take her mother away, who knew what it would do to Flor.

Papi released a long breath. "I—"

"—I don't want to talk about it," Flor interrupted.

Silence swept through the car.

"Well," Papi said. "You don't have to talk about it, but can you listen about it?"

Flor sighed in her seat.

"Muñeca, I have three sisters—"

"And two brothers and two aunts and a mother and a papá. What's your point?" Flor snapped, cutting him off without even turning to look at him. When he drove silently, guilt prickled over her body like a rash. "I'm sorry. Tell me what you were going to say."

Watching the street signs pass through the window, Flor felt him turn right when he should've turned left to get to their house.

"It's okay, baby. I was just going to say: I watched them go through the Change. I knew them before and after. They stayed who they were. They didn't become someone they weren't or someone they didn't want to be. I know it must feel strange, but you shouldn't worry."

Flor turned onto her back.

"I've already become different," she said, motioning at her pink skin. "I didn't want to become a walking strawberry shortcake!"

Pulling to a stop at a red light, he gave her a knowing smile. "Yes, you have turned pink. For today. But nothing between your ears has changed. You'll learn to control this, and then it'll just be something else you can do. You are still you whether you're pink, periwinkle, or kryptonite green."

He watched her process the information. Part of her wanted to tell him the truth, that she was also afraid of what the Change would lead to if it led Mami so far away, but she didn't want to watch his face crumble at the mention of her. Not now. Instead, she bent her elbow over her eyes, blocking the sun.

"Kryptonite green? You've been talking to Mateo about comics, haven't you?" she asked, peeking at him from under her elbow. The light turned green. He turned back to the road.

"He'll talk to anyone who will listen about comics." He laughed. "The boy has a problem."

Flor pulled the lever on the side of her seat, and the back-rest shot upright. She looked out the window and saw that he'd pulled into the drive-through of her favorite ice cream parlor.

"What can I get you, sir?" said the chipper server wearing a sun-yellow uniform at the drive-through window.

"She'll have two scoops, one chocolate chip cookie dough, one cookies and cream. I'll have two scoops of whatever flavor you have that's as pink as she is," her papá said, winking at Flor.

The server leaned forward and blinked at Flor in surprise, nearly hitting her head on the window frame. Then she tentatively said, "So, two scoops of strawberry shortcake?"

Flor snorted.

The next month had been a time of constant discovery. Flor found that her skin could return to its original color, but emotions triggered different hues if she felt them strongly enough. Her hair, though, always stayed silver no matter how her skin changed. Art class became even more fun, as she could press her palm to the paper, and the images in her mind would bloom on the page as if by magic. If she focused hard enough, she felt a click in her mind, as if the image were locking itself into place. Then she knew that it would not fade even after she moved her hand.

When he'd seen her do it, Mateo rolled up his sleeve and said, "Think you could tattoo 'I Heart Mom' on my shoulder?"

She'd laughed, and they'd spent many lunch periods coming up with the most ludicrous tattoos that she could create. But outside of art class, she grew frustrated by how obvious her emotions became. She'd change colors, and other students would ask her if she was feeling okay—if she was feeling moody—making her more annoyed, which in turn proved their suspicions.

Today, during a strenuous math exam in Mr. Maralopez's class, she'd turned burnt orange in frustration. Mr. Maralopez, whose Adam's apple was so bulbous it looked like he was constantly trying to swallow an egg, promptly asked her to take the test in the hall so she wouldn't distract the other students, especially the boys. Fuming, she'd gone outside, left the test blank, and skipped class instead.

After a long lecture from her papá and the empty threat of being grounded, she was left to collect her thoughts and write an apology letter for Mr. Maralopez. Just after dinner, Mateo knocked on their door and her papá, always a softie, let them talk in their gated backyard.

While they sat on the grass, legs splayed out, Mateo passed her a plastic container. She popped the lid off. Inside were mini empanadas, and Flor didn't have to ask him if they were chicken and cheese. Those were her favorite.

"Mami thought you could use some after today."

Flor stuffed a whole one in her mouth and then another.

"Thanks," she said, her voice garbled by the food.

"It's okay, Mr. Maralopez sucks."

She swallowed. "He really does."

"My sister didn't like it at first either, you know?" Mateo began, rubbing his palms together uneasily. She shot him a look. "I know that all girls aren't the same, and you and my sister aren't the same. I know, I just asked her about it, in case you might want some advice . . ."

Flor shut the container of empanadas. The last time she'd seen Gaury, she was standing in front of her and Mateo's house, making the spring buds in their garden bloom under her touch.

She seemed pretty comfortable about the ability that the Change gave her.

"Fine. What did Gaury say?"

"She told me to tell you that other good things come with all of this stuff."

"Like what?"

"Well, since she went through the Change and got her flower ability, she loves flowers even more, and she knows she wants to be a florist or a landscape gardener when she grows up. And you love art class, so maybe this makes sense, a little." His voice fell at the suggestion, knowing full well that she was a minefield of color-coded emotions.

"Maybe," Flor said, glancing at him with her arms crossed.

"She said you'd learn to control it, and less embarrassing stuff will happen. Everything will become easier in a little while," Mateo said, glancing at her out of the corner of his eye to make sure he hadn't said anything to upset her. "And she said other good stuff happens too now that you've gone through the Change, but it's a little gross."

"What could be worse than this?" Flor said, gesturing to her pale blue skin. Her calm color. She was relaxed enough to focus and let her skin fade to its usual brown, but she wasn't embarrassed by her colors when just Mateo was around.

"I mean, a lot of things could be worse. I think it looks nice." Flor watched a flush roll up his neck and face. She could feel her skin shifting to a shimmering, deep pink, a color she hadn't turned yet. She'd taken for granted the days where her skin was too dark to blush. Now her whole body was a mood ring.

"What gross stuff did your sister say would happen?" Flor pried, wanting to distract herself and shift back to blue.

Mateo cleared his throat. "It's not gross stuff about you guys—girls, I mean. It's stuff about me—I mean, boys."

"Okay," she said, watching him rub the back of his neck. "What about boys?"

"Well, nothing changes about us on the outside, you know, besides getting taller and beards and all that basic stuff. But Gaury said we all get more mature on the inside."

"Like how? Smarter?"

"I don't really know," Mateo said, his eyes darting away from hers. "But she said that's why we all start dating and stuff around this time. Because we're getting more mature and stuff . . ."

There was a pregnant pause. Then Flor made a retching noise and followed it up with wet, smooching noises. "Ew. That is gross. Like I want to taste what you had for lunch."

"I had a peanut butter and banana sandwich," Mateo mumbled. Flor felt the pink of her skin brighten even more.

"I should probably go inside now," she said, her voice sounding too loud.

"Yeah."

"Probably."

"Okay."

She pressed her palms against the grass to ready herself to stand but thought better of it and sat back down. "Before I go, wanna see what color I can turn you?"

Mateo's spine straightened in excitement at her proposal. He'd been begging her for weeks, but she enjoyed holding things over his head. His incessant whining made it fun. She'd practiced by Change her bedroom walls on a fairly regular basis for the last three weeks. Last week, she'd even tried it on her papá, stamping him with the colors of his favorite football team. He'd been ecstatic at first, but she'd done too good of a job, and the color had lasted over a day. He had some explaining to do at work the next morning, but now she'd practiced enough, and she was certain she could control herself and paint Mateo without any permanence. Worst case scenario, he'd go to school tomorrow in a shade of her choosing.

"Yes, please! I want you to!" he yelped before pausing and collecting himself. "But, you know, only if you want to."

"What color do you want?"

Mateo shrugged. "I dunno. You decide. I won't limit your creative process." Flor rolled her eyes at him, but her smile remained intact.

After a moment's hesitation, Mateo shuffled closer to her, nodding in encouragement. She let her mind fall exclusively on him. The way he swung his backpack onto his shoulder carefully, as if the science fiction trilogies in his bag were made of glass—how his tongue curled when he yawned in history class. She flexed her fingers and thought of his body as a breathing, blank canvas. She covered her hand with his, her palm over his knuckles.

As if he were a white T-shirt dipped slowly into a tub of dye, color began to seep through his pale skin, snaking up his arm in tendrils until it covered him from head to toe. It wasn't one shade

but a myriad of deep blues. Even his hair shifted in color, trans-
forming into a fringe of skyline. Then pinpricks of light flickered
against the blue, dusting him with freckles of pure starlight—
soft and calm starlight, so different from what she'd seen in her
mother's eyes.

"I—" He stared down at himself in awe, his eyes widening.
"You made me look like space—the sky!"

"Guess I did." Flor smiled, feeling very cool. Her color shifted
from pink to a royal purple. Deep purple meant confidence or, if
she let herself admit it, vanity.

She left her hand on his for a while to give him time to admire
himself. She didn't know which of them had laced their fingers
together, but it looked like she was holding hands with the galaxy
itself. Abruptly, she pulled her palm from his. The color began to
fade, the flecks of starlight snuffing out one by one. Mateo held
his arms out and watched the colors lighten. Flor stood, brushing
the grass off the back of her pants.

"Anyway, I'm supposed to be in bed soon. So I'll see you tomorrow."

Mateo's skin returned to its original shade.

"Okay," he said, still a little breathless. He stood and made his
way toward the gate in the backyard.

"Oh and—"

"Yeah?" Mateo turned away from the gate to face her, his voice
high pitched.

"I was just gonna say I won't be at lunch tomorrow. I have to
make up the math test."

"Right," he said, nodding. "Okay. I'll just see you later then."

When Flor lay in bed that night, shifting her sheets not only from color to color but also from pattern to pattern (stripes to polka dots to paisley), she felt feather-light. She wondered if the next time she held Mateo's hand, she could make shooting stars streak across his skin.

Just as sleep began to whistle its first notes through her, Flor heard a familiar tapping at the bay window nestled between bookshelves on the other side of her bedroom. She wondered what Mateo could be throwing pebbles about at this hour. Last time he had done it, her papá had noticed, and the next morning he'd joked, "Mateo's a bit of a romantic when it comes to you, isn't he?"

Flor had made gagging noises to cover his laughter.

Her mind still stuck in the crawl space between dreaming and waking, Flor slowly rolled over to face the window, her silver curls mashed down on one side. A lithe figure with long, grass-green tresses floated behind the glass, centered in the window frame like a moving portrait.

Flor's mother pressed her face to the glass and knocked.

MAGICAL OFFERINGS

by

Nina Moreno

Hidden within the swamps and once-thriving citrus groves of Florida, at a crossroads that led nowhere new, was an abandoned miniature golf course that a charismatic Cuban showman swore he could turn into a kingdom. The alligator wrestler across the way from him disagreed. They fought about everything, but the wrestler figured he was right about this one since their dying neon signs only attracted mosquitos and moths. No one ever took their exit off the highway. Not when those vacationing families and tourists were headed to see magical castles, roller coasters that shot out to space, and water parks that called themselves paradise.

Luz Pérez had been exiled to that rusted kingdom.

Selling magic to sad girls again? Her mother was furious.

They were small spells! Luz argued. Simple rituals to find lost things—charms for luck. Ways to conjure up good news and grades for them. And extra cash.

Magic is never small, her mother said to Luz, again and again, like a lullaby. Or a curse. *One day you'll open a door you don't know how to close.*

This time the pastor's daughter complained all over town about a failed love spell, and angry mothers had screamed witch. Getting kicked out of another high school and being sent to the alternative one was one thing, but getting kicked out of that one just days before graduation was her mother's final straw. Because Mami finally felt settled. She had a good job bartending for old vets at the Legion and a breezy apartment with gleaming white tile by the beach. She didn't have another move in her to escape whatever mess Luz had gotten herself into this time.

From the bus window beside her, Luz watched the sunrise over an interstate lined with trucks selling orchids and billboards warning travelers about their mortal sins. Luz had been born not too far from here in a tiny house that stood on stilts at the edge of the swamp. She could still sometimes hear the raucous song of rowdy frogs.

She hadn't been back in so long.

The relief of arriving shriveled the moment she stepped off the bus into a heat that bore down on her without mercy. There wasn't a single breeze to cut through it out here. She was so far from the sea.

"Lucero!" Abuelo Berto waved from beside a pickup truck so old and rusted she couldn't even begin to guess the color. Berto Pérez still had a full head of dark hair, but it was now going gray. There was grease on his linen shirt and probably new gold in his teeth. She loved the rasp of his Cuban accent when he spoke Spanish and how his English tumbled into a Southern drawl.

He wrapped Luz in a big bear hug that she was vulnerable

enough to lean into for one, shoring moment. She'd missed him so much.

"I'm so happy you're here!" he said, not minding the scandalous reason for her arrival, simply ecstatic that she was finally back. He grabbed her bag and tossed it into the truck's bed before moving around to the other side and grandly opening her door. "Your chariot, mi amor."

Ten minutes and three dirt roads later, Abuelo Berto pulled up in front of a small house that reigned over a pile of junk.

"You like it?" he asked proudly, his chest all puffed up.

It was something between a junkyard and a broken-down carnival. The putting greens were overgrown with tall, weedy grass, and all the supposed obstacles were either falling apart or strewn about with empty shells of cars and appliances. A windmill that had fallen over, a water tower painted to look like a lighthouse. The lightbulb up top was hanging by a wire for dear life.

"It's definitely something," Luz said as they got out of the truck, and he led her deeper into the mess.

"Every time I saw this place, I knew I could fix it up. Your abuelo Berto knows this land, and a big idea when I see one."

A bold statement about a place that looked like a graveyard of bad judgment, but her abuelo was an incurable optimist who always had his eye on his next big scheme. She picked up a broken bicycle tire. "This is where big ideas go to die." She tossed the tire back.

"Ay, you're just not thinking big—"

She laughed, and it was a relief after this never-ending day. "Oh, I'm thinking and seeing plenty. I've been cast out from another town, and my punishment is to help clean up this mess."

Something sad shadowed her grandfather's eyes. "You used to believe too, mi niña." He led her forward through the tall grass. "When you were growing up, you told me silly stories about frogs and lizards who knew your name. You chased them into the woods before running out with your hair braided with orange blossoms and rosemallow." A shadow darkened his bright smile before it fell away.

"And then I disappeared."

For an entire week, no one could find seven-year-old Luz Pérez after she slipped into the woods to play. The whole town had searched for her. Luz's memories were hazy, painted strange by her wild imagination. When she reappeared seven days later—telling stories about feasts beneath the moonlight and a king who sat on a throne of roots—everyone's fear had turned to anger.

They called her a troublemaker. They called her single Cuban mother much worse.

Mami had flown through the house like a hurricane, packing whatever would fit in their car, and with Abuelo Berto in the rear-view mirror, they'd left their tiny house at the edge of the swamp.

Luz hadn't been back since.

"Yo las extraño a las dos." Abuelo Berto scratched his neck and sighed forlornly. "You were so young, and she would never come back. Pero está bien. I'll fix this place, and then you can both come home."

Home. Standing here, between her abuelo's dreams and these woods beyond it, the word had weight.

They reached the back of the property that butted up against dense swampland. Crooked trees draped in moss hid much of the land beyond it, but Luz could see murky, still waters and the low-lying fog that rolled over scattered islands. From here, the wetlands looked like they went on forever. A sharp whistle sounded, and Luz continued in that direction until her abuelo stopped her in front of a broken tractor.

"Ah, *now* I see," she said, and her lips quirked into a smile. "You need a mechanic."

He grinned big and snapped his fingers. "You're a magician with metal, mi amor, and I need this thing to move all this stuff around."

She kicked at the flat tire then screamed bloody murder as an alligator crawled out from behind it.

Her abuelo set her aside from him and grumbled a curse about the wrestler across the way. "Voy a matar a ese tipo." But instead of acting on the threat of murder, her abuelo approached the huge alligator as if it was a neighbor's dog that had gotten into the house, snapping his fingers and whistling as he called, "Let's go, Shakey."

Luz leaped back as the alligator patiently followed after him. Baffled, she asked, "Shakey?"

"Shakey the gator," he grumbled on a sigh. "He lives with the loco wrestler across the street, but Shakey gets lonely over there." He puckered his lips and blew an air kiss at the reptile as they left. "He's a good boy, but if you feed something, it always comes back."

The gator wrestler. Right. This place was too hot, sticky, and so far off the map *and* its rocker. And yet, part of her had missed it. There was a peaceful stillness here, even though it was never truly quiet. It hummed, sang, and growled. The land was a wild green that wasn't afraid of death.

Luz lifted the corroded hood on the tractor. The elements had not been kind to it. No hoses, no belt. Not even an exhaust or steering wheel. It was true she knew her way around some engines, though she wouldn't call herself a magician. But she hadn't thought herself a witch either.

She had to hand it to her latest school, where she'd learned her new favorite thing ever: welding. Teaching a lovelorn teen how to burn the right candle and braid their hair with someone else's before slipping it beneath their pillow hadn't made Luz feel powerful. But an electric current sparking from her and shaping metal to her will? She'd become a goddess.

Luz didn't feel anywhere close to that power as she smacked away a mosquito and sighed at the rusted tractor in front of her.

Inside the house, she dropped her bag off on the couch and plugged in her phone to check in with her mother. Mami had been worried about Luz returning. But she wasn't seven anymore. And her imagination was locked tight.

Her phone showed zero service. "Abuelo, you got Wi-Fi?"

From the kitchen, he laughed like that was the funniest thing he'd ever heard. "Wi-Fi? ¿Qué Wi-Fi? I got Lo-Fi!" He handed her a battery-operated radio.

Luz held up the artifact. "Let me guess," she said and yanked the antenna out. She pointed it toward the junkyard outside. "You found this out there?"

"¡Claro! All of this is ours now." He offered her a hopeful smile.

"Y no te preocupes. Yo voy a llamar a tu mamá." He picked up the old landline phone and dialed. He shot Luz a confident wink before turning his attention to the call. "¡Hola, mi amor! ¡Sí, Luz está aquí!"

His big smile slipped at whatever her mother was saying. He turned away and lowered his voice into an urgent whisper, reassuring her that Luz would be too busy working to mess around in town with locals or get caught up in any more brujería.

Luz slipped outside to avoid hearing more. She stood on the porch from where she surveyed their prized loot. Despite her abuelo's infectious optimism, it really was a junkyard of half-formed dreams. She walked amongst the busted theme park castoffs and abandoned garbage, following the radio's every crackle. It finally clicked with a promising sound when she reached the tractor. The scratchy blues song was a relief. Luz set the radio down on the tractor just as another sharp whistle brought her head up.

She expected to see a crow or her abuelo. But there was only a barren tree.

It looked different than the many ancient cypress trees beyond it. Those dug into the dark water with their thick, gnarled roots, but this one stood apart. Closer to the edge of her abuelo's land. It was only a couple feet taller than her, the leafy top gone. A lone branch on the right side stretched out like an arm. The trunk narrowed into two roots. On this tree, they looked like legs.

Luz moved closer to touch the bark. She found herself humming along to the song as she dragged a finger down the solid branch. When she reached the end, she stopped and did a slow spin beneath it.

A tiny laugh flew out of her. It felt good to laugh and let go a little. The song sped up, and Luz spun faster, too, kicking up dirt. The song grew stormy. The rhythm shook and stomped. The world around her flickered as moonflower petals scattered. Memory and dreams. Static and song. A deep laugh. Spongey grass beneath her bare feet. Eerie lights floating in the dark mist, leading her off the path. A table made of wild vines overflowing with a feast. A tiny strawberry cake drizzled with wildflower honey that had tasted like home.

"*¡Lucero!*" Abuelo Berto desperately called out from beyond the door.

Luz crashed to a sudden stop.

She stumbled against the tree, shaky and dizzy. The music was gone. With both hands gripping the trunk, she tried to catch her breath. The radio had lost signal, and the clamorous static sounded as loud and grating as Abuelo Berto's next shout. "¡Sabes mejor que eso!"

That strange daydream crumbled and blew away like dust. Frustrated, she returned, "I'm not disappearing or getting into trouble, Abuelo. I was just . . . dancing." She pointed an accusing finger at his radio like it was the one to blame.

A battle took place on her abuelo's usually warm and charming face. "Whispering voices out there," he warned, then prayed protective words in Spanish under his breath before kissing the charms at the end of his gold chain.

She recognized the small, black azabache stone and pair of protective eyes—ojos de Santa Lucía. Her abuelo was one of the

bravest people she knew. He'd lost an island but was always trying
to find them a new home—one with roots that would last. Something soft in her gave when she looked at this mess, knowing he
was trying to build something great here.

But he was afraid of these woods. Maybe of her, too.

Luz woke the next morning to a rooster crowing and her abuelo
shouting at the gator wrestler. The sheets stuck to her bare legs,
and the useless, slow-moving fan above her could do nothing to
combat the burdensome heat. She stretched but stayed in bed for a
long moment. She pressed a finger to her lips and wished she could
recall yesterday's daydream and the taste of wildflower honey.

After a cool shower, she found a pair of boots waiting for her
out in the hall. Abuelo Berto was in the kitchen, where it smelled
like burnt bacon and sweet cigar smoke. When he saw her, he
laughed, delighted by her getup of cutoffs, T-shirt, and busted-up
boots.

"¡Bueno!" he cheered from the corner of his mouth, the cigar
held tight between his teeth. "¡Pareces a una guajira!"

"Yup, I'm a regular country girl now." Her chair squeaked
against the linoleum. She smiled as she twisted her wet hair up
into a knot before carefully asking, "What did Mami say?"

Her abuelo scooped up the charred meat and dropped it on
plates. "Tu madre está feliz de que estás aquí."

"Abuelo," she deadpanned.

He shrugged like he'd been caught. "You are eighteen now, mi
niña. She knows you have to live your life, and you weren't happy
there."

Luz and her mother had moved from one sunburnt seaside

town to the next, and no matter what she did, trouble always seemed to find her.

"What's the plan?" Abuelo Berto asked—optimism back in his voice. He puffed on his cigar. "The tractor?"

Luz made a big show of getting to her feet. "The plan is to help you turn this pile of sh—"

"Shiny treasures!" he interrupted.

"Right," she agreed with a quick laugh. "Let's turns these treasures into a tourist trap."

He clapped then pointed at her with his cigar. "¡Eso!"

Just a couple of dreamers and schemers. Luz grabbed an orange on her way out.

The day was as suffocatingly hot and humid as yesterday. The tall grass tickled her calves as she walked and peeled the fruit slowly. The orange was bright and juicy on her tongue.

She reached the strange tree she'd danced with and considered its oddly humanoid frame.

"How'd you lose your arm?"

The way it stood separate from the other trees felt sad to her. And Luz understood loneliness. The shape of it. How quiet it could be. The way that silence sometimes felt like loss.

"What's all that behind you?" she asked before popping another orange slice into her mouth. She couldn't help her curiosity over the swamp beyond it.

"Do you remember me?" It felt dangerous to ask, and her pulse drummed. Luz's disappearance all those years ago changed everything, but because they never talked about it, and because she couldn't *remember* it, that lost week sometimes felt like it had happened to someone else. One Luz slipped into the forest, and a different one returned.

Sweat dripped down her neck, and her hands felt sticky from juice. She finished the last slice of sweet orange and then tossed the peel toward the tree. It had no answers, but Luz found that she liked talking to it. Her sad, lonely tree.

She turned on the radio and set off to search the maze for parts to build the tree's other arm.

After dinner, Abuelo watched her weld the sheet metal and spark plugs into fingers at the kitchen table.

"That's for the tractor?"

"No, that has a diesel engine."

"¡Diesel, qué diesel!" The eternal optimist, he then assumed she was making some kind of robot for his twisted little golf course. Perhaps she could eventually.

Beneath the summer evening sky that still burned with light, Luz kicked over a nearby bucket and stepped up onto it to attach the arm. Another silly impulse, but it didn't matter out here. Because for the first time in a long time, Luz no longer felt so lost. She could weld and create something whimsical. She could talk to trees and play in the woods and not be called a witch or troublemaker for it. Fixing this tree was like a lodestone that grounded her here.

She held the new arm up with her shoulder then fastened the base to the trunk. The radio's static won over the song, becoming a cacophony of noise. After the third screw, she felt a tickling sensation on her neck. She finished the fourth and hopped back. She grinned brightly at her work.

Two arms, two legs. A face, though still sad. The sight inspired Luz to find more parts.

Buried away in a shed, she found the tanned hide of an alligator that must've been first cousins to a damn dinosaur. Luz dragged it back to the tree, where it became a sort of hooded cape around the tree's shoulders.

Next came the chain of gator teeth she draped like a necklace. A piece of cowhide was cinched tight around the middle with a rope. Nearby cattle ranches had mostly died out with the citrus groves, making her wonder what other wayward animals Abuelo's neighbor found to wrestle out here. She tied off the knot and stepped back to consider her work. It made an imposing figure now, with its metal arm sticking out from beneath the alligator cape.

But it all came together when she found the bull skull.

One of the horns was cracked in half, and the bottom part of its snout was gone. Inexplicably mournful over the broken face, Luz dragged her thumb across the rough edge.

And sliced her skin.

"Son of a—!" She nearly dropped the skull but grasped it tight to her chest for a moment of dizzying relief that it didn't break further.

The skull fit perfectly on top. She looked closer at her work, and her heart dropped when she saw the blood that stained it. Her blood. Her mother's dire warnings rang out in her mind. *Doors and windows. Blood and demands.* Luz wasn't even allowed to get her hair cut if she was on her period. She hurriedly pressed her shirt against the cut then swore at herself.

Superstitions. That was all they were—silly stories to scare kids about their own bodies. There was nothing magical about her;

a nowhere girl and troublemaking dropout. Her pulse pounded in her thumb and a cold sweat prickled along the back of her neck.

When a whistle sang out sharply, spooking the nearby birds that had been picking through the dark water for bugs, Luz's head jerked toward the thick grove of cypress trees. Another piercing whistle had her backing away from her tree, which now looked every bit the sentinel at the entrance of a forbidding swamp. Luz's heart battered her ribs like a wild thing trying to get free. The whistling sounded further away now, and she tried to find comfort in that. Her pulse continued to pound in her bleeding thumb as she turned on the radio for noise and found another song from whatever pirate radio station was able to reach her, the reception rough enough to sound miles and years away from broadcast.

"¡Oye!" Abuelo marched over to her, and she was relieved to be snapped free of her spiraling imagination. "¿Qué es esto?" He stopped and considered her work for a long, strained moment. She had no idea how to explain before he moved up to it, the intention to take it apart clear.

She leaped between them. "¡Abuelo, no!"

Abuelo Berto's face fell. "Luz," he said, her name filled with confusion and wariness.

Her arm hairs rose in warning just before a crack of lightning lit the sky and struck somewhere in the swamp beyond them with a thunderous boom she felt in her teeth. It stole her breath, and before she could even scream, a heavy deluge of rain fell in a sudden, violent downpour. She and Abuelo Berto ran toward the small house, and after crashing inside, he looked at her cut hand, and his brown skin paled.

How could a girl feel so inconsequential and dangerous at the same time? Luz said nothing as she went to wash the blood off her hands.

Rain continued to lash at the windows for hours as the summer storm raged. Near midnight—unable to sleep—Luz dug into her bag, past her cards, herbs, and stones, and plucked out a candle. She prepared it, and the space around her as best as she could then struck a match. The lights above her and the candle before her flickered. It had been a long time since she'd done any kind of ritual for herself. Magic had become orderly—spells her currency. But now she sat on the floor as she whispered the wild words that grew somewhere in her middle, bloomed up her throat, and tickled her tongue. The promise of them jingled like keys.

Doors and windows. Blood and demands.

Monsters and magic.

Luz and the thunderstorm continued long into the night.

When a harsh shout sounded, Luz blinked against the bright sunlight. Still on the floor, she jerked up to sitting, guilty over last night's magic and disoriented by the hour. Another angry curse outside her window made Luz throw herself out of bed, panicked that Abuelo Berto was acting on the fear she'd seen in his eyes by the tree. In her haste, she knocked over the still-burning candle. She snatched it up off the floor, hissing at the burn of melted wax spilling over her cut hand as she raced outside. She crashed to a stop on the porch. Abuelo wasn't on his way to the tree with a pitchfork—he was out by the road, embroiled in another morning shouting match with the wrestler across the way. This time it was a custody battle over Shakey, the gator, who waited in the dirt between them.

"Come on, gator!" the wrestler shouted as her Abuelo called, "¡Shakey, vámonos!"

She tried to catch her breath. But right off the porch, in the dirt, was a trail of seeds that led toward the woods. Luz was still holding the candle. She was a mess. A loose cannon who had promised her mother she'd stop getting into trouble. But she very badly wanted to know where those seeds led.

Luz set the candle aside and tugged on her boots, her heart pounding with an undeniable sense of anticipation as she set off to follow.

The trail led right to the tree. Oranges were piled on the ground around the base of it. They sat purposefully, like an offering. Her confused gaze traveled up the tree. The skull and cape were in the same place, but it all looked . . . different this morning. *More*, somehow. Luz took a careful step closer. The branch was now bent halfway down like an elbow. And the bark looked softer. Luz touched it and found it inexplicably warm. As she pressed her fingers harder against it, the tree tore itself away from its place and sprang toward her.

Luz screamed and fell back hard. The tree was no longer buried in the ground. What had just been roots were shuffling like feet through the dirt as it circled her. She slammed her eyes closed. The bull skull was right in her neck.

She choked on a strangled whimper as a hot, frustrated huff escaped the mask and heated her neck. Breath. Skull. *Bones.* Her mind frayed from the disconnect between reality and the living, breathing tree standing over her.

And then it was gone. Luz jumped to her feet and ran like a bat out of hell.

"¡Abuelo! *¡Abuelo!*" He was right. They were all right. Luz was a troublesome witch who played too much and had now awoken a monster.

"What? What?" he called from the driveway.

She grabbed his hand and made him run with her, which he complained about the entire way. But once there, the tree was just that again. Back in its place. Her decorated silent sentinel.

Abuelo studied it for a long, strained moment before stepping back. "Desarmarlo, Lucero. ¿Me entiendes?"

She nodded, her throat dry.

"And burn everything."

Her gaze skipped to the tree. As afraid as she was, the idea of taking it apart was immediately unthinkable.

Abuelo turned away then patted the tractor's cold, dead engine. With a determined look, he solemnly promised her, "We are going to fix this place, and then everything will be okay."

Luz watched him go. And then she went to look for a machete.

She found one in an old freezer of all places. She sharpened the blade then hid behind a broken gas pump to lay in wait. Several feet away, the radio sparked to life with another ancient song. It sounded like a big band war relic.

Luz gripped the machete tighter and exhaled slowly. She searched around the tractor and radio. A shuffling sound brought her gaze swinging back to the tree.

Luz glanced up, and her bravado crumpled as she watched the very humanoid tree lean forward. The form beneath the alligator cape shifted like shoulders as the metal hand—the one she'd built—picked up one of the oranges. It straightened, and she saw a wide chest of living bark. Those spark plugs worked as fingers as it studied the peel. The branch now bent into the shape of an arm, too, but both metal and wood appendages struggled. Luz muttered her abuelo's favorite prayer, and then, with the machete firmly in hand, she left her hiding spot and carefully moved closer.

The bull skull was turned away as the tree monster continued to struggle with the fruit, ignoring her. Or at least pretending to.

Luz stopped beside the tractor and climbed up to take a seat, never giving the tree her back. This close, she could see that the bark beneath the bull's skull was greener now.

She wanted to see it eat. She needed to know what she was up against.

The metal hand finally broke through the peel. She watched it tear off a slice and slip it beneath the broken end of the skull. She couldn't help but lean closer. There *was* new growth behind the bull skull. Lips parted.

Swamp thing, Luz thought, both terrified and a little bit fascinated.

Another slice of orange disappeared into its mouth, and that new neck moved like a throat. Once it finished eating the orange, it finally looked her way. Luz gripped the machete again, but the tree monster simply tossed the peel toward her just as she had yesterday.

Luz waited for it to do something else, but it only proceeded to eat another orange. The broad, tall form moved fluidly now. Roots had twisted into thick, corded legs. The right branch bent as smoothly as a limb, the bark now green with life.

Luz tried to mentally measure their height difference. She stood at five and a half feet, but the tree had to be . . . eight? It studied its metal arm, flexing the spark plug fingers.

It had been a tree—a stuck-in-the-ground, typical tree. She was sure of it. But now, it looked up and watched her steadily. The wooden hand went to the corner of the skull and touched the spot with her blood. Luz couldn't breathe as that hand went to its mouth. Shadows stirred behind the skull's empty eye sockets just before they glowed.

The monster was quick because before she could even react to it tasting her blood, it was right next to her as it leaned into her throat again. Luz swallowed a scream and froze. Was it smelling her? She felt hunted before it let go of another unexplainable huff of frustration and stormed away.

Luz scrambled off the tractor and bent at the knees to greedily inhale a much-needed breath. After another minute, she dragged her shaking hands through her hair and stood. The agitated monster paced the edge of the property. The radio became lost to static. Within that scrambled white noise came a deep voice; garbled, angry, and low. It sounded far away and crackled like thunder. **"This . . . is your . . . language?"**

Luz's head shot up. The monster moved closer. She snatched up the machete and uselessly held it up between them as her arms trembled.

The monster stopped beside the radio and static cleared as if an antenna had found an open window. The skull cocked to the side.

"These . . . are . . . your . . . words."

The tree had a voice. A brooding growl that matched those hot exhales of irritation she could still feel on her neck.

"Who are you?" Luz's gaze darted to the shadows and hint of the full mouth she'd seen.

Grainy static echoed again, and the volume jumped erratically. **"What . . . are . . . *you?*"** The words were sulky and feral.

Luz took another step back, putting the tractor between

them. "I'm just a girl," she said as the monster circled her, moving closer. She tracked it in return. "I'm no one."

It stopped in front of her.

"I . . . am . . ." The metal hand went to her chin, but she jerked back. "A . . . huntsman," he continued solemnly. The cold hand fell to her throat, gently circling her skin.

She stilled. "A what?"

"And . . . you . . . are . . ."

She waited, breathless and desperate for answers.

". . . a curse."

Stunned, she shoved his arm away. "I am not the curse. You're a talking tree!" Luz paced. "Jesus, this is nuts. It's not real. Monsters aren't real. Magic isn't—"

"Luz . . ."

She stopped. Not only did he know her name, but the exposed rage in his voice rang louder and clearer now through the radio's speakers. He moved close again, his metal hand carefully returning to her neck. She couldn't say why she didn't push him away this time, only that she couldn't stop thinking about the fact that she'd built that hand. Welded those fingers. And now they were slowly exploring where her neck met her shoulder. This monster huntsman seemed confused as he explored the soft skin there. Confused but bold.

Luz felt the same.

She carefully placed her palm against his chest. She didn't find a heartbeat, a racing, pounding pulse to match and ground her own in this impossible moment, but he radiated with life as his hand slipped down her arm.

"What are you hunting?" she dared to ask.

The radio scrambled and screeched. The huntsman swung both hands up in front of her. He shook them at her.

"Unchain me!" he demanded.

Nothing was binding him.

"Unchain . . . me . . . *witch!*"

Luz scrambled back, accidentally dropping the machete into the dirt between them in her haste. Her terrified gaze swung between the weapon and the furious being. Was she faster? She didn't want to get close enough to see. The monster leaned forward and reached for the machete. She was deathly still but prepared to run in the other direction. The metal hand picked up the sharp end. And then handed it back to her.

The radio found a song again as Luz took the offering.

"Luz!"

She spun toward her abuelo's shout, afraid of a hundred things at once. The radio scrambled, clicking impatiently between stations.

"¡Teléfono!" Abuelo Berto called from closer to the house.

The monster's attention snapped beyond her and her machete shot up between them. Her hand didn't shake this time. Not with Abuelo somewhere behind her and this mystery in front of her. The huntsman watched her, measuring her conviction. The hood had fallen back off his broken horn. After a moment, he slipped back into place at the edge of the swamp. She knew that was as close to compliance as she would get.

Luz hurried inside. Abuelo glanced at the machete but didn't ask as she reached for the landline in the kitchen. Luz tried to keep her voice level for her mother. She listened to her latest funny stories about the old veterans who looked out for her and even smiled as her mother considered signing up for surfing lessons.

"I think you should go for it," Luz said, meaning it. She wanted more than endless work and worrying for her. Mami deserved rest and adventures.

"Maybe I will," she said with a laugh before sobering. Luz braced herself. "And you're okay? Everything is . . . okay there?"

Luz still clung to the machete in her clenched fist. The monster she'd awoken had just called her a witch. She wished she could rip herself open like a book and give her mother satisfying answers for everything. Ones that would erase the years of worry and make all the heartache worth it. Maybe then Luz wouldn't have to hide or lock up all the messy parts of herself. She could own her wildness, the words that bloomed in her heart, the power that stirred in her blood. The mystery of it all would be hers to solve instead of bury.

She just needed to remember.

"Sí, Mami," she told her now as the sun sank into the horizon in a glorious painting of oranges and pinks. The sweet smell of cigar reached her through the window screen from where her abuelo smoked on the porch, in his old rocking chair, his one heirloom from the island. A familiar gator sat comfortably at his feet as if it was a dog. "I'm happy here."

The next morning when Luz headed toward the woods, she feared she would find nothing waiting for her. Another memory lost like a forgotten dream.

But the huntsman waited.

He loomed at the edge of the swamp, and instead of oranges at his feet, there were now salvaged parts beside the broken tractor. A new tire. A water pump. A steering wheel.

Luz swallowed around a lump of helplessness as she considered the offerings. "I don't know how to unchain you," she admitted and gestured to his unbound hands. "There's nothing there."

The radio clicked on. Static crashed and clattered. He shifted closer and held his metal arm out toward her. The hand snapped closed into a fist. **"I . . . am . . . here. Witch."**

"I heard you the first time!" she snapped.

Witch or not, she had no idea what to do with a chained tree monster throwing a temper tantrum. But with these parts, she did know how to fix that tractor. After a frustrated exhale, she turned away to gather some tools. The huntsman brooded from the edge of the wood as she worked. His hooded robe flared around him as he paced. She took the engine apart and racked her brain for some mythological answer. He strode along the edge of the woods, then turned and did it again over the same ground. She measured it at about fifty feet. Was he cursed? Could *she* break it? She rubbed her finger across the healing cut on her thumb.

His focus turned to his hands, but she could see no chains between them. He studied his right arm. The metal one scratched and tore at the wood. They both stared as new vines grew like veins. The song on the radio drowned beneath the defeated static that rang out like a howl.

Her hand tightened around a wrench as his anguish reached out to her.

"I don't have any answers," she pleaded with him. "Do you? Because I disappeared into those woods, and it ruined everything. *I* ruined everything, and I can't even remember it. So, no, I don't know how to help you or fix this damn golf course for my abuelo or make sure that my mother is happy enough that I don't drown from the guilt or fear that I'll ruin it all again."

He moved closer, and his metal hand tentatively reached for her. She pushed him away.

"I don't have your answers," she answered hollowly.

"Witch," his deep, despondent voice called from the radio.

"Fine! I'm a witch," she shot back. "You want me to light you a candle? Read your cards? Connect with your ancestors?" Luz dragged her hand through her hair and returned to the tractor. "Or some seed, I guess," she muttered.

"Witch," he said again, slower this time, and she nearly crumpled beneath the suffering in it.

He was so much bigger than her. So terrifying and monstrous and . . . trapped. He was a beast caught in a snare. The trap was invisible to her, but it was there all the same because why else would he be pacing the fifty feet of dirt between those wild woods and her abuelo's attempt at a tourist trap?

Her gaze moved to the abandoned miniature golf course. The pirate's shipwreck. The overgrown maze. The rusted castle with a broken drawbridge. Her abuelo's busted kingdom was like a twisted fairy tale, monster included. Luz studied the enigmatic space where she'd first found the huntsman and noted the way the light shivered there.

Witch, they all said.

So be it.

"Come here," she told him, surprised by her command.

The radio crackled. The way the huntsman focused on her felt predatory. He stalked closer, stopping just in front of her. The air around them was electric and hazy, like a brewing storm. She trailed her finger along the edge of the skull, still stained with her blood. He dipped his head closer to her, and she didn't flinch when his broken horn brushed through her hair. The skull slipped into the crook of her neck, and she tipped her head back as bark scraped gently against her throat.

Luz touched his metal forearm. Her hand sliding carefully higher beneath the leather cape. Over the ridge of his shoulder and up to his neck.

"Luz."

Her heart pounded, but not from fear. New words stirred within her as unexpected warmth rushed her skin. A sweet heat sparked before magic melted over her tongue. It felt like sunlight but tasted of wildflower honey. She wanted to free them both. Because maybe it wasn't a curse or sad story. Perhaps it had always been a fairy tale.

And those had taught her one way to break a curse.

She lifted up onto her toes and pressed her lips against the column of his neck. She closed her eyes and saw a wild, green field of orange blossoms. Her lips moved beneath the edge of the skull, and she found his mouth, as real and alive as hers.

A shocked inhale just before strong arms wrapped tightly around her, and he kissed her back. Whispered words bloomed between them. Her mind and world flickered, and the discovered memories played like long-lost songs. A young girl slipping into the woods, her wild magic opening a door between worlds. The huntsman who traveled its crossroads, cursed to stand at the edge, to now guard it. Stuck until the witch returned.

Doors and windows. Blood and demands.

Heat sparked from Luz's hands, and the huntsman flew back from her, startled, his eyes glowing as he raised his own hands and studied them with wonder.

"*Luz*," he said, the word ringing out from the radio with wonder and reverence. He was free from his post at the crossroads that led somewhere else, but didn't leave. He was staring at her.

He offered her his metal hand.

Monsters and magic.

A marvelous world waited for her on the other side. One she had played in as a child, leaving a piece of herself there. Luz had tried to seal it all away, locking up her memories tight along with her enigmatic imagination. But it hadn't worked. The potent magic inside her had sung out through these wild woods and opened the door again. Luz had never felt so awake.

But there was also *her* whole world *here*. Abuelo was working on the fence today. Her mother was paddling out into the Atlantic Ocean.

Magic is never small, her mother said, again and again.

But perhaps Luz never had been either.

At midnight, she slipped into the kitchen with a letter for Abuelo Berto, reassuring him and her mother of her return. She unexpectedly found a note addressed to her. She opened it, and Abuelo's gold necklace with the black azabache stone and charm of Santa Lucía's protective eyes fell into her hands.

> *Lucero,*
>
> *Sometimes home isn't where we begin. Be safe, and don't be a stranger.*
>
> *And thank you for the tractor, mi amor.*
>
> > *Te quiero siempre,*
> *Berto Pérez de Shakey's Gigante Putt-Putt Kingdom (coming soon)*

Luz smiled. Just a couple of dreamers. She slipped the necklace around her neck then tugged on her boots. She picked up the ancient radio, and by the light of the full moon, she followed the huntsman's voice to the edge of the liminal land. She stopped at the crossroads. He towered above her—fearsome and otherworldly—but she felt just as mythical as him. She offered the waiting monster an orange.

The radio sounded with a low chuckle.

He reverently bent his head and offered her his cold metal hand again. Luz took it as she followed her huntsman into the wood. The radio crackled between static and song as they slipped between the exposed roots of a huge, ancient cypress tree. They followed a pathway within the dark water, only a bit of moonlight peeking between the trees to guide them until strange, eerie lights floated out from the mist. Vines slithered like snakes, and unseen beasts called out to each other. The huntsman's hand tightened protectively around hers. The lights drifted closer, surrounding her. She now had the undivided attention of a curious, growling swamp. The radio whined as it tuned to a new station.

"*Luz,*" they called.

Light gathered and shimmered around her like sunlight, illuminating an open door. Luz stopped and kissed the black stone at the end of her necklace. She took one last deep breath before grabbing the huntsman's hand again. They moved forward and crossed the space between worlds together. Roots and moss swallowed the entryway behind them on the final notes of an old love song.

OTHER TIMES, OTHER REALMS

ROGUE ENCHANTMENTS

by

Isabel Ibañez

When people walk into La Hechiceria in Monterisa, they expect to find something extraordinary. An outdoor market full of purchasable spells that add color and convenience to one's life. They say love can be found at a stall near the end of the lane, while lost memories can be bought at a booth near the food quarter. If you need to curse an enemy, then look no further than the back end of the market, right next to vendors selling dried frogs and snakes to mix into potions.

Here's what I know for sure: No one in their right mind would move into their shop during the opening of the day. For one thing, Monterisa is murderously hot this time of year, when the days are long and the mosquito-riddled nights too short. For another, shoppers from every corner of the world crowd the main cobbled path lined on either end with wooden stalls painted in a riot of colors. It's impossible to take anything other than a few half steps forward.

I clutch my woven baskets, one layered high above the other, wildly teetering as I try to push my way through. From every-where comes the steady sound of hooves clacking against stone, the hum of patrons buying one thing or another, chattering in var-ious languages, and of people hollering the prices of their wares.

One sol for an encanto to heal diseases and wounds!

Twenty-five soles for a spell to ensure a long life!

Two scudos for a spell to grow your hair half an inch!

Absolutely outrageous! Two scudos for half an inch? That's thirty-two soles!

Fifteen soles for an encanto to keep a plant alive forever!

Wait, that's actually a great deal.

I abruptly stop and think about spending what little I have on the spell. I peer at the vendor as a shopper presents a dying dahlia in a pretty ceramic pot the exact color of maracuya, a deep and golden yellow fruit. The seller pours a green liquid onto the packed soil, glittering like mica under the bright sun. Immedi-ately, a mist rises and swarms around the dying flower. Within seconds the plant straightens from its wilted state, the colors deepening, the stem and leaves becoming plump and healthy. The shopper hands over the soles and walks off with a delighted smile in place.

After a moment, I reluctantly press on. My poor fern will have to wait. Maybe one day, I can figure out how to brew a po-tion that will save all of my plants. I can never keep them hale and thriving, even the heartier cactuses that are supposed to be difficult to kill. Apparently not for me.

The buyer's grin stays with me every step I take. In a matter of hours, that will be *me*. I'll have been responsible for bringing a smile to someone's face.

I push forward, and people scatter, glancing nervously at the tower of baskets in my hands. Overhead the sunlight assaults anyone within reach. Sweat slides from my neck and down the length of my back under my best tunic, a soft purple the exact shade of lavender. I stitched the floral embroidery myself, a pretty pattern showcasing gold and red thread woven down to my ankles. I'm wearing my mother's leather belt and sandals, a deep whiskey hue that complements my deep olive skin and dark, curling hair I keep wild and free.

The scent of smoked duck drifts over the market like a stubborn mist over a lake. I ignore the growl of my stomach. I simply don't have time to eat. This morning I have to paint, sweep, and clean, and then decorate my booth in order to not miss out on the day's potential customers.

It's important that I make a good impression.

One can't just open a new store in La Hechiceria. No, there's a lengthy application process, managed by La Gerencia, who have rules and processes. The hours we have to keep, the type of goods we can sell, and of course the hefty rent to operate our stall at all. Their ordinances are stifling. Everything has to be approved and backed by paperwork and licenses. It's a logistical nightmare but completely worth it because of the hundreds of customers, locals and foreigners alike, La Hechiceria hosts every day. They will come, whatever the weather.

The only reason there's an empty booth at all is because my abuelita died. La Gerencia gives family members first rights to the space before opening it up to the general public. Now's my chance to make a name for myself.

To finally have something of my own.

I peer around the baskets, unfortunately still teetering rather dangerously, the tight weave digging into my skin, and attempt to find my bearings. My stall is in a prime location, right in the middle of the mercado, surrounded by other popular booths and situated on the main thoroughfare—a cobbled path where only people on foot and four-legged creatures are welcome to traverse. No carriages or wagons allowed. I look wistfully toward a stall selling single-use encantos guaranteed to make you stronger for a period of time.

But I can't afford the magic.

My savings were depleted purchasing a license, buying ingredients to enchant my art supplies, *paint*—my abuelita had covered her stall in an awful yellow, straddling the line between sludge and pee. Not to mention the soles for a new tunic. La Gerencia has strict rules about that sort of thing. If you're a vendor, no tears or stains on any clothing. Every gold, silver, and copper coin I had went to my new life in this legendary market.

Someone knocks into me, and I let out a small yelp as the top basket slides. A hand reaches up and catches it before it can fall onto the uneven path.

"Sorry," they say in a rush.

I peer around my stack. Staring down at me is a tall boy with a mop of wavy dark hair, friendly brown eyes, and pale skin dotted with freckles. He has a dimple on his left cheek, and his answering smile reveals a charming gap between his two front teeth. He's my age, or close to it, and I can't help how my attention lingers on the breadth of his shoulders, the sinewy strength of his forearms.

I glance away, blushing.

His voice is a deep bass. "¿Te hiciste daño?"

I shake my head. "I'm not hurt. Honestly," I say in between huffs, "I'm amazed I'm still standing. I can barely see what's in front of me."

"Well," he says, "we can't have that." And without my having to ask, the handsome stranger reaches out and plucks my things from my hands. The stack looks manageable in his arms, while on me, it must have looked like I was attempting to cart around an enormous mountain dog.

"Where to?" he asks.

I hesitate. So far, I've had to do everything on my own. My mother passed away ten years ago just after my eighth birthday. My father lives miles and miles from Monterisa, working hard on the farm. For the longest time, it's been just me against the bustling city. Papá despises it here with its loud nights and high prices and refused to move away from the verdant hills. And while he writes every week and supports my dreams, I know he'd prefer I try my hand at growing maize. I can't stand the taste of corn.

A furry creature at the boy's heels catches my eye. Brown and black spotted with big eyes and floppy ears. His paws are enormous.

"Who is your friend?" I ask.

My companion looks down and barks a laugh. "That's Felipe. He's a monster."

The dog yips happily and then trips over his own feet. The handsome stranger rolls his eyes and scoops him up while still balancing my baskets. It's an impressive feat. I reach out and pet the adorable pup, cooing softly.

"He makes friends everywhere he goes," the stranger says with mock disgust.

"And you don't?"

"Not as easily as this mongrel."

"What's your name?"

"Mateo Salinas, formerly of Hispalia."

"Hispalia? That's a long way from here."

"Six weeks by boat." He shuddered. "The constant rocking and terrible food, sleeping on a hammock with no pillow. Never again."

I laughed. "Then why make the voyage?"

"Dragon attacks," he said grimly. "My whole family perished in a fire. I wanted to live in a more tropical climate and start somewhere new."

I'd heard about Hispalia and its dragon problem. "I'm so sorry," I said.

"It was years ago." He shoots me a curious look, and swiftly changes the subject. "Where did you buy these paints? I haven't seen them in the market before."

"They're mine," I say proudly. "I mean, of course they are, but what I meant is that I'm selling them. I have brushes and canvases, too."

The stranger's grin falters. His brow furrows, and he pulls his lip with his teeth. He lets the squirming Felipe down and the dog bounds ahead, barking happily. "What's your name?"

The sudden change in his mood makes me stiffen. "Graciela."

"Graciela with no apellido?"

Unease sweeps through me. I don't like the forced smile on his face, don't like the sudden nonchalance in his stance as he shifts my things onto one arm and holds out a hand.

I hesitate and finally take it in mine, noting the many nicks along his fingers. "Do you also have a cat?"

He looks down at where I'm staring. "No, I carve figurines. I sell them here in the market. You didn't answer my question."

But before I can reply, the sight before me snags my attention.

We've reached my abuelita's stall—but it's completely wrecked.

The boards were ruined by paint splatter, dried bits of food, and debris littering the area. Shame rises up my throat, scorching hot. The vendors on either side of my stall pointedly ignore me, going about their business, pretending not to see what's been made clear: I am not wanted in La Hechiceria.

My cheeks are on fire, and I clear my throat, forcing myself to blink away the burn of tears threatening to embarrass me in front of all these people.

I will not cry. I will *not* cry.

Next to me, Mateo's brow puckers with dawning realization. "You're Maria's granddaughter." His gaze drops to the basket. "You're selling art supplies."

I blink rapidly, panic flaring in my blood, making it roil under my skin. "Y-yes."

Mateo shifts on his feet, still clutching my baskets, and opens his mouth to say something, but then closes it the next second. Dimly, I hear the pulse of chatter rise around us. He lets out a low whistle, and Felipe runs back toward him, yarn dangling from his mouth.

Mateo and I stare at each other, the air between us awkward, even with the puppy sitting on both my feet. He narrows his gaze, no doubt seeing the tears in my eyes, my blotchy cheeks, and shaking hands. Something in his expression softens.

"¿Graciela Mamani?"

I turn at the sharp voice as two men dressed in matching red and pink striped tunics march toward me; one is short and squat, stepping hard onto the cobbled path like an enraged bull. He wears his frown like a thick cloak to guard against impertinent weather, foreboding and stern. His companion is younger and an apprentice, judging by the stitch of yellow fabric pinned near his collar. His rich bronze skin sets off the amber hue of his eyes. The people step aside, and the encargados, enforcers of La Gerencia, cut through the crowd as if they were a sharp blade. They stop a few paces away.

Mateo stiffens next to me.

"You are Graciela Mamani, correct?" the older encargado demands.

I suddenly wish I had something in my hands. They're trembling too noticeably, and my only choice is to grasp them tightly, hoping no one notices.

"I am Francisco, and this is my apprentice, Suri." Francisco pulls out paper from the depths of his red tunic and then yanks out a slender quill. He scratches something onto the parchment and then lifts his eyes, hand poised over the roll.

"Your stall is in violation of several market stipulations." He points to the debris, the bits of food stuck on the overhang, the dried egg running down the length of the side.

"I just got here," I say, fighting to keep my voice steady. "And was unaware of the mess. It's my first day in the mercado as a vendor."

Suri's attention swerves to my stall, lingering on the cracked eggshells. There's a downward curve to his mouth, a pinch of disapproval.

"Let me see your license," Francisco says.

Mateo sets down my baskets next to my stall and stuffs his hands deep into his pockets. His eyes move restlessly over the crowd of onlookers. I expect him to walk off with Felipe at any moment, to forget about the moment he helped me with my paints, but he remains motionless. The pup tries to amble over to the trash on the ground, but Mateo scoops him up and tucks him close to his body.

I rummage through my canvas bag and pull out a small roll of parchment and hand it to the encargado. Francisco looks it over, and Suri peers into my basket. Tension snakes up my spine.

"Everything should be in order," I say, hating the quiver in my voice.

The crowd around us thickens, curious spectators wanting to see La Gerencia at work.

Suri steps closer to me while his companion is distracted, dipping his head toward mine and in the barest of whispers says, "A cleaning encanto ought to take care of the mess. Try Hortensia's, ten stalls down."

Mateo narrows his eyes at the apprentice.

Suri straightens and walks toward my belongings. He bends and picks up one of my brushes, the copper handle glinting in the sun, and then lifts it to his nose. He shoots me a look, lips parted, eyes widening.

"Is that . . . fig I smell?" He sniffs again. "And locoto?"

Francisco stops reading and glares at his apprentice.

"That's right," I say, surprised. "No one's been able to identify it."

"Probably because it's not ever mixed into a potion," Suri says. "What made you think of it?"

"It just made sense to me." I swallow, thinking quickly. There's no rule against using food in spells, is there? "I like experimenting, especially with fruit, and so I tried several mixtures until I got the result I was looking for. The locoto adds longevity to the encanto."

"And what does the spell *do?*" Suri asks.

I glance around uneasily, fully aware of how closely other vendors and patrons are listening to our conversation. "It's meant to assist people in completing paintings or sketches. The brush helps them sketch faces, capture pets, and draw straight lines."

"It's unexpected, just like your abuelita," Suri says, and then he gingerly replaces the brush.

I blink. "Did you know her?"

"She helped me once, when I first became an apprentice," Suri says softly. "I was sorry to hear of her passing." He pauses, his gaze flickering to Francisco, who visibly didn't appreciate the turn of the conversation. But Suri shrugs, as if to say he doesn't care about what the encargado thinks. "When you're open, I'd like to buy a set of paints."

I grin as Felipe barks in agreement.

"That's extraordinary magia," Mateo says. "Who was your instructor?"

I run my fingers along my skirt, and fist the fabric in my palms. "I never actually finished my learning at the Colegio de Magia." The years at one of the most expensive schools in Monterisa weren't cheap. I ran out of money when I only had one more year to complete my training. But I had a knack for potion brewing, so it wasn't the failure I thought it'd be.

Francisco sniffs but thrusts the license into my hands. "Everything is in order, but I'm writing up a warning for the state of the stall. Several code violations will need to be remedied by the close of the market."

"I'm getting a warning?" I whisper. "On my first day? In the first . . . *hour*?"

"The *only* one you'll get before you're permanently removed and your stall can be taken over by someone else."

"But that," I gesture helplessly toward the mess, "isn't my fault. Please reconsider—"

"You're the owner of this stall. It's your responsibility to maintain order," the encargado says. "I'll return to make sure your area complies with our standards."

He stalks off, and Suri darts after him with a quick look of sympathy in my direction. Something wet clings to my cheeks, and I wipe away the tears. I didn't realize I'd started crying.

Mateo clears his throat. "They will never leave you alone, you know. Not until you're gone."

I snap my head around. "Who are *they*?"

"The other vendors. It's no secret they wanted this stall to be filled by Pilar Fuentes."

"I'm not Pilar, sorry," I say, my voice trembling. "I'm my *own* person with my *own* things to sell. Besides, this was my abuelita's stall. It's mine by La Gerencia's own rules." With a shaking finger, I point toward the mess. "Can you tell me who did this? Were *you* a part of it?"

"Pilar has waited years for a spot available in the market,"

Mateo says flatly, his face wooden. I've offended him. "She's a friend, but even so, I wouldn't destroy someone else's property." He brushes past me and then pauses. "I wouldn't leave your things tonight without a guardian spell if I were you."

I bite my lip. I can't afford one, not even a cheap cleaning encanto.

Mateo disappears into the crowd, and the rest of the people resume their business.

But I still feel the weight of their disapproval, crushing and relentless.

I waste hours cleaning. Picking off sticky residue, gathering the trash, scraping up the runny egg that's dried like glue onto the boards. Across the path, Mateo sells his figurines—charming wood creations that come to life for various amounts of time. A tiny bird flutters its wings and chirps, a doll dressed in a ruffled flamenco dress stomps her feet, while a llama spits little wooden pellets. It's clever magic, and he's never short of customers. The stall next to his sees as much traffic, a booth specializing in selling ingredients for potions: dragon teeth and horns all the way from Hispalia, turtle shells, dried eyes of various animals, plucked hairs from people of various ages, and feathers from various owls.

I wipe my brow—the Monterisa sun is positively murderous—and resume scrubbing the awning that hangs a foot beyond my stall. When it's clean, I take a step back to look at my shop; it still needs a fresh coat of paint, but at least everything complies with regulations. Francisco can't have one negative thing to say. I use one of my brushes to smother the whole thing in a bright, crisp white—it will be a beast to keep clean, but no one has a white booth in the rainbow of colors decorating the other stalls. My awning is black and paired with the white, the results are striking.

My booth is finally ready.

It's rectangular shaped with sturdy boards and a front stoop decorated with a few pots filled with girasoles. Sunflowers have always been my favorite flower. Inside, there's room for three or four people to come to browse the products sitting on various rows of shelving. My abuelita left me a beautiful rug woven in strands of blue and bright pink and lavender, and I left it exactly as she had it, right in the center of the stall. In the corner sits a wooden stool and a little end table where I'll tally everyone's purchases. I spent months making cloth bags and painting them with the new name of my store: Artesenia. At the front of the shop, there's a ruffled curtain to draw closed at the end of each market day.

I pull out all of my wares and place them onto the shelves: rows of brushes and paints, small canvases, thick rolls of parchment, and an assortment of planters filled with various ferns and succulents. A single beam stretches from one end to the other across the middle of the wood ceiling, and I hang dozens of long ribbons in a riot of colors. The ends rustle with the lazy breeze drifting in and out of my store. The effect is whimsical and so lovely, I nearly cry on the spot.

I step outside, a smile on my lips, but it quickly fades. The market is closing, and already the main hubbub only has a smattering of people ambling toward the main exit. On either side of Artesenia, the vendors are locking up—their stalls have doors—and leaving quickly for home. I think about packing, but I hesitate, remembering Mateo's warning. I have enough money for cheap food for the week: huevos, queso, and arroz. What I wouldn't give for a plate of salteñas or silpancho. Both dishes are a source of comfort, ones I grew up eating with my parents in the middle of the morning. But I can't afford the expense, not when I can't even pay to affix a door at the entrance of my shop.

I know there's a powerful enchantment guarding the main entrance from anyone trying to come inside, but that only works for people who don't have a stall in the market. There's nothing to protect your booth from other vendors.

I'll have to stay the night and every night until I make a profit. But a chill cuts into my skin when I remember one very important thing.

During the day, La Hechiceria belongs to the living, but at night the dead rise.

These are the duendes, ghosts who appear in the form of children. Mischievous fantasmas from the other side, who like to sneak into people's stalls and steal one or two things. Not enough to ensure disaster, but just enough to know that you've been visited.

Abuelita used to say, "Mira, Graciela, you must never enrage a duende. If you do, they will come after your children."

My palms are slick with sweat. I don't want to make *anyone* angry.

I step back inside the booth. The sweltering heat from outside permeates, and I immediately start fanning myself, when a voice startles me.

"¿Tienes hambre?"

I turn, surprised to find Mateo at the entrance, leaning against the wood frame, two bowls filled with fricasé. I firmly believe my mother's stew, filled with seared pork, chopped onion, red peppers, plenty of garlic, and several spoonfuls of ají amarillo, was the best in Monterisa. But my stomach growls the second the savory scent fills up my small stall.

With Felipe at his heels, Mateo smiles shyly and steps inside, like my stomach ushered the invitation. His eyes take in my day's work and exclaims, "¡Mira esto!"

I flush. "It looks better, right?"

"I wouldn't have recognized it." He looks around for a place to set down the dinner but then decides against the stool and instead drops onto the plush rug in one fluid movement. I smile to myself and settle onto the ground, and he hands me my food. Felipe curls up at my ankles. Mateo pulls out a scrap of dried beef from within his pockets and chucks it at the dog—who yips happily.

I lift the bowl as a kind of salute. "Gracias."

We settle into our meal, and everything is crisp and delicious. He only brought one clay utensil, and we have to share it to eat. The back and forth is strangely intimate, and we laugh when I delay his turn by continuing to eat.

I stare at him in between bites, and his brows inch toward his hairline.

"Yes? You have something to say?" he asks. "Or maybe I have something on my face?"

"It's a handsome face." I clap a hand over my mouth. What possessed me to say such a thing? Mateo merely laughs, and I struggle to find something to say and finally come up with a question. "Why did you bring me dinner?"

"Earlier, I was very angry," he says slowly. "You had a smile on your face walking through the market this morning, and the moment we got to the stall, it completely disappeared. I haven't been able to stop thinking about it."

He'd been thinking about me all day? I place the bowl on the ground. "Will you please tell me who's responsible? I ought to report them to La Gerencia."

"I have my suspicions," he says carefully. I open my mouth to ask, and he quickly shakes his head. "They're friends, and I won't share their names, but I will be speaking to them because what they did wasn't right. It was *terrible*, and I won't let it happen again." He sighs. "I know they want Pilar in this space, but they went too far."

"How long have you been a vendor?"

"I began at sixteen," he says. "I'm nineteen now."

"Sixteen?" I ask, impressed. "Have you enjoyed running a store?"

He nods. "For the most part. You can make very good money every week, as long as the rules are followed." Mateo hesitates. "Your abuelita liked to get in the way of that—made things difficult for everyone, and La Gerencia came down hard on all the vendors as a result."

That was my grandmother. When something wasn't fair, she said so. I wished I could be more like her, but sometimes the words got stuck in my throat.

We finish eating, my eyelids heavy with sudden exhaustion, and Mateo wishes me a good night with a soft smile, and Felipe licks my face. I walk them both out of the booth, and as they disappear into the twilight, I can't help but think that I've made a friend.

An ally. Someone who might want me to do well, despite my

abuelita. I settle into the rug, my vision darkening, and let out a huge yawn. After careful consideration I leave what I didn't finish of my meal outside on the front stoop. Then I tie the curtain off, enclosing myself inside Artesenia.

Surprisingly, sleep takes me quickly, but I'm thankful.

I don't hear the duendes throughout the night.

When I wake, it's to the sounds of La Hechiceria coming to life. I gingerly sit up, sore and with a sharp sting aching my shoulders. My temples throb, and I rub them until the pain subsides. From under the ruffled curtain, the scent of freshly baked marraquetas wafts into my small shop, and my mouth waters. Someone grinds coffee beans and horses neigh as they strut past my store. I jump to my feet, a shiver of anticipation pulsing in my blood.

Today is the day.

I can hardly believe it. After months of planning, waiting for my paperwork to come in, it's finally here. The start of my new life.

When I brush the curtain to the side, it's in time to see Mateo arrive at his own stall across the lane. His eyes unerringly find mine through the bustle of people. He's carting a stack of wood in one hand, a steaming mug in the other, and in his mouth is a leather strap, an iron key dangling at the end. He can't smile, but his brown eyes crinkle at the corners, and he dips his chin. Felipe darts over to me, runs around my ankles once, twice, three times, barking madly before dashing back to Mateo, who somehow manages to open his store and disappear inside. The stall to my right hasn't opened yet, but I swing my head around to the shop on my left, eager to meet my neighbors.

The owner stands a mere three feet away from me, a canvas

apron around his waist and a scowl bending his mouth. He's average height, round around the middle, with an impressive thick beard and heavy brows. There are sharp lines dividing his weathered face nearly in half. I hadn't heard his soft approach.

I open my mouth to greet him but his words beat me to it.

"The right thing to do would have been to give up Maria's stall," he says in a deep voice.

No hola. No buenos días.

My smile fades and with a forced cheer, I say, "I'll make a friendly neighbor, I promise." I stretch out my hand. "Mi nombre es Graciela. What's yours?"

He looks at my palm as if it were a wild snake. Then he lifts his gaze. "It's not too late."

I let my arm drop. "Actually, it is. I've put everything I have into this enterprise. I—I have a right to be here."

He sniffs. "So you say."

"What does that mean?"

His eyes gleam with sudden malice, and then he's gone, ducking into his booth. It's as if someone hit my belly with a hammer. But I don't have time to dwell on it. The mercado is officially open, and the pathway fills with shoppers. I step aside and smile at everyone who passes, and eventually, a few people walk into Artesenia.

My heart races. "¡Hola!" I wince at the high note. I clear my throat and strive for a polite, professional tone. "My name is Graciela. Please let me know if I can help you find anything."

They absently nod before examining the brushes and paints. I stand off to the side, not wanting to crowd any of them but bursting to ask them a dozen questions. One of them walks out without another word, and my stomach flips, while another picks up a brush with short, blunt bristles. The shopper looks at me inquiringly.

"The handle is made of copper. The bristles are llama tail," I say proudly. "Those brushes have been sealed with a spell that allows the painter to draw straight lines. The pile next to them— also made of copper—helps with portrait drawing. The encanto lasts for one year."

The shopper gives me a delighted smile. "Extraordinary! How much is each?"

I fidget on my feet. I want the sale so badly, and I'm tempted to offer a discounted price. I almost feel bad asking for so much— but the effort was enormous, and the ingredients were expensive. Hours hovering over a steaming potion, getting the measurements exactly right. With a slight tremor, I say, "Sixteen soles."

She gasps. *"Each?"*

My stomach plummets, but I force myself to nod. "That's right. A lot of care and unusual ingredients went into each po-tion. The spell turned out thick and smoky, a very pretty purple mist—"

But she put the brushes back and walks out of my shop.

I flap my hands as I pace around the booth, nervous and wor-ried. What if I seriously miscalculated? What if no one purchases any of my supplies? I've made them too expensive, too complex.

I stand outside my booth for most of the day with the same results. Many shoppers are impressed by my magia and the long-lasting effects, but no one wants to splurge on any of the art sup-plies, not even some of the ones priced at a handful of soles.

Maybe this was a mistake. Maybe I don't belong here.

I lace my fingers tightly and hear Papá's gentle voice in my mind. *Hijita, no matter how much easier it is to believe the worst about yourself, remember to be kind and always tell yourself the truth.*

Here's the truth: I made a good product with quality ingredients, and the price is fair given the time and labor spent on each item. I do belong here. I have a right to be here, like anyone else.

And it's silly to have assumed that on my first day, I'd sell out of everything.

But still . . . I'd like to sell *one* thing.

With three more hours to go, an idea streaks through my mind: a demonstration.

That's what I need.

Unless I can show people the kind of artwork made possible with my brushes and paint, I can't expect anyone to purchase my wares. I scramble inside and quickly use one of my own personal brushes and an old canvas to quickly paint a sign that reads FREE PORTRAITS! WHILE SUPPLIES LAST in whimsical, loopy lettering. I use a rich black against the cream of the canvas, hoping the bold color will draw notice.

I walk outside, careful not to smear the lettering and hold it up high. Someone in the crowd steps forward and gestures toward my painting.

"Is this for today?"

I quickly nod. "Would you like to sit? I'll hang the painting in my shop for a week, and then you're welcome to keep it. What do you think?"

She grins. "Mi nombre es Camila. No one has ever painted my likeness before."

She's a pretty young woman, with curves and luminous eyes, wearing a bright ruffled top and matching skirt in the boldest of reds—the color of fire and anger and ambition. I motion for her to wait as I drag out my stool, easel, and new canvas. Next, I pull out my stash of supplies and gesture for her to have a seat. I mix paints, swirling my brush to create a palette full of colors delicious enough to eat with a spoon.

I settle into the sketch, and soon a crowd surrounds us as I capture her likeness. The magic in the brushes vibrates in my palm, and I frown slightly—it's never done that before. I sniff the air. Instead of the sweet and spicy smell of the fig and locoto pepper, there's a musty note that I hadn't caught before. Perhaps from prolonged exposure to the heat? But my lines are straight, Camila's face slowly appearing on the canvas, lovely, full of life. As I paint, I make sure to talk about each brush I use, as well as some of the ingredients.

When I'm done, Camila hops down from the stool and rushes over to my side to see the final result. She lets out a delighted squeal. "This is so beautiful, gracias!"

The crowd claps loudly, and soon I have several people drifting inside my booth. Two people buy brushes, another buys a set of paints, and a third person buys a canvas. Once the crowd thins, I hold up the sign, and another person volunteers to sit for me. This time, it's an older caballero, with a bowled hat and leather sandals. There's a gleam of humor lurking in his dark eyes.

"¿Cómo te llamas?"

He offers a kind smile. "Mico. And you?"

"Oh, I have a tío named Mico." I tell him my name, and he's quiet for a moment. "That's very lovely."

"Well, my mother was a lovely person." There's something about this gentleman, quiet and strong, that warms my heart. I want to make sure he has a nice home to go to, enough food to eat. "Gracias."

He sits on the stool, and I begin, the painting coming to life as I lay down broad strokes and then work a smaller brush to get the details many people wouldn't notice: the smattering of freckles on his right wrist that reminds me of a constellation, the sharp lines of his collar bones that disappear under his vibrantly colored vest. He has blunt hands, square-shaped and calloused, and I take extra care to make sure I capture the strength of his palms.

We chat idly as I work, and I finish much too soon, enjoying his sincere and earnest conversation. Mico stands and comes to look at the finished result.

"A pretty present for your family," I say.

"It's just my grandson and me," he says softly. "I'm thankful for the painting. It's been a long time since I've seen my face."

I can't think of a thing to say to that, and before I can let out a word, the caballero tips his hat and strolls away in a gently sloping walk. He disappears into the thickening crowd, and I'm sorry to see him go. The front of my booth swells with people as they stream inside. I quickly follow, and the next hour is a blur as my inventory dwindles with each sale. I can hardly believe the money I'm making. I can't help the grin that stretches from ear to ear. Mateo comes to help, and Felipe rests under the stool, a lazy bark coming from him every time someone buys something.

At last, the booth empties until it's just the three of us.

His shy smile returns. "Can Felipe and I bring you dinner tonight?"

"Por supuesto."

After they leave, I spend another night in my store. This time I hear the duendes murmuring as they walk past my curtain, ruffling the fabric. Cold air seeps into every inch of my shop, and goose bumps spread up and down my arms.

They'll leave me alone if I stay quiet.

Hopefully.

I shut my eyes and keep myself tucked under the blanket, too scared to sleep, too terrified to blow out the candle. Too scared to draw notice to myself.

The next morning, I step outside of my booth, stretching and yawning, thrilled there are no more duendes. Tonight should be my last night sleeping on that rug—I made enough money not only for a door but to replenish my shelves and, if I spend it wisely, for a little food that isn't arroz.

A vaguely familiar woman strides up the path. She has a large cloth hanging over her head that nearly covers all of her face except for a cutout for her eyes.

"I must speak with you," she says when she reaches me and then points to inside Artesenia.

"I—all right," I say, taken aback.

She waits to speak again until I draw the curtain closed. I glance at her nervously, having trouble placing her. "May I help you with something?"

"Oh, I think you've done enough," she snaps and then yanks her covering clean off her head.

It's Camila, but *not* Camila.

Her once dark hair is now a startling shade of gray, her skin sags under her eyes, and deep lines crease her forehead and the corners of her eyes.

She's aged sixty years overnight.

"You did this to me," she hisses. "Now make this right."

My throat is dry. I open my mouth but no words come out.

"Well?"

"I can't believe it—this has *never* happened to me before," I say. "I've painted dozens of portraits—lo siento, I can't understand it."

"Oh, I understand perfectly," she says. "Your magic is atrocious." She thrusts her purchases from the day before into my hands. "I want my money back."

"O-of course," I stammer, fighting tears. I pull out the drawstring bag and hand over the soles.

"How long before I can return for the counter-spell?"

Panic claws at my edges. I don't know any transformation encantos. Wouldn't know where to begin, what ingredients to use, or where to find them.

Camila must see the worry on my face because she shrieks, "This can't be permanent!"

"I'll fix it," I say, choking back a sob. "I only need time."

Camila bends and picks up her cloth. "I'm reporting you to La Gerencia for this."

She covers her face and storms out.

Outside, the mercado comes to life, loud and impatient for the start of the day. But inside my little store, it's deathly quiet. I can hardly breathe. My heart thuds against my chest, one ferocious beat at a time.

Doom. Doom. *Doom.*

I clutch my throat, unseeing, as someone I don't recognize jerks the curtain back and stalks inside, carrying a turtle in his arms. He's young with strong arms and a broad chest and wind-swept hair the exact color of a mountain cliff. His rich bronze skin is flush with anger. Like Camila, he looks vaguely familiar. His eyes narrow into slits.

"Are you Graciela?" He demands when he comes to an abrupt stop in front of me.

I can barely speak, still reeling about Camila, but somehow I manage a nod, my attention on the laces of my sandals.

"You painted a portrait of my abuelo yesterday—"

My eyes snap to his. The young man regards me coldly and I flinch.

"—and this morning, he's turned into a *tortuga*. His shell has paint streaks!" He holds up the animal, and I gasp at the sight of the miserable creature gazing at me with bleak eyes.

I'd enchanted Mico into a turtle.

A *turtle*.

That kind, older caballero. My heart twists and tangles into knots. "Lo siento, por favor, I'll make this right—" I swallow, and it's painful. The words sit on my tongue, refusing to come out. I don't want to lie to him.

I don't know if I *can* make this right.

The man's grandson glowers at me. "Oh, you had better. He's the best person I know, and I refuse to let him waste a single day as a damn turtle."

He walks out of the booth, and I follow him, wanting to offer something—money, another apology.

"Por favor—I'm so sorry."

The young man whirls around, despair written all over his face. "He's the *only* one I have left. Bring him back to me."

"I'll do anything," I say in a rush.

"You better," the young man says fiercely, holding the turtle tucked close to his lithe body, as if it were the most precious treasure in the world.

Before I can say another word, a terrible sight robs me of breath. Francisco and his apprentice, Suri, are fast approaching, Camila at their heels. Several vendors step out of their booths—including the disgruntled neighbor to my left. The one who refused to give me his name.

Francisco reaches my little storefront, hands on his hips. Mico's grandson steps aside to let Suri draw closer.

"An extraordinary claim has reached me, Señorita Mamani," Francisco says in a cold voice. "Is it true your magic has wreaked havoc on your customers?"

Shame pricks my heart, angry needles sinking deep. "It's true. I painted portraits yesterday, and some of the brushes I used were . . . faulty. This has *never* occurred before. I've created these potions a hundred times. I don't know what's happened, I don't know how it *could* have."

Suri snaps his head in my direction, visibly weighing my words. Then he ducks inside my booth without a word to anyone. A large crowd gathers around us, and from the corner of my eye, I see Mateo and Felipe easing their way forward. Mateo shoots me a questioning look, and I respond with a helpless shrug.

Francisco regards me as if I were an annoying mosquito. "Whatever you might claim, we cannot have rogue magic sold in the market. From this day forward, you will never operate another stall."

I clench my eyes, fighting to keep myself from crying.

"You will also cover the costs of magic to rectify all damages done to your customers."

I nod reflexively, desperate to make things right.

"Now," he snarls. "Pack up your things and go."

"Good riddance," my neighbor yells out. Several other vendors voice their agreement.

I turn away, shoulders hunched to protect me from their terrible words, when Suri steps out of the stall, holding several brushes.

"A moment, Francisco," he says in a clear voice. "There has been foul play here."

"¿Qué?" Francisco snaps.

From the corner of my eye, I catch sight of Mico's grandson. His face is steeped in suspicion, but his lips lose their hard line.

Suri holds up one copper-handle brush. "This brush has the exact same scent as it did the day she moved in. Honey, fig, and locoto." Then he holds up three other brushes. "These have the same scent, but there are other smells: yarrow and rotten eggs. I believe some of her inventory has been tampered with."

I gasp. I *had* detected something different while painting.

"It could still have been her negligence," Francisco says, dismissive. "Her magic might still have been applied incorrectly."

"True," Suri concedes. "But given her stall had been vandalized on the day she moved in, I highly doubt she sabotaged herself on both counts," he adds dryly.

A muscle ticks in Francisco's jaw, but he remains silent, considering. No one moves, least of all me.

"If you find proof someone has tampered with your inventory by tomorrow afternoon, then you may stay, and the culprit will be punished."

"Tomorrow *afternoon?*" I ask with a hoarse voice. I'm still reeling from Suri's discovery. I should have suspected, but I was too quick to blame myself, to shoulder the failure. Too afraid to defend myself.

"Tomorrow afternoon," Francisco repeats. "An hour before sundown."

And then he's gone, disappearing into the crowd so fully that for a moment, I wonder if he'd been there at all. But no, his apprentice remained behind, watching me intently.

"Do you have a plan in mind?" Suri asks in a hushed voice.

I blink—sweat beads at my hairline. He's standing in front of me, back to the crowd, trying to get me to focus, but all I can think about are Camila and Mico. The crowd glares at me, and my neighbor curses my existence, wanting me gone. They don't believe that I've been wronged.

"For the proof?" Suri prods. "Graciela?"

"No sé," I say, at last, averting my gaze from my furious neighbor. "I don't know where to begin—where to look."

Suri casts one furtive glance behind his shoulder, and then he meets my eyes again, low and urgent. "Well, I know one person you can ask. Someone who sees everything that goes on in the market."

"¿Quién?"

He leans forward and whispers, "The duendes."

Another night sleeping in La Hechiceria.

I don't know how I'll be able to stand it. I sit in the middle of the shop, the sounds of shoppers drifting past, eager to be gone and out the front door before becoming trapped inside. I clutch my arms, wishing I hadn't sent Mateo and Felipe away—but what choice did I have?

No one wants to deal with duendes.

I leave a bowl of fruit outside on the stoop because Papá once said it was an easy way to call for one. With more considering, I leave another, leading into Artesenia. The minutes go by until all is quiet on the other side of the curtain. And then I hear it: the rise of low voices, fast and chaotic, as if the speakers are in a rush, moving from one place to another. Sweat drips down my face as the curtain rustles. I ignore the yawning pit deep in my belly and slowly crawl forward, my fingers skimming the fabric. I swallow hard and push aside the ruffled hem so only a few inches are visible.

I unlock my jaw. Loosen my tongue.

"¿Hola?" My voice is a soft croak. Barely audible at all.

A shape materializes from out of the darkness, nibbling on a banana.

I push down the gasp rising up my throat. This duende is a young girl of eight or nine, with dark hair tucked under a large sombrero. Her skin is deeply tan like mine, and she wears a simple shirt made of a light fabric, dark colored pants, and on her feet are abarca sandals made of leather and rubber.

"Hola," I squawk again. "Do you like the fruit?"

She grins, a toothy smile that makes the hair at the back of my neck rise.

"Why do you call for me?" The duende's voice is high, like the soft ringing of a bell.

"I have a question."

"Ask," she says. "But the answer comes with a price."

"What is it?"

The duende looks over my shoulder, and I follow her gaze to where I have propped up the cursed portraits. "Would you like me to paint you?"

Her gaze flickers back to mine and her face brightens. "That is acceptable. Do we have a bargain?"

"Almost," I say, thinking fast. "Your answer will take but a single moment to say. My painting will take me a whole day."

"Clever," she says in her high, girlish voice. "What do you require?"

"I want the answer to three questions."

The duende is silent and then flashes that same quicksilver grin. "All right." She pauses, her smile still stretched from ear to ear. "Is this about Diego?"

I furrow my brow. "I don't know a Diego."

She says, "You will know your love one day. If not now, certainly later."

Disappointment clouds my vision. Maybe she was mistaken. I think about how Mateo brought dinner my first night, how he stood with me as everyone else cursed me. If I were to fall in love, I'd want it to be him.

"What are your questions?"

I blink, attempting to get my thoughts straight. "Have you seen anyone come into the shop and ruin my supplies?"

"Yes."

I wait for more but the duende says nothing else. In an instant, I realize my mistake and groan. "*Who* has ruined my supplies?"

"There was only one who took your things and dipped them

into a vat of something foul and rotting. Awful, smelly magic."
She tells me the name.

My breath catches at the back of my throat. I jump to my
feet, pacing up and down, wringing my hands. I only have one
more question left, and I must not waste it. But I have so many, I
struggle to land on the wisest course.

"Would you like to know how the spell is activated?" the duende supplies helpfully.

I think hard and then slowly nod, deciding to trust the fan-
tasma. "Yes, I would."

The duende whispers the answer, and then I paint the duende's
likeness into the long night, relief that it feels as it normally does: a
wonderful escape. Creating something always takes me away from
the humdrum of daily life, and especially after today, painting is
a delight. When I'm done, I stare at my work: the luminous dark
eyes, the soft curve of her cheek. I've seen her before. I know it like
I know my own reflection.

I give her the painting and the duende thanks me.

"Wait!" I blurt out when she has one foot outside. "I know
you. How do I know you?"

The duende glances up at me with a soft smile, and she looks
so small, she might come up to my hip. "Take care of my shop."

The duende vanishes just as I whisper, "¿Abuelita?"

In the morning, Mateo brings me coffee, and I gladly accept the
cup. Monterisa's café is very strong, and always gives me heart pal-
pitations, but I'm going to need the boost. I barely slept the rest of
the night. I set the drink on the stool and continue painting a sign
in bold red lettering, taking up nearly every inch of the canvas.

Mateo reads over my shoulder, using his foot to keep Felipe away from my artwork.

"You're going to paint another portrait?"

"Yes," I say from where I'm kneeling on the ground, adding the last swirl. "My whole life, I've wanted to have something of my own. Born from nothing except my dreams. I won't give up, even if everyone wants me to." I straighten, propping my hands on my bent knees. "I have to do this one last thing."

"Are you sure that's wise?"

"No," I say. "But it's the only thing I can do."

"Without proof, you'll still have to pack your things. Besides, no one will volunteer," he adds gently.

I draw in a breath; he's probably right. Which is why I'm going to paint a face entirely from memory. "Will you help me spread the word? I'm going to paint the portrait at fifth bell."

Mateo hesitates but then agrees.

By the fourth bell, everyone has heard of my plan. Several people come to my store, shouting at me for my stubbornness, for my stupidity to risk another person's life.

It takes everything in me to not yield. To stay the course. I know what I'm doing, and I won't accept my expulsion from the market lying down.

When the fifth bell tolls, I step outside of my booth to meet the immense crowd that's gathered on the lane, curious to witness my fate—not just shoppers but also dozens of vendors because the news has spread up and down the street, into every stall within the market.

Francisco makes his way to the front of the masses, Suri at his heels.

"What is this?"

"I'll gladly explain," I say in a loud, clear voice. I'm answering Francisco's question, but I'm addressing the people circling my booth. "Today, I'll be painting a portrait from memory, using the very brushes that have been tampered with. The destructive spell is only activated by my signature, which I will leave off—but *only* if the culprit turns themselves in to La Gerencia."

The crowd gasps.

"You *know* who is responsible?" Francisco demands.

I nod. "You asked me to provide proof, but I will provide the culprit instead. They won't want to suffer the effects of the magic, believe me."

I search the crowd, and my gaze snags on the one who ruined my brushes while I slept, unaware that the duendes were watching. A chill slithers down my spine as I force myself to keep my gaze moving, resisting the urge to glare at the person responsible.

And then I begin to paint.

My canvas faces my store, away from the onlookers, and I can feel their impatience. Only Francisco and Suri stand next to me. As the general shape of the culprit solidifies, their eyes skip across the crowd, trying to find the right person. The colors become bolder, highlighting the figure of a young man: a friendly face, adorned by warm brown eyes and pale skin.

Suri sucks in a deep breath. Francisco places his hand on his hips.

I finish the painting, and true to my word, I leave off the signature. I raise my voice to address the crowd. "It's ready. Remember, it's up to you if I add my name."

I flip the canvas and show the spectators the face of the culprit.

Mateo.

He jerks his head back in surprise.

"Is this true?" Francisco demands as Suri darts across the street, disappearing into Mateo's booth.

Mateo shakes his head. "She's a liar!"

"Am I?" I ask, proud my voice isn't shaking. I bend down and begin lettering my name and then—

"Wait! ¡Espera!" Mateo yells.

I freeze, my hand hovering over my half-spelled name.

"I did it for Pilar," he says.

I can't meet his eyes. I drop my hand away from the canvas and walk into the booth, cries of outrage and loud accusations and disappointment following in my wake.

I let the curtain drop and whisper, "Gracias, Abuelita Maria."

It's Suri who forces people away from my stall, ushering them away and toward the mercado exit. He raps on the wood of my stall, and I let him enter.

His dark eyes are full of sympathy. "How are you feeling?"

I shrug, helpless. "I ought to feel pleased, I suppose. But he was my friend. At least, I *thought* he was. And now those poor people have to live with the effects of that awful spell."

Suri nods, thoughtful. "Mateo got rid of most of the ingredients of the spell, but I found a sleeping drought."

My heart races as I remember my exhaustion after the meal we shared. "What will happen to him?"

"He's out of the market and forbidden from returning," the apprentice says. "And responsible for paying for the counter-spell."

I gasp. "*Counter-spell?*"

He smiles briefly. "Yes, I managed to come up with one. Everyone who needed it was given a vial this morning."

Relief courses in my blood. I feel as if I can run for miles and miles. "That's wonderful! How did you—?"

"I didn't know Maria for long, but she helped me when I needed it the most." Suri waves his hand, dismissing the praise. "Don't let them push you out of La Hechiceria. Your magia is unique, and you belong here."

"I won't." I thank him for his help, knowing the words would never be enough. I grab the brushes he'd admired and hand them to him. Suri's eyes widen. "Please take them, with my sincere gratitude."

I walk the apprentice out of the booth and stop short.

An older caballero with graying hair and freckles on the back of his hands stands outside. His grandson is with him, but he's lost his scowl. Not that I blame him for his anger. If someone put a spell on my grandfather, I'd do more than scowl.

Mico's grandson smiles at me sheepishly, his warm brown eyes meet mine, and my heart skips. "I saw what you did." He clears his throat and blushes. "It was very clever."

"Well"—I duck my head, and gesture to the apprentice—"I had help."

Suri inclines his head, then disappears into the crowd of shoppers, milling from one booth to another.

"Graciela," Mico says. "Can I show my grandson the painting you made of me?"

"Of course! I'm happy to see you looking like yourself again," I say with a grin. "Though you did make a handsome turtle."

Mico laughs. "My grandson disagreed. Said I pooped every-where. Have you two officially met?"

My eyes flicker to the young man. "Not exactly, no."

Mico's grandson holds out his hand and I grasp his calloused palm. A warm feeling zips up my arm, and my heart skips.

"I'm Diego."

SUMAIKO Y LA SIRENA

by

Vita Ayala

When the sun shone, Suma belonged to the plantation—the cloth that needed mending, the thirsty people who toiled in the fields waiting for her to bring them water, the watchful eyes of the men—but at night, Suma dreamed of the sea.

The plantation, and the mill attached, were under the power of two brothers, the elder called El Gordo, who was contrarily quite thin, and the younger called El Flaco, who was almost a head taller than the next tallest man.

El Gordo was ten years older than his brother and had fought in The War (which war, Suma didn't know, and no one bothered to tell her). He was a pale man who turned red in the sun and liked to have Suma sing church songs for him on days when her work as a seamstress brought her to the big house. He rarely smiled, but he rarely frowned either—his gray eyes were flat and calculating. He made Suma feel cold when he was near, like a heavy cloud covering the sun.

El Flaco was tall and broad, and his bright white smile and smooth tanned skin made him the subject of much-giggled whispering among the women. He was quick to anger but just as quick to forget and was fond of the strong rum made from the sugar. While El Gordo ran the mill, El Flaco lorded over the fields, dispensing punishment and favors liberally. From the time she was twelve, he liked to make Suma sit on his knee and sing love songs while he took his lunch. He always ran too hot, his body scorching Suma's back and thighs like an out-of-control fire.

The plantation itself was of a good size—the second biggest on Vieques—and consisted of the cane fields, the mill, and a small distillery.

The people who worked the plantation were of two types—those who belonged to El Gordo and those who owed El Gordo. The former mostly worked the fields, and the latter mostly the mill and distillery, though the real difference between them was that eventually, those in debt would be free.

Suma was neither, but she was not free to go.

When she arrived on the island, the girl had been old enough to speak, though she rarely did. One of the men who worked the plantation fields found her sleeping on the shore of la bahía reluciente.

Legend had it that the shining water of the bay was magic and that if one wished hard enough there and gave proper offerings, they would receive their deepest desire.

The man—who had no children of his own and had recently lost his wife—took the girl home. He had been coming to the bay for almost a year, leaving gifts at the water's edge and praying. He knew his prayers were answered.

The girl's dark curly hair was tangled with algas marinas, her dark skin sparkled like the night sky, and her eyes were the color of the darkest storm clouds. She wore a dress of shining, golden scales, which sounded like soft bells on the wind whenever she moved.

The man knew that if he ever told the girl of where she came from, she would return to the sea, so he washed the shimmer from her skin, untangled the plants from her hair, and burned her shining dress.

He gave her the last of the fish he had stored to eat. "You are a gift from Atabey, to whom my wife prayed every day," he told her, smiling kindly and tousling her soft curls. "I will name you Sumaiko in her honor and care for you for all the rest of my days."

And so Suma lived on the island, as sweet and beloved as the sugar cane, never knowing that she was anything but a field hand's daughter.

The people of the plantation accepted Suma as one of their own. The women always had small bites of food for her when she came by and made her new clothes of scraps of cloth when she outgrew hers, and the men whittled her toys and taught her to use a slingshot and make nets to catch fish so she could supplement the diet provided by El Gordo.

Her father was paying off seemingly insurmountable debts to El Gordo, and so soon as Suma was able, the women taught her to mend and sew so she could help him. Days were spent working and learning, and evenings after supper were hers to do with as she pleased.

There were very few children on the plantation, so despite no shortage of doting aunts and uncles, Suma was a lonely girl, which made her wander. Vieques was not a large island, and by the time Suma was sixteen, she had walked around the edge of it four times.

She knew the plantation like the skin of her palms but was just as well acquainted with the black and white sand beaches nearby. The sound of water was a soothing rhythm, and when she could, Suma wandered the shore, singing along with the crashing waves. The sea called to her, and she only ever truly felt right when she could feel the warm water lapping at her legs.

When Suma's body ripened, El Flaco took notice of her. Often, he would make extra trips to wherever the girl was working, staring at her in ways that felt oily along the back of Suma's neck. His attention was heavy on her skin, so to escape it, Suma avoided the big house as much as possible. She always found something else to do when El Flaco's footsteps thumped near.

Her father tried to protect her, making sure to dress her in ragged clothing and to hide the shine of her hair and dark skin under smudges of dirt, but it was no good. The girl was as beautiful as her voice.

For a time, her father forbade her to leave their home unless he or another of the plantation men was with her, but Suma almost seemed to wilt when kept away from her wandering, so he begged that she should wait until the night had fallen to go. He gave her his best knife and told her never to be seen.

When Suma was eighteen, her father fell ill. He was well-loved by the people of the plantation, known for being generous and kind, and all the men and women took turns watching over him as he wasted away.

Suma was alone with him, however, when he passed at last.

He smiled up at her, warm brown eyes pinched with pain, and touched her cheek gently.

"Thank you," he said. "For staying so long. For being with me."

"Of course, Papá," she replied, her chest feeling very tight. "I am your daughter. I could never leave you."

A look of guilt passed over the old man's face, and he shook his head. He whispered to her then the stories he had kept from her growing up, the stories the people of the island told about the bay, and about the strange creatures that sometimes swam there. About the fish who were sometimes women, about their beautiful voices and shining scales. He explained that the scales could be removed, and once they were, las sirenas would not be able to transform back from their human form until their scales were returned.

He told her then about finding *her* in the shining water. He told her about her dress, about how he had burned it, and how without it, she could never return to the sea.

"You belong to the sea, girl," he admitted, taking her hand and holding it as tight as his frail body still could. "You were just visiting here, but I couldn't bear to let you go back. And now I've doomed you to this place. Lo siento, mija."

Suma's heart ached, and her mind raced, but before she could ask him anything more, he faded away.

After his death, Suma found her way back to la bahía reluciente.

Her father had always warned her that it was too dangerous, and being dutiful, she had kept away. But on the night of his death, the moon was full and her grief scorching and dangerous, her feet moved in the forbidden direction. Without fully meaning to, Suma entered the bay.

The breeze was warm but gentle, inviting her to come closer to the edge of the shore, to the lapping water.

The water shimmered brilliantly—green and blue and gold—as if there were a sea of stars under the surface, bursting to life with every swell of waves. The sound of the surf breaking on the shore was like the beat of a song Suma had long ago forgotten.

When her skin touched the water, it was welcoming, tugging at her dress and tickling her legs. She shouted for joy, voice clear as bells on Sunday morning, and let herself wade in up to her waist.

Suma had felt a small spike of fear when the water crept up her back—she had been forbidden by her father to learn how to swim (a ploy, she knew now, to keep her from returning to the sea)—and wasn't sure if she would drown.

Curious, she bent her knees deeply, dipping below the surface, and took a deep breath.

The pain was immediate, sharp, and red, ripping into her throat and lungs. Suma burst above the water like a shot, coughing harshly and flailing her way back to the shore.

He had told her the truth.

Heartbroken, the girl threw back her head and wept. She was alone now, and she could never go home.

The first time she sees la sirena, Suma mistakes her for a shark.

Having taken to coming to the iridescent bay when she can't sleep, Suma often finds herself singing to the sea, hoping her song will convince the zemi that she belonged.

On this night, she sits on the sand under the light of the full moon, pouring out her heart in a haunting melody. As her voice swells with emotion, she spies a bright glow in the water as a gently rounded fin breaks the surface.

The sight of it stops the song short, and in the silence, the large shimmering shape under the water flicks its tail—sending a splash towards Suma—then disappears. A heavy thumping beat of power lingers in the air, vibrating against the girl's skin as she watches the glowing thing agitate the water, leaving a trail of shining light in its wake.

Trembling, she stands, fear and elation warring in her chest, and retreats to her home.

She knows she has been heard. But the question is, by what? Is it a generous spirit, here to grant her heart's deepest desire, or something else . . .

Along with the stories of the benevolent zemi, there were stories of the hungry ones, who would lure hopeful wishers into the water with sweet songs that promised the world, and all that would be left was gnawed-up bones in the shallows.

She stays away from the bay for many days—almost a month, throwing herself into her work and caring for the people of the plantation. She is up with the sun and in bed only when her fingers shake, and her eyes blur too much for mending by candlelight.

But too long without hearing the sea, and she begins to feel restless, trapped. She decides that as long as she stays on the sand, the glowing thing cannot hurt her.

Suma straps on her father's best knife and marches with determination all the way to the shore.

Her voice shakes at first, but after a time, she loses herself in her song again, becoming one with it. It's only then that the shape rises from the depths, the fin breaching the water like a brilliantly shining blade.

Suma's voice wavers again at the company, and the tail fin flicks against the water with impatience, so the girl closes her eyes and continues, forcing herself to ignore the trembling in her stomach.

She sings until she feels warmth on her skin, and the backs of her eyelids glow red with the dawn.

When she opens her eyes, the shape in the water is gone, and there is a speckled shell the size of a large coin at the edge of the water, gleaming like gold in the morning light. Suma takes the shell and holds it up to her ear—inside, she can hear waves cresting on the shore.

It isn't the deepest desire of her heart—to go home, back to the ocean—but it is a little piece of the sea she can have with her wherever she is. It makes her feel less restless, less alone, and for that, she is grateful.

Suma spends more and more time at the bay, her songs changing from those she was taught to ones she invents, to tell the truth of her heart.

She sings her pain and loneliness, but also her hope and what little joys she's had, and in return, the glowing thing with the shark's fin leaves her gifts.

El Flaco's eyes follow Suma everywhere she goes. She can feel them burning into her skin when she takes the field workers water at noon, and when she sits in the shade of her tree and sews torn work clothes and bedsheets in the afternoon, and when she makes her way home in the evening.

Sometimes he insists on walking her home, and she lengthens her stride to make the trip shorter, so she can hide from the unwelcome heat of his gaze behind her door.

More and more, he finds her and presses wrapped parcels into her tense hands. A crucifix and chain of gold, a fine crystal glass, an expensive dress for church, a mother of pearl comb for her hair . . . so many expensive things that feel like weights on her back.

On the evening that she comes home and finds one sitting on her bed (a beautiful dark wood brush and small, gilded mirror, wrapped in golden paper), she pays one of the men half of her meager savings to install a lock on her door.

El Flaco refuses to take any of the gifts back, insisting that it is bad luck. He shames her for even suggesting it, reminding her that no other woman on the plantation has things so lovely.

She keeps them all in the wrappings they came in, tucked under her bed and out of sight.

One night at the bay's beach, not long after she began to sing, her eyes closed and face tilted towards the sky, Suma heard splashing in the water. It grew in power and frenzy as she sang until she couldn't ignore it.

Opening her eyes, she saw the water near the roots of a mangrove tree roiling with fury.

Among the foaming white of the water, she spied something new—the rough ropes of a net tangled around a shimmering tail.

Without hesitating, Suma jumped into the water, wading over and using her father's knife to free the shining thing. It wasn't until it was free that she felt fear grip her heart, but it was short-lived—

the rough skin of the shining shape brushed against her side like a grateful caress, and then was gone.

A day later, before she began her singing, Suma checked the roots of the mangrove trees for nets, cutting up the one she found, then settling closer to the edge of the water and closing her eyes.

Before long, just under the sound of her voice, there was the sound of something leaving the water and clumsy footsteps on the sand.

Startled, Suma opened her eyes: before her wobbled the most beautiful person she had ever seen.

The woman wore a long, scaled dress that shone like moonlight. She was tall, almost as tall as El Flaco, and thick with muscle, though her hips were flared and her stomach looked soft. Her eyes were dark and unknowable, but her smile was inviting.

"I tried to stay away," the woman said, voice like gentle waves on the shore. "But your song . . . it calls to me no matter how far I swim."

"I'm . . . sorry to disturb you," Suma said, but it was clear to them both that it was a lie.

"Have you liked my gifts?" the woman asked.

"Yes, thank you. Are . . . are you here to grant my wish? To help me come home?"

The woman's smile turned sad, and she shook her head. "I am sorry, but your scales were destroyed. Without them, you are stuck in this form—you would not survive in the sea."

The disappointment was almost unbearable, and Suma turned away to try to stop herself from weeping. "I see."

"Will you sing for me some more? And in return, I will bring you gifts from the sea?" the woman asked.

Suma wanted to say no. A flash of anger and resentment burned through Suma's chest but disappeared just as quickly. It was not the woman's fault she could not go home.

Turning back, Suma nodded, clearing her throat. She enjoyed the company, and the gifts she had received were some of the only joys she had. If this were all she could have of her true home, she would take it.

Closing her eyes again, Suma lifted her voice and sang.

This continued for many weeks. Sometimes, la sirena would join Suma in her singing, and together, their voices would bring dreams of the sea to the people of the plantation.

It was in these moments that Suma could taste freedom. It was then that she began to know love.

"Sumaiko, your father has been dead for more than a year, and it is high time you had another man in your life." El Gordo's voice is firm but not harsh. He has come to her in a small shaded area around the back of the mill, where she prefers to do her mending during the day.

Suma feels as if she has swallowed a red-hot stone.

Clearing her throat, she puts down the sugar sack she is mending and turns her full attention to the master of the plantation, waiting for him to continue.

"My brother has had his eye on you for quite some time. He tells me you take his gifts but do not reciprocate."

"I can give them back," Suma says quickly, trying to keep her fear from her voice. "They are untouched."

Frowning, El Gordo shakes his head.

"No. You have accepted them. There is no changing that. But

that is beside the point. A woman cannot live *properly* without a man. And it is *my* responsibility, as the master of this house, to make sure that everyone is healthy and living up to their full potential."

"Am I not working to your satisfaction?" Suma asks, a little of the desperation in her gut leaking up into her voice, making it thin. "Have I not earned my keep?"

El Gordo sighs, looking off to the side for a moment in what could be shame.

"You have not wavered, even when el viejo murió. But it isn't *right*." El Gordo sounds resolute, unwavering as the foundation of his plantation. "If you will not marry my brother, you must choose someone else. But, it is my belief that he will take good care of you."

His words sound final, like a nail in a coffin, and Suma can only smile wanly and go back to her mending. It takes all of her strength not to burst into resentful tears as El Gordo gives her a smile and pat on the shoulder on his way back to the house.

Despite El Gordo's words, Suma can't bring herself to spend a moment more than is strictly necessary with El Flaco.

As days turn to weeks, El Flaco becomes more and more agitated, short with his workers and more physical with her. He never forces her to do anything that he wouldn't talk about in church on Sunday, but she feels the weight of his expectation like a heavy lead on her back.

He gets into the habit of serenading her house in the evening, the sound like metal on rock, and she finally agrees to see him if he will leave her alone most nights. He views this as progress and insists that she come to the Big House for dinner twice a week.

His gifts become more elaborate, more expensive as if he is buying her affection. He buys her pretty dresses whose starched material chafes her skin and golden crucifixes that feel like a tightened noose around her neck.

The only time Suma feels free is when she sneaks away to see la sirena.

"They will force my hand soon, and I will have no choice but to marry him," Suma tells la sirena one night.

La sirena scoffs, flicking the water with a long leg, like an agitated fish.

"It is not their place to *take*. It is your place to give *if* you so choose. You don't belong to them any more than the sea belongs to the boats that glide on her back. They must understand this. You must make them understand."

Suma doesn't know how to explain that things are different on land to one who has only known the freedom of waves and the cool darkness of the sea, so she smiles and nods.

La sirena nods back, once, convinced things are as they should be.

"Now, would you do me the pleasure of sharing your song with me?" she asks, and Suma's smile goes from forced to genuine.

"For you? Always."

La sirena grins, her teeth a little too sharp to be human (though that has never bothered Suma at all), and shimmies completely out of the water so she can sit pressed against Suma's body. She leans down and presses a cool, salty kiss to the corner of the girl's mouth.

Pure, giddy joy bubbles up in Suma's chest.

"A gift for a gift," la sirena says and closes her eyes.

Taking a moment to compose herself, Suma gazes at her companion, marveling at the shimmer of her scaled dress, her rich brown hair, tangled gently with water plants, the glow of her skin (a light tan on the front side of her body and darker than Suma's own dark skin along her back)—the rise and fall of her chest.

Overcome with a burst of bravery, Suma touches la sirena's hand, which already rests, relaxed, on her knee.

La sirena opens one eye, looking down at Suma lazily. "Hmm?"

"Kiss me again?" Suma asks before she can stop herself.

She feels as if this will be her last taste of freedom, happiness she didn't know she could feel, and she is desperate for it.

La sirena looks delighted to be asked, leans down the short distance, and kisses Suma again, slower this time like they have all the time in the world.

Suma sighs, a tear escaping her closed eyes, and pushes into the kiss, deepening it, reaching up to carefully thread her fingers in la sirena's hair.

They lose time in that kiss, both feeling light and carefree as the foam on a cresting wave.

Neither of them notices the dark, angry shadow that watches them from the trees.

The day following their kisses, Suma drifts through her day thinking of la sirena. Even inside, she smells the strong, wonderful saltiness of the sea and hears the waves caressing the shore. She still feels la sirena's cool, firm touch on her skin.

The men in the fields take off their hats and compete for her attention when she brings them water, and the women whisper good-naturedly behind their hands that Suma has the look of a woman in love. Suma feels giddy to hear that word but doesn't let herself think about it too hard, for fear the feeling will pop like a fragile bubble.

When El Flaco comes around at lunch to ask her for a song, she doesn't begrudge him, even smiling at him once or twice. She is sitting in the shade of the sugar mill, having just finished bringing the men in the fields water.

"You're so light and carefree today," the large man says when she's finished, tilting his head to look at her sideways. "What has you in such a lovely mood?"

There is something *different* in his eyes, but Suma doesn't know the warning signs.

"I visited the sea last night, and she taught me a new song," she replies, cheeks aching from her smile.

"All this from the *sea*, eh?" El Flaco asks, and even distracted, Suma hears the danger in his tone. "What would a man have to do to get such smiles from you?"

Suma knows to look down, be demure and flattering, even though all she wants to tell him is that there is nothing he has that could possibly bring her joy.

"Kindness and generosity are the virtues I value most," she says. "And there is no man here who would say he is kinder or more generous than you."

The words feel heavy and hot in her mouth, though they are

at least not lies. No man would *dare* say anything negative about El Flaco, lest he suffer the master's wrath.

El Flaco smiles a sharp smile and tips his hat in what some of the women around the plantation would mistake for a gallant gesture.

"It pleases me to hear," he says. "I hope to be the master of your smiles soon."

It's supposed to be a lover's promise, but to Suma, it sounds more like a threat.

The night after Suma kissed la sirena, El Flaco brings three men with instruments to her door and has them play Plenas. Frustrated, Suma watches for a while, hoping that they will leave soon if she smiles and applauds, but they seem to go on forever.

Eventually, the girl grows tired and retires back into her home, and the men play on until the moon is moving towards the horizon line.

By the time Suma feels safe enough to venture to the bay, el gallo is beginning to crow.

Suma doesn't know why, but she feels desperate. The water of the bay seems darker, emptier somehow.

She shakes, her voice wavering as she attempts to sing, and la sirena does not come.

She finally gives up when the sun peeks above the ocean.

For many nights, Suma goes to the bay. Each night, her songs grow more desperate, rawer, and the bay loses a little more of the shimmer, but her cries go unanswered. El Flaco does not come to call while she mourns, and it is the only silver lining of this time.

Some evenings, she thinks she hears la sirena calling out for her, but when she reaches la bahía reluciente, there is no one there.

Then, after about a week of lonely nights and listless days, El Flaco comes around with his new woman. She's shorter and frailer than Suma remembers, her features completely human, but there is no mistaking that the dazed creature El Flaco shows off to the men of the field is la sirena.

Their eyes meet—Suma and la sirena—and for a moment, Suma hears the roars of the ocean as she watches recognition spark in the other woman's eyes. But in a blink, the moment is over, and la sirena looks away as if she knows it is dangerous to acknowledge Suma.

La sirena wears a dress of the finest cotton, light and brightly colored, but compared to her scales, it is dull and coarse-looking. There are fading bruises around her wrists and ankles that make Suma ache down to the bone.

"I could not wait for you forever," El Flaco says, his voice knowing and cruel when he reaches her.

Suma has no response for him. Her heart beats too hard in her throat.

"There will be a wedding next week, on Sunday," the towering man continues, casually bringing a large hand to rest around the back of la sirena's neck. His fingers are so long they almost meet at the front of the woman's throat like a collar.

The men, who are too taken with la sirena's beauty to see the fear and sadness in her eyes, cheer and whistle, many coming forward to pat El Flaco on the back.

Suma feels bile rising from her stomach, burning her insides. She knows, without having to be told, that this is her fault. That if not for her, El Flaco would never have been able to catch the woman.

"I was hoping that you would agree to sing for me, girl," El Flaco says, but all of Suma's attention is on la sirena. He takes her silence as acceptance, and grins, tilting his hat. "Good."

A wave of emotion crashes over Suma, and without knowing it, she is rushing forward, taking la sirena in her arms so that they share a tight embrace. "How?" she whispers, afraid to be overheard.

"I heard your singing, but it was far away. I came looking for you, but I found him instead," la sirena murmurs into her ear, voice thick with regret and barely controlled anger, understanding that they have little time and no privacy.

"Your dress?"

"He has it. I must do as he says."

Before anything else can be said, El Flaco's voice cuts through the air. "Time to go now. We have much to prepare."

They are ripped apart, la sirena tense and jerking against El Flaco's hold before relaxing into a limp sort of walk, moving like she is biding her time. Suma watches them walk away, and it feels like dying.

Suma goes to El Flaco the day before the wedding. She has searched and searched but has not been able to find the dress. At night, she can hear la sirena's sad song on the wind, and she can't bear the thought of her lover being trapped there like she is.

She goes to him in the prettiest dress he gifted her, wearing his jewelry and perfume, with her father's knife tied to her thigh with a piece of thick twine.

"You win," she says when he opens the door, shivering under his gaze but still meeting his eyes.

"Oh?"

"Give her back her dress, let her free, and I will marry you."

El Flaco laughs, but the sound is cruel and hollow.

"She has *many* dresses, all of which I have given her. And she is free to leave—there are no chains keeping her here," he says, pausing for a second to regard Suma. The look he gives her is like a snake watching a songbird land nearby. "But, if you think I am making a mistake choosing her over you, perhaps you can convince me."

Taking a deep breath, Suma nods once, allowing him to lead her through the Big House.

They pass through many rooms, the building almost like a castle from the fairy tales her father used to tell her as a child— stories he learned from his mother, who came from Spain to reap the rewards of the lush little island but found love with a poor fisherman instead.

They reach El Flaco's quarters, and Suma notices a large, ornate chest at the foot of the bed. It is locked, but the lock looks old and rusted, and she thinks it would give easily under the butt of her knife.

He takes her in his arms, and she allows him to pull her close.

His lips find her neck as her hand finds the knife, and her knife finds his neck as her lips find his ear.

Hot spatters of blood tap against her skin, like a summer rain.

"Reap now the rotten fruit you sowed."

The lock gives way as easily as Suma thought it would, and inside the chest is *the* dress.

Feeling it in her hands, it is cool and soft. The scales call to her like a memory of something that was once hers.

It would be so easy, she thinks. *To do something for myself, for once. To be Free.*

As Suma stands, paralyzed with deep wanting, a mournful song rises. She knows the sound of that voice, and though it twists her stomach to think of giving up the scales, she knows what she has to do.

She finds la sirena in the room next to El Flaco's, unchained as promised but looking no less trapped.

"Come," she says, throwing the dress at the weeping woman without looking. "They will discover what was done here soon. You must get to the water before they do."

"I don't know the way," la sirena says, but her voice is breathy, excited.

Without looking back, Suma leads them away, towards la bahía reluciente.

They make it to the edge of the plantation before someone sounds the alarm. Standing among the sugar cane, Suma looks at la sirena again at last.

She is beautiful, more magical than anything else Suma has ever seen.

Unable to help herself, Suma kisses the woman, cutting her lips on la sirena's once-again sharp teeth.

Pulling back, she grabs her hand, pulls her into the woods, and drags her towards la bahía reluciente.

They run, la sirena awkward and stumbling on her legs, as the sound of dogs and men grow louder behind them.

When they burst from the treeline by the bay, they are both panting, la sirena bruised and bleeding, the men moments away.

"Go," the girl says, looking down and away but pointing the woman towards the water with her blade. "I will hold them off." She pauses for a moment, eyes closing, tears burning them. "I'm so sorry."

A cool, strong hand grabs her knife away, and there is the sound of ripping.

"Do not apologize for the actions of others."

Suma looks up, and la sirena is nude, the dress cut in two at the midsection in her hands. She holds out half like a promise, and Suma shakes as she reaches for it before snatching her hand away.

"But, you won't be able to transform fully. You—"

"Would happily share myself with you, forever," la sirena interrupts, eyes large and scared as they flicker between Suma and the trees—the sounds of furious men crashing through the forest, so close. "Take it. Come *home*."

Trembling fingers catch the edge of the half-dress as El Gordo and his men tear into the bay.

El Gordo, a soldier trained to charge into battle, moves forward, a rifle in his hands.

"Which one of you witches killed him? Which one of you took my brother?"

"Your brother," Suma says, still covered in El Flaco's blood and feeling rage and fear bubble up inside her, "stole from the sea and paid the price."

El Gordo advances, but the rest of the men, who knew Sumaiko when she was a child and have loved her in one way or another most of her life, stay back. They knew El Flaco to be cruel and covetous, and while they followed their master here, they will not mourn the passing of such a man.

El Gordo raises the rifle, and Suma positions herself in front of la sirena.

"You will pay," he snarls. "We will take you back and make an example of you both. Your blood will feed the sugar cane."

Now the men move forward, and Suma braces herself, but instead of lunging for her, they grab hold of El Gordo's arms and take his gun.

"Go, now," they say.

Whatever else happens, the men will not punish a desperate girl for wanting to be free.

Suma slips the scaled half a dress over her head, and the world disappears in the sound of waves pounding the shore, in the comforting, cool rush of power crashing over her.

When she opens her eyes, things are different. Colors sharper—smells more intense.

She feels la sirena take her hand, and she smiles at the spooked men. Together, they turn and rejoin the sea.

. . .

Though it has been many, many long years since the mill was shuttered, and the plantation is forgotten, la bahía reluciente still shimmers in the dark. It is said that on clear nights, two glowing shapes can be seen frolicking in its water, the laughing sound of their joyous song carried for miles on the wind.

RIVER PEOPLE

by

Yamile Saied Méndez

Malena had skills that no one could explain, not even her. When they were alive, her parents thought that her ability to speak to ghosts meant she was a bridge between this world and that of spirits, between their ancestral home in Ireland and the new one in Argentina. She was the only O'Rourke child born in the land at the end of the world. But her parents had died a year ago, and she had never even heard a whisper of their voices. Not even to give their grief-stricken children their last instructions or a simple I love you.

For this reason, her oldest brother Miguel concluded the voices were a product of her overactive imagination, or even worse, tricks of the devil, the father of lies. Instead of being a bridge, Malena was the cause of tension in what remained of her family—three children who didn't know how to function in the world after so much loss.

But even in her grief, Malena only knew not to refuse a gift. Ignoring the voices was worse than refusing.

So when the river Paraná spoke, she listened.

She lived by it all the sixteen years of her life, but it was only during the last few months that she'd discovered the river god could speak in actual words. The first one he said was her brother's name: Miguel.

A warning hummed under the surface of the lapping waves of the powerful river.

The warning confirmed her suspicions. Ever since their parents' death, with the growing responsibilities of becoming the head of the family, her older brother had changed. Especially after he started spending time with the rich man, Don Osorio. Her brother had become moodier, distant, bitter. She feared for him.

In her quest to find out what was wrong with her brother, she went down to visit Paraná every moment she wasn't needed at Los Hermanos O'Rourke Pulpería, the family's dry goods store. Perhaps if she learned more about the river, she'd be able to understand its secrets.

She knew its moods by its currents. The color of its waters told her where to fish. Malena could tell by the roar of its voice if it had rained in the north where the river was born and if their town, Los Teros, should prepare for Paraná's voracious hunger. The more water it carried, the more the river devoured, and the people were tired of the river taking away their cattle.

Lately, it had been different. Underneath the whirlwinds, the dappled gold and copper of its waves and thunderous voice, there was a humming in Malena's ears when she thought of the river or touched its waters. The river wanted to tell her something, and she didn't understand what, only that it had to do with Miguel, the patriarch of their family at twenty because he was the oldest.

Now February was coming to an end, and the murmurs and gurgling had become urgent, frantic. Malena didn't have time to learn the river's language. Early the next morning, she'd be on her way back for her last year at the nuns' school in Rosario. Back to blistering shoes and stiff white shirts and long silences from home. Miguel wasn't a good correspondent. He was too busy with the pulpería. The youngest of her brothers, Patricio, was seventeen years old. He only wrote because his days in the seminary were too long to fill with only prayers and the lives of saints. But he didn't have news from home. Miguel didn't write to him either.

Early in the morning, while she did her chores before the customers arrived, Malena asked Tomás, the youngest brother, what she should do about the river. Maybe because he was a ghost, he knew things others couldn't see. The SS *Dresden* had been both the first and last place he'd known. To his parents' grief, he'd died without being baptized. Perhaps that's why he'd lingered behind, his spirit growing along with Malena. Sometimes he was the only brother who listened to Malena and didn't brush off her worries as unimportant girl's fancies. But by the way his image flickered in the sunlight when she was hanging sheets on the clothesline, she knew he also didn't know what to do about the river. Tomás placed a hand on her shoulder. The air smelled of green grass and salt water, and her mind filled with the words, "Listen with your heart, just like you listen to me."

The white sheets flapped in the wind filling the air with the scent of lavender and lemon soap.

"Gracias, Tomás," she said, and although she didn't know how to open her heart to the river, she could at least try because although she didn't understand it, she loved it. She'd loved it all her life.

She didn't have time to waste; she'd be needed in the kitchen soon. Malena ran down las barrancas, the bluffs where the teros, the riverside birds, nested. Her dress tangled around her legs. She lifted her linen shift when she stepped on the muddy beach. Paraná reached his hands and pulled Malena farther and farther into its depths. Soon her hem was wet, stained reddish-brown like the river. She wiggled her toes in the clay, and her skin broke into goose bumps because the water was cold. She brushed her fingers on the surface of the rippling waves. A carancho flew above her, and its peevish cry echoed on the tops of the paradise trees.

Paraná whispered.

Malena lowered her head to hear better, but the words didn't make any sense. As if it were desperate, Paraná pushed her down, and under the water, Malena heard her name for the first time.

"Malena . . ." The river's voice was deep and ancient. The jumbled words gurgled in her ears, and stars popped in her eyes.

"Cattle . . . Miguel . . . devil . . . lost," she thought the river said. "Cattle . . . Miguel . . . devil . . . lost . . ."

Her lungs clamored for air, but still, she didn't know what the river meant. Maybe it repeated echoes of things it had heard in its travels, in its journey to the end of the world. Maybe it played with her; it teased her about staying in Los Teros and not becoming a learned woman with the nuns and their rules.

"Cattle . . . Miguel . . . devil . . . lost . . ." the voice whispered in her heart.

Malena pushed herself up to the surface, and the river let her go. When her head broke through the gleaming water, her name resonated down to her bones.

"María Elena!" cried a voice.

At first, she thought she could join the rapturous birds in their joy greeting the sun. She understood the river's voice!

"María Elena!" she heard again, and when a cloud covered her head, she wanted to hide in its grayish cotton. This voice wasn't the river's. Only one person called her by her proper name. Even to the nuns, she was Malena.

She whipped around and saw Miguel standing furiously atop the barranca. His golden hair blew in the breeze, but the frown on his face seemed set in stone—so much weight on his young shoulders. Even through the distance, she felt his piercing green eyes following her every move as she waded out of the water in his direction. He never went down to the river. Without a command, Malena knew her time with Paraná was over.

Malena reached him and stood in front of him in silence. His boots were smeared with reddish mud, just like her feet and her dress.

"Patricio was scared el Pombero had kidnapped you in the night," Miguel said.

El Pombero!

The Man of the Night could never set foot inside their house to kidnap her. She always made sure to leave an offering of honey or tobacco outside her window, and she never wandered into the trees unaccompanied once the sun had set.

But Miguel sounded angry. The lilt of Gaelige, which he clung to stubbornly, melded into the words of his Castellano, which he resisted. Malena knew it wasn't a good idea to laugh at him.

"Aren't you going to explain yourself?" he asked.

Malena looked up at him. Behind her, she felt Paraná waiting for her explanation too. "I'm sorry, Miguel," she lied.

She wasn't sorry she'd gone down to the river. She was only sorry her brother had found her. If she told him she'd heard a warning, he'd think she was deranged. He'd brush her fears off, but the river dripping from her clothes told her to *try, try, try* . . .

Malena did as the river wanted. "The river speaks to me, Miguel. It wants to tell me something, but I don't know what."

Miguel's face remained unreadable. He removed the poncho from his shoulders and covered her with it. The wool retained his warmth, and Malena noticed the air carried the promise of frosts from the south. Soon, the paradise trees would turn gold, and the swallows would leave their nests for sunnier homes.

"You're a señorita now, María Elena—"

"Malena," she said, and her voice sounded sharp.

"That's not a proper Christian name."

Malena felt as if he'd slapped her. She was underwater again, her lungs bursting for the pressure to talk back, but she held her tongue. There was a sadness in her brother's voice, underneath the current of impatience and frustration. She tried to listen with her heart as he spoke, but it was hard to do when his disdain for her name made her shiver with anger.

"I think you're making up excuses not to help in la pulpería. Is that it?" Miguel said. He led her back home through the narrow trails between the trees. She followed him, careful not to step on the anthills or the small branches the Pampero wind had ripped off the trees in his last visit through Los Teros.

Miguel continued, "All summer long, los arrieros and the

farmhands take long detours for your *mate* cocido. I never understood how these people like their heathen tea, but they come for this drink and stay for the food and supplies. I thought you'd help me one last time?"

"One last time before I return," she added quickly. Didn't he know it was dangerous to say such careless words? Any spirit might hear him say *one last time* and take his words to heart. He should know better. He'd grown up in Los Teros, but he resisted the place, the people, the land, and the customs. For all his religiousness, he was ungrateful.

She resented the way he talked of her gift preparing *mate*.

Mate was the tea of the gauchos, the cowboys of the Pampas, a gift of the goddess of the Moon for her people. After so many years, how could he be so ungrateful to this land that was their home since he was a young boy? But she said none of this to her brother. After cholera had taken their parents the year before, he was the head of the family, and he deserved her respect.

Miguel was too dignified to roll his eyes, but she sensed his annoyance. "Such superstitions, Malena. If the nuns can't teach you to behave like a lady, I hope they teach you how to be a proper Christian. Now, go make yourself presentable, and run to the kitchen. I have important business to take care of. Remember, we have a reputation to uphold. Don't dishonor the family name."

Three horses were tied to posts at the pulpería already, and Miguel walked ahead as he'd already forgotten her. His customers were all-important. More would arrive with the first train.

Back in her room, Malena said a prayer to the saints she had met at the church and school and to the spirits of nature that had watched her grow up. "Help me understand the river's warning. Help me not disappoint my brother."

She braided her long black hair and changed into working clothes before heading to the kitchen. Patricio was already slicing bread he'd baked in the mud ovens in the backyard overnight.

"I'm glad the Pombero didn't take you."

She made a face at him, and he added, "I already brought you water for the *mate*, Malena. The sugar is running low, but Miguel said we'd get more in the train tomorrow."

She stood on tiptoe to glimpse into the sugar canister. There was only a fistful left. She set to work on her first batch of tea. Even if she hadn't deciphered the river's secret, she would ponder the words in her heart as she worked.

She listened to the song the bubbles made in the iron kettle over the fire. She heard the sigh of the *mate* leaves when the water flooded the cup. She felt it in her skin and blood when the tea was ready for the cream and the sugar. She said a word of thanks to the house spirits no one else could see, the spirits who'd lived in the land since the dawn of time and those who'd clung to the family's trunks during the crossing of the Atlantic and the equator.

Malena shivered when she felt Tomás's presence. He was scared.

"Our brother," he said, and the urgency in his voice was like Paraná's.

Patricio was outside, feeding the chickens in the coop. He spoke to them as if they were people when he thought no one was listening. When Malena peeked through the curtains to check on him, she saw the chickens gathered around his feet, enraptured with his words. Malena never teased Patricio about it.

Her brother's heart was tender, and she didn't want to bruise his gentle soul. Patricio was out of danger.

But where was Miguel?

Armed with a pot of *mate* cocido and two teacups, she walked toward the dining hall, but Miguel wasn't there. She headed to his studio, a small room with a few books and a map that showed the emerald island of their ancestors gilded in silver and gold. She tiptoed the last few steps when she heard the voices in serious negotiation. She peeked inside the door, holding her breath and willing her thumping heart not to give her away.

A man sat with Miguel. He had smoldering eyes like la luz mala, the witch light that guided wanderers to their death.

"All you need to do, O'Rourke, is to get *my* cattle across the river," the man said. His pointy beard was like Mandinga's, el diablo, the devil of the stories.

"If I were discovered, I could lose my honor, Don Osorio," Miguel said, sounding just like Patricio when someone told him off.

"You're the one who invited me into your home for business. I didn't go looking for you," Osorio said.

"When a man is desperate, he may do unthinkable things he'd never consider under other circumstances." The stony mask had slipped off Miguel's face. Underneath the coldness and harshness, he was a scared boy.

Malena wanted to embrace him.

Don Osorio laughed. "That's true," he said. "But the world belongs to the adventurous only, chamigo!"

Since when were Miguel and this man such good friends to call each other chamigo?

Don Osorio continued, "One would've thought you'd learned something from your father. May he rest in peace. Juan wouldn't have been afraid of crossing a few heads of cattle. Perhaps courage skipped a generation? He was rash and irresponsible, but he was no coward."

Malena couldn't take it any longer. She crossed the threshold into the studio, knowing she was breaking all the rules of decorum.

Don Osorio's gaze fixed on her, and she squared her shoulders against its force. Miguel's forehead was covered in perspiration, although the rain had cooled down the temperature.

"Disculpa, Miguel," she said.

He didn't return the smile.

Osorio had pale skin and dark hair like a moonless night. He regarded her with a calculating look. "Ah, the famous little O'Rourke, la nena with the magic." The slimy aftertaste of his words turned the phrase into an insult.

Miguel felt it too. He wasn't completely oblivious then. He took a teacup from Malena's hands and placed it before the man. "Don Osorio, this is my younger sister, María Elena O'Rourke."

"Malena," she corrected him without thinking.

Miguel clenched his jaw, and Malena wished she hadn't corrected Miguel in front of this man, but it was too late. Her brother grabbed the teapot from her and poured the fragrant sweet *mate*. "Drink up, Don Osorio, por favor. I wouldn't say my sister has a magic touch, but she sure knows how to prepare tea."

The man smiled and took a long gulp of the *mate* cocido. Before he swallowed, his face turned red like the coals beneath the tea kettle. He turned away from Miguel and spat the tea on the floor.

Miguel looked at Malena with so many questions in his eyes. But she hadn't done anything differently. If the man was going to complain, it should be because the *mate* was cold. She'd been eavesdropping for so long.

Malena remembered Paraná's words. Cattle. Miguel. Devil. Lost.

Had the river been warning her all summer about this man?

Miguel stood up and went around the table to bump Don Osorio on his back, as was the custom in this kind of mishap.

When the man finally swallowed, he groaned and clutched his hands on his throat. "It was burning! And bitter! What did you put in my tea, girl?"

He said "girl" like he meant "scum." Dirt. Garbage. Nothing.

Malena lifted her chin. His words didn't offend her. She had no doubts about this man's identity now. He couldn't drink her *mate*, prepared with love for her brothers, reverence for the Moon goddess' gift. He was the devil, the enemy of humankind, the collector of souls who relished in making the noblest of them fall and then gathered them in his sack of midnight and sorrow.

"Lo siento, Don Osorio," Miguel mumbled. "María Elena, please bring some lemon water for—"

"No," Señor Osorio said, his smile stretching into a grimace. "She's done enough."

Miguel sent her a look with the slap of lightning when it hit the quebracho trees in the middle of a storm. Without a word, she went back to the kitchen.

Patricio was waiting for her. In his eyes, she saw the reflection of her fear that had crawled under her skin—a warning of an impending threat.

"Don't you feel it too?" she asked.

Patricio pulled out rosary beads from underneath his work shirt and placed them around Malena's neck. She twisted the beads between her fingers and remembered Paraná's urgent warning.

The beads were made out of rolled river mud left to dry in the sun. Patricio had painted them himself, with her favorite colors, green and brown. Green like the llanura. Brown like the river.

"Pray, Malena," he said fervently, his skin flushed and clammy. "The devil is here, and we're so small compared to his power. What can we do?"

"We can find out what he wants with Miguel," Malena said.

Patricio hesitated, and then he sighed. "Ask Tomás to listen for us. I know he trails behind you like the tail of a kite and that you can hear him."

Malena looked at her brother until he smiled.

"I can't see him or hear him, but I feel his presence—an angel watching over us." Without another word, Patricio went back to his chores.

"Go, Tomás," she said. "Listen and tell me all the man says."

Her ghost brother left like a breath, and Malena waited, twisting a kitchen towel and tying knots on its corners to stop Miguel from giving his word to the devil. The time passed, and Malena had to attend to the customers—the regulars—who wanted one more cup of *mate* before she left for school. She served them all, and they all left with hope in their hearts. When she returned to the kitchen for biscuits and fried bread, the sound of a horse's gallop told her Don Osorio had left.

She ran outside, but all she saw was a flock of teros flapping back to eat the drowned ants in the puddles the rain had made on the road.

Tomás joined her outside. "Osorio wants Miguel to take stolen cattle across the river . . . He'd been pestering our brother all summer, and Miguel finally went looking for him."

The rain was soaking her only dry working dress, but she didn't care. "But why?" she asked. "Miguel never goes near the river. He can't even swim."

Tomás took her hand between his cold palms. "He promised him enough money to pay for la pulpería's debts. He's scared of losing the business, the fruit of our parents' sacrifices. So much money that you and Patricio would never have a care in the world ever again. But you can't let him, Malena. No money can pay for lost honor or lost life."

Was this the message that Paraná had tried to give her all summer long?

Malena found Miguel in the studio. He stood in front of the map, looking at the place their family had come from and where they would never return. For better or worse, the O'Rourkes had taken root in the Pampas.

She didn't remember her father's face anymore, but she remembered the lesson he taught his children over and over. Material things come and go, and Juan O'Rourke didn't leave many possessions to his children, just la pulpería and a legacy of hard, honorable work. If Miguel accepted the deal with Osorio and carried it out, her father's legacy would be gone.

"Miguel," she said. "You can't—"

"I can't what?" he snapped at her. "I can't keep Papá's business the way he did? I can't take care of the clients with Patricio gone to the seminary and you to your school?"

The pain in her brother's soul roared louder than the words that still reverberated in her ears. Malena wanted to speak, but she knew Miguel enough to understand that whatever she said would make the situation worse.

"You're only a girl," he said. "What can you know of the weight it is to keep a legacy too big for my shoulders? Now go back to work. The clients are waiting."

He walked away from her before she could tell him that he was walking into a trap, that the man was the devil who only wanted his soul.

All day, Malena served her *mate*, empanadas, and cakes while Patricio took care of the animals. Miguel avoided their eyes, and in the early evening, he left without saying goodbye.

Malena sent away the last of the customers and went out looking for her brother—her heart in her throat. At the edge of the town, she stood and gazed at the raw llanura, the endless plains, where the wheat danced for the wind. The grass was long and soft, like the ocean Miguel talked about when he was melancholy for Eire.

Now in the darkness, she knew better than to step onto that ocean of vegetation. The Little Folk that had followed the immigrants had infested the fields. Combined with the native plagues of the land and the wild animals that prowled the night, Malena was safer skirting the precarious constructions of the village than risking a meeting with the mischievous folk or el Pombero. Malena clutched her rosary beads. How long had it taken Patricio to roll them, dry them, paint them, string the mud and transform it into a powerful talisman?

It was raining again—this unrelenting rain. Without even trying, Malena heard the roaring of the growing river beneath the deafening song of the raindrops, frogs, crickets, and birds of the night. Above the trees, a bat swooped down time after time, tasting the still ripening nísperos in the trees. The medlar fruit was an immigrant like Malena's family, its ancestor brought as a seed in a ship all the way from China, and now it covered the fields as if it had been here since the beginning of the world.

Go back home, she heard the voice of the river say. *Warn Miguel that he's walking into a trap.*

For the last family dinner, Malena arranged Mamá's china, noting the empty spots at the table Papá had built from quebracho wood, the hardest wood in the land. She placed an extra setting for her departed parents and for Tomás.

Patricio was in the middle of a Padre Nuestro when Miguel arrived. When Patricio said Amen, Miguel sat at the table, but he didn't touch his food, the asado she and Patricio had prepared. Malena couldn't swallow even though the meat was the best she'd had in years.

"It's cold outside," Miguel said, his voice hoarse as if the words scratched his throat.

Patricio and Malena exchanged looks.

Patricio begged her with his eyes. Although he'd soon be a priest, he didn't have a way with words that would reach Miguel's heart.

It was all up to her. She served tea for her and Miguel. "Please, Miguel," Malena said, "whatever you promised that man, you don't have to do it."

Miguel lifted his eyes from the plate, and he looked like a stranger, strong and unmovable.

"Don't risk crossing el Paraná with that stolen cattle. You don't even know how to swim," she said.

It was the wrong thing to say, and Patricio clasped her hand under the tablecloth.

Miguel rose gingerly as if his legs couldn't hold his weight. "María Elena, how do you know of my plans?"

She met his eyes with equal strength. "The river warned me about you, and then Tomás, the spirit of our brother, told me of your plans with that . . . that man, Don Osorio."

Miguel's stony mask slipped for a fraction of a second. Enough for Malena to see he was scared of her words. "I can't go back on my word," he said. Then his eyes hardened, and the distant, stubborn Miguel was back. "Such ridiculous notions! What are the nuns teaching you?"

He threw the embroidered napkin on the table and stomped out of the dining room, slamming the door.

Patricio smiled sadly and cleared the table, gathering the scraps for the chickens. "Are you packed?"

She nodded. She couldn't disobey her brother.

"Wake me up when you leave," Patricio said.

She finished putting things away in her trunk. All the material things were there. But she couldn't pack the smell of the rain in the clover field or the scent of the river when the water glinted copper. She didn't know how to pack the sound of the Pampero caressing the trees or the feeling of being both small and immense when she stood next to the river or gazed at the sky. She couldn't pack the noises of her family home in the nighttime when she felt they were all protected under one roof and that in the morning, the petty disagreements would be forgiven.

Shé lay on her bed awake all night, trying to memorize every creak the wood made as it settled for the night, the scurrying of rodent feet on the roof, the call of the owls from their nests. The front door slammed shut, and the clatter of a horse's hooves echoed in the night.

She wanted to run to her brother, stop him from making a mistake he'd regret all his life. Any money he received for crossing stolen cattle couldn't pay for his soul, but what could Malena do? She sat by the window, dressed for her journey, until the teros and the swallows started chirping.

While Patricio got ready to take her to the train station, she went to the kitchen to prepare one last cup of her famous *mate cocido*. She found a pouch with coins for her expenses and a note in which Miguel had scribbled his last goodbye.

Miguel. Why was he so prideful and stubborn? Maybe if he had confided in her and Patricio, they could have found a way to save their parents' pulpería without any of them having to sell their soul to the devil.

He was going to end up dead, or worse.

He knew his way around the animals, but not around water. He'd never made friends with Paraná, and instead of honoring the river, he ignored it.

Miguel was right. She was just a girl. What could she do?

She could talk to the river, beg for her brother's safety. He said there was no going back now that he'd given his word, but Malena wouldn't let him lose his soul, not for all the money in the world.

There was only one place where Miguel would attempt a crossing. In a section of the river, where the siblings played when they were little. Back when things were happy, even if they were difficult. Back when their parents were still around.

Malena headed there without hesitation. She smelled the cattle first, and then she heard the lows of dissent. The cattle were smart. They wouldn't get into the barges, but Miguel prodded them until they did. Miguel always reminded her and Patricio of the family's honor, but he had agreed to take the tainted money the devil offered. If Miguel succeeded, their parents' legacy of honesty and integrity would be destroyed.

Malena remembered Paraná's warning. The river wouldn't be complicit. He'd stop her brother even if it cost Miguel his life.

Malena ran.

"¡Arre!" Miguel called to the cattle and led them toward the flat barge. His foot slipped off the edge of the barge.

"Miguel!" Malena screamed.

Even in the gloom of not yet daylight, Malena saw an arm made of water and shadows grab her brother and pull him down the whirlwind. Miguel didn't struggle. His limp body in the hands of the river shook like a rag doll. The cows were quiet in the ship that drifted back to the shore. Miguel bobbed above the water in a last attempt to breathe.

Without thinking, Malena kicked off her boots and waded into the brown waters of Paraná.

The thrashing calmed at once, and a breeze of warm air, like the sigh of a condemned soul that sees salvation ahead, ruffled her long brown hair.

She swam to her brother—his dark curls plastered against

his face. He didn't breathe. She saw his spirit underwater thrashing against the water hyacinth, trying to break free, trying to get back to his sister. So full of regret.

Malena dove underwater and reached for her brother's soul. With the pressure of the water in her ears, she understood that Paraná loved her, that the resident god just wanted to be loved back.

"Paraná, I love you already. Take me instead. Miguel is rash and thoughtless, but he's a good man. Let him raise a family by your waters. Let him learn that life at your side is beautiful."

She let the water cover her head. Miguel's body was snatched from her grasp.

A girl wasn't enough to fight a river. She opened her mouth when her lungs were bursting, and she swallowed water. She loved this river and its life, and its story and all the things it had seen. If she had one more chance, she'd tell her brothers of the river's love for their family. She'd sail its waters from its birth until it joined the great ocean.

"Malena," the voice of the river spoke in her mind. "I don't want to take your life. I want to tell you my stories. Will you listen to me?"

The warmth of the river's embrace enveloped Malena's soul. She closed her eyes and said, "Yes, Paraná, tell me your story. I promise I'll listen." And she did.

She woke up to the song of teros and newborn sunshine tickling her face.

Patricio rose from his knees with a *hallelujah!* that rattled the glass panes in the windows. The ghostly hand of Tomás glinted like a diamond from next to the altar, on which sat the picture of her family before boarding the ship to America.

"Where's Miguel?" Malena croaked, and water gurgled in her throat.

The curly head of her beloved brother peeked from behind the curtain.

Miguel's face crumbled, and tears fell on his face. "What did you do, Malena? Why?"

She didn't know how to answer. He'd called her Malena.

Patricio said, "I found the *mate* on the table, but you were gone, so I ran to the river. I arrived as Miguel crawled back to the shore with you in his arms, dripping river and leaving a trail of stars in his wake. I helped steer the cows back to the town. They're back to their owner."

"And Don Osorio?"

"I had holy water in my pocket, and the river told Miguel what ancient words to say to shun him from our midst."

Malena closed her eyes, satisfied.

She understood the river's words, and so did Miguel. They weren't just superstitions.

Malena kept her promise to Paraná. She listened to his stories and wrote them down in books. She sailed his waters and learned his secrets. And although some of her posterity moved to seek new prospects like her family had once done, the O'Rourkes always heard the song of the river.

Thousands of miles away from Los Teros in the Argentine Pampas, one hundred years after Malena had addressed the river god and listened to its stories, one of her great-grandchildren sleeps in the night and dreams she floats in the brown waters of a river she's never seen, but whose song she can hear in her soul. Its waters run through her veins, and when she wakes, she murmurs, "Paraná," and greets the newborn sun.

MOONGLOW

BASED ON A TRUE FAMILY STORY

by
Sara Faring

ARGENTINA, 1910

Dear Diary, I know it is only safe to write you in my head, where I will forget bits of you, but I shall do so anyway.

It is the night before Nochebuena, and I've been without him for thirty-five days, but every hour feels like a gluey-long eternity. If I shut my eyes and tense all of my muscles, I feel his lips on my neck, the scratch of hay on my back, the flush of warmth when he is nearby. Sebastián, Diary. Father's head rancher's son, that muscled Romeo, plucked straight from all of the stories I ever heard the maids tell. These tales of ladies and their ranch hands are well-known for a reason; who else was I meant to meet in the hell and gone besides my brother Pedro's ghost?

You know Sebastián well, Diary, even though I had to start writing you afresh in my head in Buenos Aires (for if anyone found your pages, I would be dead, deader than the hen whose body Sebastián cleaved in two and brought to the cook once, apologetically almost, because Sebastián is as soft as he is strong). I swallowed your pages back in Bragado, all forty-two of them, moistening them in milk and balling them up. And if I weren't such a paper-eating coward, maybe Sebastián and I would be halfway to Uruguay now, nearly by the white dunes of Punta del Este—

You'll be a mother soon, I hear whispered in a gravelly voice.

And I know, without opening my eyes, that he is there. Not Sebastián, Diary. Pedro. I could wring his neck if he weren't dead.

The night before Nochebuena, that bastard's at the foot of my bed again, eyeing the wadded up, sweated-through sheets that I kicked there (wouldn't *you* want to kick your sheets off one last, sticky-hot night?). He clears his throat until I open my eyes with a groan.

You'll be a mother soon, my brother repeats, his ghostly voice warped, as usual, like he has a mouth full of sand.

For thirty-five nights, he has come to tell me this. Every night it sounds like a graver insult. But I suspect he only speaks these words to tease me, to remind me how very small my living world is.

Pedro never took anything seriously when he was alive, so of course, he doesn't take things seriously when he's dead. Once in Bragado, three years ago, Mother asked him to take some old worn-down shoes to the cobbler for repairs—están hechos mierda, Father remarked—and instead, Pedro boxed up some dog shit and dropped it on the old leather man's door. Special delivery. When Mother asked Father to punish him, Father only laughed and left us to smoke cigarillos on the windy, chilly porch.

Now it is almost Christmas, and Buenos Aires is so humid I would peel my skin off if I could. Maybe I could even drape it around Sebastián's neck then, so he could always keep me close to his fingers. It's so hot in this God-forsaken city now that the twins come to me nightly and beg me to blow on their foreheads, their cheeks, the back of their necks. The first time I heard Pedro's noises—like the rustling of leaves—I thought it was them, keeping each other cool beside me and watching for hadas up to evening mischief.

But it was Pedro.

You'll be a mother soon, he tells me again, the donkey.

He can't know about the seed I feel burning in my belly—can he? He can't know about the times Sebastián and I touched each other under the cloak of night. In the haystacks, we laid down beyond the barrels where we once crushed grapes with our feet.

Although the pervert always did observe us, *little women*—as he called my sisters and me—to stay abreast of our differences from his *bolder* sex.

I'll admit: I might've spied too, had I free run of the house and Father's favor. How else would we learn about these differences, much less how a child comes to be? I did the little I could: I eavesdropped when the maids told their stories, then observed farm animals in heat.

Bewildering.

"I told you, Pedro, and I'll tell you again," I tell him in a harsh whisper, lest I wake up the twins. "You'll speak to me clearly, or you won't speak to me at all. Don't come around here stirring shit up to entertain yourself. I'm sure you're plenty busy like we are."

Pedro blinks, and the mosquito bites colonizing my flesh flicker like velas in church. Then he smirks to show he is responsible. He is only a shadow of his former self, this glossy, half-formed thing, but the smirk is unmistakable.

"Oh, you devil," I tell him, scratching at the bites until they bleed.

Pedro shrugs, repeats his message in that garbled voice, and walks out of the window, disappearing into the humid air above the piles of garbage in the street.

I am new to Buenos Aires, Diary, but I needed only two minutes in this stinking place to know that it is a city of stale air, smoke, and shadows. I don't just miss Sebastián. I miss the freshness of the country air. I miss the home where we grew up in Bragado, its sprawling flatlands full of sweet nutria the size of hounds and quince trees begging to be climbed. We all do. Except for Pedro, presumably, because he died there two years ago in a riding accident, yet he still finds his way here to me, my mother, and siblings.

I fluff up my sheets and settle back into my pillow, and shut my eyes, the burn of the bites turning my flesh into a bag of bursting stars. That's when my door creaks open, and I hear the patter of little feet.

"Sara, Sara," the twins cry, out of breath. "The hadas are here, and they're whispering about the gifts we're going to receive! Come see, won't you? Come see!"

If I were smarter, like my mother, perhaps I would, in five simple words, convince them that their place at night was in dreamland.

If I were tougher, like my father, I would boom at them a single word—¡basta!—that would send them scurrying back to their bedroom.

If I were crueler, like my father's mistress, I would tell them three dozen clever, quiet words all while smelling of sweet lilac:

a meandering tale where little children who don't stay in their bedrooms the night before Nochebuena would have their presents taken away, then be eaten by the monstruos that roam the halls at night.

Of course, what the adults don't understand is that the twins are very different, that they process these words like food, that the tale that wounds Paloma's heart will poison Berta's liver, that in five years, you won't be able to recognize these girls if you stamp on their small joys.

Paloma is a wisp of a thing, so slight I sew heart-shaped stones into the hems of her dresses to keep her on earth. She hardly eats anything fit for humans, preferring shreds of paper, dust, and dew. And her pupils are like inky coins at night; she sees places I cannot believe exist, and I do not know who shows them to her, for she smiles and holds a finger to her lips whenever I ask.

Berta is solid and unyielding, like a bag of freshly milled grain. She smells of fresh earth because she always has evidence of life under her fingernails. She asks me for lemons, and she eats them, sliver by sliver, beneath her covers, her fingers and lips smelling of sunshine.

"Let's see what the ladies have to say this evening," I tell them, setting aside all sticky dreams of Sebastián and rising from my bed, though I've never once seen the hadas myself. It is barely three, and I haven't slept more than an hour. "Did you know some fairies are so small they can fit inside a thimble?"

My grandmother once told me that the more struggles we face in life, the more beloved we are by our ancestors. For the most beloved of us are given the most trials to face by their ghosts. But I want to be the beloved one because the twins must know more joy than pain, Diary.

Dear Diary,

Berta sees the carriage first on the morning of Nochebuena, our father's carriage barreling down the street like it's carrying messengers from hell. She races to find me, Mother, Delia, Paloma, and Alfredo, but of course, we are all watching it from the window—me, leaning out so far I might catch my death, just so I might glimpse Father's face, because . . . What if?

What if he's discovered the truth about Sebastián and me and has come to skin the soles off my feet and chain me to the Buenos Aires sewing table?

Mother watches the carriage with this terrified grin like she's been enjoying peace and quiet during this city banishment and has been caught. She snaps a finger at Delia, who knows to smooth the tablecloth and fetch the tray of sweets we always have on hand. Best not to be caught unawares when Father comes.

Pedro was the favorite, but Alfredo is the only boy left living, and even though he is bow-legged and flat of foot, he is the new favorite, so Mother licks her fingers and cleans his dirty face, and he is dispatched to greet Father at the door.

The treats are sweating on the porcelain plate on the table like overripe fruit when Alfredo returns with a very large crate in his arms, his cheeks flushed pink as a newborn rat.

Mother looks at him, and everyone in the room knows she is asking, *Where is he?*

"There is a note," Alfredo says, nodding his head at the lid of the crate, where a little white slip waves like surrender.

¿Un regalo?

¿Un regalo?

¿Un regalo?

¿Un regalo?

¿Un regalo?

This is what runs through the women's heads. Not because we love gifts but because Father does not know what gifts are. Father told us the house in Buenos Aires was a gift for us, the gift of living in a cosmopolitan city, but really, this was a gift for his mistress, the gift of all of us becoming nothing more than ghosts at our ranch.

Delia, the sweetest peach and the best at reading and keeping secrets, lifts the note from the crate with trembling fingers.

"Fragrant summer tomatoes from the garden for your Christmas feast," she reads aloud. Alfredo sets down the crate, and Mother, disbelieving, nods at him to open it.

I lean back, expecting a bomb but too afraid to admit it. We know such evil things as bombs exist in the world, and they would love nothing more than to exist inside this crate.

But inside lie six ripe tomatoes the size of a giant's fist, their juicy crimson striped with gold and royal purples—one tomato for each of us. The skin looks so tender it could burst, but not a one is marred by the journey—the only evidence of the kilometers they've traveled the glowing white dust upon them. I'll admit I breathe a sigh of relief at their mundane grotesquerie.

"Can we eat them?" Alfredo knows to ask.

We wait for the reply. Paloma has not once looked up from where she draws figures in the dust. Berta eyes the tomatoes hungrily, and I know she wants nothing more than to squeeze their flesh in between her fingers, to throw them at walls and paint with their guts, if she is allowed. Delia, the tender thing, turns to Mother and me with a smile that says Father is a changed man.

But people don't change unless they want to, and for Father, want is nothing but a small-hipped woman with a serpent's tongue and color-changing eyes, riding his lap.

"We will eat them in a Christmas sauce," Mother says, clasping her hands together, and I know Mother thinks she is full of grace by welcoming these tomatoes into our house and our bellies. And she *is* full of grace, and hope, and all sorts of delicious soulful things that devils would very much like to eat.

I will not eat the tomatoes.

Delia will try one and decide she does not like the taste (dirty water, unwashed flesh, a heady perfume). She will push it around her plate apologetically.

Paloma will nibble at the edges of the green food on her plate to please Mother and then wait as she always does to lick the savory dust from her cupboard later.

Berta will ask for her tomato to be set aside, for she has secret plans to throw it from the window in a parachute made from rags. The parachute will fail, and the tomato will explode, which is what Berta wanted all along.

Alfredo loves steak, and he will eat so much steak he will not know what to do with the tomato on his plate, which looks like a watery steak that God forgot to fill with fat, sinew, and bone.

Mother eats her tomato dutifully, in small, elegant bites, then eats each of our leftover tomatoes because to refuse a gift made out of kindness on Nochebuena is to spit in the face of all things good in the world.

After gifts are exchanged, and small cups of good wine are drunk, and cheeks are kissed, and heavenly lobes of pan dulce are savored, we wake to Mother's screams of agony and find her clutching her stomach, covered in vomit in bed.

Dear Diary,

Mother lives, though she resembles the ghost of Pedro more than her former self. She sits in bed all day, head dangling like an old flower, smiling with damp skin like a frog's when we approach, on tiptoes, fearful of interrupting her rest. When the city pollution coils through her open window, she coughs thick flecks of green phlegm into the threadbare handkerchief Father gave her when they were newlyweds, which—you'll remember, Diary— Berta once used to wipe her bottom.

Mother will not say a word of what happened. She will not admit there was a bomb in that crate—a bomb meant to destroy what remained of us so that our father's mistress could have the cleanest of slates with him. We dab her brow and feed her broth and whisper in her ear to convince him to let us all return, to convince him to let her recover in the country.

While I am bathing, Mother dictates a letter to Delia, who writes it in her finest hand—these painstaking loops that leave her fingers cramped—and sends Alfredo to post it. It is Berta who overhears its message, Berta who was rolling marbles down the hall and stooped outside Mother's room to dislodge one from a crack in the tiles.

Mother asks Father if she might recover in the country, that all of the children would do well to spend some time in their campo—that perhaps he could pass the time in the city, see a show, and visit the newly opened fine French restaurant in Recoleta. What is unwritten fills all the space between the lines: Father's friend will be charmed by this, surely, for she was charmed by the lilac-scented tissue-wrapped boxes of French lace underthings Father brought her.

This is like Mother: to offer the finest French soup in a porcelain tureen when someone deserves less than shit in a box.

But Diary, I burn for Sebastián every minute, and I hope my devil of a father takes what Mother dangles before him. Perhaps a return to the country would also mean a respite from Pedro's taunts: his nightly hauntings continue, for he is so callously undeterred by the havoc caused by Mother's illness. He might have warned us, the devil. And yet.

Alfredo returns with Father's reply a few days later. I would not have known of it were it not for the sniffling I heard coming from her room, for the smell of burnt paper.

I squeeze Delia like a grape, and she tells me what Father wrote. Wife, he has replied. Letizia sees no problem with you coming to the country to take the air for a few days.

We pack our dresses, our marbles, our books, our orthopedic shoes, our hadas, our fears and longings. I overhear Paloma telling Delia the hadas don't like the little house in the country, and Delia patiently reminds her we are more fortunate than most. Our home in the country is not little at all, but rather an estancia that a thousand wild horses could comfortably roam. I spit on the ground and wish those horses would ride from heaven and trample those who try to hurt us. The twins appreciate the bravado of my gesture.

Dear Diary,

My belly aches today as my eyes search every corner of the house, the yard, for a glimpse of Sebastián, but on our first day back, he is nowhere, and I hardly have a moment to myself to breathe.

Delia salvages Mother's old dresses, the ones we could not pack last time, to scavenge the fine fabrics, and she needs my help carrying them.

Paloma sets up a tea party in her closet for the hadas, and she asks if I will brew her a calming tilo.

Berta finds a hammer and wrench to break open the secret wooden compartment where she hid all of her treasures so they would be safe until her return, and she asks if I will make sure the coast is clear.

Alfredo plops himself in the kitchen and persuades the cook to assemble him a feast fit for kings and queens, and he asks me to pick out the best wine Father won't miss.

Mother, Mother is given the bedroom where our abuela died from a sweating sickness only a few years ago because from there, you cannot hear Father's evening reactions to his Francophile friend's French lace. But she looks brighter here; she takes the sun on the terrace, and it flushes her pink.

There is no time to think much about the seed in my belly, beating sharply like a ruined heart.

On the first day, Father and Letizia do not make themselves known, and another person might view that as a kindness. But like gifts, Father does not know what kindness is, and I know we remain but ghosts in the house, for her lilac stink is everywhere. Cheerful ghosts, more so than Pedro, but still.

Before dinner, I hear shouts in Father's hall, those same sloppy shouts that follow long afternoons kicking up his carpincho-skin boots on a wine barrel and tasting his new vintages. I worry the steel toes of those boots found one of my siblings, or worse, Mother.

I pace our hall, wearing down my own calf's-skin soles as I peek around the corner to Father's rooms. I see nothing for many long minutes. But then I glimpse the slender shadow of a man's back, and I dig my fingernails into the meat of my palms.

The man turns and winks at me.

It's only him, the donkey. My brother, Pedro, shimmering in the air. He must've hitched himself to our carriage, and now he is not content to sullenly taunt me. He does a jaunty little jig. The nerve of him. He had free rein of our world as my father's little prince when he was alive and even freer rein of it when he's dead.

I dare myself to float toward him. Toward Father's hall and the chamber where Mother once slept. Pedro's figure flickers with curiosity at my boldness.

Mother's old door is open. The room inside looks much the same, except her favorite mirror bears an unfamiliar crack. I creep closer, smelling smoke, and trip over myself when I notice *her* in the mirror's reflection: Letizia.

Hair mussed, face swollen, her French underthings riding up

her thighs. Limbs slack as a doll's. She holds a lit cigarette with a detachment that gives me pause.

She is so still until she brings the smoking butt to her lips and holds it there. I cannot stop myself from shuddering.

I expected to find a venomous snake. I see a faded picture of a lost woman instead, much like Mother on those days she didn't leave her room. I smell her lilac, as pungent as something dead.

I pinch my thighs through my skirts to remember my anger and back away to find my lurking brother. But it seems that Pedro, who so enjoys observing our sex, has melted into the walls.

When he visits me that night, he makes his pronouncement only once, shakes his sandy head, and disappears.

On our second day, Diary, Mother sends us to collect fourteen different kinds of flowers, knowing it will take us all day in the campo, exploring the land we grew up on and getting the color back in our cheeks. Making flower crowns with Delia, I lose sight of the twins and Alfredo, and for the first time in weeks, I do not worry. This land raised us. We drank the wine we made from crushing its grapes beneath our feet. We tended its gardens and ate its fruit. They are safe here.

And I must find Sebastián. I tie up my skirts, and I run past the quince trees, the apple blossoms, and the thorny bushes. I enter the first barn, the second, then the third, where the pigs often hide in corners, and I find him there, smelling of hay and something sweeter, wiping the sweat from his brow with the folded corner of his work shirt. He is shy and golden, a lamb in the body of an ox, and I would eat him whole if I could. Instead, I rush up to him and press myself into him hard and fast, and we tumble into the pile of hay behind him.

Our reunion is sublime; he is all tenderness and affection, as he always was, kissing my neck, my ears, my lips like they are the only ones on earth. He has never felt the hot, soft flesh beneath my dresses with his skin, but he has made me feel loose-limbed and tingly with the pressure of his fingers, with the sharp corners of his hips. I will say I keep sniffing at him because he smells different, somehow; saccharine sweet. But the work changes with the seasons. Maybe it is the smell of newborn pigs playing in the flowers.

"I may be carrying our child," I whisper to him when I can't bear it any longer. We will go to Uruguay to live among the exotic trees in the famed arboretum of the sands, or I will rid myself of what is in my belly. I will know from his reaction.

And Diary, he is but a man, so he tenses up and then softens into me, kissing my neck again. "You joke."

I push him off of me and look him straight in the eyes with the fire I reserve for moments like these.

"It can't be possible," he whispers to me, pleading almost, and I see the confusion in his eyes, but he is a country sort, despite the noble French blood his father brags about when drunk, and I love him for his sweetness.

Alas, I could not go to Uruguay with a lamb.

"Are you even a woman yet?" he asks. "You're, what—fourteen?"

I rise to my feet, affronted. "How *dare* you," I tell him, brushing the dirt flecks off my skirts. "Now. We must sort this out." For I have heard the maids speak of a woman who changes conditions, a woman who helps those in need, and I never have only one plan. I contain multitudes.

He agrees and tells me to meet him in the back garden after dark. His pulsing hands are wet and rough, too large for his body.

Dear Diary,

With those hands of his woven through mine, he tugs me forward, hard and fast like a horse pulling a carriage, and we tramp past the gardens, past the haystacks, and through the field of rich loam, stinking in the dark. We walk so far that my feet blister in my leather shoes, and I worry the sun is rising, but no, it is the eerie glow that permeates the terrain around the lagoon.

When I was young, I heard stories about this lagoon, about a magnificent wild horse that evaded capture by soldiers again and again until one day, they cornered it by a ravine. It leapt into the lagoon, dying to escape them one last time. They named our town Bragado after it.

We find the thatched-roof hut in the lagoon's swampland. It is filthy, but I follow Sebastián toward it, entranced by the flickering candle flame inside. He hesitates by the open doorway, but he does not knock. Diary, I shiver with the sense he has been here many times before.

A woman stands by the hearth in a heavy black gown in tatters. She is neither beautiful nor ugly. She has the kind of face you would forget immediately were it not found in such a strange locale. She eyes me and breaks into a smug grin, then grasps for a nearby jug of wine and takes a long pull.

"Can you help us?" Sebastián asks.

The woman nods at the table, and I blink at her until

Sebastián pulls a bottle of Father's finest wine from his satchel and sets it on the table. The woman burps and smiles wide, her teeth so clean and straight they do not seem real.

"What do you want?" she asks.

"We—"

"You," she continues, speaking over him.

With shaking hands in fists, I stand up straighter. "I want whatever is in my belly out." I don't mention how I ate fistfuls of my diary paper those weeks ago, how Mother was almost murdered by Father's tomatoes, how Pedro insults me nightly, how my belly throbs even more ever since we returned to this countryside, how I suspect all of this is connected.

She cocks her head at me again, then takes another slug of wine. I wonder if she has heard me, but then she turns and rummages through her many unkempt baskets of rotted foodstuffs. She tosses her things every which way, and I swear I spot a skein of precious French lace resembling the fineries Father gave Letizia. She plucks a wet-looking bundle out of a repurposed bassinet and holds it out to me.

I hesitate—not out of fear; out of suspicion—but before Sebastián can open his mouth, I reach.

But she withdraws. "You alone put them there by devouring your ardent love, but this will take them outside of yourself," she tells me, dangling it in the smoke-choked air. "Eat them after dark and bury what results."

I seize her bundle and stuff it in my pocket—they feel like grapes under my fingers, old sugared grapes—and leave with Sebastián. The trek back is shorter, for he is tender with me, kissing my fingers and assuring me this will work.

I settle into my bed, exhausted, but I am sure to down the soggy bundle, and it tastes of a chalky sweetness, of the sweating candies we used to leave out for Father but with the flavor of false grape. Soon, I am asleep, my cotton-stuffed limbs so blessedly far from this plane that I wouldn't hear Pedro if he could scream.

Oh Diary,

I wake from a dream of pain in more agony still, delirious, and dripping wet. I feel my cheeks and believe it can only be blood, but indeed it is sweat. Something has ruptured inside of me, and I scramble to the outhouse to rid myself of it, but my legs must be tired from the exertion in my nightmares, for I must drag myself stone by stone until I can't bear it anymore and a rush of foulness streams from between my legs, staining the stone and filling the air with a sweet stench.

I have killed myself, Diary, I have killed myself just as my mother was almost killed by the tomatoes, and my mind drifts into darkness until, until—

I wake to pale-faced Paloma fanning me with her fingers, to blood-stained Berta poking at the ground beneath me, around me, at these bloodred clotted, swampy masses, with her fingers. My blood. It is unlike any blood I have ever seen.

"Stop that," I manage to gasp. Berta holds her filthy hands out to me, red as old rotted berries, and I gag, heaving onto the floor, but nothing comes up.

"Look," she urges, and that's when I see, coated in ruby muck, these shiny seeds in her hands that are big as opals and full of moonglow. Five of them. I know without asking that she found them in my refuse. I know without thinking that that woman turned the seed in my belly into these.

"We must bury them," I tell the twins, and in their infinite wisdom—the wisdom of children whose minds haven't been chopped up and squeezed to fit into boxes—they understand and agree immediately.

Dear Diary,

In the morning, my skin is refreshed, and I feel purged of my heaviness, my weariness. My underclothes are stained with spots of watery amber, but the pain of last night is passing. In certain moments, I feel aglow with clarity, like a gauzy curtain before me has been pulled away, and I can understand the entire world's feelings. The entire world! Oh, Diary, the woman of the lagoon did as promised. Triumphant, I find Sebastián by the stables and inform him the deed is done and the cursed fruit is out of me.

He looks bemused as ever and smells of pig hay. Oh, he is a sweet simpleton.

"I buried them," I clarify, speaking as clearly as I can.

He looks at me as if last night never happened. "What is it that you buried?"

I sigh and grab him by the wrist, tugging him out to the back garden. I will show him the five lumps where the twins and I buried the seeds; I will dig one out if I must and show him their moonlike sheen.

But in the spots where I buried them, there are empty pits, as if someone dug the seeds out. The twins wouldn't dare, not after they saw me half-dead. An animal, foraging for its morning meal?

Sebastián crouches and touches the soil by the pits. Traces

of chalky residue lead away from them and deeper into the garden—fading snail trails. Before I can stop him, he tastes the chalkiness on his fingers, as Paloma might.

He scrunches up his face, as puzzled as ever.

"I swear I buried them," I whisper, and that is when I hear the screams.

Dear Diary,

Paloma writhes, her face pale as a dead pig's, the stench of death on her and her vomit-flecked bedclothes. Mother, only half recovered herself, cries as she tries to feed her spoonful after spoonful of tepid, fatty broth. Dripping rancid-smelling yellow stars all over, she prays that Paloma won't die from whatever afflicted her only days ago. Alfredo has been dispatched to the cook to ask about spoiled tomatoes. Delia holds a cold rag to our sister's head and startles every time Paloma screams. Berta sits on the floor beside the open maw of the closet, covering her face with dirty-knuckled hands.

I crawl on my hands and knees over to Berta and pull her into the dark closet, where the hadas flit.

"Tell me how she spent the morning," I beg her.

She looks at me with two glossy-black eyes and brings a filthy finger to her mouth to silence me.

"Fine. Ask the hadas alone, and I will return," I reply, leaving her there in the damp dark.

I return to Paloma's bedside and examine the insides of her eyes, her ears, her mouth. Her tongue is coated in white residue. I smell her, sniffing the back of her throat as best I can, and I curse under my breath. She reeks, of course, of the chalky moonglow.

I close myself into the closet with Berta anew, where a little voice inside of her whispers that Paloma likes to lick the sweet garden wall. So I pull Berta out there, back to where we buried the pits, back to that ghostly trail of filmy eggwash white leading to the very back of the garden.

Diary, the back wall is pocked with hives of powdery ivory, moonlit from within. It is a glorious, infernal monument made by . . . *them*. Could they be like the hadas or a wicked, ambitious cousin?

Berta stands there, gaping. This is as familiar and incomprehensible to her as it is to me, born from my womb as it is.

"We must destroy this," I whisper to her. "Mustn't we?"

She shrugs, trembling, and I send her to Mother to alert them all while I look for a hammer—for anything we can use to crush the home they've made for themselves overnight. This property is no place for them, no. Imagine if my father were to see them, so fresh and new like little buds made of snow? But there is no hammer anywhere in the house, so I run on to the barns, to Sebastián's collection of shears and tools and—

I stop, some meters away, for my father, that hulking mountain of a man, has crossed my path at last. He holds a scrap of shiny lace in hand and shouts at someone inside the barn—no, he's terrorizing two cowering someones, the brute.

Mother walks up behind me, cheeks tear-washed, breathing in short sips because she can sense, at a distance, my father's rage. She settles her hands on my shoulders, and they feel like birds' wings.

My father takes no notice of us as he takes the scruff of Sebastián's neck in hand and pries open his jaw with the other, stuffing the lace inside his mouth until it looks like his eyes may pop from his skull.

Understanding comes down on me like cold rain, and I feel the early shivers of something righteous and uncontainable inside me.

Sebastián makes a choking sound and pitches forward, scrabbling to free his mouth of lace, and only then do I see it. The lace is covered in moonglow, too—have *they* not left anything untouched in this house?

Her voice cuts through my thoughts—Letizia, who speaks through sobs. At first, I think she is saying more clever, quiet words.

"It's the little ones," she says, supplicating at Father's feet. "It's always them, up to some mischief. Take pity on me. Take pity." And she glances behind him. At first, I think she watches me, but her eyes lock on their monument. The beast of my father swings around to look, his red eyes snagging on us.

"Do not dare touch my children," Mother cries, her arms pulling me to her chest, and Letizia's face looks saintly in its confusion and horror. She reaches out a hand as if to stop my father from barreling toward me, but from the corner of my eye, all I see is my father's arm rearing up, this ungainly meat hook. I feel my mother's heartbeat against my spine before el brillo de la luna overpowers us all—this *wave* from an ocean whose feminine power I've only felt and never before seen. *Them*, sweet Diary. My children.

Dear Diary, forgive me for not writing.

It is like Pedro said, I am a mother now. My peculiar children wake when I am sleeping, and I do not get a minute's rest. They like me tired, complacent, and if I turn my back for a second, they'll decide to make mischief, to lure another around us to danger, so that it will be just me and them, me and them, me and them forever in their moonglow.

You'll be surprised to know, Diary, that Letizia has become close to Mother, me, and the girls. She stayed on, though Father hardly knows her after his infarto, and it has been left to us women and children to care for him—so soft now—and them both.

Sebastián has gone, bones and flesh melted into the air like fragrant smoke. The bolder sex, indeed! At first, I fizzled with rage, but his loss pains me less each day. I know more now: I know these children were born from me alone—well, from me and my diary.

You see, Letizia tells me she, too, had a diary full of lumbre once. She tells me in her clever, quiet words how best to care for my children, for she has learned how to tend to her own after many a visit to the woman of the lagoon. She assures me that we are the beloved ones, given more trials to face by the ghosts of our family. And Diary, I must insist upon believing her.

My children are calling for me now. The children will never stop calling, but I know how to handle them, and now, well, Diary, I really must go—

How bittersweet it is to live in their moonglow.

THE END

KILLING EL CHIVO

by

Claribel A. Ortega

I was standing on a bright grassy knoll beside my family's house, sunshine warm on my back, when the first bomb from my magic hit just a few yards away. It shook the earth around me, sent chickens and rabbits scurrying up into the surrounding mountains. The ground split beneath my bare feet, and I looked down just as the light extinguished from my hands.

"Good, but could be better."

My older sister Yesenia circled me, her eyes like a halcón as she inspected my hands. They were dirty with soil and bruised from the use of my powers. Every time I invoked it, pain prickled over my skin, and continued use had discolored my hands and arms purple and blue.

"Next time, pull from your stomach." My sister placed one hand on my abdomen. "And think of something that angers you."

That would be easy. "El Chivo." I clenched my teeth, and light began to bloom inside my palms once more.

"No, Zaria." Yesenia folded my hands over gently. "Not him. You know it can't be him."

She was right, of course. Of all the people on this island who inspired anger in my heart, El *so-called* Jefe, the purported leader of our island, was the worst. I looked back at our house, the wind winding through the valleys and ruffling my long brown hair. It was more like a hut, with a metal roof and a dirt floor and concrete walls, but once, it had been home. Once, it had been filled with laughter, and the smell of habichuelas con dulce, and the soft thump of my parents' feet on dirt as they twirled and spun to merengue music. I was often tempted to ask Yesenia to silence those old memories with a hex I knew not many but her were capable of. To take away the painful reminder of what was. Now there was only silence, hushed discussions on devious plans, and occasionally, a scream of pain as my magic manifested in me unbidden.

The last time I had tried to conjure my powers by invoking his name, I'd nearly blown up our house and everyone in it, then been sick for weeks—my bones breaking, stretching, coming back into place. I had almost died. At first, we believed it to be the work of a bruja, a hex or mal de ojo, but we had ruled that out with the use of Remedios and our sole tía who knew about our powers and shared in them.

"Not a curse," she had said, standing over an enormous metal pot that most people used for making asopao but that our tía used for divination. "This is something to do with your own powers, I think. Do not use his name again. It is not safe."

Some nights, my magic still exploded, and my bones ached almost every morning. As if I were becoming something else.

And so I hadn't thought of El Chivo since, not on purpose. But when I thought of hate, I thought of him. When I thought of the darkest night when my parents were taken from their beds, when the wails of my two sisters should have been enough to wake the village but didn't because fear kept them tucked in their beds— I thought of him. But I wasn't convinced that this hate was the cause of my intensified powers or my bones breaking, or my near visit with death. My aunt had seemed worried and distracted, in a rush to get out of our house. She had packed her caldero, her wooden spoons, herbs, rats, and poisons and had barely kissed us on the cheek before riding her donkey into the mountains in the dead of night. It was like she was fleeing from us, and she hadn't been back since. This made me think there was something evil about my magic, and I did not particularly care if there was. So long as I could use it to kill him. The only thing we knew for certain was that my power was untamed and that we only had a few days until he rode through our village. It would be our only chance to stop El Chivo once and for all.

Our youngest sister, Milagros, waved at me from our doorway. She had fashioned a helmet out of a pot and old ribbons, in case my magic came too close. It had made me laugh the first time I saw it because nothing I did could hurt Milagros. She was the diffuser to my bomb, as strong as any blast I could dish out. I was glad that our mission was to kill El Chivo and not someone like her. The moment we had taken the chance and told the other rebels what we could do, we knew that it would be what they asked of us. In fact, we very much hoped they would. We had been lucky that they did not try to burn us alive or drown us in a river as is customary whenever there is an accusation of witchcraft. It was bad enough we had to look over our shoulders for El Jefe's men because we were rebels, but we also had to be wary of every neighbor or wandering eye because we were witches.

"Again," Yesenia instructed. She took an old coffee tin from the pile we kept stacked in our yard and set it on the spikes of the fence around our property.

I let the magic pool in my stomach fill slowly this time, imagining a pond of golden light in my belly. It filled and filled and rose until it was a lake, one with lapping waves and fish. When the waves felt strong enough to turn over a small boat, I unleashed it onto the target.

Light filled my eyes and mouth as I anchored my bare feet to the ground. I felt the hot soil, then dug my toes in and felt the cool beneath. The sensation calmed me, helped even out my magic. The light erupted from my hands and mouth as I shot out toward the coffee tin and heard the sharp, melodic chime of my magic destroying my mark. When I was sure it had been destroyed, that I had pushed my magic as far as it could go without also blowing up the mountain, I closed my mouth, eyes, and palms, extinguishing the golden light pouring from them. My eyes fluttered open, and Yesenia stood before me, holding the blackened remnants of the tin up, a giant smile on her lovely brown face.

Milagros whooped from the doorway, and I collapsed to the ground, sitting for the first time in hours. My magic was like energy made up of all the things around me, but mostly it fed on my own emotions. When I let the energy fill up inside me, I could release it through a burst of power—the stronger the feeling, the stronger the magic. The light I unleashed from my hands, mouth, and eyes was not like fire or anything that potent. Only the most powerful witches could wield something as pure as fire. Instead, my magic was like a spark that reacted with my emotions creating an explosion.

"I'm thirsty," I said as a pitcher of ice-cold water hovered beside me, drifting in from the house like a buoy in the ocean. Yesenia waved her wrist in elegant loops as if weaving a costly blanket and a metal cup came floating in from the house, settling beside the pitcher for me to drink with.

"Thank you," I said as I poured the river water and the metal cup became cold. I drank greedily.

"I could have done that, you know," Milagros said as she sat beside me.

"I need to practice as much as I can. We must all do our part." Yesenia sat and completed our small circle in the grass.

We had been planning and practicing for almost a year now, mostly at night if we were sure there would be no sound, or during church or festivals when we were sure it would be too loud to hear my explosions. On Sunday mornings, when the village was busy at church, their hymns drowning out any noise from our mountain, we used the noisier tin cans to let Milagros rest. On days when we must not make noise, my younger sister was used as a mark. Her thick metal-like skin absorbed any noise we might make, but the sight of me setting her alight was not pleasant. She looked charred and mutilated after each practice, but in the blink of an eye, she dusted the dirt off, her joints popping back into place. We were not certain if Milagros regrew her wounded skin, if the impact simply did not affect her, or if she somehow absorbed it, but one thing was certain: of the three of us, she was the most frightening.

Our plan was simple enough in theory, but the execution would be much more complicated. El Chivo would ride into our village in a few days, a cavalcade of cars and horses surrounding him. The village would always be forced to stand on the sides like they were watching a parade and not the march of hangmen. It would be impossible to get him from the sidelines. One of our neighbors, out of loyalty or fear, would stop us or attempt to. We could only attack from one place without being killed and killing innocent people in turn: above. Since none of us could fly, we devised a plan for Yesenia to use her telekinetic magic on me as I sat atop the highest tree near our point of attack. It was dangerous, but you cannot shy away from danger when it comes knocking on your door. You must confront it.

Yesenia had practiced on Milagros first. At fourteen, she had not reached her full height and was slimmer than I was. After three months, she was finally able to get her level with the trees. After six, she was sending her so high above us we could barely see her. She had fallen a few times, but that was not an issue for her. I did not possess the same gifts.

Our practice had gotten off to a horrible beginning. We'd spread as many burlap sacks of grass as we could find or steal on our yard, with only a prayer to keep me from falling anywhere outside our perimeter. I had fallen and become unconscious on our first try—sprained an ankle, broken an arm, and a leg on others. Eventually, though, Yesenia had been able to hone her magic enough to carry me up and over our home for five minutes at a time. Five minutes was all we had. Five minutes to fly up and over a crowd of innocents and would-be traitors. Five minutes to hover above the man who had killed our parents, who had plunged our island into darkness and fear. Five minutes to kill El Chivo.

We knew he would stop at the statue he had erected in his honor to stare at himself and give the people a chance to clap for him and bask in his nonexistent glory. That was our moment. Once I was above him, in position, I would send the most powerful wave of magic I could muster directly onto him. It would take a lot out of me, possibly kill me if the fall didn't, but my only concern was for the horse he rode upon. Milagros's task was to absorb as much of the crossfire of my magic as she could and to keep the rest of our village safe. My two sisters would possibly get away unscathed, but I would not. Someone would see me. Even if I succeeded, there are those who would remain loyal to El Chivo. I told my sisters that no matter the outcome, after our strike, they should flee.

"We will wait for you," Yesenia had insisted.

"And get us all caught and killed? No. We did this for Mami and Papi and our people. You two at least should survive to see the fruits of it," I had responded. "Besides, who will make sure my legend is told the way I want if you two also get taken?" A sly smile had spread across my face, and Yesenia had shaken her head in exasperation.

It was the way I dealt with most things these days. I made jokes, or brushed them off, or faked bravado that deep down I did not feel. But I felt it was the very least I could do. Yesenia worried enough for the three of us, Milagros was the youngest, so it was my job to try to lighten the heavy load we had been given to carry. But if either of my sisters could see how I felt, if they could somehow read the thoughts I kept buried just beneath the surface, they would know I was terrified. I did not want to lose my sisters. To lose them was to lose my own life, and I did not want that either. I wanted, despite everything we had been through so early on, to *really* live without fear or unending grief. I wanted to live. And this was our chance.

"We also need to try again if we fail to kill him," Milagros had said. The youngest but ever the most practical.

"That too, I suppose," I had said.

I awoke that night to a shadow in the doorway of our house. Our home was one room, with three hay-and-wood beds lined up against the far wall, a small clay oven on the other end with pots and pans hanging from a wooden rack my father had made. Beside the stove hung a portrait of El Jefe. His white and brown fur seemed to move in the wind sometimes, his inhuman snout sneering down at us, his beady black eyes fixed in a stare to never, ever give us a moment's rest. This was a requirement of all households—that you put up a picture of him in the center of your living room so that everyone could see it. Not having this was enough for one of his men to come and take you in the night to the jail, La 40, where they would torture you before they killed you. Some say the portrait, much like El Chivo himself, had a hold on people—an enchantment. But it would not work on us. It disgusted me to have his picture here, the person who was responsible for our parents' death, but it was necessary. When you are fighting a war, it is impossible to fight every battle and make it out whole. Instead, you choose carefully. Besides, inside of the frame was another picture, also of El Chivo but turned upside down, his eyes blacked out with the slash of a small knife—a perpetual hex upon him.

Moonlight spilled into the room and lit up El Chivo's portrait, making his horns gleam in the night. Milagros snored softly beside me as I sat up, rubbing my eyes. The mosquitero's netting around my bed broke my sister into tiny pieces. With the light of the moon in my sleep-tinged vision, it was like seeing her through a kaleidoscope.

"Yesenia?" I asked, my voice hoarse.

"Shh, go back to bed," my older sister whispered from the doorway. She was wrapped in her heavy shawl, the one we shared for nighttime excursions.

"What are you doing?" I asked.

"Chula got out of her pen. I'm just putting her back."

"Again?" I asked.

Chula was our pig. We were meant to kill her for spoils, but after we'd gotten her, we couldn't bring ourselves to do it. Instead, she became one more mouth to feed, and she was forever escaping to the Fernandez family's farm downriver. I couldn't blame her. Their farm had more food than our conuco could manage to produce for her, and she had taken a liking to their oranges. This was the fourth time in the past few weeks she'd escaped in the middle of the night, and Yesenia was always the one to get her. Older sister duties, she said.

"Do you want help?" I asked.

"No, go back to sleep." As Yesenia moved, her shadow was long and crooked as if there were two large humps on either side of her. Almost like wings. If I did not know it was her, I might have been frightened. I drifted back to sleep as my sister slipped from our doorway and into the night.

A rooster crowed three times and woke me the next morning. I sat up, my body still sore from our practice. Milagros and Yesenia were already outside.

It was my turn to get coffee and oranges from our neighbors so Chula would stop escaping and visit the pulpero to buy meat for our dinner. I would also bring the leaflets Milagros had been hard at work on, using the notebook paper meant for a school she could no longer afford to attend.

¡QUE VIVA QUISQUEYA! it read in bright red letters. Quisqueya meant mother of all lands in the native tongue, Taino, of our people. A language we only held onto by bits and pieces now. The rest of the pamphlet spoke of revolution, freedom, resistance, and in coded language below, of our next meeting place. I stuffed the pamphlets into the waistband of my skirt, grabbed a basket from the entrance, and made my way down the road to the center of our village.

A boy held a basket of warm, yellow bread on his head, and my mouth watered, thinking of spreading butter on them fresh from the oven. Men I did not recognize rode in on motorcycles from other towns to visit family or their mistresses, I imagined. People bartered food for work and bought sugar and alcohol with pennies from small bags. There were those with more money than us who came into our village sometimes, those who had heard through a web of whispers and secrets that there was something happening here.

I reached our neighbors' land. They had a cafetal where my sisters and I helped gather coffee in exchange for more coffee and oranges and sometimes plantains. Mr. Fernandez was on the edge of the farm, repairing a fence. Probably because of Chula, I thought, and my face became hot with shame.

"Zaria." Mr. Fernandez smiled as he saw me approach.

"Hola, Don Fernandez. Sorry about Chula," I said. A sharp smell stung my nose then, and I tried not to let it show in case

Don Fernandez thought me rude. But it was awful and familiar. It was the smell of blood.

"Oh, this wasn't her," he said. "I don't think she could have broken the fence this way. I think it was some sort of dog or something . . ." He looked beyond the fence at something I had not noticed. Lying between two rows of coffee plants was an animal. Its body had been split in two, seared on each end. It looked almost like . . . an explosion had hit it. I tried not to think of that or let the guilt show on my face. Even if I knew it was not my doing, the fear of being discovered built in my stomach. It was not enough to be part of a clandestine group trying to stop El Chivo. To be a witch as well was unforgivable.

"What animal can do that?" I asked, desperate to think of anything but my power.

"No sé," Mr. Fernandez said. He made the sign of the cross, thinking what I had been thinking. No dog, no animal, could do this. This was the work of something sinister. I flinched again, and fear gripped my heart. The sight of the mangled creature made me incredibly uneasy but felt just as familiar.

"You're here for your payment, yes?" Mr. Fernandez asked. He wiped his hands on his jeans and stood up.

I nodded.

"Of course. I have it ready for you." He took a bag filled with coffee beans he'd taken from the ripe, red coffee cherries we'd helped gather and about ten oranges and placed them in my basket.

"Gracias," I said and took off toward the store before he could say anything else, desperate to get away from the smell of blood. I would ask Yesenia about the animal. Maybe she knew what happened.

The pulpería was not so much a shop as a small stand, big enough for one person to stand and work, handing out products to patrons waiting in line in a dusty clearing. When I reached the store, there was a small line of people waiting and even more milling around talking. That could only mean there was gossip to be heard.

"Did you see the animal at the cafetal?" one older man with liver spots on his hands asked.

"Brujería," said a younger woman, mirroring the sign of the cross Don Fernandez had made. She looked up to the sky as if asking for help. She looked like a statue of La Virgen María. Around her wrist was a red cloth. Other villagers sported similar protections on their wrists or ankles. It was meant to keep witches away. I held back a smile at how horribly they were currently failing at that task.

"There has been a witch walking through the corn at night," the old man said.

"Yes, she walks on our roofs at night," another person waiting in line interjected.

"A witchbird," whispered the old man in response.

"I heard it. I heard it cawing as it flew," someone said.

I nearly snorted. Witchbirds were only a story. An old island legend of a powerful witch that can transform into a giant, deadly bird. Witchbirds sucked the blood from your toes or navel, the stories said. They kept their skin in a tincture when they transformed. Witchbirds slept beneath the platano trees and hid in the shadows. They were reviled and feared but how silly of my neighbors to fear something from a storybook when I was right beside them.

"The trickiest of devils. We must all be careful and not let them tempt us with their *gifts*," the younger woman said. "They always come at a price."

As if on cue, the gossiping villagers all did the sign of the cross at once. The story of the witchbird goes that if she does not wish to kill you, which is unlikely, she has the power to give you a gift—the gift of becoming a witchbird. The price they imagined was clear: their souls.

The storekeeper, Don Hermes, shook his head and smoothed his enormous bushy mustache. He often shared complaints of his patrons with me, always in private, of course.

"They gossip about things they have made up but ignore the real dangers right in front of their faces. There are people being snatched from their beds at night, and they only speak of witches," he'd say, his face red with anger.

Don Hermes was a good man, an honest one, but I knew even he would be afraid of me if he knew what I truly was. If he knew I could blow up everyone in our village in the time it took to fry a circle of salchichon, would he still look at me with kind eyes or look up to the sky for mercy instead? I knew that despite his anger at our neighbors, that he feared the stories about witches too. Everyone did because they knew they were true. The vision of Yesenia hovering in our door the night before came to me unbidden, and fear riddled my heart. Before that moment, I had not thought much of waking to find her in the doorway every night. But what if the witch my neighbors spoke of was her? What if somehow she had done . . . whatever had been done to that animal? I shook my head to rid myself of those thoughts, but now that I'd let them take root, they would not go away. By the time I'd reached the front of the line, the rest of the customers had gone home, which was a lucky thing. I got the package of meat, wrapped in brown paper and string, and placed it in the basket beside the coffee and oranges, then walked behind el pulpero. I glanced around, and there did not seem to be anyone nearby. Knocking twice, softly, I waited until the shopkeep opened a tiny window at eye level.

"¿Viste la mariposa?" he asked softly.

"No, pero vi la bomba," I responded.

The exchange was how the shopkeeper knew we were who we said we were, which was important when magic can change your face. When he asked if we'd seen the butterfly, we responded with no and our code name. I blew things up with my power, so I was La Bomba. Don Hermes thought we dealt in homemade explosives—that we were clever with building bombs and not magic. The leaders of our rebellion, another group of sisters as luck would have it, thought it best we kept our powers a secret from the others to prevent them from being afraid and turning on us.

He opened the door, and I slipped the stack of flyers to him as deftly as I could manage. He took them and placed them beneath an overturned wooden box. The entire exchange happened in less than a minute, and my heart raced with terror the entire time.

"Mañana llega El Chivo," he whispered so softly I almost did not hear him.

I nodded curtly, afraid to make eye contact for fear that my happiness would betray me and I would cry out. El Chivo knew, deep down, that he was hated. No matter how much he insisted otherwise. And that meant he kept his schedule purposefully erratic and hard to find. But finally, we had a firm date. Tomorrow!

After all these months of planning and practice, he would be here tomorrow.

We also need to try again if we fail to kill him. My youngest sister's words haunted me. There was always the possibility of failure. I did not want to think of what would happen if we failed to kill El Chivo but were caught instead—if all of the people who trusted us failed in turn. We could not let that happen, and I would give my own life before it did.

I parted ways with Don Hermes and ran home to tell my sisters. We would need our rest tonight. Tomorrow, we would kill El Chivo.

That night I dreamt of a witchbird. She crept to the foot of my bed just as a cloud passed over the moon. With one mud-crusted hand, she lifted the blanket from my body and touched the soles of my feet. Pain, cruel and hot, shot through my body at her touch, and in the dream, she began to tell me a story. Witchbirds suck the blood from your toes, she sang. With that blood, they take your life force, and then you shrivel into an aged and dying version of yourself. They steal your life to fuel their own, to fuel their power. In my dreams, the witchbird's teeth were sharper than the knives we used to cut meat into strips for cooking. She smiled at me, crouched at the foot of my bed, her mouth covered in my blood, her eyes completely white. I awoke with a start, drenched in sweat and terrified from my dream. The moon illuminated our home in slivers of white. Against the doorway stood a shadow, long and still. I put my hands up instinctively, then looked to my left— Milagros was in her bed asleep. To my right, there was nobody. Yesenia had gone again.

"Yesenia?" I whispered at the shadow, but this time it did not respond. Fear rose to my throat, but I did not move. I did not even move the netting around my bed. I just sat there, hands up and prepared to attack. I did not strike.

"No soy Yesenia," the voice warbled, low and sweet like a lullaby sung by a crow.

I pulled the netting aside now, ready to drive this thing from my house. One foot touched the soft ground, and the other landed in a pot of something cold and slippery. I pulled my foot back reflexively, looked down, and disgust overtook me. There, in a metal basin filled with what looked like one of Yesenia's tinctures, floated strips of flesh. I leaned closer, struggling to see in the dark. It was not just any flesh, I realized, seeing the pattern of beauty marks in the shape of the moon. My beauty marks.

I jumped from the bed, fear propelling me up and over the basin of my . . . my *skin*, my heart thundering, my chest tight with anxiety.

Then I heard my sister's voice.

"Where are you going in such a hurry?" Yesenia asked.

A bright light pushed me back, and I shielded my eyes.

My sister was by the stove, brewing coffee. The sun was just rising beyond the mountains on the horizon. It was morning.

"I . . . thought I saw . . ." I looked at the doorway, where the shadow had been. Then back at the foot of the bed where the grotesque basin had sat. But there was nothing there. It had all felt so real, but I guess it was all a dream. But why was I dreaming of witchbirds?

A witch's dreams could sometimes be warnings, and dreams of witchbirds were an omen of death. I was probably just nervous about our mission. That must be it.

"You should get a few more hours of sleep. You will need it," Yesenia said, turning back to the coffee.

I just nodded and slipped into Milagros's netting. She was asleep still, and I envied her ability to rest through anything. I lay beside my youngest sister, my heart still racing, and somehow I dozed off.

By the time Yesenia woke us, the sun was high in the sky. We dressed and ate a small breakfast in silence. The tension in the air rippled like waves of heat on a scorching hot day. The three of us were nervous, tapping our feet, winding our thumbs, and throwing excited and fearful glances at one another. My stomach ached the entire morning, and soon it was time to make our way into the village for El Chivo's procession. The last one he would ever have.

We reached our spots—me atop the tallest palm tree I could climb, Milagros on the ground beside the tree, Yesenia on the other side of the road, parallel to us. She was wrapped in an enormous shawl so that her hands would be covered. When El Chivo was in position, Yesenia would send me up higher and over El Chivo directly so that I would not miss, so that as few people would get caught in the crossfire as possible. We had experimented with me shooting him from atop the tree, but the impact from my power was enough to split the tree in half or send me flying in the opposite direction. The best way was this. We had arrived before anyone else so that nobody would see me atop the tree. It would still be three hours until he rode through. Yesenia and Milagros hugged me tightly, and I bit back tears, not knowing if this would be the final time I embraced my sisters.

"You remember the plan?" Yesenia asked, her voice shaky with nerves.

"Of course," I said. The calm of my voice surprised me. It did not betray the fierce fear in my heart, how my body seemed to vibrate with anxiety.

Milagros squeezed my hand, her palms sweaty, and gave me a small smile. "It will all be okay," she said. I nodded, returning her smile but unable to lie and say yes. I did not know if it would all be okay. It had not been okay in so long. I had almost forgotten that was a possibility.

When I was safely in place in the palm tree, Yesenia and Milagros went home, glancing back at me until they went over a knoll and disappeared.

The sun rose higher and higher in the sky, and my dress stuck to my back as I waited. Finally, the villagers trickled in, then filled both sides of the road like ants. I watched as my sisters arrived and got into place. My heart beat wildly with anticipation. And then, he was on the horizon. El Chivo's horse was infamously a bright blue the color of the sky. The moment I spotted it, my stomach lurched. I looked all around us, at the people from our village. They were smiling. Their mouths spread wide and tight like invisible hands were stretching back their skin. They wore their best clothes, the ones reserved for church on Sundays, that wealthy people from the city would have their servants use as rags for cleaning. Among the crowd of farmers stood Don Hermes, his smile as bright and wide as the others, but a fire behind his eyes I hoped nobody else could see. A few feet from him stood my sister. She gripped a small flag in her hands, and unlike those standing around her, her smile looked genuine. My sister waved the flag of our island and cheered alongside our neighbors, and her voice was a battle cry. In her cry was the suffering we'd endured. Losing our parents, going hungry, watching our friends and neighbors disappear, or leave us behind. I felt the suffering of our lives in every echo of her voice, and it pummeled my heart with pain. Today, the suffering ends.

The sound of hooves clopping down the rock-filled dirt road came closer and closer. Animals grunted under the weight of the soldiers they carried, and the cheers of people further up the road filled the air. A cloud of dust approached us, and I knew El Chivo's party was only a few feet away now. The smell of his freshly washed fur wafted into the crowd and mixed with the smell of coffee beans and fresh soil. The villagers closed their eyes and breathed in, ecstasy washing over their faces. Moments later, their eyes opened and looked at him atop his horse, and their looks turned to disgust. El Chivo's magic was like that. It enthralled people. It forced their eyes on him only to be betrayed by the reality of his cruelty. The villagers quickly corrected their expressions and cheered loudly. Their voices sounding more like pained screams than celebratory acclamations. He was inches away from the spot we'd decided on now, and from my perch in the tree, I looked at Yesenia. She nodded, and her hands shifted beneath her shawl. Thankfully, we did not have to worry about our neighbors seeing us. The crowd on the ground stared at El Chivo adoringly, his magic fooling their senses and their hearts. Many of them had lost family to this monster, yet he demanded allegiance through his magic. We did not know exactly how he maintained this hold over them, but our best guess had been a sort of pheromone emitted from his fur. It explained why a burst of wind would make it more potent, as we'd learned from other rebels. It kept them enthralled and helpless because they did not have magic of their own to combat it with. But *we* did.

El Chivo stopped at the enormous statue in his likeness, just as we knew he would, to soak in the adoration of the crowd. He took in the cheers hungrily, just as Yesenia made her move. But I did not budge. She tried again, and nothing happened. Panic grew in my belly. If she was not able to lift me soon, we would lose our chance. Just as El Chivo's horse began to move on, Yesenia risked taking one hand from her shawl and hurling her magic my way.

"No," I whispered, too late.

As the magic passed over him, El Chivo sensed it. She had aimed wrong. He whipped around toward my sister. His mouth opened hideously like a cavern. I jumped down from the tree, not worried about breaking bones or being discovered, just as El Chivo sent a stream of fire directly at Yesenia. The flames engulfed her, crackling horribly as the crowd around her maintained their smiles, their eyes on El Chivo.

"YESENIA!" A scream ripped through me, and my voice was not my own. It was high pitched and melodic like . . . like a bird song. I did not want to hear anything beautiful, not now, not ever again. Not while my sister's body lay charred on the ground, smoke coming from her chest, the crowd dissipating while El Chivo stared down at her from atop his horse. Milagros held me in place, her strength too much for me to match.

"Zaria, no. She's gone. There is nothing we can do. We must run," she tried.

I heard her, but her words bounced off me like ricocheting bullets. I refused to hear that Yesenia was gone and that El Chivo was still here. Anger and grief ripped through me, my entire body shaking with the force of it. I did not know if I could handle the pain and felt moments from collapsing. Milagros released her grip on my shoulders and instead took my hand. She was steady, her hands not even betraying a small tremble, but her eyes told a different story as they bore into mine. I could see there all that had been taken from us: the childhood, the love, the lives. El Chivo kept taking, taking, taking, and I could not see an end to it unless I made that ending myself.

We were still behind the enormous tree, its trunk concealing us from El Chivo and his men who were still lingering. I did not think they had seen us, or they would've already descended on us. Yesenia's magic seemed to be aimed at El Chivo and not at someone else, but still, we had to be cautious. People stared at us, whispering as they passed. They were happy not to be us. They were judging us for whatever it was that caused El Chivo to attack Yesenia. Because it surely could not be his fault. Not even in their private thoughts were they brave enough to accept a plain truth.

"Qué lástima," they said as if we had shattered a vase and not just lost our sister. Members of our rebellion pulled their hats down and pretended they did not see us.

"Cowards," I said. My voice shook with rage.

"Zaria, please, maybe if they leave her body, we can take her to tía." It was the first thing that made me snap out of my anger. Our tía was a powerful witch, one that could, if we did not wait too long, bring Yesenia back. It was close to impossible, but there was still some hope.

So we waited in silence, so still, not even the breeze could rustle our hair. El Chivo was still staring at Yesenia's body, relishing his work, then finally he looked up and signaled to his men. They began to ride away. My body tensed in anticipation, our next moves—Milagros picking her up, me making a veil of dust and dirt with tiny explosions if necessary—taking Yesenia, her body, home. I took a step out from behind the tree, Milagros holding tight to my skirts.

Just as his blue horse was about to disappear over a hill, El Chivo stopped. We scrambled back behind the tree as he turned around and came back to the body.

Please, please, please, I begged in silence, not to this monster, but to any god that would still listen to a witch. And then his horse trampled over Yesenia. This time, Milagros screamed, and before I could react, she ran into a slide—dirt and dust making a halo around her. She as beneath El Chivo's horse now, protecting Yesenia, and his face was one of shock and horror as he brought the beast's hooves down on my Milagros's back, but she did not break.

"¡Diabla!" he screamed in a horrible bleating voice. His horse at least was a frightened at the sound and took a few hesitant steps back. El Chivo urged his horse forward, but he did not listen. The poor animal was frightened, as was everyone else around them. El Chivo's men were cowering at the top of the hill, afraid of Milagros or their boss or both.

Only a few feet away, El Chivo dismounted, his own hooves crashing into the ground and cracking the dirt as if it were concrete. Turning his anger at his still unmoving horse, he placed one hairy, gnarled hand on the horse's chest, and the poor beast withered—turned to skin and bones before us, and then collapsed to the ground. He was not dead. El Chivo was not that merciful. The horse would suffer a long, languorous death from whatever curse he had been inflicted with. Just one touch was all it took. If El Chivo fought my sister himself, he would kill her. And then he would have killed everyone I love. Milagros chanced one sad glance at Yesenia then bounded at El Chivo. It had felt like an eternity behind this tree, but in reality, it had only been a minute, maybe two. I prepared to shoot my magic at him, the way we'd practiced. It would not hurt Milagros, but it would kill him.

As I ran out from behind the tree, my hands up, my skirts flying in the wind behind me, El Chivo swiped at Milagros, quicker than a serpent, and a stream of blood erupted from her face and neck.

"No!"

I was alight with rage, but as I unleashed my magic, no explosions came—no burst of fire. Instead, my bones began to break. I could feel each one crack, split, then rip off my skin as blood soaked my clothing. It was a pain like I have never known, pain that was so searing and hot it felt like the death of my parents one hundred times over. I blinked, and blood dripped from my eyes, and they began to roll as if in slow motion to the back of my head. Before they did, I saw a hand twitch. Yesenia. I saw her fingers weave lightly through the air in my direction before my body lifted into the air and a final burst of pain set my body alight. Then I was in the air. I did not recognize the sensation of floating I'd come to recognize from our many practices. This was different. This time I was truly flying.

El Chivo's men were screaming, running. Milagros was alive, scampering away. Yesenia's body was still, but the hope of her being alive propelled me forward. I turned my head, and through new eyes, I could see enormous wings on either side of me. Black feathers, glossy and tipped with bright blue span—large like a thing I had only seen in my nightmares. I was the thing the monster from my dreams had warned about, the thing that crept on its clawed feet in the darkest night. The thing that had killed the animal in Don Fernandez's cafetal, who awoke as a human with sore bones and tangled hair in the mornings. I was a witchbird. I remembered then a forgotten part of the story from my dream.

A guttural caw came from my throat as I swept high in the air, and untapped visions flooded my mind. Our village blanketed in moonlight from high above, my bones breaking and stretching over and over as I cried out in pain, a blast from the sky killing the animal on the cafetal. Transformed, it was as if my memories came back to me. Suddenly, I remembered everything, and I knew Yesenia had used her memory magic on me after all. The rumors of the witch stalking through our village at night were true. It was Yesenia. She had somehow found a witchbird and had traded something, perhaps her life right now, to give me this power. Perhaps, she had traded my soul. But I was not concerned with my soul or heaven or redemption. My only concern was, as it ever was, vengeance.

Grim satisfaction flowed through me as I realized El Chivo had mounted one of his men's abandoned horses and was fleeing. With no audience to watch him, he revealed what he truly was: a trickster—a coward. Instinctually, I let the magic gather inside me, and I shot out toward El Chivo. A stream of fire erupted from my wings and licked the hooves of El Chivo's steed, but they did not stop him. Even now, he was quick, so fast that I knew a human eye would probably miss him streaking by. It was fortunate then that I was no longer a human. I swooped down, low enough to smell the sulfuric scent of his fur, to see the gleam of his horns, to see the sweat dripping from his sharp chin. I extended my legs, opening my claws and digging them into his shoulders. As El Chivo screamed, my skin burned from touching him. It was a pain I did not know if I would survive, but if it meant killing him, it would have been worth it. I picked him up off the horse, who I was glad to spare, and flew high, high up into the sky.

El Chivo bleated, and soiled himself, and cast hex after hex in my direction. He unleashed his wicked tongue and licked my jagged legs, sending acid running over my body. I did not relent.

I took him over mountains, past villages like my own, metal roofs and chickens, and farmers and families unaware that above them flew two devils. My claws dug deeper into his flesh, and though he was wounded, El Chivo continued to fight. The old me would have relented, would have succumbed by now, but Yesenia in her wisdom had given me this gift for this very reason. Only a monster can kill a monster.

We reached the sea, glittering and blue as the tips of my wings. Now El Chivo wailed, for he knew my plan. Glee erupted in my heart as I soared toward the water and plunged El Chivo in. He screamed the whole way down, water bubbling in his throat as the waves smothered his scream. I cawed in delight as I made a loop back into the air, up and up as high as I could go, until I could see all of Hispaniola, and then I let him fall.

When he hit the water, I dropped with him, the pain of his hexes snaking their way into my heart. I watched El Chivo struggle in vain and die, the water turning a deep red around him, before swallowing him whole like a hungry beast. The ocean turned the most beautiful shades of blue, and a sigh came from the earth, from my island. I welcomed my death as the water took me away. The waves opened like the arms of my mother and father. They opened like the broad smile of Milagros's face, like the rough palms of Yesenia's hands, and carried me home.

TAME THE WICKED NIGHT

by
Zoraida Córdova

This isn't the story of war, though the kingdom of Lutríste has been clashing on some distant border for nearly five years. Nor is it the story of the worst drought ever experienced by the provincial town of San Mercurio, though it does play a part in the events. No, this is the story about the boy who would unleash an ancient power for the sweet sin of a banished god's love.

The boy in question is Aurelio Saturnelio. The Saturnelios were farmers when the earth was on their side. And the year he turned thirteen, the earth was always on Aurelio's side.

That was the same year the draft arrived and took his elder brother, along with all sturdy youths over the age of thirteen. Gangly, tall, and thin as a blade of mountain grass, Aurelio had been three days short of being drafted.

For five years, Aurelio was nothing but a boy who preferred to talk to plants and his goat more than others, including his younger sisters. People were difficult. The goat protected him, more or less. Plants understood him. They danced to the lull of his voice. Erupted from their seed pods at the treble of his playful baritone. Potatoes sprouted when he sang as he paced up and down neat dirt rows. The purple hearts of bananas grew in size when he slept under their shade.

Aurelio's curious ability to make things grow elevated his family from poor farmers into decent merchants with a year-round market stall offering the ripest, sweetest, crispest fruits and vegetables for up to three towns over. The secret, Mamá Saturnelio said, was their venerable blessing from God.

There was doubt and questions about the boy's powers. After all, why would San Mercurio bless a family of no consequence such as the Saturnelios? But when the drought settled in and a fine layer of dust perpetually clung to the air, no one bothered to question how Aurelio tended the Saturnelios' fields. Instead, he became something to be desired.

It was a period of change and hardship in the kingdom, and Aurelio was ready to rise to any challenge. He was not, however, ready for a thing like marriage.

His mamá had even arranged a promising match with the daughter of a marqués. Aurelio neither accepted nor declined the idea. He knew that with Julios at the front lines, he was the oldest. He had to care for the family. He'd simply thought he'd have more time to find his true love, that was all.

And so, on the day of the Feast of San Mercurio, Aurelio was determined to get to know her and then make his decision.

The Feast of San Mercurio celebrated the saint that used his final breath to banish the violent serpent demons that once roamed the land. Lanterns lit the town square. Chiffon gowns billowed in the arid, dusty heat as accordions, guitars, and tambourines shook the sorrow and worry from all who listened and danced.

Aurelio dressed in his best clothes and his only pair of leather shoes and socks that matched. His tawny brown skin had been scrubbed, but he was a farmer, and there was little he could do to get all the dirt from beneath his fingertips.

The Marqués Montrose wasted no time in bringing his daughter before Aurelio. She was very pretty, with high cheekbones and hair like powdered cinnamon.

"Marisol," she said, offering a shy smile.

"Aurelio," he offered because she'd used her given name, and he'd feel like a fool if he didn't. "Would you have this dance with me?"

She blushed as she took his hand. He wasn't used to the way girls reacted to him lately. Once, he'd been dismissed as the goat boy who talked to plants. Since his gift, he'd transformed. His muscles filled out and hardened from arduous farm work. His wispy hair grew into soft waves he'd stopped trying to tame. His voice no longer scratched like silver on porcelain every time he spoke.

Even now, dancing with the wealthiest girl in town, he still felt like the runt of the boy he'd always been. He didn't want to be anyone else. Would marriage to Marisol change him?

"Tell me," he said. "If you could be anywhere in the world, anywhere, what would that place be?"

They spun under the stars, and he was keenly aware of everyone watching.

"Here, in your arms," she said, batting long, pretty lashes.

He didn't know why he was disappointed with her answer. And now he couldn't tell her that he wished he could be on a ship sailing to the faraway Kingdom of Pearls where it was said existed a hundred types of oysters because he'd never tried seafood. He couldn't even swim, but he wanted to try.

He couldn't say any of that because he'd be a jerk and a fool if he said he'd rather be flailing in an ocean gobbling shellfish instead of with her.

All he could think to say was, "Ah."

"I remember you, you know," Marisol said, a bit bolder as the song progressed. "From school. You told us that plants grow better when you talk to them, and you brought a foot-long sunflower that you claimed you'd grown that very morning."

He remembered that day, too. Everyone had laughed at him and called him a liar. She hadn't, though. Lady Marisol, the marqués's daughter who went to school just like any other girl because the queen had ordered the nobility to spend time being educated like their subjects.

"Did you like it?"

Her hand fell from his shoulder to his bicep. "I did. It was a very clever story. Father says your ancestors were lucky to have settled on the most verdant spot of land in the region."

Story. Lucky. That's what she thought his gift was. What would she think if he got on his knees and whispered to the ground to revive the parched grass and weeds at their feet? What would she say if he asked the trees that lined the temple to sway with him? Would she be afraid of him?

He swallowed the knot in his throat because he knew that it wasn't Aurelio that Marqués Montrose wanted. It was their land.

As if he'd conjured the man, the marqués returned to their side. "Come now, Aurelio. Let us talk among men."

The marqués, a head shorter than Aurelio, ushered the produce farmer into the candlelit vintner stall and ordered two glasses of wine.

"My daughter," the marqués said.

That's all he said. As if Marisol were a thing for either of them to trade. Frustration burned under Aurelio's skin like a seedling trying to take root, but the soil of his body was not made for such things. He was only sure of two things. He loved his family, and he aspired to be a good man. Marrying Marisol wouldn't be good for his family if all the marqués wanted was their land. Marrying Marisol wouldn't be good for his spirit. He'd be a cruel man, a terrible man. A liar. He couldn't have that.

"Marqués, you honor me, but I cannot accept marriage to Marisol."

The music staggered to a stop. It seemed the town had been waiting for the proposal because they all turned to him. But he looked at Marisol, at his sisters, his parents. They deserved better than him.

"Can't or won't?"

Aurelio swallowed. "I will not marry until I find my true heart."

The marqués was still for a moment. Then he snarled as he withdrew a bejeweled dagger and tossed it at Aurelio's feet.

The townspeople of San Mercurio gasped.

"I have offended you. I acknowledge that," Aurelio said but could hardly hear himself over his racing heart. "I accept your challenge."

The Marqués Montrose sniffed at the air. "If my daughter is not good enough for the likes of *you*, then to satisfy my honor, I require nothing less than for you to tame the wicked night."

There was a murmur in Aurelio's ears like a hive of wasps let loose. He knew taming the wicked night was a fool's errand.

It was the solution to an impossible dispute. He'd have to bring back the head of the beast that dwelled in the Midnight Mountains. No one returned from the Midnight Mountains.

Aurelio saw his paths before him. He could marry a girl he did not love, bind himself and his lands to feed the wealthiest man in the province. Or he could journey into the unknown regions of the south and remain true to himself. Even if he died trying.

"I accept," he declared. But Aurelio did not return the dagger to the lord as was customary when one settled a dispute. "I will bring you the head of the beast."

The Midnight Mountains were located a fortnight south of San Mercurio in the desolate ends of the kingdom. The earth was black sand with bits of jagged stone that sliced the skin at the barest touch. Neither rain nor sun gave the land reprieve though a thick blanket of clouds clung around the mountain peaks. One legend, in particular, said it was once the battleground where a millennia ago, San Mercurio defeated the demon gods. Logical men said it was the remnants of volcanoes. Whatever the cause for the darkness that isolated the area, entering the Midnight Mountains was not for the faint of heart.

No one knew what lived within. They guessed at a beast of legend with wings, sharp claws, sharper teeth. They weren't completely wrong. But if they truly knew what lived in the dark, *who* lived in the dark, they might have done a better job of keeping Aurelio Saturnelio out.

Victoriana drove Aurelio as far as the edge of the San Mercurio forest on the family wagon since no one in town would sell him even a lazy donkey. He had enough food to last him two weeks. He had coin in his pack, and, most importantly, he had his gift.

Some might have run and started a new life in a new place. But if he wanted to return to his family and spare them the marqués's wrath, he had to see the challenge through. What good was he if he could not keep an oath?

Aurelio walked the rest of the way, trailed by Rigoberto, the dumb stubborn goat.

In the Fields of Sighs, Aurelio plucked several of the sigh flowers, named such because of the delicate sound they made in the breeze, and tucked them in his shirt pocket. They slept in a field of dead grass. Crossed a dry river. Replenished his food by reviving an abandoned garden.

When they reached the base of the Midnight Mountain, Aurelio froze. He took in the shadows and peaks that disappeared into a nexus of clouds.

Rigoberto made a terrible sound.

"I don't disagree," Aurelio said, sweat trickling between his shoulder blades as he lit his gas lamp. He glanced back once at the path he'd traveled, then walked ahead.

On and on they went, ascending the narrow path. It's important to note that Aurelio Saturnelio had never killed another living creature before. But he kept a vise grip around his mother's cleaver. Though she'd shed no tears, she must have been afraid because the blade was truly her favorite.

Higher up the mountain, black clouds obstructed his view of the rocky path. He held up the wisp of light in his lamp, but it was no use; this was what it must have been like to be swallowed by the night. A tight coil gathered in the pit of his stomach and pulled at him. Run. He needed to *run*.

But he couldn't. He wanted inside the mountain, and now it was taking him. He pushed Rigoberto to safety and let the trap swallow him whole.

Aurelio woke. His mouth was dry, his body, though conditioned with hard work, ached in ways he'd never imagined possible.

When he touched the ground, he was surprised to discover he was on a bed. A canopy bed draped in a gauzy fabric that gently moved in the draft.

"Hello?" he asked the hollow room.

A slight chill answered, and he discovered he was naked under the covers, in someone else's bed. He had the ridiculous notion that beasts and monsters couldn't have had decent beds—could they? Then again, he'd never met a monster before, had he? The covers were made of a fabric he had no name for. Soft as the skin on a ripe peach. He inhaled the cold air. Tasted minerals and dust.

He tried to recall how he'd ended up there, but the last he remembered was the vise grip of darkness and a rumble of thunder—or was it laughter? He'd been unconscious. Vulnerable. So why wasn't he dead?

"I—I should thank you for sparing my life and putting me up in such luxe accommodations."

He kept the soft bedsheet around his waist, and when his feet touched the ground, something moved in the darkest corner of the room. He recognized the crush of fabric, the speed of a gale. He stilled, but no one and nothing made itself known. Or it had vanished.

Aurelio blinked to adjust his eyes to the dim light. Gold phosphorescent orbs of varying size drifted lazily along the crest of the craggy cavernous ceiling. One sank low enough to touch, and he reached out with wonder. It was hot to the touch, and he hissed when he made contact with his calloused fingertip.

He wanted to see more.

Curiosity replaced his fear as he ventured out of the bedroom. More golden orbs moved through the hall like pollen in a slow breeze. He followed the narrow stone path into a cavernous dining hall. The slap of his bare feet echoed. There was nothing else in the hall but a banquet table fit for two dozen people. Its surface was an unbroken slate of marble, and there was a single wooden chair at the head of the table.

"What a lonely way to dine," he said, thinking of the crowded, lopsided kitchen table his family squeezed themselves around at supper time.

"Careful, stranger," his captor said, finally. "Or you may find yourself upon it."

Aurelio spun around expecting to see the being who lived down here, the one whose head he was supposed to bring to the marqués. But the disembodied voice seemed to come from the ether.

"Is that why you cleaned the dirt off my skin and put me to sleep?" he asked, feeling his heart rate spike. "I'd like my clothes back, by the way."

"Perhaps I want to devour a pretty thing." Her voice caressed the skin at the base of his back. He turned around then, but there was no one there. "Don't humans dress their game anymore, or have you returned to eating your pigeons raw and bloody?"

"Who are you?"

"I am the remnant of the old spirits, and you are in my domain."

Aurelio adjusted the bedsheet around his waist and trailed his eyes along the unadorned stone walls of the dining hall. Golden light played tricks on the shadows. He walked the length of the banquet table and ran a finger over the fine layer of dust.

"I've never heard of old spirits," he confessed. "Perhaps you can enlighten me more. Face to face."

"How dare you give me orders in my own home?"

"It's merely a request. You do mean to devour me, do you not?" A nervous laugh worked up his throat. "If not now, eventually."

She made a short growling sound at the back of her throat, and a part of him lit up with a thrill he'd never felt before. "The others cowered as I dragged them. The others screamed when they woke on this table."

Why hadn't he awoken on the table? he wondered.

"Would you prefer I cower?" he asked.

"Yes," she snapped.

"Why?" he asked, breathless. His heart raced, waiting for her reply.

"Because I am an ancient thing. I am the night that devours the dawn. I am the terrifying—"

Aurelio chuckled. Perhaps it was nerves. Perhaps part of him knew that he was in a cave with a being who apparently ate those who trespassed, and therefore he wanted to die laughing. Perhaps he was more curious than he was afraid because he was a fool—a goat boy who spoke to plants and hoped for true love, and so why would he not want to be foolish to the very end?

And then, she appeared before him.

His captor.

She had a mane of black waves that framed a heart-shaped face. Dark, wide eyes fringed by inky lashes watched him with cold anger. Her round nostrils fanned as she snarled, "Are you laughing at me?"

Aurelio was struck by several things at once. The red pout of her lush mouth, the paleness of her skin despite the olive undertone. Her dress was a wrap of black silk, like shadows made to hug her sweeping curves. When she pulled her upper lip back, he saw the sharp point of her canines. He wondered if her bite would hurt, which he shook instantly from his mind. He'd come here for her head. His eyes fell to her throat. She was the most beautiful and impossible sight he'd ever witnessed.

"I apologize. It's just that—if you're terrifying, you really wouldn't be telling me you were terrifying, would you?"

Then, he heard a sound he hadn't expected to. The familiar *clip-clop* of a goat.

"Rigoberto!"

The loyal creature trotted into the hall. He picked up the old goat into his arms and rubbed at the spot between his horns. "You silly beast. You were supposed to run."

"He followed you all the way here." His captor circled him slowly. "I tried to devour his spirit, but he's unlike any satyr I've ever known."

"Satyr?" Aurelio scoffed. "This is a goat. Satyrs are things of legend like winged snakes and chimeras and, well—you."

Rigoberto agreed vehemently.

Aurelio put him down, and the goat proceeded to eat the leg of the dining chair.

"Stop it. We're guests."

"Legends?" The beautiful girl said the word like a question. "Tell me, what age is it?"

Aurelio backed up as she took a step toward him. Doubly aware of his indecent state, he secured the ends of the bedsheet and tucked them securely under his midriff.

"I'll tell you if you answer one of my questions," he said.

"I could devour your soul here and now instead."

He grinned. "Again, you're set on consuming me, being terrible and all. Why don't we get answers before you have me?" He cringed. "I mean—kill me."

Her eyebrow cocked as she considered him. Her eyes were so black, like jagged tourmalines, like a starless night. That stare raked over his torso, his face, and his whole being felt tight and warm. He took another step back from her and found himself against the edge of the banquet table.

"A question for a question," she posed. "Agreed."

"It's the nineteenth century in the kingdom of Lutríste. The year 1897, to be specific."

"Eighteen ninety-seven," she repeated. Something like pain knit her brow for a second. "What—"

"My turn." He waved a finger between them. He gave Rigoberto a gentle kick and pulled the chair for her to sit, then he hopped up on the table. "What's your name?"

She glared at him. "That's a waste of a question. Ask again."

"I want to know what to call you. I can call you my captor. My executioner. My reaper, if you'd like. Though the villages, including mine, do call you *the wicked night*."

Her lips quirked, and he wished he knew what was flitting

through her mind. Meanwhile, Rigoberto resumed gnawing on a different leg of the chair.

"I suppose it's been so long there's no one to remember my name. I am Solana."

"Solana," he repeated, lingering on the way his tongue touched the roof of his mouth. "I'm Aurelio."

"I didn't ask."

"I've volunteered it."

"Your kind has gotten more foolish. Or you've simply forgotten your sense of self-preservation."

Aurelio shrugged. He was here both because he was a fool and wanted to preserve himself—and his loved ones. "I am afraid that whether it's by your hand or another, I am already a dead man."

Something about the way he said it made her flinch. It was the barest thing, but he caught it. He was overwhelmed with the need to know everything about her. Who was she? Why had she spared him? How long would that last?

"Why are you looking at me like that?" she asked.

"Because I want to understand why people call you the things they call you."

She lifted a shoulder. "I do not know why others do anything."

"Are you alone?" Then he made sure he was specific. "Here, I mean. Before Rigoberto and I arrived?"

That question brought a devastating, slow smile to her lips. "Yes. Why have you come to disturb my solitude?"

He felt his throat dry up, but the way she tilted her head, he knew that *she* knew. "To tame the wicked night."

"I see," she said, licking her canines. "I would have thought that perhaps someone like you might have had a more interesting story. The others who entered here wanted pride and glory. They ended *begging* and yelling and—"

"Screaming? Yes, I got that." He regretted phrasing it as a question and raked his fingers through his tangle of hair in frustration. "I've always been the village idiot."

"Then they sent you here as punishment?" Was she mocking him?

"They sent me here, Solana, because I chose to face you rather than marry a girl I did not love."

He watched her mouth unfurl into a perfectly parted O. He was overcome with the desire to tap her chin, but he did not want to touch her until she asked him to.

"Why would you do that?"

"Ah, it's my turn, remember."

She frowned but let him continue. He had a million things to ask her. Where was the rest of the furniture? Do your sharp canines hurt? Where are those other travelers who *did* end up on the very banquet table he was perching on? But he kept coming back to her—Solana. Solana. Dressed in her black gown, wandering these cold halls alone, trapped.

"Who trapped you in this mountain?"

"Trapped." She glanced at the ceiling. The faint phosphorescent orbs pulsed their strange rhythm. Her stare fell to the other end of the banquet table. "I chose this."

It wasn't his turn, but he blurted out, "Why?"

She stood up abruptly. Rigoberto had eaten through the leg of the chair, and it fell with a hard snap. "Enough questions!"

He stood to stop her. She couldn't leave again. He wrapped

his hand around her wrist, then after he blinked, Solana had him by his throat. Her nail grew sharp, digging against the pulsing vein there. He grabbed at her hand and was surprised—not that she was trying to kill him, but that she was so warm to the touch.

Their eyes locked, and he could see anger and frustration in her strange midnight eyes. Then she cried out as Rigoberto rammed into her.

Aurelio grabbed the goat and restrained him. His horns hooked onto the sheet, and then the stubborn goat ran away, leaving Aurelio naked and awaiting his lonely death.

Solana nursed her thigh, then blinked several times. He couldn't be sure because of the dim light, but was she blushing? The terrible, wicked night was blushing because of him.

She gritted her teeth then returned to seething. "I'll deal with you later."

Then she vanished into the dark.

Aurelio picked a direction. He had a goat, and clothes for that matter, to find. He hurried down the same hall he'd entered, but the path seemed longer. He found nothing but empty bed chambers, a dirt pit, and a kitchen that hadn't been used in decades.

Then, he approached a heavy wooden door bolted with iron sigils. The smell overwhelmed him. He remembered one summer when plague hit San Mercurio, and the pile of dead bodies got so bad they set fire to them. This was worse. Still, he opened the door. Hadn't he wondered what she'd done with the bodies of the others?

There were hundreds, perhaps thousands of skeletons piled high. At the foot of the heap was a man in his first year of desiccation, a leather satchel on his waist, his skin drying on his bones like a withered oak. The last visitor Solana had had in the mountain.

Aurelio ran, searching in vain for a way out. He'd seen evidence that there wasn't a way out. Every turn he took seemed to lead him to a dead end. He realized he hadn't had water or food since before entering Solana's lair. The labyrinthian halls finally emptied in what might have once been a throne room. The gold throne and dais were covered in cobwebs and layers of dust. What had this place been? Where was she?

He could barely think as he retraced his steps and finally slumped on the cold ground. He was faintly aware that Rigoberto had found him, the bedsheet slowly vanishing between the goat's crooked teeth.

"Give me that," Aurelio said, feeling too weak to pull the fabric back.

Rigoberto peered with curious eyes at his friend and nudged him awake.

"I know we have to go. I just—don't know if I'm looking for a way out or if I'm looking for her," Aurelio confessed. "Not that I could covertly leave because I'm with the loudest chewer in the world, really, Rigs. Could you be *any* louder?"

The old goat sniffed at the air and bit his best friend at the ankle.

"I'm sorry," Aurelio said. "I'm sorry, all right. I know what I came here to do. She has fangs and claws and can vanish into thin air, not to mention a disgusting room of death. I have—well— you. Even if I had my weapons, I don't believe I could hurt her."

Rigoberto bleated loudly.

"What do I want?" Aurelio felt the headache pound at the

base of his skull. He licked his lips. They were starting to crack. "Food. Water. I want to find her. Feed her ripe berries that match her cruel, bloody mouth. Listen to me. I don't talk this way. I— She's a monster. Isn't she?"

Rigoberto huffed.

Aurelio felt himself drift. He'd never felt so lost, and he'd never been more afraid of whatever dark thing might be lingering inside his wild heart.

He woke up in the bed again. He didn't remember getting there, also again. His body always woke with the sun, but inside the mountain, there was no sun to speak of, only the orbs of phosphorescent light.

"You make noises when you sleep, do you know that?" she asked.

It took Aurelio a moment to realize that he wasn't dreaming and that Solana was standing before him in glittering chainmail and leather pants.

Then, he remembered her hand at his throat. The stench of those bodies. Him losing consciousness. His head still pounded.

"What happened?"

Solana pressed her lips together and glanced at the goat, chewing the silk bedsheet while he slept.

"You wandered through the mountain halls until you fell unconscious. There's no way out, foolish boy. If there were, I wouldn't have to survive on souls who wanted into these caves."

"So you brought me back here?" He rubbed the sleep off his eyes. "If I didn't know any better, I'd think you're starting to like me."

She pursed her lips. "Get dressed. We have a game to resume."

And then she left.

There were fresh clothes, along with his own clothes, though they were too filthy to wear. He dug into the pocket of his trousers and found a pouch filled with mint leaves. They were wilting, so he pressed his finger to them. They did not spring back to life. That had never happened before.

"How odd," he said and blamed it on his exhaustion and lack of nourishment.

He found that Solana had also filled a silver basin with salt water and left behind a sponge. He cleaned himself and rinsed his mouth. Chewed on a wilting mint leaf. Then he dressed in his new pants and blood-red tunic, though they were tighter than he preferred his clothes to be.

He let Rigoberto sleep off his stupor and returned to the dining hall where Solana was waiting for him. To Aurelio's surprise, the dining table was covered with the contents of his pack. The marqués's dagger and his mother's cleaver. Fruits and vegetables. Stale bread and his water reserve. The bunch of sigh flowers. He grabbed that first with trembling hands and drank half of his water canister before remembering he didn't know how long he needed to conserve rations.

Solana picked up a bright purple maracuya, like she was holding up a fragile diamond, and said, "My mother loved these. She called it passion fruit."

"Have it," he offered.

"I always found them too bitter for my liking." She set it down. She gestured to a second chair that was now positioned beside her. "Sit. I want to know more about the world before I devour your soul."

He sat, and his stomach cramped with hunger. He picked up an apple, dusted it on his sleeve, and ate it in four bites, all except the seeds, fully aware that she watched him the entire time.

"You haven't killed me yet," he said. "Not that I'm complaining."

Solana held up a finger to silence him. "That's not how our game works."

"Right. How could I think we could have a polite conversation?"

"Are monsters of legend polite, Aurelio?"

He felt something shift within him, like a brush from within his rib cage. It was a sensation he usually got when he was in his garden, making something grow, coaxing a sprout out of the ground in a spiral of green.

"Why haven't you killed me, Solana of the Wicked Night?"

She narrowed her eyes, but he saw the tiny quirk at the corner of her smile. "Truthfully? I don't know. I meant to. But when you stepped through the mountain, you didn't try to save yourself. You saved your satyr."

"Goat."

"You're—" She stopped like she was searching for the right words.

"Not like other farmboys?" he offered.

She only lifted her gaze at him, and a well of sadness lay there. "You remind me of someone I knew long ago, that's all."

"Your turn," he said, attempting to pull her back to him.

She bit her bottom lip, a canine showing. "What's the world like now?"

He blinked. "How *long* have you been here?"

She held up a finger again.

"Right, our game." He rubbed his hands over his face and

recalled what he knew of his brother's letters. Lutríste was at war on all sides, and if he was honest, he didn't know why except that the king believed the war was for the future.

"War and drought," she said, disappointed.

"My turn," he said, eager to know. "How *long* have you been inside the Midnight Mountain?"

"It feels like an eternity," she said. "But I suppose it's been three hundred years."

He nearly choked on his words, but he let her ask her turn.

"Why couldn't you marry that girl?"

Aurelio hadn't expected that, but he didn't hesitate. "Her father only wanted me because he wanted my family lands. And I did not love her."

"Love is for children," Solana said, like a mantra.

He sighed. "Would you marry someone you did not love?"

"I suppose I too was a fool when I was young." There was strain around her eyes, and he knew he'd hit a nerve. She picked up one of the sigh flowers from the table. Like the mint leaves, it was wilting. She blew on it, and it gave a small, sad sigh, then the petals fell.

"Let me," Aurelio said. He took the green stem between his calloused fingers. The first time he'd discovered his power was on the equinox. The orchard was dying from an infestation of strange fungi. His mother was pregnant with Luciana, and news of the draft had made its way to San Mercurio. Helpless, he'd prayed. Not to the God that everyone worshiped in the temple, but something older. Something he had no name for. He prayed to the sky, the rain, the dirt, the roots, the seas. He knew, in his heart, that if he'd uttered those words in public, he'd be lashed or worse. But the words came to him unbidden like they'd been asleep within him and awoke during his time of need. He'd fainted in the heat, and when he woke, he lay his hand on the bark of the grapefruit tree and felt the pull of life. It bore fruit that very night.

Now, in the Midnight Mountain, at the marble banquet table sitting beside Solana, he meant to use the same power to give life back to the sigh flower. Only, after long moments, nothing happened.

He cracked his fingers and shook out his hands. He took deep breaths. He stretched and slapped his face once. He panicked.

"What are you doing?" Solana asked.

"It's not working. I've made a thousand potatoes sprout from nearly dead earth. I—"

Realization dawned on Solana. "Do you have the gift of Viridae?

"Viridae?"

"Can you whisper to the earth and make things grow?"

Aurelio stared at her. Had his gift had a name? He nodded and told her of the first time it occurred. He'd never even told his family the whole story, only that one day it was a miracle.

Solana blinked rapidly. "Your power wouldn't work here. Nothing can grow in this place. It's cursed."

"But you said you chose this."

She shook her head. "I—I made a mistake, and now I am forced to remain here. I can only be freed when something grows within this dead mountain. But the mountain is cursed never again to hold life."

"So there's no way out?"

Solana shook her head. "You've doomed yourself, foolish boy. The only way out of here for *you* is to slay your beast."

Aurelio watched Solana's features darken. Her nails became jagged again and drummed on the table. He looked at his mother's cleaver, pictured the ease with which she decapitated their dinners. Even if he could catch Solana unaware, could he do it?

He realized, "That's why you eat souls."

"The strongest life force." She huffed bitterly. "There are many things I miss, but the one thing was truly the banquets. Tierra Dorada was full of festivals."

"Tierra Dorada? Why do I know that name?" He scoured his memory from school. Tierra Dorada was the name of the age of the demon gods. The time when monsters roamed and beings of incredible power shaped the land, the stars, and people. They were chaotic before San Mercurio brought order. Speaking their names was sacrilege, punishable by flogging or having your tongue cut out. Even though a small part of him suspected, he'd never attributed his gift to anyone other than San Mercurio. He stared at Solana with renewed wonder.

"Who—*What* are you?"

"Solana Segunda," she said. "Goddess of the Suns. Or, I was."

"Suns?"

She nodded. "There were two suns once, long ago. Una and Segunda. We rotated the suns around this world. This was our palace, our birthplace. Then, I lost everything, everyone. I am the last of my kind."

He brushed his hair back and breathed hard. "Sweet merciful Mercurio. I'd have my tongue gouged out if I ever uttered this."

Solana stilled. "What did you say?"

"Which part?"

"Mercurio?" Aurelio told her of the holy saint who became God, the one his town was named after, who'd given birth to the kingdom.

Solana slammed her fist against the table, and a fissure ran along the marble from one end to the other.

Then she vanished, and he did not see her for two days.

During those two days, Aurelio Saturnelio devised a plan. He rationed his water and organized his food supply.

He returned to the place he'd once thought was a dirt pit. It wasn't. In fact, the earth was practically black sand, like at the base of the mountain. Dry stalks stuck out from the ground like the remnants of a razed forest, nearly petrified. But he should have recognized it for what it might have once been.

A garden.

. . .

The garden was dead. But Aurelio Saturnelio was an optimist and patient. He'd once waited an entire month to coax a patch of pumpkins to take root, even during a sudden frost. He used a bit of his water, doused the seeds from the apple he'd eaten with it. Then planted them.

"Come on," he said. "Come on."

On his knees, he pounded a fist on the ground. This was his one gift. The thing that made him special. He could whisper life into seeds. Make things grow. What had Solana called it? The gift of Viridae.

But as he knelt in the garden beneath the mountain, the place where Solana had walked and lived and spent a thousand solitary years, the only thing that seemed to grow was his doubt. His gift, his blessing, had never failed him before.

At the end of the second day, he sat on the hard dirt eating a cucumber before it began to rot when Solana joined him. Her arms were crossed over her chest, and she looked down her nose at Aurelio.

"It's not going to work."

"How do you know what I'm doing?" he asked. "Are you spying on me?"

Solana rolled her eyes and sat beside him. The spot where he'd scooped out cucumber seeds looked unchanged. "My mother was the queen of the whole world, Aurelio. When she was angry, everything and everyone felt it. If she didn't want anything to grow in this place, nothing would grow."

Aurelio refused to listen to that. "Perhaps your mother is the reason for my gift. Perhaps that's why I'm here."

"Fool." She shook her head, but for the first time, she truly smiled at him. It knocked the wind out of him, and he had to remember to breathe.

"Don't you see?" he asked. "If I can make something grow, even a tendril of a root, I could accomplish two things at once."

She arched her brow. "Is that so?"

"First, you'd be free from this cursed place, and then, you'd come to my town. The marqués said to bring him your hair, but he didn't say it couldn't be attached."

Solana laughed at him, and so did Rigoberto. "You've thought of everything, haven't you?"

"Nearly," he said, as she left him once again.

On the third day, nothing yet had grown.

On the fourth day, Aurelio busied himself in the kitchen. He scoured the iron skillet in the stream of salt water and then gathered some to make salt.

He coaxed the flame in the iron stove using the remnants of old furniture, and Rigoberto finished the rest.

Solana kept her distance, and Aurelio gave her space. But he wanted to surprise her. He didn't know what she ate before she was relegated to consuming souls, but his mother's chaolafán was a town favorite. He chopped garlic, onions, and cut sage into neat ribbons. Diced root vegetables and potatoes. His hunger nearly overpowered him when he stirred everything together. But he wanted to share this with her.

He returned to the dining hall and set two bowls down. She appeared in moments, dressed in a deep blue velvet dress that fell off her shoulders. He'd never been quite so fascinated by anyone's shoulders the way he was with hers.

He nudged a silver fork closer to her while she stared at her bowl. "Hungry?"

Her eyes fell on him, half-lidded. "Ravenous."

"Eat."

Solana inhaled the salty and sweet herbs and garlic. "What is it?"

"Chaolafán. You stir fry every vegetable in the pantry, but it usually has corn oil. My mother makes it with rabbit or lamb when we celebrate something."

"There's always your satyr," she said and delighted in the horror on his face.

From somewhere in the other room, Rigoberto bleated his objection.

Aurelio leaned in and waited for her to eat first. Her face was still, savoring, chewing, then she shut her eyes. He heard a sweet, satisfying sound come from her.

"Good, isn't it?"

She nodded, and then he ate his share.

When the food was all gone, Solana scrapped the bottom of the bowl and sat back, embarrassed. "Thank you."

"It's the least I can do since my goat and I have taken over your bed."

She leaned forward, inches from his face. "That, my sweet farmer, is not my bed."

His heart raced with her face so close. "Whose bed exactly am I in?"

"One of my sisters, Nitxi. She once held power over the night sky. She created the constellations." Solana stood and moved her fingers in the air. The phosphorescent globes of lights twinkled. "I ferried the suns."

He touched the fissure that she'd created in the glass days before. Watched the light above pulse, like the steady rhythm of a heartbeat. "Is that light—is that made from you?"

"The remnant of my power, yes." When she paced, her feet made no sound. She was more wraith than she was a young woman. More beautiful than the first light of day. "I used to think I'd miss the suns. But over time, I missed my family more. I miss them every day, and I live every day knowing that I'm the reason they are gone."

Aurelio hadn't realized he'd stood and went to her. She stopped pacing in front of him and took his hand in hers. "What do you mean?"

He could feel her want to go, so he threaded their fingers together. He felt a pulse between the core of their palms, the radiating glow that blinked faster and faster around them.

"Please, Solana. Please don't go."

She wavered. There was an eternity of anguish and unspoken words in her dark stare. In the center of her irises, light sparked, and he could see the things that she couldn't put a name to. The mountain as it had once been, floating in the clouds. The ancient gods in their splendor. And Solana standing there as it all collapsed.

She showed him that terrible day when the mountain fell. When her light was extinguished, and she was cursed to live out the rest of her immortal life without her true power, and without her family, and with the knowledge that she could have stopped it all. But she hadn't shown him *why*—only the aftermath. He wanted to press, but he felt her sadness crest again. How could he feel that?

When she let his hand go, he felt the same chill as on his first day. "You shouldn't have shared your meal with me. Your days are running out."

The following day Aurelio took stock of his food. He had, by all accounts, two days' worth of rations if he was very careful. Perhaps three if he skipped supper and slept longer. But he was hungry after every meal. Only it was a hunger he hadn't quite felt before.

He spent all day and night in the garden. The cucumber seeds had dried up. The apple seeds hadn't taken root. He tried to dig deep and to search for the bottom of the ground where there was, perhaps, something other than death, but he only ended up with long cuts on his fingers.

Solana found him that way, and then she left.

He hadn't expected her return, but she had returned with salt water and a clean cloth. She took his trembling hands in hers and cleaned his wounds.

"Why are you trying so hard, Aurelio?"

He didn't answer her for a long time. He bit his tongue to stop himself from crying out from the sting of his wounds. Instead, he shut his eyes and welcomed the touch of her delicate hands on his rough ones.

That pulse returned, like the light of her orbs. Only it wasn't in his palm. It was in the pit of his stomach. In his solar plexus. In his throat.

"Once," he told her, "boys from my town chased me in the woods on the way home. Their parents claimed I dodged the draft. But I hadn't. I truly was just three days short. My gift was new, and I didn't know the extent of it. I was frightened. A runt of a thing, then. And so, I made two elms spring up and move. I could feel the roots move like an extension of me." He tapped the skin over his heart. "So much so that one of the branches hit a boy so hard, I thought I'd killed him."

"Did you?" She wrapped threads of cloth around his finger.

"No. But I came close. I felt cursed. I felt so many things." He stopped her hand. "I'm doing this because I don't believe that I'm cursed anymore. I don't believe that I found my way here, to the heart of this mountain, by accident."

Solana looked away, but he whispered her name. She smelled honeysuckle in the sea breeze.

"I want you—I need you to believe, too."

She faced him then, brushing the curve of his cheekbone with her thumb. He felt that pull again, like the day he'd been trapped inside the mountain. A force was tugging him closer to her. He cupped the back of her neck and traced the length of her spine. He felt the exhale of her breath against his cheek.

"Kiss me," she said.

Aurelio had never kissed anyone before, but he'd dreamed of it, dreamed of her. He pressed his lips against hers and tasted salt. His heart raced under her palm, pressed hard against his chest. It was then that he put a name to his hunger.

He hungered for her.

Solana.

Solana, the goddess of twin suns.

His wicked night.

His beautiful, cursed girl.

He felt a bright pain, then tasted iron as she bit his bottom lip. Solana recoiled and slapped her hands over her mouth.

"I'm sorry."

Aurelio was dizzy and smiled. "It's all right. I'm all right."

She shook her head and put space between them. "Don't you see? This ends two ways. You run out of food, and I devour your soul. You do what you came here to do—"

He jumped to his feet, the cuts on his hands nothing compared to the sting of her words. "Believe in me, Solana."

She whispered, "I can't."

Aurelio was so hungry on the sixth day. He ate a potato without cooking it, like an apple. He spit out the eyes and pushed them into the dead garden.

On the seventh day, he slept and slept. In and out of consciousness, he felt Rigoberto's warmth at his side. Then he felt her appear in the room, even before opening his eyes.

She sat on the bed. "If you don't slay that satyr, I will."

It hurt to laugh, but he felt delirious. His mouth felt like a cotton flower. "Too old and stringy. You could put me out of my misery. Why don't you?"

"Too old and stringy," she said, but he heard the strain in her words.

"Come here." He held out his arm to her.

Carefully, like she was climbing into a bed of serpents, Solana climbed into his arms and rested her head against his chest. His heartbeat was steady but too slow. Breakable.

"Do they still sing during the harvest equinox?"

"It's called the Feast of San Mercurio now."

She tensed against him, but then asked, "Sing me something."
He did.

That night, Aurelio stumbled out of bed.

He returned to the garden and plucked out the dead leaves.

There was no change. Once, he'd made miracles. Now he was wasting away. Now that his life depended on it, now that he needed his gift the most, it failed him.

And still, Aurelio tried because he had to try. He had one fruit left. The maracuya. He tried to break the purple shell with his thumbs, but he was too weak even to do that. It fell out of his hands and rolled away. He tried to reach for it, but dizziness came over him.

He rested his head on the ground and felt tears run. He pictured his family back home and whispered their names as if somehow, they'd hear him. He sang the same song Solana had asked of him. He'd once held a handful of seeds in his hand and sang a cluster of carnations to bloom right there. He wasn't the goat boy who talked to plants anymore. He was something else.

"You're an utter fool," Solana said, appearing beside him. She was in a sheer nightgown made of a gold material that shimmered on her skin. If he could see one last thing before he died, he wanted it to be her.

"Yes, but remind me why specifically this time?"

"Because there was someone willing to learn to love you, and you couldn't do the same, so you chose to die instead."

"I didn't choose to die," he corrected. "I chose to be *true* to myself. That's all I've ever tried to do."

"Was it worth it?" she asked, propping herself on her elbow to better look at him.

The sun. She was the sun, and someone had locked her in here and taken her light. But not all of it. He could see it within her. A pulse, steady but slow. "Yes. If I had the option again, I would still decline the marqués. I'd still have trekked for a fortnight."

"Because Marisol wasn't your true love," Solana said plainly.

He entwined a lock of her hair around his finger. "Correct."

"I was in love once," she confessed. "He promised me the kind of love you seek. True. Real. Passionate. He told me that the only thing that stood between us and forever was my family."

Aurelio made a sound of understanding, encouraging her to go on.

"My father, the king of the gods, lord of the sky, had a spear made of the strongest light of the galaxy. Sun, star, and moon. It was the kind of alchemy that was sparked from the dawn of the world. And I stole it for Mercurio."

"San Mercurio." He repeated the story that had been hammered into his head. "He defeated the demon gods of the world and gave birth to our kingdom. His descendants rule the world. He stole your light. He's the reason you won't believe me."

Tears sprung from the corners of her eyes and into the ground. He caught one and brushed it with his thumb against his heart. Solana let go of a deep sigh. "I haven't cried since that day. I don't like it."

"No one likes to cry, Solana." He took her hand and kissed her knuckles, the heart of her palm.

"You can't know that for sure."

"I suppose babies like to cry."

"Why are you like this, Aurelio?"

"You have to be more specific," he said.

"Why are you someone I want to keep?"

He bit his lip. There he was, and the most beautiful girl in the cosmos, a literal goddess, wanted him. To keep him. And he was fading. He wanted to tell her that he didn't want to go anywhere. He didn't want to leave her. But he felt the ground beneath him soften, just the tiniest bit. No one except a bearer of his gift could tell the shift in the earth. His eyes were heavy, and his pulse slow and steady, still. He felt Solana's hands against his torso and his arms. He heard her shout his name.

Then, a sweet, bitter liquid passed through his lips. The bright scent of maracuya made his eyes flutter open, and he nearly choked on the seeds. He swallowed it whole, and his whole body felt a surge of energy.

"You have to leave here, Aurelio," she said, and he felt the hitch in her breath as she helped him sit up. At her words, he was awake, alert. She tried to feed him the second half of the maracuya, but he steadied her hand.

"You said there were only two ways out of here."

She looked away. Her ancient stare held so many more secrets he had yet to discover. "There's another way I didn't think possible. It may not be, but we can try—"

"And you'll come with me?" His heart swelled. The orbs of light above them flickered. He felt strength return to his veins.

"Kiss me again, and I'll tell you."

And how could he deny her anything? Aurelio had only ever dreamed of her. He pulled her against him, kissing her hard, harder than he meant to. As close as she was, he wanted her closer still. He tasted the salt on her lips, the tears that he wanted to consume until he took away all of her sadness. This was the feeling he'd wanted. He wanted to fall, dive headfirst into the kind of love that rattled him to his core. He chased the feel of her, brushing his tongue against hers, and she welcomed him.

He relinquished her mouth, breathless, and kissed the hollow of her neck, the sheer fabric between her breasts. His mind raced because he had never done this, never held anyone this way. His skin heated under her touch, like the light buried under her skin was spreading.

Aurelio pulled back, but she tried to catch his lips with hers. She kissed him fervently, her sharp canines drawing a surprised hiss from him. This time, when he tasted iron, he smiled against her mouth and they tumbled around the dirt. He wanted to beg her to do it again. Instead, he was stunned by her confession.

"I love you, foolish boy."

And he didn't hesitate, not for a moment. "I love you, my wicked night."

She shut her eyes, and her sadness returned. What had he done wrong? He tried to wrap his arms around her, but a heavy weight enveloped him. It forced him to his knees, then to his feet. He strained against the invisible force, too bewildered to cry out at first. Aurelio was on his feet, then slammed against the wall.

"What's happening? Solana, what's happening to me?"

Solana touched her lips, pink from his kiss. His blood on her tongue. She brushed it with her fingers, then rested her hands on the ground. The ground he'd whispered to, and cried into, and sang into. The ground littered with stubborn seeds that would never, could never take up room. Because she knew her curse, and she would not curse him, too.

"I'm sorry," she said. "I wasn't certain it would work."

He tried to fight, but the invisible force sustained him—held him in place as a vacuum opened at his back. It began to drag him away, the same way the mountain had pulled him in. Only this time, he didn't want to leave. He struggled against the current.

"Solana—"

"My sister added her own punishment to the curse. Should there ever come a day I was foolish enough to fall in love again and that they should love me back, they would be expelled from these halls with no way back."

"No."

"Goodbye, Aurelio."

The wind picked up, and he strained against the powerful hands that punched his body. Sand and dust created a funnel around him. He drew on his power, tugged at everything he'd ever dreamed and wanted.

"Solana!" He screamed her name. He screamed her name, eyes locked on hers before the world went black, and then he vanished.

He reappeared on the outside of the mountain, without a way back in, without a way back to her.

Aurelio, being who he was, tried to find a way back in. For a day, he roamed the nooks and crannies, the clouded cliffs, and nothing. Nothing. There was no way back. That had been her punishment because she had loved him back.

Solana loved him.

He had gotten everything he'd wanted, and in the same moment, it was gone. He screamed and beat the earth, but it was useless.

When he was dizzy and delirious, he made the trek back down the mountain. Desperate, he reached the only living forest on the fringe of the mountain and called forth an apple from an oak tree. He ate the bitter fruit. Resented every single bite because his power, his gift, was alive and well.

Useless.

He was nothing but a fool.

Nearly two weeks later, Aurelio Saturnelio, who'd been gone for well over a month by then, staggered into the town square of San Mercurio.

He hated the name. Hated that he lived in a place that celebrated a fraud. That Solana had loved the false saint before she'd loved him, and that was the reason she was still—

He couldn't go there again. He walked past the townspeople on their way home from the temple or the market stalls, but he kept walking despite the stares he drew. At first, no one recognized the man dressed in black and blood red. They didn't recognize the haunted look in his eyes or the serious set of his mouth.

Despite his time away, which felt like a day and an eternity all at once, his muscle memory had him passing through the market. He heard a series of gasps, recognized his name uttered by his parents and sisters.

"Aurelio?" Luciana asked, approaching him like someone might a wild animal.

He couldn't quite meet her eyes, but he lowered himself to her height and hugged her tightly. He was home. Surrounded by people, screams, tears, he let them welcome him back. They began to close up shop to retire home early, and he promised to tell his story when he was ready. Though he didn't know when that would be.

The moment of relief was cut short as the commotion had drawn other attention. Marqués Montrose and his family blocked their way out of the stall.

"What a surprise, Aurelio. We were on our way home from the temple when we were alerted you'd returned. And you're still alive," the marqués observed.

Aurelio began to shove past the marqués. He'd traveled for weeks, had barely slept through it all. He'd lost Solana and Rigoberto by uttering foolish words he couldn't take back. He couldn't, wouldn't, deal with this today.

The older man grabbed Aurelio by his shoulders and squeezed. "You owe me the head of the beast."

Perhaps it was his weary, broken heart or having that pig call Solana a beast, but Aurelio spat, "I owe you *nothing*."

The marqués grabbed Aurelio by the collar and tried to choke the life out of him. He heard people scream. Other merchants and his father tried to pry them apart.

But Aurelio did something he had never done. He let the gift within him take root. He let his unfettered rage fight back. A blade of grass wound around the marqués's ankles and sprouted thorns. The marqués opened his mouth and cried out in a shock of pain, and let Aurelio go.

Aurelio wagged his fingers, and the grass unfurled at his command, returning to the earth.

"We're not done here, you common little—"

Aurelio Saturnelio, the goat boy who talked to plants, would have gathered his family and gone home. He would have chosen a middle ground. But that lost farmer was gone. In his place was the boy who had kissed the darkness and let her kiss him back. And so, he grabbed the pistol from the man nearest to him.

He threw it on the ground at the marqués feet. "I failed in my quest, and yet I returned. To satisfy your honor and mine, I challenge you to a duel."

The marqués nearly frothed at the mouth as he cursed the Saturnelios. But it was his turn to walk away.

"What's gotten into you?" Victoriana asked, trying to hold him back from threatening the marqués further.

His sister's voice, familiar, sensible, worried, snapped him out of his fever. It wasn't until he was back home, crawling into the tangled vines of his gardens, that Aurelio Saturnelio let himself break apart.

Solana knew that exchanging her love with Aurelio would be the thing that struck her sister's curse. And yet, she did it anyway. It was, after all, the only way she could save him.

The man who called the earth awake with his voice. Long ago, her mother had gifted mortals with that power. If she hadn't spent a thousand years alone, if she had remembered what hope felt like, she would have imagined that Aurelio had been gifted by the mother of the gods. For a moment, as she'd watched him toil in that dead garden, she'd almost believed that he'd succeed. But he didn't. She was the decrepit thing under the mountain. The traitor that toppled the kingdom of the old gods, her family. She was where she belonged.

When Aurelio was gone, she remembered his screams for days. She remembered his touch. His blood on her tongue. The treble of his laugh. The desperate way he thought, like sunshine. The sunshine she had once tamed with her bare hands and guided across the sky.

All she had left was an empty mountain waiting for the next soul to devour. The next time, she wouldn't waste any time. She'd simply add a body to the pile of bones.

It was days still before she realized that she was not alone. When she sat at her table, the chair gave way under her. One of the legs had been chewed.

"Rigoberto," she hissed. "Of course, you'd get rid of the first man I've loved in three hundred years, but you'd leave behind a goat!"

And yet, it was Rigoberto who kept her company through the day, wandering the labyrinthian halls of the mountain, sleeping in the chamber with the hole in the ceiling. She could see the sun, the moon, the stars. She could see the centuries pass but only ever in the sky. Other times she wandered into her sister's old chamber because the bed still smelled like her foolish farmer.

One day, she couldn't find him. She panicked. This goat. This half-cocked would-be satyr was all she had of Aurelio.

She found him in the garden.

"There you are," she said. "Come, you silly thing, I want to look at the storm."

But the goat refused to move, and she realized why.

In the place where she'd kissed Aurelio, where they'd wept,

and bled, and crushed seeds into the earth, was a new bloom. A spindly green shoot weighed down by a single sprout—maracuya, the fruit of love and desire.

Something had grown here.

She had a way out. A way back to him.

Her heart thundered as she knelt to pluck it. She held it in her hand. It wasn't ripe yet, but she'd developed a taste for bitter things.

Solana devoured the passion fruit.

The world was different. The permanent clouds around the Midnight Mountain cleared. Solana stepped out of the caverns. Her eyes hurt, and she felt like an ancient creature the earth had spit out. In many ways, she was. In all corners of the kingdom, across the valleys, rivers, the capital where the descendants of San Mercurio reigned, they felt the ripple of power that had been unleashed.

In the lush orchards of the Saturnelio lands, a young farmer with the gift of Viridae heard the whispers of every green thing. Something was stirring. He felt a strange warmth pulse in his heart, but he didn't dare to hope. Not anymore.

Solana had an entire kingdom to reacquaint herself with. But first, she set off on a long road with a loyal goat at her side. Her true heart was out there, and she was going to get him back.

ACKNOWLEDGMENTS

This anthology wouldn't be possible without every single author you've just read. Vita Ayala, David Bowles, J. C. Cervantes, Maya Motayne, Mark Oshiro, Lilliam Rivera, Anna-Marie McLemore, Romina Garber, Sara Faring, Isabel Ibañez, Nina Moreno, Daniel José Older, Claribel A. Ortega, Yamile Saied Méndez, Circe Moskowitz, and Linda Raquel Nieves Pérez. Thank you all for trusting me with your words. Your stories taught me about love, magic, and hope. I love and admire you all.

As always, my family for their continual support, especially my brother Danny Córdova. To Dhonielle Clayton for always being my sounding board, confidant, and friend. To Alys Arden for coffee, king cake, and long discussions about romance and fairy princes. I couldn't have written "Tame the Wicked Night" without you and Dhonielle there to keep me honest.

To Victoria Marini and Irene Goodman Literary Agency for championing this anthology and finding the best home.

To my brilliant editors Eileen Rothschild and Mara Delgado-Sánchez. This project has so much of my heart, and I couldn't have asked for a better publisher to see it through. To the entire Wednesday family, including Lisa Bonvissuto, Rivka Holler, Brant Janeway, Meghan Harrington, Erica Martirano, and Alexis Neuville.

To Faye Guanipa for the truly breathtaking cover illustration, and Olga Grlic's expert cover design.

To my agent Suzie Townsend, Danie Segelbaum, and the wonderful team at New Leaf Literary and Media.

Finally, to the Latin American diaspora. Here, there, everywhere. Your voices matter. Your voices are the future. We are waiting for your stories.

ABOUT THE EDITOR

ZORAIDA CÓRDOVA is the acclaimed author of more than a dozen novels and short stories, including the Brooklyn Brujas series, *Star Wars: Galaxy's Edge: A Crash of Fate*, and *The Inheritance of Orquídea Divina*. In addition to writing novels, she serves on the board of We Need Diverse Books and is the coeditor of the bestselling anthology *Vampires Never Get Old*. She is the cohost of the writing podcast Deadline City, and writes romance novels as Zoey Castile. Zoraida was born in Guayaquil, Ecuador, and calls New York City home. When she's not working, she's roaming the world in search of magical stories. For more information, visit her at zoraidacordova.com.

ABOUT THE CONTRIBUTORS

VITA AYALA is a queer Afro-Puerto Rican writer born and bred on the Lower East Side of New York City, where they grew up dreaming of dancing on faraway worlds, fighting monsters on the block, and racing the fish along the bottom of the ocean. Their work includes *The Wilds* (Black Mask Studios), *Supergirl* (DC), *Xena: Warrior Princess* (Dynamite), *New Mutants* (Marvel), *Livewire* (Valiant), *Quarter Killer* (Comixology Originals), *Jessica Jones: Playing with Fire* (Serial Box), and *Submerged* (Vault), among others.

DAVID BOWLES is a Mexican-American author from south Texas, where he teaches at the University of Texas Río Grande Valley. He has written several titles, most notably *The Smoking Mirror* (Pura Belpré Honor Book) and *They Call Me Güero* (Tomás Rivera Mexican American Children's Book Award, Claudia Lewis Award for Excellence in Poetry, Pura Belpré Honor Book, Walter Dean Myers Honor Book). His work has also been published in multiple anthologies, plus venues such as *The New York Times, Rattle, Strange Horizons, School Library*

Journal, and *Apex Magazine*. In 2017, David was inducted into the Texas Institute of Letters.

J. C. CERVANTES is the *New York Times* bestselling author of books for children and young adults, including *The Storm Runner* series and the forthcoming, *Flirting with Fate*. Her books have appeared on national lists, including the American Booksellers Association New Voices, Barnes and Noble's Best Young Reader Books, and Favorite MG Science Fiction/Fantasy Top Ten Books, as well as Amazon's Best Books of the Month. She has earned multiple awards and recognitions, including the New Mexico Book Award and the Zia Book Award. J.C. lives in New Mexico (otherwise known as the Land of Enchantment), can read, write, and talk backward, always roots for the underdog, and believes in magic.

Born in Los Angeles, **SARA FARING** is a multilingual Argentine-American fascinated by literary puzzles. After working in investment banking at J.P. Morgan, she worked at Penguin Random House. She holds degrees from the University of Pennsylvania in International Studies and the Wharton School in Business. She is the author of *The Tenth Girl* and *White Fox*. She currently resides in New York City.

ROMINA GARBER (RUSSELL) is a *New York Times* and international bestselling author whose books include *Lobizona* & the Zodiac series. Born in Buenos Aires, Argentina, and raised in Miami, Florida, she landed her first writing gig as a teen—a Sunday column for the *Miami Herald* that was later nationally syndicated—and she hasn't stopped writing since. Romina is a graduate of Harvard College and a Virgo to the core.

ISABEL IBAÑEZ is the author of *Woven in Moonlight*, which is a finalist for the William C. Morris Award and was listed among *Time Magazine's* 100 Best Fantasy Books of all Time; *Written In Starlight*; the forthcoming *Together We Burn*; and an as yet untitled YA duology. She was born in Boca Raton, Florida, and is the proud daughter of Bolivian immigrants. Isabel has a profound appreciation for history and traveling, and loves hosting family and friends around the dinner table. She lives in Asheville, North Carolina, with her husband, their adorable dog, and a serious collection of books. Say hi on social media at @Isabel-Writer09.

ANNA-MARIE McLEMORE (they/them) is the queer, Latinx, nonbinary author of *The Weight Of Feathers*, a 2016 William C. Morris YA Debut Award Finalist; 2017 Stonewall Honor Book *When the Moon Was Ours*, which was longlisted for the National Book Award in Young People's Literature; *Wild Beauty*, a Kirkus, School Library Journal, and Booklist best book of 2017; *Blanca & Roja*, a New York Times Book Review Editors' Choice; *Dark and Deepest Red*, a Winter 2020 Indie Next List title; Junior Library Guild Selection *The Mirror Season*; and the forthcoming *Lakelore* and *Self-Made Boys: A Great Gatsby Remix*. Find them online at annamariemclemore.com.

YAMILE (sha-MEE-lay) SAIED MÉNDEZ is a fútbol-obsessed Argentine American author. Her titles include the acclaimed picture books *Where Are Your From?* and *What Will You Be?*; *Blizzard Besties*; *On These Magic Shores*; and *Furia*; a Reese's Book Club Selection and the 2021 Pura Belpré inaugural YA gold medalist. An inaugural Walter Dean Myers Grant and a New Visions Award Honor recipient, she's also a graduate of Voices of Our Nations (VONA) and the Vermont College of Fine Arts MFA in Writing for Children and Young Adults program. She's a founding member of Las Musas, a marketing collective of women and nonbinary Latinx children's authors. Find her online at yamilesmendez.com.

NINA MORENO is a YA writer whose prose is somewhere between Southern fiction and a telenovela. She graduated from the University of Florida and now lives by a swamp outside of Orlando. Inspired by the folklore passed down to her from her Cuban and Colombian family, she writes about disaster Latinx teens chasing their dreams, falling in love, and navigating life in the hyphen. Her first novel, *Don't Date Rosa Santos*, is available now. You can find her at NinaMoreno.com.

CIRCE MOSKOWITZ is a wanderer at heart and firmly believes home is anywhere she can sit down and read. These days, she lives in Kentucky. To learn more, visit her at circemoskowitz .com.

MAYA MOTAYNE thought of herself as a writer long before she could even read. She spent her elementary school years carrying around a notebook full of what she called her "million-dollar ideas," though it was mostly full of doodles and scribbles. She pursued degrees in English Language and Literature and Creative Writing at the University of Maryland, College Park. After that, she worked as an editorial assistant at Random House Children's Books for just under two years before leaving to write full-time. *Nocturna* is her debut novel.

LINDA RAQUEL NIEVES PÉREZ is an Afro-boricua writer born on a rainy night in Arecibo, Puerto Rico, which she often blames for her obsession with writing water goddesses with stormy tempers. Her goal is to see more curls and fat bodies portrayed in the books they read. When she's not buried between casebooks and sketchbooks, you can find her talking about her latest reads and *Pride and Prejudice* on Twitter (@MissLindaBennet) and Instagram (@linda.reads).

DANIEL JOSÉ OLDER, a lead story architect for Star Wars: The High Republic, is the *New York Times* bestselling author of the young adult fantasy novel *Ballad & Dagger* (book 1 of the Outlaw Saints series), the sci-fi adventure *Flood City*, and the monthly comic series *The High Republic Adventures*. His other books include the historical fantasy series Dactyl Hill Squad, *Star Wars: Race to Crashpoint Tower*, *The Book of Lost Saints*, the Bone Street Rumba urban fantasy series, *Star Wars: Last Shot*, and the young adult series the Shadowshaper Cypher, including *Shadowshaper*, which was named one of the best fantasy books of all time by *TIME* magazine and one of *Esquire*'s 80 Books Every Person Should Read. He won the International Latino Book Award and has been nominated for the Kirkus Prize, The World Fantasy Award, the Andre Norton Award, the Locus, and the Mythopoeic Award. He cowrote the upcoming graphic novel *Death's Day*. You can find more info and read about his decade-long career as a NYC paramedic at danieljoseolder.net.

New York Times bestselling and award-winning author **CLARIBEL A. ORTEGA** is a former reporter who writes middle-grade and young adult fantasy inspired by her Dominican heritage. When she's not busy turning her obsession with eighties pop culture, magic, and video games into books, she's cohosting her podcast *Bad Author Book Club* and helping authors navigate publishing with her consulting business GIFGRRL. Claribel's debut middle-grade novel, *Ghost Squad*, is out now from Scholastic and is being made into a feature film. Her forthcoming books include *Witchlings* (Scholastic) and the graphic novel *Frizzy* (First Second). You can find her on Twitter, Instagram, and Tiktok @Claribel_Ortega and on her website at claribelortega.com.

MARK OSHIRO is the author of *Anger is a Gift*, winner of the 2019 Schneider Family Book Award, and *Each of Us a Desert*, both with Tor Teen. Their middle-grade debut, *The Insiders*, is out in 2021. When not writing, they run the online Mark Does Stuff universe and try to pet every dog in the world. You can find them on social media at @MarkDoesStuff or on the web at markoshiro.com.

LILLIAM RIVERA is an award-winning writer and author of children's books, including her latest young adult novels *Never Look*

Back, a Pura Belpré Honor winner; *Dealing in Dreams*; *The Education of Margot Sanchez*; and the middle grade Goldie Vance series. Her work has appeared in *The Washington Post*, *The New York Times*, and *Elle*, to name a few. Lilliam lives in Los Angeles.